BY JACKIE FRASER

The Beginning of Everything
The Bookshop of Second Chances

The Beginning
of
Everything

The Beginning
of
Everything

A Novel

JACKIE FRASER

DELL

NEW YORK

A Dell Trade Paperback Original

Copyright © 2023 by Jackie Fraser
Book club guide copyright © 2023 by Penguin Random House LLC

Published in the United States by Dell, an imprint of Random House,
a division of Penguin Random House LLC, New York.

DELL is a registered trademark and the D colophon is a trademark
of Penguin Random House LLC.

Random House Book Club and colophon are trademarks
of Penguin Random House LLC.

Published in the United Kingdom by Simon & Schuster UK, London.

Library of Congress Cataloging-in-Publication Data
Names: Fraser, Jackie, author.
Title: The beginning of everything: a novel / Jackie Fraser.
Description: New York: Dell, [2023]
Identifiers: LCCN 2023007729 (print) | LCCN 2023007730 (ebook) |
ISBN 9780593723920 (trade paperback) | ISBN 9780593723937 (ebook)
Subjects: LCSH: Self-realization in women—Fiction. |
LCGFT: Romance fiction. | Novels.
Classification: LCC PR6106.R45443 F73 2023 (print) | LCC PR6106.
R45443 (ebook) | DDC 823/.92—dc23/eng/20230224
LC record available at https://lccn.loc.gov/2023007729
LC ebook record available at https://lccn.loc.gov/2023007730

Printed in the United States of America on acid-free paper

randomhousebooks.com
randomhousebookclub.com

2 4 6 8 9 7 5 3 1

Book design by Alexis Capitini

This one's for Katie.

The Beginning
of
Everything

Chapter One

It's nearly a month since I ran away, if you can call it that. I suppose you can. After almost three weeks camping damply in the cemetery—a good choice, although you mightn't think it, a quiet, empty place (empty apart from the dead, I mean) where I was able to almost relax—I found something more weatherproof and substantial, although equally quiet and empty.

Only temporarily empty though—the house has been sold, quite recently, I think—so I can't stay forever, but I'm really hoping I can get myself back on track before the new owners appear. I don't much want to have to deal with anyone who might discover me lurking in their new property. That would be awkward, right?

The house is one of a long row of semidetached 1930s houses on a road that leads down from the cemetery into the town. It has a name—Sunnyside—and a big bow window. There's stained glass in the front door: stylized flowers, a nice bit of provincial art deco. It's been empty a long while, I think, judging from the state of the garden. The electricity's still connected (this doesn't seem very efficient, but I guess it's far from being my problem), so I can charge my phone even if I can't put a light on. And I can cook on the ancient electric stove. This is a lot better than the mostly soup- and noodle-based meals I was making with my Primus, hidden away among the graves.

I didn't have to break a window or anything to get in; I used my lockpicks. I know most people don't own lockpicks, but luckily I was quite an odd child. The picks were a gift from my brother, long ago. I hadn't used them for years—not since I was at college, saving friends the cost of a locksmith when they locked themselves out—but they used to often come in handy, especially when I was seventeen or so and lived for a while with a bunch of people who sometimes required access to odd bits of vacant land, apparently secure behind padlocked gates. The sort of people who might own bolt cutters, let's face it, but who found my facility with the picks hilarious as well as useful.

Anyway. Here I am, wrapped in my sleeping bag in the back sitting room of this house. It has three empty, dusty bedrooms, a solidly period bathroom, a bright and sunny front room, and a kitchen quite urgently in need of modernization, as they say on property programs. The whole house has loads of potential, but it does need a lot of work. Whoever's bought the place will have plenty of fixing up to do.

I lived in a house, once, that needed a lot of work. It was exciting to begin with and eventually exhausting. But maybe the new owners of Sunnyside are the sort of people who can manage this kind of task, more successfully than we were ever able to.

❧ ❧

I stretch out on the sofa and shift the phone to my other ear. It's dark, and cold, and I'm wearing multiple layers. My hands are freezing. I should maybe see if I can find some fingerless gloves somewhere, or a pair of those wrist warmer things. Despite what might seem like a negative situation, however, I'm feeling quite chirpy.

"So, wait, you're living in an empty house? Does it have a roof?" says Noosha.

"It's empty, Noosh, not abandoned; of course it's got a roof. And water and electricity. A palace!"

There's no arguing that a tiny tent, two hundred miles from what was once my home, is five-star accommodation. Sunnyside, even unheated, does feel like a palace compared to where I was living until yesterday. This might explain my positive mood.

"But how? I don't understand. Is this what you were talking about the other day?"

That's when I told her I'd "had an idea"—and this, indeed, is the result.

"Yeah. The security was quite poor."

There's a pause while she thinks about this.

"Have you broken into someone's house, Jessica?"

"Well, technically, yes."

"Technically?"

I laugh. "Yeah. No, okay, that's definitely what I've done."

"Squatting."

"I guess I am, yeah. It's a bit nicer than Wharton Road though."

Noosha laughs. She never went to the squat, but I've told her stories about it. I was in my mid-teens, had just left school, when I met the people who lived on Wharton Road. It was pretty grim; I didn't like going there. I found the chaotic nature of the things that happened—even midweek afternoons could descend into anarchy—quite frightening, although I pretended not to. Even at sixteen I felt sorry for the neighbors. This is a bit different, though; no one's stolen all the wiring, and it doesn't smell of bonfires, hash, and unwashed clothing. I wonder idly what the people who lived in the squat are doing now.

"What if you get caught?"

I shrug, not that she can see me, and look around the room. It's dark, but even in daylight there's not much to see; it's essentially empty, although there is an offensively ugly non-period fireplace with an elaborate electric fire that I'm too scared to turn on. There's no furniture in the house except for some unattractive built-in wardrobes in the master bedroom, a frameless full-length mirror leaning against a wall in the front bedroom, and this large floral sofa, where I slept last night. It's not amazingly comfortable, and my back doesn't completely love it, but it is at least big enough for me to lie full-length. And it's better than a bedroll in a cemetery.

"Hopefully I won't get caught. I'm seeing someone about a job later. It might only take me a month to save up enough money for a room. So with luck I'll be gone before anyone catches me."

"I dunno, mate, it sounds risky."

"It is risky," I admit, "but it's indoors risky, and I'm prepared to take the chance."

"Seriously, though, I could lend you some money. I don't want you to get caught. Would you get arrested?"

I consider this. "Probably not. Anyway, it's fine. I don't want your money. I'm going to do this myself."

⁂

I've deleted lots of people from my phone, or blocked them, and I never answer mysterious calls. All the location stuff is turned off. I blocked loads of people on Facebook, too, and haven't been on there anyway, except to write a reassuring holding statement. I don't want the police looking for me, after all. I'm not missing, I'm just—somewhere else. *I am safe. Please do not speak to Mitch about me, I do not want to have any contact with him,* it says. *I will not be checking my messages here, please be assured I'll be in touch later.* I should probably have deleted the whole thing, but I didn't want anyone to worry.

I'm lucky that a lot of my stuff never made it out of my sister's attic to Mitch's anyway, so I didn't have to abandon much. I've been extremely fortunate. To be honest, I've got enough money to live on for a while, but I wanted to see what I could do, how I'd cope if I really had nothing. Hence the tent, bought in the summer, when I first thought seriously about running away.

I sent my sister a postcard of the castle when I first arrived, letting her know that I'm safe, adding: *Will be in touch soon.* This evening, as well as Noosha, I called Lizzie, my best friend from school, who was relieved I was no longer camping and tried to be upbeat about the whole situation. I know she's still worried about me, though. She wanted me to go and stay at theirs, but it's too close to where I was living before. Noosha's the one I've spoken to the most since I left, messaging or speaking every day, even if only briefly. She wants pictures of the house, now, but somehow it seems rude to take any.

She was always suspicious of Mitch. I wish I'd paid more attention. I couldn't stay with her because it's the first place he'd look for me, assuming he has any interest in where I've gone. On the one hand, I can't imagine him giving enough of a shit to try to find me. But on the other hand . . . he does have a terrible temper. So much better to disappear entirely.

I know when some people have to escape it's a lot harder. Mitch might be a prick, but it's not like he stopped me having a bank account, or a phone. In fact, some people probably think this whole thing is me being melodramatic, and I suppose they might be right. I don't know, though. I think he was close to fundamentally losing it when I walked in on him. Not the best afternoon of my life. It's funny, because it should have been me who was angry, shouldn't it. I wasn't, though; I was almost delighted, and relieved—definitely relieved.

※ ※

Mid-November. I've been living at Sunnyside for a month. I've got a job, now—as a dishwasher at a restaurant in town, cash in hand. It's a busy place, popular, open all day on Saturday, Sunday for lunch, and for lunch and dinner Tuesday to Friday. It's called Cenhinen Bedr, which is Welsh for "daffodil," although the direct translation—and this made me laugh—is "Peter's leek." St. Peter, I suppose. The days are long—I work both shifts, lunch and dinner—and I'm on my feet, so it's hard work, but my colleagues are friendly and my boss, Maura, is great. I get two meals a day, and since she caught me eating leftovers from people's plates (I know, disgusting), she lets me take food that's reached the date on its "best before" catering sticker. I'm saving money, and it won't be long until I can start looking for somewhere to rent.

Saturday morning, earlyish. On Saturdays I get the bus out to the Leisure Center to use the showers before going to work. The rest of the week involves strip washing with a tiny kettle full of hot water, reminding me of my grandfather, who washed himself at the kitchen sink when I was a very, very small child.

My bag ready on the counter, I'm standing in the kitchen in my coat (the house is colder than ever), drinking coffee, eating toast before heading out to wash my hair and luxuriate in the endless hot water. I gaze out at the crisp autumn garden. It's long and leafy, with mature trees on the boundaries protecting the house from nosy neighbors. There are mildewed asters stiff with frost, ancient fruit trees, a greenhouse with white-painted windows, a patio with rusting outdoor furniture. I watch the birds eating berries from the cotoneaster that clambers over the fence.

I always keep the kitchen door closed, so there's no risk anyone peering through the mail slot will see me, a nebulous figure warped by the stained glass. That's why I don't hear anything until the door is pulled open. Someone says:

"Yeah, anyway, so this— What the fuck? Who the hell are—"

And maybe more, but I cram the final piece of toast into my mouth, grab my phone and my bag, and am out of the back door before they can finish. I glance back at the man standing, astonished, in the kitchen doorway, but I don't hang about to see if he has anything else to say. I'm off down the garden, heading for the loose fence panel.

"Hey! Hey, wait!" he shouts, but I don't.

⁋ ⁋

Ten minutes later, I sit cursing on a bench beside a playground somewhere in the estate of newbuilds that sprawls behind the house. Damn. All my stuff—wash bag, sleeping bag, rucksack, all my clothes, my small and ancient teddy bear, the library books I've naughtily borrowed using the personal details of Sunnyside's previous owner—everything's in the house. I'm such an idiot. But I reckon I'll be able to get my tent—that's in the garage, along with the bedroll, my attempt at sensible risk management—even if that guy is the owner, which he presumably is. He won't be sleeping at the house tonight. Or will he? He might've had a van full of stuff parked outside, just about to move it all in. Maybe I should walk past the house to see. Say he didn't, and he was there to measure up or whatever, then I could get the tent, later. But probably not the rest of it. He's bound to bolt the back door, isn't he? And who could blame him. At least I've got my phone—although no charger—and my bank card, driver's license, and passport, safe in my bag. And a towel and some shampoo. Great. I press two fingers to my forehead.

Do not let this overwhelm you, I tell myself. *You've coped with worse. It will be fine. You can still have a shower; you can still go to work. You can get the tent and have somewhere to sleep. Or you could ask Maura if she can help; she might have a spare room. Or a sleeping bag.*

I wonder about this. I think she'd help me, if I asked her, but I really don't want to. I don't like asking for help. That might be why I'm in this mess in the first place.

After a while, I walk down the hill to the bus station, trying to pretend everything is just the same as it was yesterday. I take the bus to the Leisure Center, have a shower, and then walk slowly back into town. It's quite a long walk, but I have nothing else to do, and at least the sun is shining, even if it is freezing cold. It's a glorious day, in fact, a hard frost gripping the gardens I pass on my way back to town, furring the walls and railings. The sky is triumphantly blue, and it's hard not to feel hopeful. I'm always surprised by this. For the last couple of years I've been inclined to think I was no longer a hopeful sort of person, that I might have grown out of it, or had it taken from me.

I'm early to work, which is lucky for Maura, as it's very busy. I wonder if it might be better to ask one of the waitresses—Eirwen, or Alys, maybe (they're my favorites)—if they know someone who'd let me sleep on their sofa. Probably not, though—like the chefs, they're all so young, at an awkward age, most still at home with their folks, others living in shared houses. I suppose I can camp, even if frosty mornings will look less enticing from inside a tent.

❧ ❧

I have three hours off in the afternoon, from three until six, so I walk back up the hill to see what's going on at Sunnyside. A casual saunter past. No car in the driveway, but there's a dumpster in the front garden, ruining the lawn. Maybe they'll pave over it.

I crane my neck to see what's in the dumpster—maybe he'll have chucked out all my stuff? Sadly not—just a big flappy roll of carpet, from the front room. I wonder where he's gone. Properly away, or a quick trip to B&Q? I cross the road and then turn back. I may as well go round the back and see what's going on. Perhaps he'll have piled all my things on the patio. What would I do, in the same situation? I'd put the person's stuff where they could get it and make sure the house was secure.

He hasn't attempted to fix the fence, anyhow, and I slip easily through. Everything looks the same as ever, but I approach the back of the house with caution. He was talking to someone when he opened the door, wasn't he—partner or friend or parent—and they might still be here.

On the back doorstep there's a piece of paper—or, in fact, an envelope, taken I guess from the pile of post that's built up in the porch, an unsteady slather of circulars and takeaway menus. The envelope is held in place with a pebble. Written on the back in pencil is a note.

> *Hello. If you're reading this, I guess you're here for your stuff. I'm sorry if I scared you earlier. You scared me, too. I can see you haven't done any damage (in fact, the kitchen is spotless, thank you) and if you need to sleep here tonight, please do. Your stuff's all here, and the door's open. The boiler's working now as well. I'll be back in the morning, about half nine, and I'd really like to speak to you if possible. I'm not angry or pissed off about you being here. I'd like to help you if I can.*
> *Gethin Thomas*

"Huh," I say. "Well."

I open the back door. My camping kettle and pans are still on the worktop, along with my plate and bowl and cup, all "borrowed" from the restaurant, and my cutlery. The plastic bottle of milk, the butter in the stainless steel 1970s butter dish. Nothing's changed in here, anyhow.

I stand silent, listening. Nothing. There's no one here. In the back room, Bear and my sleeping bag are still on the sofa; my rucksack, untouched, leans against the wall. I go to look at the floor in the front room, where he's pulled up the carpet. Parquet, the same as in the back room but in much better condition. It already looks like a room in progress, with tools heaped on the floor, wallpaper scrapers and bottles of sugar soap, a paint-spattered stepladder leaning against the wall. On the cupboard opposite the door sits an elderly radio/CD player, with a plastic crate full of CDs.

I think for a moment and go to bolt the front door. I'll unbolt it in the morning before I leave, but I don't like the idea that anyone might just arrive while I'm sleeping. Even though, of course, this has been a possibility for the last four weeks. It's different now, though. I make a cup of tea and sit on the sofa for a while, trying hard not to worry about the future, before heading back to work and locking the back door behind me.

❧ ❦

When I get home, at nearly midnight, I have a bath, despite the shower I had earlier. It's the first bath I've had in weeks. I put the landing light on, figuring it doesn't really matter now if someone sees it. It's odd, though; I've got used to living in the dark—which is why I don't put the bathroom light on. The bath is large and ancient, cast iron and enamel. It takes ages to fill, the pipes groaning in protest, but the water is hot and it's amazing to lie here in the half-darkness. Then I go to bed, and sleep surprisingly well.

Chapter Two

I'm up early, to pack up my things and clean the bathroom and kitchen. I'm not sure I want to stay and talk to this Gethin person. There's nothing he can do to help me, and even if there was—well, it's better not to have obligations, isn't it. I take my rucksack outside and put it on the grass behind the greenhouse, following it with the tent and bedroll. It's another bright, sunny morning, so even though it's cold, I sit down at the rusty iron table on the patio, with its peeling, bubbled white paint, attempting to read my book but mostly glancing at my phone to check the time. It's nine-fifteen now, and there's a car pulling into the drive. I suddenly panic that he's called the police on me and stand up, ready to run. My heart beats painfully in my chest.

It's just a normal dark gray car, though, and there's only one person in it. He opens the driver's door and gets out. I retreat a step farther, onto the lawn, watching cautiously as he leans back into the vehicle. Then he's balancing a takeaway coffee cup on the roof of the car, another in his hand, and closing the door. He glances toward me briefly, smiling, and walks round the front of the car and onto the patio.

"Hello," he says. "All right? I thought you might like a coffee."

I back away another step farther, saying nothing. I didn't

really get to see much of him when I ran away yesterday, so today I'm paying more attention. He's maybe five years younger than me, or perhaps he has good skin. Fortyish, anyhow. Springy dark hair, graying a little, tallish—about six foot, I'd guess. He's dressed in jeans and a dark shirt, a tweed jacket. He looks okay, but most people do. You can't tell fuck all about someone by how they look.

"I'll put the cups on the table," he says, "and sit down." He suits the actions to the words and sits down, his back to the coal store. This means I can sit closer to the steps that lead down to the lower lawn, my escape route clear. I approach slowly. He's digging in his pocket for sugar and stirring sticks. He arranges the coffees next to each other. "Nice to be dry enough to sit out, in November," he says. He nods at the coffees. "Both the same: lattes. D'you want one?"

I haven't had a latte from a coffee shop in a very long time; they're an unjustifiable expense. It's tempting.

"I'm Gethin, anyway."

"I'm Jess. Sorry I broke into your house." This isn't strictly true. I'm sorry he caught me, is all. But I have to say something, and this seems polite.

He laughs. "That's okay. Thought they might have left the door open."

I shake my head. "Picked the lock."

"Wow, did you? How did you do that?"

"Lockpick."

He looks startled. "That sounds a bit professional."

I shake my head once more. "Just a hobby."

He laughs, again, at this. I look at the coffees.

"Have one," he says, "go on. Otherwise I'll have to drink both."

I lean forward and take the one on the right, and some sachets of sugar. I don't usually have sugar in coffee, but I feel the need for it.

"Thank you."

"You're welcome."

We sit in the sunshine, looking at each other. Our breath steams, mingling above the table with the steam from the coffee. I feel slightly calmer now, my heart no longer hammering in my chest, although I'm not exactly relaxed. I pour two tubes of sugar into my coffee and stir it slowly.

"I won't ask you why you needed to sleep in my house," he says, "although you can tell me if you like. How long have you been here, though? If you don't mind me asking?"

"A month, more or less. I thought it wouldn't be long until you were moving in, or doing it up anyway. Are you going to live here?"

"That's the plan, yes."

"By yourself?" I ask, although really, how is that any of my business.

He nods.

"It's such a nice house," I say, turning to look at it.

"It is. I'm pleased with it. I always liked these houses, since I was a kid. Needs a bit of work, like."

"It does, but there's nothing you couldn't live with. I mean, easier to decorate before you move in if you've got somewhere to stay. Have you sold your other house?" I smile at him, slightly awkward. I'm surprised at myself, at this easy return to social chitchat.

"I'm staying with my sister at the moment, so yeah, the plan was to get it all done before I move in. The other place was sold a while ago."

"Where was that? Local?" I realize this sounds incredibly nosy, but he doesn't seem to be bothered.

He shakes his head. "Cardiff. That's where I work. Or have been working. Only another two weeks to go and I start a new job in Swansea."

"Oh, much closer." This is about the sum of my knowledge of Welsh geography, if I'm honest.

"Yeah, commuting to Cardiff is a pain in the arse. I've been staying with a mate there during the week. Since the other place was sold."

"What do you do?"

"Oh, it's not interesting. IT stuff," he says, shaking his head.

I laugh. "I'm a dishwasher at the moment. It's probably more interesting than that."

"You're working? Where are you doing that? In town?"

I nod. "It's okay, I don't mind it. I need the money. I'm saving up so I can rent a room. Not much further to go." I stop, wondering if I've already said too much. It won't do, will it. Although none of these details is risky, or dangerous, as far as I can tell.

"That's cool."

"Yeah, well. I was lucky to find your house, it made things much easier than they would've been otherwise." I frown, at myself more than at him. It's true, but I can't imagine he'll quite see it that way.

"Were you sleeping rough, then? Before?"

"Only for a couple of weeks. I've got a tent," I add. "I'm not from round here, I don't know the street people."

"No, I can tell from your accent you're not local." He grins at me.

I laugh. "No."

He's got quite a strong accent, himself, but three weeks in the kitchen means I don't notice like I would have done when I first arrived. It won't be long until I begin to pick it up; I find it hard not to accommodate, with accents.

"But you'd been living here? In Caerwyddon?"

"No. Picked it at random. Or—not quite at random." I did have some criteria, not that I'm going to tell him what those were. "It's quite good here, though. Not too big. I wouldn't know what to do in Swansea or wherever."

He nods. "Do they feed you? At the restaurant?"

"Yeah, you get two meals if you do nine hours. And they give you leftovers, if you want them."

I frown again, thinking of Maura catching me eating from the plates I was supposed to be scraping into the food waste bin. She didn't say anything, but later she asked, apparently uninterested, if I wanted to "help out" by taking unwanted stuff for her. She also asked if I wanted to do front of house, because the money is slightly better, but I explained that I'm not much of a people person. I find the general public, and busy places, rather intimidating. A constant stream of pots to wash is much more my sort of thing. I think she can tell that this isn't what I usually do. She's never asked me what's changed in my life to make it necessary, for which I'm grateful. I try to make myself as small as possible at work, as dull and uninteresting as I can. I don't want anyone to wonder about me or ask questions I don't want to answer. I don't want to lie, either, so it's best to just be a quiet middle-aged woman. Luckily that's exactly what I am, and it makes me essentially invisible.

Gethin and I sit for a moment in silence. Then he says, "And what will you do now?"

"Oh, well." I put my cup down, forced to face reality. "I don't know."

He runs his fingers over a rusted patch on the table and then glances across at me. "You could stay here, if you want. Until I move in, anyway."

I'm shocked. I stare at him. He smiles, an open, friendly smile.

"I don't think—that's kind of you, but it seems like—I don't really know why you'd offer?"

"I won't be living here for a while yet. So you could. Stop anyone else moving in," he says, and laughs.

I shake my head. "I can't afford to pay you and save for a room."

"Oh, God, no, I don't want your money."

"Yeah, so, I know I've been staying here rent free, but I couldn't do that now I've met you. And I don't"—I pause here, trying to find a way to say what I mean without getting upset, which suddenly seems a lot closer than usual—"I don't want to, you know, owe anyone anything."

"That's fair enough," he says. His expression darkens, slightly, a faint shadow crossing his face. "Can't blame you for that. But maybe you could help me with the decorating. In exchange? You could help me strip all the wallpaper. It's a massive pain, isn't it, wallpaper. There's woodchip wallpaper in the small bedroom. I'd really like to get everything back to the plaster. You could help me."

This is also surprising. I frown at him. "You don't know me, though," I object. "Or anything about me."

"That's true."

We sit in silence. I'm confused. I know he said, in his note, that he wanted to help—I don't know what I thought he meant.

Pull some strings at a shelter, maybe, or give me a reference for a landlord. See, I can imagine why someone—a man—might think it would be worth their while to help out a woman with no visible means of support. Even a woman like me. This interaction doesn't feel remotely sleazy, but, like I said before, you can't really tell anything about someone when you first meet them, not if they're hiding their true self. I mean, most people don't—they show you what they're like all the time, and you should pay attention—but if someone's trying to conceal themselves, and they have experience at being deceptive, you might not spot it.

"Why do you want to help me?"

He's drinking his coffee and looks over the rim of the cup at me. He puts the cup down on the table and clears his throat.

"My brother lived rough for a while. I was too young to be able to help him. He was—he wasn't . . . well."

I watch him. He looks away. I guess I know what he means—some kind of unfixable situation. Drugs or mental illness is my guess.

I've known plenty of people whose lives are lived at the edges. A year after I met the people who lived in the squat on Wharton Road, more than twenty-five years ago, I was living somewhere almost as chaotic: in a trailer on that previously mentioned vacant lot, up at the far end of one of the business parks. Our neighbors there were a loose collection of ex-punks and New Age travelers (not that any of them ever really went anywhere). I thought it would be freeing, living on site, but to be honest it was as bad as, if not worse than, being at home, compounded by a lack of washing and toilet facilities and the fact that I was living with an arsehole.

I got used to thinking of Fitz that way years ago, but more

recent developments suggest he could have been a lot worse. I may have to recalibrate. He was just a bit of a knob really, and to be completely fair, he mostly meant well. Although he tried hard to pretend he'd never had an upbringing, he was often thoughtful and probably didn't treat me any worse than any of the posh boys he went to school with would have done. I should have known better than to leave a relatively stable situation at home to move in with someone like him, but I was your averagely foolish seventeen-year-old. My subsequent mistakes have at least all been different. I sigh and return my attention to the present, to the chilly November morning and this unexpectedly friendly stranger.

"Yeah, I'm not . . . unwell. I don't have substance problems," I tell him. "Or mental health . . . issues. Or, not more than everyone does. I just . . . ran away."

It sounds silly, doesn't it. People run away from school, or from home, but when they say "ran away from home" they mean from your mum and dad, your family. They mean children, or young people, with no agency. Can you say you "ran away" when you're my age? I don't know. That's what I did though. I didn't just leave. I ran away, escaped.

I feel the need to explain further. "I mean, I didn't . . . I didn't *do* anything. I'm not running away from the consequences of my actions. Or at least, I haven't stolen anything. Or killed anyone." I wonder if this makes it sound as though maybe I've done exactly that.

He nods. "Does anyone know where you are?"

"My friends know I've been staying here. I told them the address," I lie, wondering, suddenly, why I have in fact done nothing of the sort, "and that I was meeting you this morning. And my mum and my sister—they know I'm safe, or not dead, anyway." I laugh, although it's not funny. I think about my mum, about the message I sent her once I was sleeping at Sunnyside.

Am safe don't worry.

She didn't reply, but I didn't really expect her to. She replied to the first one I sent after I got here—a terse OK. This is fine. I have no idea whether she ever thinks about me when I'm not in a room with her. That's fine, too.

Gethin interrupts these thoughts with further questions. "You couldn't stay with them? Your family?"

"My mother—our relationship is . . . well, I haven't lived with her for a long time. And she lives . . . it's sheltered accommodation, so there's no room for guests. My sister's busy; she's got a houseful. I'm not interested in being a burden to anyone." I'm surprised at myself, just coming out with this; it's quite a personal thing to tell a stranger. The things I'm concealing have exposed something else.

"They probably wouldn't think it was a burden?"

"Maybe not. But I didn't like the idea. And I wanted to be . . . farther away."

"You'd stay here? In Caerwyddon, I mean?"

"Why not? It seems okay. People are friendly, it's . . . the countryside is beautiful, from what I can see of it."

He nods, watching me.

"And there are loads of shops and things. I mean for work, if I get bored of washing dishes."

"What did you do before?"

"Oh, all sorts. Care work. I've worked in schools, and at the library." All this is true, but also nicely nonspecific. I don't know if I'd be able to get a job in a school now; it's a long time since I worked in education.

That was my first job after graduating. I was a teaching assistant when I met Johnny—another posh boy with a chip on his shoulder, like Fitz—at a festival (there's a story) and moved away to live with him in Brighton. He thought teaching was bourgeois oppression of the masses. I didn't exactly agree, but he was quite persuasive. That was another life of fluctuating finances. We did house clearances and sold things at antiques fairs, sitting in the van in the cold, up at four in the morning to drive round the country. For far too many years I lived in a freezing doer-upper with someone who didn't actually want to do anything up. That house is probably worth a million quid, now—or it would be, if anyone ever got round to doing the work—an enormous dilapidated Georgian pile, on the cusp of Hove: six bedrooms, sea views, mice, a roof that leaked, electrics constantly on the fritz.

I did that until Johnny stopped coming home because he was too busy sleeping with someone else. I moved back to my hometown and lived (gratefully) in a shared house, with central heating and double-glazed windows and a complete lack of either sea view or mice. That's when I worked in the library, my favorite job. I didn't give that up until I was made redundant when they closed the library.

It's funny how much you can think about in a few moments. I suppose because you know your own life so well. But I need to concentrate, don't I, to listen to this man who's so calm about my appearance in his life.

"You've got a bank account?" asks Gethin.

"Yeah. Got my paperwork. If I wasn't sleeping on your sofa"—I manage a half-smile—"you'd never know I was homeless."

"No. So, what do you think? Would you like to help me?"

I hesitate, anxious. "I don't know."

"I realize you've no reason to trust me."

"Well, or you me," I point out.

"No, but—"

"How long will you stay at your sister's?"

"Oh, until it's done, probably? Or maybe not . . . she's all right, my sister—in fact, she's been brilliant—but it's not what either of us would choose, I don't suppose. But anyway, another two weeks at least, until I'm finished in Cardiff."

I nod.

"There's a bloke coming on Monday to start the rewiring," he tells me.

"How long will that take?"

"He reckoned five working days. Should be quick 'cos there's no furniture."

I nod again.

There's a pause while we look at each other, cautiously, and he also looks around, at his new garden, his new house.

"I thought you were younger," he says, "when you ran off, yesterday. Not that I'm saying you're old," he adds hurriedly, a slight look of panic on his face.

"Yeah, I'm not young." I shake my head, amused.

"You must be my age, so that's pretty young." He nods, showing he's joking.

I laugh. "Or not. I'm forty-five."

"There you are then," he says. "I'm forty-seven."

"Really? You look loads younger." I don't mean to say it; it just bursts out of me.

This makes him laugh again. "Well, thank you very much."

I'm embarrassed. I feel like he might think I'm trying to flirt with him. I clear my throat, awkward, and drink some coffee.

"It must be quite unusual . . ." he starts, and then, thinking

better of it, begins again. "I suppose there are more homeless
people our age than you might think. Newly homeless, I mean."

I shrug. "Probably."

"I suppose everyone always assumes you have to have all
kinds of problems, to end up in that situation."

I shrug again.

"Everyone has an idea of what it means, don't they, of the
typical person. I bet there aren't any typical people."

"I don't know, I think there are things that happen to people
that make it more likely. Life is quite precarious for a lot of
people. And like you said before. Substance abuse, whatever."

"But you're not—?" He pauses.

"Yeah, I'm not a—" I search for an appropriate word, but
they all sound quite old-fashioned. "I'm not an addict. If that's
what you're asking. Although that's what I'd say if I was, I expect, so—whatever."

"No, I . . . you know that's not what I meant."

"Isn't it?" I tilt my head, and he laughs.

"Okay. Maybe."

"I don't blame you; addicts are complicated."

He looks serious again. "Yeah, they are." Another pause. "I
know no one chooses that, but . . ."

"But still. You wouldn't want to get involved, would you. I
wouldn't either." I wrinkle my nose. "Are you one?" I mean, he
could be. I don't really think there's much chance of this though.
I'm . . . not joking, exactly. Sort of joking.

"Always seems like a lot of effort. Often ends badly." He
looks stern for a moment, or sad. I wonder what happened to
his brother. Maybe he died, and my attempts at humor are
painful and clumsy. I wouldn't be at all surprised; I frequently
say the wrong thing. I think perhaps I ought to apologize, but

then he grins at me, eyes crinkling. "I admit I've never fancied it much. Anyway," he adds, picking his phone up, "I've got to go. Collecting a fridge at ten."

"Right."

"And then I'm going to look at a washing machine—the pictures were shit, so I haven't said I'll definitely buy it. Then I have to get a hoover."

"The fun never stops."

"It doesn't." He stands up and collects his empty cup. "You done?" I nod and hand him mine. "Are there bins?"

"In the garage."

"Okay, cool. Anyway," he says, putting his phone away, "um, so if you decide you don't want to stay, could you lock the back door and put the key through the cat flap? But if you do—and honestly, it's completely fine—then I'll see you later. Are you working today?"

"Yeah. But I'll be back this afternoon. If I decide to stay. Or even if I don't, I suppose. Have to get my stuff. But . . . so, I'll be back. If that's all right."

"Of course. Might see you later, then."

I regard him for a moment, impassive, and then nod again.

"And if you decide not to . . . d'you think—I'd be worrying—have you got a phone? You could let me know you're okay? I'll give you my number," he says, and rummages in his pocket, producing a business card. "This is for the job I'm leaving, so . . . but that's my personal mobile number."

I take the card. "Okay." I can't exactly imagine texting him. What would I say? *Back at the cemetery, it's cold but I'm not dead*? I appreciate the gesture; it's thoughtful. He seems nice. I don't much want anyone else worrying about me, though. Or thinking about me at all.

Chapter Three

I watch him drive away and then fetch my stuff from behind the greenhouse. I'll pile it all in the back room for now. I can't decide what to do, so I'm not going to think about it.

Instead, I'll do something useful. I fetch the bucket from under the sink, run some hot water into it, add a squirt of washing-up liquid, and then go to look at the decorating equipment. I select a wallpaper scraper and find a sponge in the cardboard box full of brushes and rollers. I take them upstairs, roll up my sleeves, and begin to soak the horrible wallpaper in the box room. Woodchip wallpaper's bad enough; why anyone thought navy blue was a good color for such a small room, I have no idea. Mind you, it wouldn't look better in a big room. It's awful.

Warm water runs unpleasantly up my arm. You have to really soak woodchip. It's messy. Sticky, unpleasant, the wallpaper coming off in annoyingly tiny pieces. I've stripped woodchip before, and it never gets any better. Do they still make it? Surely not. Eventually, I suppose there'll be none left; even the most determined landlord of shitty student rentals and multiple occupancies for migrant workers will finally get round to removing it.

I sing a line about woodchip wallpaper from a Pulp song. I

remember the first time I heard that, and how poignant it seemed even to my much younger self. Everything's poignant now, of course, every memory dipped in the greens and purples of disappointment and betrayal. I sigh. This is no good. I think of the ancient CD player in the sitting room; maybe I could play some music and distract myself from the thoughts that are always looming on the horizon and threatening to sweep down and overwhelm me.

I go back downstairs and look in the plastic crate full of CDs: a random selection of sixties girl groups, Motown, eighties pop, and the sort of thing vaguely alternative people of roughly my age liked at university—Nirvana, Nine Inch Nails, Jane's Addiction, Violent Femmes. I'm not quite able to face this, however, and instead choose the sort of compilation album that motorway service areas were full of in the nineties and aughts. I go back upstairs to play the Supremes and the Ronettes. When you're by yourself in an empty house, you can really belt out "Be My Baby."

When I was a kid, the sixties were five minutes ago. It's hard to believe these songs are nearly sixty years old, Ronnie Spector nearer eighty than seventy. When I first heard "Be My Baby," the people who were eighty would have been born in the nineteenth century. It does my head in. How did I get to this point? Where did the time go? Spent, wasted, frittered away, stolen. It doesn't make any difference; it's gone all the same. I shiver.

There's bare plaster showing now, in places. In other places there's evidence of older wallpaper under the woodchip. That comes off more easily. I tug at it and tear a wide, angled slice off, all the way to the doorframe. Very pleasing. It's deceptive, though; the next bit's as hard as it was to start with. I wonder if a steamer would make it easier. The horrible dark blue color certainly doesn't help. Steamers are bad for the plaster, but if he's having the rewiring done, it will all need to be re-skimmed anyway.

I'm amused at how quickly my head's filled up with practicalities. I might never have owned a house, but I've done quite a lot of decorating. And I've watched a lot of property programs, too, always fascinated to see how other people live.

I flick tiny pieces of dark blue paper off my arms. It gets everywhere. And what time is it? Okay, better stop. I empty the water from the bucket into the toilet, and then collect all the soggy scraps of wallpaper into the bucket. I take it downstairs, empty it into the dustbin, and then scrub my arms at the kitchen sink. Time to go to work. Well. I'll come back, this afternoon, and decide what to do. I could collect my stuff then, if I want to.

Or I could stay.

I pick up my bag, check my phone's in my pocket, and leave the house, locking the door behind me.

ॐ ॐ

This isn't the first time I've given everything up and started again. If I had to come up with a theme for my life, it's probably that. Gave up living at home for a life with Fitz in that caravan. I gave *that* up when he said we ought to have a baby. I was basically still at school, and thought this was properly bonkers, so I went home for a bit and finished my A-Levels. I think people expected me to give that up, actually, but I didn't.

When I was young, I spent a lot of time trying hard to do the opposite of what people expected. I don't think anyone thought I'd manage to get my exams, but I always did my homework, even when I was living on site. I used to write essays in the college library before I went home, so I didn't have to keep my books in the trailer. Like I said, it wasn't quite as chaotic as the squat, but you never knew what might happen. We came home from a festival once and the police had turned the whole place over. All our things strewn across the field. The men all ranting about "the system," Tansy in tears because they'd emptied out a whole tin of formula, "looking for drugs," and she had nothing left to feed her monstrously hungry baby. I was glad my college copies of *Tess of the d'Urbervilles* and Christopher Hill's book about the English Civil War had escaped all this by being safe in my locker.

Anyway, I gave that up and moved back home. My mum was pretty unwell at this time, so living at home wasn't brilliant. I spent a lot of time at Lizzie's house, because it was better. Clean sheets. Clean towels. Proper food. If I stayed over on a college night, her mum would make me a packed lunch, a good one, with ham sandwiches, crisps, an apple, and a carton of Ribena. I still feel bad about leaving Natalie—who was only twelve—to deal with Mum by herself. That was selfish, but I was too young to see it.

I managed all of university without giving up anything, which is quite impressive when you think about it. When that was over, I moved back to my hometown and lived with some girls who had proper jobs in banks and offices. And then I met Johnny and gave that up for something rather less secure, although—let's be fair—a lot more fun. My life's been a series of changes, sometimes quite abrupt, and the choices I've made have probably often been . . . stupid. Not careless—I've thought long and hard about them—but wrong, anyway, in one way or another.

I'm pretty much the only person I know who could run away

like this—the only person without children, without a house of my own, without a career or even a job I cared about; without any stuff, really. It all seemed more carefree and fun when I was younger, but now, not so much.

I'd like to live a different kind of life. I'd like to give up with the giving up. I'm not sure running away is the best way to do this; in fact, it seems like the opposite might be true. There wasn't anything that could have been fixed by hanging about, though.

"Are you okay, Jess? You're very quiet. Got a serious look on your face."

Maura is one of those people who's a good boss because she pays proper attention to her staff. The rest of the team all treat her like an extra mum. It's a cliché to imagine your workplace as a family—and even the nicest workplace is still quite a dysfunctional family—but she seems to have an enormous capacity to care about her employees. You get a bit of drama when everyone's young, but Maura always sorts everyone out.

"Oh, yeah. Yeah." I scrub busily at roasting pans. "Yeah, just trying to decide what to do about something."

"Is it anything I can help with?"

"Thanks. Probably not. Thanks though." I smile at her, and she looks searchingly at me before hurrying back out to the front of house. It's busy: Sunday lunch, usually the busiest lunch service of the week.

Talking about it would mean explaining, and I'm still not inclined to do that. It would be a long and complicated story, and really, what good is advice? No one ever follows it. You do what you want, however you might try to dress it up. Although when you don't know what you want, it's harder. What do I want? I rub my face with the back of my arm. My gloves are a size too big, and dishwashing makes my face itch, probably because it's difficult to scratch it. I always get soaked, as well; the front of my shirt is wringing wet. I need a waterproof apron.

I could stay at the house for the next two weeks, couldn't I? Until the rewiring is done, and the make-good plastering. If this Gethin person isn't going to move in quite yet, then why not? That would be okay. I don't much fancy the idea of sharing a house with him—but it's not like he's suggested that. And two weeks should be long enough to find a room somewhere, shouldn't it? Admittedly, then I'd be living with whoever else lives in the house I move to—maybe several other people— and I don't fancy that much either. But it's not like I have any choice. I can't afford to live on my own. And I've always known that; I've never imagined I'd be able to. The month alone at Sunnyside has spoiled me a bit. Even in its undecorated, unheated state, it's pleasant. And so lovely and quiet. That's one of the best things about it: the heavenly silence, the emptiness of the rooms.

⁂ ⁂

My inability to decide what to do reminds me of earlier in the year, when I was seriously thinking about leaving—leaving my job and the town as well as the place where I was living. For some reason I couldn't quite make myself take the final step. Why did I wait? I'm not sure. I try not to think about the things that wouldn't have happened if I'd left in August, or June, or last spring. I realize it's possible that equally awful—or even worse—things will happen if I stay at Sunnyside, or indeed if I don't. This thought makes me sigh. I wish . . . I suppose I just wish my life was less insecure. I want to be safe, and I'm not convinced I ever will be, or at least, I'm not convinced I'll ever feel like I am.

It could be worse, though. I miss my friends, but it's not like I don't speak to them. I speak to Noosha all the time, telling her about the house, and work, reassuring her that I'm okay, behaving as though this is a normal thing I've done. I called Lizzie last week, on her birthday. If I needed to see them, I'm sure I could arrange something. I still think—despite everything—that I've been very lucky. Mitch always had a temper, but that last afternoon—even though, really, it should have been me who was angry—he was furious. I think of all the words for it: incandescent with rage, ballistic—all of that and more.

I'm still not sure why he reacted the way he did. I'd assumed he sort of wanted to get caught. I mean, you don't mess about in your own home if you definitely don't want to get caught, do you? I don't know why I needed that final push, but I did, and here we are.

I suppose now I just need to take things one day at a time. I can do that.

❧ ❧

Back at Sunnyside, it seems strange to walk down the drive from the street, as though I'm entitled to be there. I unlock the back door and stand to listen. The lights are on, and there's music playing upstairs: Nirvana. And someone's been busy in the five hours I've been gone—the fridge is in place, and the washing machine, which is badly scuffed but presumably deemed acceptable. I open the fridge, which is full of stuff—bottles of beer, milk, cheese, ham, and eggs. He's been to Tesco, then. I'm not sure who this stuff is for, if he won't be living here. I open a cupboard, now full of pasta and tins of tomatoes, a big box of tea bags. A loaf of bread with the end cut off stands on a wooden board, along with a shiny new bread knife, and a block of butter on a plate. Did he think it was inappropriate to use mine? That would seem—ironic. There's an equally shiny new kettle, and a toaster. In the sink, soaking, are a selection of mugs, which all look like donations, printed with the logos of garages, the local council, and various chocolate brands. I dry up a couple and put the kettle on. I make two mugs of tea and take them upstairs.

I hear him singing in the box bedroom. I don't think he knows I'm here. I push the door open with my elbow. "Hello?"

"Oh shit, bloody hell," he says, turning a startled face toward me. He presses a hand to his chest. "You made me jump."

It makes me laugh. "Sorry. I made you some tea. I just guessed—one sugar?"

"Oh, cool, thanks. Hi. You'd better put it on the windowsill, I need to wash this horrible stuff off me."

He's half-finished the wall I started this morning.

"You've been busy."

"I really have. Running around like a . . . running around thing."

We shuffle round each other so he can get out of the room. I put one mug on the windowsill and look out at the house across the road. They have a large and impressive magnolia in their front garden, the remaining leaves huge and golden, next year's buds already showing.

He comes back into the room and leans to turn the stereo down. Then he picks up his mug.

"Thanks," he says again. "Actually, I don't take sugar. Or I'm not supposed to."

"Not supposed to?"

"Well, you know, it's not healthy, is it. Used to have two, when I was younger."

"Everyone did," I agree. I look out of the window and nod at the magnolia. "You should get one of those. Or are you going to pave over the front garden?"

"Oh God, I shouldn't think so. I can park on the drive. In the garage, even, not that anyone ever seems to park in their garage these days." He looks over at the tree. "It's a magnolia, right? How old do you think that is? Take ages before it would be that big, surely."

"That one looks pretty old," I agree, "but some varieties grow quite quickly. Might be nearly as tall as the house in ten years, if you planted one in the spring."

"Really?"

I nod again.

"My grandparents had one," he says. "Great big flowers like cups."

"Yeah? They're great. I like the big fat pink ones. And the ones with skinny petals. Maybe that one was planted when the house was built. Lots of them along here—they're a 1930s sort of tree, aren't they. Kind of deco-looking."

"I suppose they are."

"I always wonder what people thought," I tell him, "when they first arrived. They came from China, in the eighteenth century. People would have planted them who'd only ever seen drawings. Imagine that." I sip my tea, musing on garden history.

He turns to look at me. "I'd never thought about that," he says. "Is that where they're from? China?"

"Yeah. Although I think some are American. So maybe they came from there, first." I frown. Then I think of something else. "You know they're extremely ancient, as a type of plant. They developed before bees even existed."

"Before bees? Shit." He laughs. "Hard to imagine a world before bees. So, what, did they get pollinated by dinosaurs?"

I know he's joking, but I shake my head anyway. "Beetles. You've got some nice trees here. I think there's apple and pear in the garden, and maybe a plum tree? Hard to tell at this time of year. They flower earlier, though, so you'll be able to tell in the spring."

"Those ones down the end?"

I nod again.

"I thought they were fruit trees, but I didn't know what kind. There was no one to ask."

"Did she die, the old lady who lived here before? Mrs. Evans?"

"Yeah. The house had been empty for quite a while, when we first came to look at it. You know a lot about plants?"

"I wouldn't say a lot. A bit. I'm interested." I grin at him. "When I was at university I used to tape *Gardeners' World* and watch it when I got in on a Friday night. Totally the coolest person on my course."

He laughs at this. "Did you have a garden, where you lived before?"

"Not most recently. But before that."

Gethin nods. "Yeah, we had a big garden. Acers, silver birch. I thought I might get one of those big round glazed pots, you know," he goes on, "and have a little Acer on the patio. We had it landscaped, the garden, when we moved in. I think maybe it would have been better to leave it. But my . . . the person I lived with wanted it all done, modern, you know, gravel and grasses and stuff."

"That can look very stylish," I say. I wonder who he lived with, and why he won't say "wife" or whatever. Maybe it was a man. People don't always want to out themselves randomly. He doesn't seem very gay, though. Whatever that means.

"Yeah, I suppose it was stylish. I didn't really get involved; we had a gardener."

I blink at him, surprised. Then I remind myself that people who are busy often have gardeners. Even if it sounds very fancy, it isn't really, like having a cleaner—loads of people have them.

"Did you live there for a long time?"

I don't think he hears me. I wonder if I should say it again. It's not important, after all. I sip my tea, watching him. We're closer, now, than when we sat on the patio. I can see the fine lines round his eyes, frown lines between his brows. He hasn't shaved for a couple of days—probably since Friday morning. His eyes are a complex hazel; they look quite different in here—it must be the light. He sighs and looks at me for a moment.

"Hm? Oh, yeah, a while. Nearly ten years. I never really liked it though, if I'm honest."

"No?"

"The house was a bit . . . well, it was the same thing, I guess, had a lot of work done before we moved in, all very"—he gestures with his free hand—"minimalist, you know. I'm not sure that's really my style."

"Right." This is all quite interesting. I didn't really mean to be interested, but that's what happens when you talk to someone, isn't it? "Did you break up?" I mean, I guess they did; this "person" isn't here, hasn't been to the house. Unless they died—shit, I hope they didn't.

"Yeah. Nearly a year ago—January."

"Sorry."

"God, no, it was a massive relief," he says, and laughs. "Jesus."

"Oh, okay. Well, that's good." I forgot even normal people can end relationships and be pleased about it.

"Yes. Anyway, so—are you going to stay?"

"I haven't decided yet," I say, cautious.

"I bought you a bed, if you want it. I mean—not you specifically. I bought a spare bed, for one of my spare rooms. Which you can sleep on—in?—if you like."

I suppose this makes sense—after all, you don't have two spare bedrooms and not put a bed in at least one of them—but it still seems . . .

"In fact, I should think it'll be easier to put together with two people. Maybe we should do that now. Then it's here if you need it."

With this, he's off, and I follow him to the large front bedroom. He's put the light on, and on the bare dusty floorboards there's a long, flat box, and against the wall, a single mattress, swathed in plastic. In a heap beside it are plastic-wrapped sheets and two sets of plain white duvet covers and pillowcases. A duvet and pillows, tightly packaged and ready to leap up and double their size, sit in the corner.

I look at all this, amazed at how much he's achieved since I left for work this morning. And how on earth did he get all this stuff in his car? Surely he didn't get a mattress in there. He must have borrowed a van or something.

I watch as he puts his mug on the floor and feels in his pockets. He pulls out a miniature Swiss Army knife, opens it, and kneels on the floor to open the box. I feel a bit uncomfortable.

"This is all costing you money," I object.

"I'll need it whatever you decide." He looks up at me. "Please don't worry about that."

"Yeah, I dunno, this is weird. I think it might be too weird? I think—"

"Look, please. I'm sure you'd be fine in your tent—even in the winter. I'm not suggesting for one minute that you can't cope with the way your life is. You seem extremely—what's the word?—self-reliant. Resourceful, too. And I know you're not my responsibility, and it's not my job to house you, and blah blah, all that. But here we are, and I do have an empty house." He spreads his arms, encompassing the room. "And I'll need a bed for the box room, probably—I mean, I don't think it will be an office—so I've bought a bed. It didn't cost much. I sold a much more expensive house to buy this one, you know. And although I only got half the money for that, obviously, I'm not short of cash. I'm not trying to . . . I don't know, whatever it is you're worried about."

I lean against the wall and fold my arms. I like the idea of myself as self-reliant and resourceful, although I'm not sure how true it is. "You'd probably say that, though. Wouldn't you?"

He shifts position so he's sitting on the floor with his back to the other wall. We look at each other.

"I don't know what happened, to make you give up your life and come here. I get that it must have been pretty—significant. I don't want to add to your confusion or trauma or pain or anything. I'd just like to help."

"Yeah, it probably wasn't that significant. And I do sort of believe you," I tell him, "but I really don't get why you'd do any of this for some random woman you just met."

"I might have run away myself if I was brave enough," he says.

I raise my eyebrows. "That bad, was it?"

He makes a frustrated noise. "Ugh, no, okay, I'm being melodramatic. My relationship was just shit, not . . . abusive, in any way. I don't want to make assumptions about why you're here. Maybe you didn't run away from an actual person." He looks at me, but I don't react. "I still felt trapped and helpless, though, and"—he gestures—"you know. I did want to escape, and I didn't know how."

Perhaps it's wrong of me to think none of this can be true, because he's a man, and they can do whatever they want. That's me being lazy in my thinking. I know it's not as straightforward as that. Nothing ever is.

"How did you, in the end, then?"

"I just waited, didn't I. Until it was unavoidable. I'm a coward." He picks at a loose thread on the hem of his jeans.

I feel a bit sorry for him. I recognize that he's trying to demonstrate empathy for my situation. Perhaps I was harsh. I, too, have been a coward.

"Yeah, well. It's not easy. Sunk time fallacy and all that."

"What's that?"

"Where you go, 'But we've been together for five years; if I leave, that's time wasted.' "

"Oh. God, yes. And it's a bit stupid really. Is any time wasted?"

I shrug.

"I mean, it all contributes, doesn't it? To making you who you are."

"Yeah, well, I did leave a relationship," I admit, "and there are some bits I could have done without."

"Once it's happened, though? You can't go back, so you have to—I won't say accept it. If it was bad. But, you know. Acknowledge it."

"I think I wasted some time. Or had it wasted for me." I think about this. "I don't know, though, because you can't know what things would be like if you'd made different choices."

It's easy to think everything would be okay if I'd never met Mitch, or if I'd refused to go for that drink with him. I'd definitely choose differently, if I found myself back at the garage, worried about how much my car was going to cost to fix, bantering with the mechanic who seemed unexpectedly interested in me. And if I'd chosen differently, I'm fairly sure I wouldn't be here, now, in this odd situation that could easily be awful but is strangely fine.

Gethin returns his attention to the cardboard box. "Anyway," he says, "are you going to help me with this?" He slices open the box and begins to extract pieces of bed frame. I purse my lips, thinking. I don't suppose there's any risk involved in helping put a bed together.

As it turns out, perhaps unsurprisingly, it's a massive bonding exercise. We wrestle with lengths of wood too long for one person to hold and manage, inevitably, to put a vital piece in upside down, not realizing until we reach the final stretch.

"But where are the screw holes for this side?" he says, puzzled, frowning at the frame. I sit back on my haunches, slightly sweaty.

"Oh God. This bit's the wrong way up, isn't it? And that means it's on the wrong side, and that means—"

"Shit, the whole lot'll have to come apart." We look at each other and he starts laughing. "I'm rubbish at this sort of thing."

"It always happens." I shake my head. "That's why you get

all those gags about flatpack furniture. If we knew each other better, we'd probably have had a fight."

"Were you holding back?"

I laugh too. "No, you looked perfectly competent."

"Clearly not, though. Shit."

"Anyway," I add, "people aren't usually annoying until you know them. Give me the thing." I hold my hand out for the Allen key. "I'll undo this side."

Once the bed has been taken apart and reassembled, and we've wrestled the mattress out of its wrapper, I'm quite tired. It's properly dark now, the window a black rectangle of reflection.

"Is it okay here? I mean, if you were going to sleep here, tonight, and in this room—"

I begin stuffing the duvet into its cover. "I'm sure it would be fine."

"Okay, good. Pass us the pillowcases."

We finish making the bed and step back to admire our achievements.

"I thought that would take, like, ten minutes," he says ruefully, "not an hour."

"Hour and a half, more like. It's gone five."

"Bloody hell, is it? Well. That's enough for today. Do you want to get something to eat? We could get Chinese or something."

I hesitate.

"Or do you want me to bugger off and leave you alone?"

This makes me laugh. "It's your house. I can hardly expect you to bugger off."

"Are you going to stay?"

I gather plastic and cardboard to take back downstairs. The brand-new bed looks very tempting. A duvet. Imagine.

"Might stay tonight."

"Good. So you can let the electrician in tomorrow?" He clicks off the light in the bedroom and goes into the box room to do the same in there.

"Oh, yeah. I could do that. When's he coming?" I try not to trip over my own feet on the way down.

"Half eight? Nine o'clock? Earlyish. Are you working? You weren't working this evening?"

"Closed Sunday evenings."

"Oh, right."

"And Mondays, although not at the moment. But I do have tomorrow off. So yeah, I could be here. Usually I go to the library on a Monday," I explain, "because it's warm and they have the lights on."

"Why did you—? Oh . . . did you not put the lights on here?"

"No, I only used your electricity to charge my phone, and cook. Which reminds me, there's money, downstairs, for that."

"For the power you used to charge your phone? You're all right," he says, shaking his head, clearly amused. "I'll treat you to your three quids' worth of 'leccy."

Back in the kitchen, he says, "I went to the supermarket, so help yourself."

"I saw, yes." I drag the packaging outside and stuff it into the appropriate bins.

"Shall I put the kettle on? Or do you want a beer?"

Should I drink beer with this man? I like him, I think; but that in itself is worrying.

"Tea, please."

"Righty-ho." He picks up the kettle and fills it at the tap. "Do you mind if I have a beer?"

"No, no, of course not. Why would I?"

"I don't know. Maybe if . . . you lived with someone who drank?"

"Oh. No. Well, not to excess anyway." As I say this, I wonder if it's true. Mitch did drink too much, sometimes, but he wasn't worse when he'd been drinking. Or not much worse.

❧ ❧

We sit, slightly awkward, on the sofa. It's strange to have someone else in what has basically been my bedroom. He brings a big bag of crisps in from the kitchen, and a stack of takeaway menus from the pile on the porch.

"What do you fancy, then? Chinese? Pizza?"

"I don't mind," I say helpfully. I pick up my bag and find my purse. "I've got ten pounds."

"I don't need your money; don't be ridiculous." He opens the crisps and offers the packet to me.

"I don't want you to buy my dinner." I take a handful of crisps, and we look at each other for a long moment. He rubs a hand across his temple.

"But—"

"No, I mean it, it's bad enough as it is."

"Well, okay," he says, "if you'd rather. Chinese? Pick something then. But promise you'll have some of mine too."

"I don't mind sharing, I just don't want you to pay for . . . everything."

"Okay."

ЗК К

We eat crispy aromatic duck rolled into pancakes, prawn toast, special fried rice. He bought some plates, in Tesco, earlier, but forgot to get any cutlery, so he uses my fork and I eat rice with a spoon. We put the cushions from the sofa on the floor and sit opposite each other, the food between us on the parquet. He drinks a bottle of Amstel and talks about when he last lived in Caerwyddon, in his teens and twenties. When he asks me questions, he's cautious. I think he's trying not to seem like he wants to find things out—you know, big, important things.

He asks if I went to university, and when I admit that I did, decides it's safe enough to ask me about that. And it is, I suppose, so we talk about college, about moving away from home and then coming back again, changed by the things you learn, and how some of your friends drop away, often without you even noticing. I was a bit different from most people I met at university, because I'd lived away from home already, and on site—I think I was regarded as somehow older and wiser, when in fact I was exactly the same age and twice as stupid. I skirt around this story but tell him enough to be amusing.

It's eight o'clock when he leaves, and it's odd to stand in the doorway and wave goodbye. He's given me a front-door key, reminded me about the electrician, thanked me for my work in the bedroom. I feel almost like we know each other. When I close the door behind him and go to wash up the plates, the house feels strangely empty.

Chapter Four

In the morning, the electrician arrives at half past eight. His name's Davey, and he was at school with Gethin, apparently. He's a big, jovial man, with a graying beard and a shaved head. He's either polite enough not to appear too inquisitive about my presence, or else he really doesn't care. He's happy to tell me about the life of an electrician. I always enjoy watching tradesmen and asking them nosy questions. Although this has got me into trouble—if I wasn't interested in this sort of thing, I'd probably never have spoken to Mitch—I don't feel there's much danger of repeating that particular error, at least not in this case.

He reassures me that he'll be able to reconnect everything each evening, so I won't have to sit in the dark, or boil water on my Primus stove. I leave him to it and, once he's done the box room, continue to strip the wallpaper, wondering how far he'll have got by the end of the day. He says it should be pretty quick, since the house is empty. And he does the plastering himself, although an actual plasterer will be required in the box room because the plaster's coming off in chunks with the woodchip.

I'm beginning to feel intensely invested in the renovation of the house. That's probably quite stupid.

I strip more wallpaper on Tuesday and Wednesday between my shifts and when I get home from work. I finish the box room (finally!) and move on to the master bedroom. It seems to me that this is the room Gethin will sleep in, so it's only fair to do it next. It's much easier and only takes a couple of hours. I take up the carpet, too, slicing along the edges of the wardrobes with a Stanley knife borrowed from Davey. This is cheating, but I can't take them apart by myself; I don't have any tools. I clean the window and wash the windowsill and skirting boards. Then I move on to the front bedroom.

By Friday, Davey's in the final room, the back sitting room/ dining room, and then he just has to check the supply to the outside loo and the garage, and it's finished. Very efficient. A man's coming later this afternoon to measure up in the master bedroom to replace the ugly fitted wardrobes and see about putting a cupboard in the box room. It's all go.

At half past three, not long after I get back from lunch service, the doorbell rings. I answer the door to a fifty-something dark-haired woman in "business dress"—jacket, blouse, tailored trousers, smart shoes.

"Hello?" I say.

She looks me up and down with great deliberation. I can't remember anyone ever actually noticeably doing that before. It's quite the mood.

"You'll be Jess, then," she says. "I'm Abby Thomas. Gethin's sister."

"Oh! Come in. Hello." I smile at her, but she doesn't smile back.

"I said I'd come round and check how it's going."

"Oh, yes, really well. Davey's almost done. Do you want to see upstairs?"

"I'll speak to him first," she says, and looks around. "Where is he?"

"In the dining room, just—" I say, but she's already brushing past me and heading down the hall.

I close the front door and look after her, frowning. Well, it's not my house; she's as much right (more?) than I have to be here. I go back into the front sitting room, where I've been reading my book, sitting beneath the bay window on a cushion from the sofa—there's no other furniture yet, except the bed. I'm not sure that Gethin owns any furniture.

I hear their voices, but not what they're saying. Then I hear Abby's footsteps as she climbs the uncarpeted stairs. I've taken all the carpet up now, and pried up the gripper rods with a screwdriver, also borrowed from Davey. Sometimes I've stripped wallpaper until two in the morning. I can't go to bed as soon as I get in from work, I need to wind down a bit, so it seems like I might as well be useful.

When she comes back down again, I go out to meet her.

"He's done a good job, I think?"

"Yes, it all seems fine," she says. "I'll call Geth later and let him know." She pauses, looking at me. She's got her best "let me speak to a manager" face on.

"I don't know who you are, and I don't know what you're after," she says, "but I want you to know that I'm paying attention. My brother's had a lot to deal with recently, and I don't want anyone making trouble for him."

I stare at her. "I'm not here to cause trouble."

"So you say. He's had a tough time and he's not in the best place, what with everything that's happened. So just know I've got my eye on you."

"Right." I'm very annoyed by this.

"You might think he's a soft touch," she goes on, "but—"

"I think no such thing," I tell her. "Why would I think that?"

"Well." She looks at the front door. "I'd better go."

"Lovely to meet you," I say, deadpan.

"You should google his ex," she says, turning back toward me. "Vanessa Winslade."

"And why would I want to do that?"

"You might find it enlightening." She opens the door and steps through it. "Goodbye."

"Yeah." I close the door. "Whatever." I stand in the hallway, frowning. "So that's the most unpleasant thing that's happened to me since I got here," I say aloud.

"I didn't hear all of it," says Davey, emerging into the hall and making me jump, "but she's very protective of Geth, is Abby."

"No shit."

"You probably shouldn't take it personally, like."

"Shouldn't I? It felt quite personal."

He pulls a face. "Yeah."

"And what's all this about his ex? It's really nothing to do with me, is it? It's none of my business."

"Maybe you should look her up. Vanessa's . . . well, you'll see." He laughs. "She went to our school as well, not that you'd think it to look at her."

"Seems a bit nosy to look."

He shrugs. "Anyway, she worries about him, Abby does."

"He seems perfectly fine. Does he need looking after?" I've met men like that; he really doesn't seem like one.

He looks uncomfortable. "You know their brother died. Evan."

"Did he? No, I didn't know that. He's the one who was homeless?"

He nods. "Bad into drugs, he was."

"Yeah, I kind of gathered that. Not sure what she thinks I'm 'trying to do,' though."

"I suppose . . . well, Gethin's not badly off, is he. I don't know how you met," he says. "You might . . ."

"Everyone's better off than me, Davey. You, for example. You think I'm trying to shag you? If that's what she's accusing me of?"

He flushes. "No, of course not. Anyway," he says, making it a joke, "my wife would have something to say about that."

"I've only met Gethin twice. It's a peculiar thing to think. I mean, he seems nice enough, but do people throw themselves at him? It seems unlikely. However well-off he might be. Pfft."

"Yeah, she's not tactful, Abby."

"You don't say. Anyway, are you done?"

"Yeah, just got to tidy up. The power's back on—put the kettle on, yeah?"

I look at my phone to check the time. "Okay."

"Cheers." He goes back into the dining room, and I go into the kitchen to make some tea.

❧ ❧

Later that afternoon, as I walk down the hill in the dark, surrounded by the glittering lights of an evening in late November, I think about Abby Thomas. I suppose it's not completely unreasonable that she's suspicious of me. I'm trying to be fair, although that's always annoying, isn't it. I've spent so long trying to stop myself having feelings, it's odd to find I'm absolutely seething with them now. So many feelings, of which irritation and outrage (how bloody dare she, indeed) mingle with, what? I don't know; anxiety is pretty much my ground state, so that's not unusual. I suppose I'm worried she might somehow . . . what if she says something weird to Gethin? I'd find that unbearably embarrassing, although I'm not sure why. Maybe I should phone him. I put his number into my phone on Sunday, in case I needed to get hold of him. I stop and scroll through my contacts. I'm not very good at walking along and doing things on my phone at the same time—there's a difference between people who had phones in their teens and those who didn't—so I wait until he answers before I start walking again.

"Gethin, it's Jess. You're not driving, are you?"

"Hands-free," he says. "Is everything okay? Davey finished for the day?"

"Yes, it's fine. And he's finished in the house; just got to do the outdoor stuff."

"Cool. Quicker than I thought."

"Yeah, I think he's very efficient." I clear my throat, wondering how I should approach what I want to say. There's no point hedging, though, is there. "Your sister came round?"

"Oh yeah, she said she might pop in."

"Yes. Look, I thought I should ring, 'cos she was quite—er—funny with me."

There's a pause. Then, "Was she? What did she say?"

I give him a summary and finish with: "And you know, maybe I'd feel the same if I were her. But the whole thing was odd, and I don't want things to be odd, and I thought I should tell you."

A pause while he thinks about this. "Do you want me to talk to her about it?"

"God, no." I'm faintly horrified at the suggestion. "No. I shouldn't think that would help. But the thing is . . ." I'm at the restaurant now, so I stop outside to finish the conversation. "The thing is, this is . . . if you don't want me at your house, just say. I'm not 'up to' anything."

"I know."

"You do not," I say, now oddly annoyed by this. "But I'm not."

He laughs. "No, okay, what I mean is, 'I believe you.' "

"Right, good. I don't even know what she thinks I might be trying to do," I complain. "But I'm not, whatever it is. Anyway, I needed to get that off my chest. I have to go to work now."

"Okay. I'll see you tomorrow."

"Okay."

છ ૬

I spoke to Maura about my hours, and even though this is a busy weekend for the restaurant, I have all of Saturday and Sunday lunch off, plus Monday, which means three whole days, and that's unexpectedly exciting. I've worked pretty much every shift available since I started, so I suppose it's not really *that* surprising that three consecutive days off is a treat. Now I've stripped the wallpaper upstairs—wobbling precariously on the ladder to do as much of the stairwell as possible—I could start painting. The plaster from the rewiring is dry up here, I think, or nearly—anyway, I could do all the walls that haven't been plastered, if that's what he wants.

If he does want any of the woodwork stripped, he'll need to buy some paint stripper, though, or one of those things like a hair dryer. And a sander. Any of which I could ask him to get—after all, he's (presumably?) not on a budget. May as well make a proper job of it. Or I could do the wallpaper

downstairs, or . . . we need to have a meeting about it. I laugh
at this idea. I suppose he's my manager, isn't he, for this job
I'm doing in exchange for board and lodging. Strangely, it
seems easier to work hard on this project because it's not my
house. And maybe because he's not been here, it does feel like
an odd combination of a job and something I'm doing for my
own benefit.

❧ ❧

I have nightmares twice during the week. It's unexpected; I
haven't had bad dreams since I stopped sleeping at the cemetery. Horrible, suffocating, running-away-from-something-
awful anxiety dreams. I had them nearly every night when I
was in the tent, so the feeling is very familiar. I'm not sure
what's been stirred up to produce them, but since I haven't
even attempted to deal with any of that stuff, I suppose it's
only to be expected. As I lie in my single bed under the brand-
new duvet and stare up at the ceiling in the half-darkness—
with no curtains or blinds in the large front bedroom, it's never
very dark, because of the streetlight across the road—I will my
heart rate to return to normal. I wonder if part of the problem
is the size of the room and the lack of stuff. The bed is in the
middle of the uncarpeted floor, where we left it once it was put
together. It does feel a bit strange, isolated away from the
walls.

It's very quiet here in the dead of night. You never hear anything much; hardly any cars pass during the hours of darkness.
I'm never afraid though, being alone here; or not while I'm
awake, anyway. And the things I'm afraid of in my dreams are
nothing to do with Sunnyside.

❧ ❧

Last night after work, following a considerable tussle with my conscience, I googled Vanessa Winslade.

Right. Okay, I see what Davey means. She's quite a big TV star—in Wales, which is why I haven't heard of her, I guess. She does local stuff, and sometimes the Welsh bits of magaziny lifestyle sort of programs. She did six months on *The One Show* a couple of years ago when someone had a baby. The pictures are all of a very much put-together, telly sort of person, in beautiful clothes, with those legs you can cross elegantly when sitting on a sofa. Lustrous dark hair, and the sort of tan you get on glam Welsh girls—from the salon. (This is a judgment on the weather, not on them.) Since she's only a year or two younger than me, I think she must have had some work done—might just be a bit of Botox though. Or perhaps it's post-production and done in Photoshop. There's an article about the house she and Gethin used to live in, in a Sunday supplement, and it's pretty jaw-dropping if I'm honest. I can see what he means about it being a bit impersonal, though.

There's a gossipy sort of story about their breakup, with no real information, and I find several pictures of them together: one with him looking slightly awkward (although still very . . . I think he's quite good-looking) in a tux at some kind of industry do; a couple of very staged images taken in their spaciously empty cream and white sitting room; and another of them together at the seaside somewhere, looking attractively casual and windblown, with a backdrop of rocks and ocean. I look at this for ages, wondering if they were already unhappy when it was taken. Photos are odd, the way they show some things but not others.

I'm still not sure why Abby wanted me to see any of this, unless it's to demonstrate that he's way out of my league. Since I'm not running a league, this isn't of much importance. It's funny, though, to see this unexpected side of him. I can see why they might have had some conflicts in their personal life; it's hard to be a normal person whose partner is famous. And he does seem pretty normal.

Chapter Five

I FaceTime Noosha from my new bed.

"Look," I say. "I'm sleeping in a bed. With a duvet!"

"Wow. Where are you? That room looks very empty," she adds as I hold up my phone for her to see.

"Yeah, I'm still at the same place. Gethin bought a bed. And I'm sleeping in it."

"Gethin," she says. "This man. Who owns the house."

"That's right."

"And where's he sleeping?"

"At his sister's."

"Right."

"What?"

She rubs a hand across her forehead. "But he's got, like, a key, right?"

"For the house? Yes, obviously. It's his house."

"Is that . . . it doesn't sound very . . . secure?"

"Oh. I bolt the front door," I tell her, "when I go to bed. If that's what you're asking. I mean, he couldn't get in at night. Not saying he'd want to."

"He doesn't mind you locking him out of his house?"

"He doesn't know, does he. He'd only know if he came here at night and tried to get in, and if he did that"—

I pause—"I probably wouldn't be that bothered about offending him."

"Okay. And at some point he'll be moving in?"

"Yes, but . . . I guess I'll be moving out, then. In like a week and a half." I frown at her.

"Right."

"You needn't worry about me, Noosh. It's fine, honestly. He seems perfectly okay." I think about this for a moment. It's definitely true. "I'm being very cautious."

"Are you? I'm not saying you're not," she says, "it just seems . . . I'm not sure I understand why he's let you stay there."

"I'm not either," I admit. "Although he was right about the fecking woodchip."

"Yes, see—although I agree that woodchip is the ultimate bastard," she says, "I'm not totally convinced I'd let a stranger stay at my house just to get out of dealing with it."

"No."

"No. So you see what I'm saying?"

"It's only for two weeks, and he's not here most of the time. It's not like we're sharing a house or anything."

"No."

"I've thought about it loads, Noosh, and I can't see . . . I can't work out how he could exploit the situation, you know, if that's what he wanted to do? I can't see why he'd want to, either, but you know what I mean. He's mostly not here, and he hasn't said anything weird or . . ."

"It's intrinsically weird though. Isn't it?"

"I suppose it is. A bit. But anyway, I'll . . . I'm sure I'll find a room, and be able to move out before he moves in, I should think. I've nearly got enough money."

"Yeah, so don't forget I have money, darling, and you can have some of it."

I laugh. "I don't need it though. It's fine. I'm fine. I have a bed and it's warm here now and I can have the lights on and he bought loads of food—"

"For you to eat?"

"I'll have to eat the stuff in the fridge or it will go off."

"Yeah. Well, just be . . . be careful, Jess?"

"I'm being extremely careful. No one," I say, "has ever been careful-er."

❧ ❧

"Wow," says Gethin. "This is amazing. How have you done all this?" He looks round the master bedroom, all prepped and ready for whatever he wants to do next.

I shrug. "The wardrobes still need to come out. Maybe we should do that today? I always hate anything where I think, 'That'd be easier with a man,'" I continue, grinning at him, "but it definitely would be."

"You might need a different sort of man," he says, looking doubtfully at the wardrobes, which are large, and fitted—and ugly—in dark wood, with louvered doors.

"Yeah, they're not very well-made; I don't think it will be too bad. Did you buy some screwdrivers?"

"One of those electric things like a drill."

"Oh, well, I might be able to do it by myself, then."

"I'm only kidding," he says. "Of course I'll help you. You've done everything else."

"The wallpaper was easy, though, in the big bedrooms. It all came off like a dream compared to the woodchip. I saved you some bits in case you were interested." Old wallpaper is social history, after all—an insight into the time it was put up, as well as the taste and personality of the person who chose it.

He nods, and we look solemnly at the vintage wallpaper.

"Can't say I'd want to replicate any of this, like," he says, holding up a piece from the front bedroom, wildly psychedelic pink florals.

I laugh. "Maybe not. Anyway, so what are you going to do in here? Put up more wallpaper? Paint? If you just want to paint, it probably needs to be skimmed."

He walks about, opening and shutting the door and gazing out of the window. "I dunno, really. I thought I'd do everything quite pale, though. Neutral. No feature walls."

"I don't mind a painted feature wall," I say. "But a wallpaper one is very aughties."

He laughs. "So much to think about. Anyway, do you want to do the wardrobes now, or can you come and look at carpet? And then I thought I might see what kitchens are available."

I'm surprised by this. "Oh, well, you don't need me for that, do you?"

"I can't choose carpet on my own. God," he says, "I wouldn't know where to start."

꧁ ꧂

"I can't remember the last time I was in a car," I tell him, strapping myself in. He drives one of those expensively understated things, a big BMW 5 Series Saloon. There's no way he put a fridge in here. Or a mattress.

"Can you drive?" he asks me.

"Yeah."

"You didn't have a car, though? To run away in?"

I glance sideways at him. "No. My car died. And two cars was considered unnecessary, so I didn't get another one." Saying this out loud reinforces how outrageous it was, and I shake my head, slightly astonished.

"Ah, right," he says. "I'll put you on the insurance if you like."

This time I turn properly to look at him. "What the hell? Am I some kind of project? Why on earth would you do that?"

"Oh, well. It just seems like . . . sorry . . . look, none of the things I suggest are intended to be, you know, offensive."

"No, okay, but . . . this is the sort of thing your sister's talking about, isn't it? She'd think it was my idea, and expect me to steal your car, or . . . you should be careful."

We drive for a while in silence, down the hill and right at the big roundabout covered in dozens of dancing red dragons. I can't believe it. Who offers to put a stranger on their car insurance? Maybe the same sort of person who lets a stranger live at their house. It worries me that he might take risks like this all the time. He doesn't seem like he would, but . . .

"I've asked you this before, but am I wrong to trust you?" he says.

I sigh, irritable. "No, but, again, I would say that. It's like . . . usually you build up trust, don't you? It's a gradual thing while you get to know someone? And we really don't know each other. But you've"—I wave a hand vaguely—"piled a massive heap of trust on me. And it's odd, and it makes me a bit uncomfortable, and also it makes me worry that you do this to everyone. And not everyone is trustworthy."

"Yeah, I do realize that."

"I'm sure you do. You don't seem like an idiot."

"Cheers."

I turn back to look out of the window. We're crossing the river now, and I gaze down at the lazy loops of it. When you see the Towy on a map, it looks like a geography lesson, with proper meanders. It's very high today, lapping level with the top of the bank in places.

I haven't seen much of the countryside since I arrived—working pretty much every available hour, in winter, and with no transport—but I've been thinking I might try to get a bike from somewhere, in the spring. Local Facebook is always full of secondhand bikes. After all, it might feel odd to admit it, and I don't think I'm quite used to the idea, but I live here now, and I should do some of the things you do when you move to a new place.

❧ ❦

At the carpet shop I realize I've never bought carpet.

"God, there's a lot of choice," says Gethin, looking round at the brightly lit room full of samples, some rolled against the walls, or laid out in huge racks, some in flappable stacks.

"It's all quite dull as well. Not that I think carpet should be interesting." I frown at the various options. "You just need it to be warm, and the right shade that you don't need to vacuum twice a day. Is this for upstairs, or are you going to cover up the parquet?"

"Bedrooms only. Oh, and the stairs and landing. Might buy a big Persian rug for the front room. I know a guy who sells them."

We wander about, poking at things. I remember a house I visited once where the sitting room was carpeted with samples, like a patchwork floor. They kept a pile of samples in a corner, and if anything got spilled, or burnt—it was that sort of house—they took up the damaged bit and replaced it with a fresh one. I haven't thought about that for years.

"Nice. So anyway, they just need to be beige, don't they? Or do you want something more colorful?" I ask.

"Beige is fine. Oatmeal, oyster, taupe . . ."

An assistant comes over and we get involved in quite a tiring conversation about wool/synthetic ratios and quality of underlay and so on. Since money's no object, it's reasonably fun, though. As soon as this becomes apparent, the assistant becomes much more enthusiastic. We sit down and he brings us things to look at. He thinks we're married, and who can blame him? We don't explain that we're not. In fact, I think Gethin finds it amusing. Once the carpet is chosen, he arranges for someone to come and measure up. It's all very easy—I suppose that's because there's no need to compromise, and also because he basically wants something expensive but dull.

As we return to the car, I say this.

"Expensive but dull?" He grins at me. "That's me all over."

"Ha ha. But don't you think?"

"I suppose so. Can't get that excited about carpet, really."

"What did you have at your old house?"

"Reclaimed oak floorboards downstairs," he says. "Carpet in the bedrooms. Acres of it."

"How many bedrooms?"

"Oh, well."

I think he's embarrassed. I wait.

"Seven," he says, glancing sideways at me.

"That's a lot of carpet."

"It was a lot of house."

"Sounds like it." I don't tell him I've seen pictures; that

would sound weird, and also involve me explaining why I looked him (or, rather, her) up. "Did you live together before you moved there?"

"Oh, yeah. We had a Victorian semi in Cardiff before that, and when we were first together, we lived in a flat for a while. Quite a nice flat—big, Edwardian, period features all over the place. My . . . she's always earned a lot of money."

"Davey said you were at school together, you and your ex."

"Yeah."

"So you'd been together since then? Like, thirty years?"

"Oh—no. No, I did know her, or I knew who she was, but she was . . . she's younger, and we didn't really move in the same circles." He laughs. "Anyway, I went to a thing—an industry thing, it was an awards do—about sixteen years ago? She was MC, you know—she used to do a lot of that sort of event. She's quite well known, locally."

"Is she?" I say, unwilling to explain that actually, I know quite a lot about Vanessa Winslade.

"Yeah. So that's where I met her. She remembered me from school, which was surprising."

"And you remembered her?"

"Yeah, vaguely. She was mates with the younger sisters of a couple of my friends. And then, like I say, she was already quite well known. I can't think of anyone else remotely famous who went to our school."

"Is she famous?" I ask, innocently.

"Yeah, kind of. She's . . . well, she's a presenter. On the telly," he explains.

"Gosh, really?"

"Yeah. Did you want to get coffee? Or shall we go and look at kitchens first?"

I take this as a deliberate diversion and vote to look at kitchens.

This is lots of fun. I'm pretty sure I'll never be ordering a brand-new kitchen for myself, so this is the closest I'll ever get to making all these decisions, discussing numbers of cupboards and whether a built-in wine rack is useful and if you need a full-size dishwasher when you're not a family of four (yes, probably). Gethin measured various things before we came out, so we can sit with a salesperson who does a rough design while we debate whether the sink could be better positioned and what kind of oven to get. We discuss worktop surfaces and the latest design elements and types of hob and soft-close drawers and so on. I find the whole thing extremely enjoyable. In fact, every time I remind myself it's basically nothing to do with me, I get a sort of pain in my stomach.

They give us a brochure and a printout of the rough plan they've done so we can take it away and discuss it further. Then we go for coffee, which I buy, because I feel as though I'm getting a hugely free ride at the moment.

We sit in a dark corner of Starbucks with our drinks, toasted sandwiches, and cake. Coffee shops are always surprisingly busy, even ones on obscure retail parks. I suppose it's not that obscure. And people are always buying tiles and hiring machinery and ordering new windows, it's just you never think about any of that when you're not doing it yourself.

"So you think I shouldn't get a tiled floor?" he says, continuing a discussion we started in the showroom.

"Oh, I don't know. It'll look good. But my sister says vinyl's better because things are less likely to break if you drop them. And it's warmer."

"Hm. I was thinking slate would be good."

"I like a slate floor. That would look amazing. But if you drop a glass—"

"Buy another glass, I guess." He shrugs.

I laugh at such profligacy. "I know. It's just another thing to consider. I don't know, I've never bought flooring." I cut my toasted sandwich in half, and then in half again.

"What did you have in your last house?"

"Really horrible cheap vinyl. Permanently sticky and curled up round the bottom of the units. My ex wasn't really interested in that sort of thing," I say, amused at my understatement.

"I'll cross that off the list, then. 'No horrible cheap vinyl.' I suppose there must be floorboards, under the lino? Or maybe it's concrete. We could look. Anyway, d'you think it needs wall cabinets on both sides?" He slides the printout toward me. I push away thoughts of the past and concentrate on the present—or future, even. We discuss cupboards versus shelves, and extractor fans, and types of tap.

He sips his coffee. "You know, this is a lot more fun than the last time I did it."

"Is it? Why's that?" I look at him, surprised. Surely it would be more fun to do this with your partner, wouldn't it? I mean, they're fully engaged with the whole thing. Not that I'm *not* fully engaged.

"My . . . Vanessa"—this is the first time he's used her name when speaking to me about her—"she just wanted to spend loads of money. So we did. And it looked like we did, but not in a good way. And it wasn't very efficient, as a kitchen. We had it done twice—when we first moved in and again about three years ago. Tried to fix the stuff that didn't work. But to be honest, neither of us ever did any cooking, so the whole thing was a waste really. Or at least, we didn't get the benefit."

"You never did any cooking?" I stare at him. "What did you eat? Did you have someone to cook for you?"

"Yeah, housekeeper."

"Blimey."

"Her hours are a bit odd. Vanessa's, I mean. So it made sense. She doesn't cook, anyway—too busy. And we were often eating at different times. Especially more recently."

"Right. So . . ."

He sighs. "Do you think I should learn?"

"To cook? Yes. Otherwise what are you going to eat?"

"Takeaway."

I think he's joking, but I object anyway. "You can't have takeaway every night." I finish my sandwich and drink some coffee.

"I suppose not. Are there cookbooks for idiots who don't know what they're doing?"

I laugh. "Yes. You can always get good cookbooks in charity shops. Oh, but I suppose you don't need to. Anyway, do you want a list? *Delia's Complete Cookery Course*. Nigella's *How to Eat*. The early Jamie Oliver books are useful. And didn't you cook before you met her?"

"Beans on toast. Do you like cooking?"

"I can cook. And I used to enjoy it. I haven't much opportunity recently, because of not having any money. And I haven't needed to, because of the restaurant."

"Shall we cook something? You could teach me. Or would it be better to wait until the new kitchen arrives?"

I laugh again. "You don't need a new kitchen to cook in. The one you have is perfectly adequate."

"I need to get a coffee machine," he says, distracted. "We had a great one at the old place. More stuff to research." He shakes his head. "Starting from scratch is tiring." He wipes his fingers on a napkin and regards his Danish pastry with some suspicion.

"At least you can afford to buy it all," I remind him.

"This is true. I've ordered myself a bed," he adds. "But it won't be here for two weeks. I might have to sleep on that sofa."

"Are you . . . when are you going to move in?" Since I'll have to move out, when he does, this means I need to start looking for somewhere else.

"I thought I might start bringing stuff tomorrow. Not that there's much; I don't really have any furniture."

"I thought you might not have."

"No. We sold a lot of it with the house. And anyway, I didn't really like it. I've been looking at stuff on the John Lewis website. They do some nice mid-century-looking chairs and things. I know that's out of period, for the house. But that doesn't matter, does it?"

"No. Anyway, it would be mad if you only bought things from the thirties. Can you imagine? Ha."

"Yeah, I don't think that's a sensible thing really. So John Lewis it is."

"How lovely to furnish a house with new things." I smile at him.

"I'm not going to go mad though. Because I think I might like some older bits? Have a wander round some antiques places, see what there is. Do you like that sort of thing? Poking about?"

I nod, trying not to look too delighted. "I used to basically do that for a living."

"Did you? When was that?"

"Oh, it's a long time ago now. In my twenties and early thirties. We—the bloke I was with at the time, that's what he did. When he wasn't at raves. House clearances, and we sold stuff at antiques fairs. House full of Victorian radiators, you know the sort of thing. Sadly not plumbed in. Furniture, kitchenalia. Retro stuff too; I was quite good at that."

"Oh, cool. So you can advise me?"

I look at him. "If you want opinions about furniture, yes, I'm full of them."

"Excellent. I think I'd find all of this a bit overwhelming if I had to do it myself."

"Consider me your sounding board for interiors."

"I will, then," he says, and we smile at each other.

This really is like a dream, to be honest. As I've mostly lived in furnished rentals, or moved in with people, I've never had to buy much. The furniture at Johnny's sort of ebbed and flowed as we used things for a bit and then sold them on. I know I'll never have a house to furnish, so talking to Gethin about this is vicarious pleasure. No less pleasurable for that, though.

"Have you got a list?" I ask him. "What sort of thing are you looking for?"

He thinks for a moment. "Dining room table and chairs. A whatsit—sideboard. I might get an old one. Well, vintage— G Plan, or Ercol, you know."

I nod. "Antiques of the future."

"I think there'll still be room for a sofa in the back room, even with a table in there. I won't need a huge table. Maybe for six?"

I nod again.

"Sofa and chairs for the front room. Coffee table, end tables, lamps and stuff. Bed—for the front bedroom—and bedside tables." He pauses. "Do you want to stay in the big front bedroom? You needn't move to the box room."

"Oh, but—" I clear my throat, embarrassed. "If you're going to move in, you don't . . . you wouldn't want me there, would you."

"Why not?"

"Because . . . well—" I think about Noosha and her suspicions. She was right the last time she was suspicious. This is different, though, isn't it?

"You can stay as long as you want," he says. "We get on okay, don't we? I think it would be fine. I like you."

I'm blushing now, not that he can see that, I hope. "But—"

"Honestly, it's fine. You can save up more," he adds, "and then get somewhere better, later, if you decide not to stay."

"But the rent—"

"I don't care about that; I don't need it."

"I'd have to pay rent, Gethin. Don't be ridiculous."

He shrugs. "That's up to you. But you're welcome to stay, and if you want the bigger room—"

"Oh, no, no. I don't need a big room. And you might want to invite people to visit."

"Hm, well. If you change your mind, just tell me." He taps his fingers on the table. "That's agreed, then—you'll stay?"

"I don't know if—"

"It would be loads easier if you did," he points out. "For you, I mean. And loads nicer for me."

I laugh. "I don't know about that."

"No, I'm pretty sure. Anyway," he says, going on with his list, "I do own a big Victorian chest of drawers that I bought when I first moved out. That's in Abby's garage. I've got some paintings. And my books."

"Have you got lots of books?" I hope he has; that would be useful.

"Yeah. Too many, probably."

"No such thing." We grin at each other.

"You say that," he says, "but there was a lot more room at the old house."

"Mm." I sit silent, thinking, for a moment. "You might find the sofa a bit short, to sleep on. It just about fitted me. It's okay, but I don't know if you can sleep on it for a fortnight. I could go back down there, though, and you could have the bed."

"God, no. I can always stay longer at Abby's. Can't expect you to give up your bed."

For a moment, I wonder if he's being sarcastic, but he doesn't seem to be. I wonder if Abby's said anything about me. I don't want to ask though. I shrug.

"But I'd rather be at the house. It feels like ages since I lived somewhere properly."

"Did you move out as soon as you split up? I suppose with seven bedrooms you don't have to see much of each other. If you don't want to."

"No, we were hardly crammed in together. I guess it was six weeks or something." He looks up at me. "Then she said she was going to bring someone home, you know—and I thought, yeah, time to go."

"Oh. Wow. That's quite . . . so she . . . I thought you left her? Not that that would mean . . . but—"

He shakes his head. "No. Eventually everything was so shit she called it off."

"Why didn't you do that, then?" This is interesting. I know he said before that he was a coward, but I thought he was exaggerating. He doesn't seem cowardly. Not being able to make a decision isn't exactly cowardly, though.

He screws up his face, frowning. "I sort of couldn't imagine anything else. I know that sounds ridiculous. It's not like . . . well. She loved that house, even if I didn't. I thought she'd be devastated. It was weird, really. She told me I'd need to move out of the bedroom—we had a really incredible row, at Christmas. That's when it all came out, that we'd both been miserable. We said we'd try to do better, but if I'm honest, I don't think either of us tried very hard. So in January she said, right, let's split up, then, why not. She said I didn't have to leave, though, as, like you said, there's plenty of room. So I moved up to the other end of the house. It was okay. She's always so busy, I didn't see much of her. But when she said she was going to bring someone home—it was funny, because I didn't really care, but it still hurt to think she'd been seeing someone else."

"Had she, then?"

"Oh, yeah. Some guy she met at work. They'd been seeing each other for a while. I think that's probably why everything had got so awful? She'd stopped trying to be nice to me. Anyway, I didn't want to be bumping into the other guy when I was getting my breakfast or whatever, so I left." He shrugs.

"And—how do you feel now?"

"I said, didn't I, before—it was a massive relief. I'd been really tense, for ages, walking on eggshells, trying not to piss her off. I always felt bad, for not being interested in the stuff that interested her. She's really ambitious. She's good at her job; she works really hard. And she's always worked in the same industry, it's not like anything changed. I always felt awkward about it though; I'm not good at social stuff, I can't do all the things telly people do. They're not like normal people. I don't mean that . . . disparagingly."

I nod. "And then you sold the house?"

"Well, we had some meetings about it." He pulls a face. "They were proper meetings, as well, with our solicitors and everything. I thought she'd buy me out, but she didn't want to. Got a bit emotional about it—'This was our house, Gethin, and I think we were happy here.' I didn't tell her I hadn't been, particularly—or not for ages. Anyway, she's bought somewhere else; she's having it done up at the moment. Whatever I'm going to spend on my kitchen," he adds, "you can bet it would be enough to buy about three cupboards in hers."

"Is she going to live with this other bloke, then?"

"Once his divorce comes through. Not sure why he's not there already. She's renting an enormous apartment in a new-build place. Anyway, yeah, he hasn't moved out of the marital home yet."

"D'you think he will?" I'm always suspicious of this sort of behavior. When people say they're "waiting for the right moment" or whatever. Funny how often there never is a "right moment." Mind you, she's rich and famous and very attractive, so maybe that makes a difference.

He shrugs. "You'd think he would've if he was going to. Although these people have publicists and stuff. So maybe they're waiting to announce it? His kids are quite small."

"Is he famous too?"

"Moderately. He's a light entertainment sort. Does panel shows and that."

"Wow, it's all a bit of another world." I regard him thoughtfully. "Did you ever feel like you fitted in?"

"No. You know the other day, when you talked about time you'd wasted?"

I nod.

"It's not the time in the relationship itself I feel like I wasted; it was all that other stuff, the stuff we had to do because of her job. Maybe that sounds ungrateful. I've had some amazing holidays and met all kinds of people. But, I try to imagine my life if I'd never been with her. If I'd been with someone else, someone . . . normal . . . maybe we'd've had kids. I mean, I don't know if we would, or if I've ever really wanted any. But sometimes I think about it."

"You could still have kids, couldn't you? Meet someone who's thirty-five or so."

He frowns at me. "I guess. I don't really know anyone who's thirty-five."

I laugh. "I don't think you have to know them *now*."

"Meet people? Shit. I don't know about that," he says. "How do you even meet people?"

"Internet," I say, eating the final piece of my millionaire's shortbread and dabbing crumbs off my plate with my thumb.

"Dating apps? I don't fancy that much." He frowns again. "Have you . . . is that—?"

"Yeah, I've never been on one. Not planning to, either. I mean, people can tell you anything they like, can't they?" I shiver. "At least if you go out with some pal of your brother-in-law you might get a heads-up. About how awful they are. I basically want references, in future."

"How did you meet him, then? Your ex?"

"Oh, he fixed my car for me. Sadly I didn't really know anyone he knew. Would've been useful."

"What, they might have . . . warned you?"

I hesitate, and then nod. "Or they might not. People don't always. Sometimes it's only afterward, isn't it."

I think of Andy Wickham saying, "Didn't he put his wife in hospital?" and Becca Morris telling him, "That was an accident!"

"And no one likes to think their mate's a psycho," I add.

"Is he a psycho?"

I don't answer this, instead standing up and saying, "So what's next on your list? Shall we go and look at Acers? Hard to choose one at this time of year; you need to see the foliage, really."

Chapter Six

Gethin and I are painting the front room. The parquet's covered in dust sheets, although I think he's going to get someone to sand it back and re-varnish it. Or polish it at least. We're listening to Primal Scream and talking about college. He went to university in Birmingham and, as far as I can tell, mostly took lots of drugs. Not anything heavy, though. Recreational. If you can call a carrier bag full of magic mushrooms recreational. His brother was already a heroin addict, and his lifestyle, says Gethin, "wasn't much of an advert for it, to be honest. He was still working, then, like, but we all knew there was something badly wrong. I went to his flat once when I was doing my A-Levels and there was a . . . situation . . . with some scary people." He looks at me. "You probably know the sort of thing. I never went back after that. It was frightening."

I nod. I've been lucky, but both Fitz and Johnny knew some people who—while not ever actually deliberately frightening to me, or to anyone I was in a room with—were clearly potentially dangerous.

"You know those adverts they used to have, in the eighties, for heroin?" I see him reconsider this phrase. "I mean *about* it, obviously. Not *for* it. That would be wrong."

I snort with inappropriate laughter and tell him, "My friend

Frances had loads of them on her bedroom wall. Her mum didn't think it was funny."

"No, well. It's hard to tell teenagers stuff. They think they know, don't they? But to be honest, you only have to see a heroin addict being a heroin addict to know it's not . . . cool."

"Did he die?" I ask. I know the answer, but I feel like I want him to tell me.

"What, Evan? Yeah."

"I'm sorry. That's awful."

"Yeah. It's my parents I feel sorry for, really. I mean, I loved him, but . . . he was six years older than me; he left home when I was still at school. I never really knew him after that. It all went wrong pretty quickly."

I nod.

"Yeah, so—it was hard. Mostly I don't think about it, though; it's easier not to. I know that's a bit rubbish."

"That's my own method of dealing with stuff," I tell him, "so I'm not going to judge you." I paint in silence for a moment and then add, "I'm always really surprised when modern famous people do lots of heroin. You know, like Amy Winehouse. Or Kurt Cobain. I suppose he's not modern anymore. It just seems like . . . I don't know. It's not cool, is it? Funny how being rich and famous won't stop you screwing up, though."

"Hm."

"I suppose because—the people I've known—it's like you imagine they'd have avoided it, if they'd had something else in their lives. Like, you know, talent. I realize that's a massive oversimplification."

He makes another noncommittal noise and then adds, "I met Kurt Cobain once."

"Fuck off, did you?"

He laughs. "I did, though."

"When was that? Wow, get you."

"Reading Festival. My mate's dad worked for Radio One. Got us backstage. 1991."

"Did you talk to him?"

"Yeah, no one knew who they were then, really. They weren't very famous. They were like two bands below Pop Will Eat Itself in the lineup."

"Bloody hell. Imagine that."

"I know, right? They were brilliant though. Which is what I said to him." He laughs. "He said, 'Hey, thanks, man!' and shook my hand. I've met quite a lot of famous people, but that's still one of my best encounters."

"Wow." I shake my head and return to my painting. "I can't think of anyone famous I've met from bands. I've met lots of DJs. But none of them are, like, Kurt Cobain famous."

The paint color he's chosen is a warm sort of vanilla. The room gets the sun in the evening, and I think it's going to look lovely. He let me pick curtain fabric (a beautiful gray and yellow mid-century-style abstract floral) and order what I wanted. They come next week. The sofa might be here by Christmas if we're lucky. It's L-shaped and has angled wooden legs. We drove to Cardiff last weekend so we could sit on it to check it was comfortable. It took me about two hours to choose the fabric— the most beautiful teal color. It's stunning. Then we went out for lunch, and it was one of the best days I've had for a long, long time.

It's a bit like being married, if being married was like it is in 1950s films, perhaps. So extremely—or, rather, utterly—chaste. It's odd to think that it must be five years at least since I was this happy.

❧ ❦

I roll up my sleeves to facilitate painting. My clothes—a large plaid shirt and a pair of men's jeans from a charity shop—are already paint-spattered.

Gethin leans past me to reach the paint tray with his roller. "What's that?" he asks, pointing at my forearm. "Cigarette burn?"

I glance down at the scars. I'm annoyed. I forget about them. Two close together near my elbow and another nearer my wrist. I don't want to lie and say "no," but I definitely don't want to say "yes," either. I say nothing.

"I used to have one on my hand." He holds his left arm out, examining the back of his hand. "Gone now though. Takes a while. Not sure how long. Years, I guess."

"Hm."

"Had a girlfriend," he says, "when I was at college: Julia. She was . . . quite into that sort of thing?"

"What, burning you?" I turn to look at him, surprised.

"I wouldn't do anything to her if she wouldn't do it to me," he says. "That was my rule."

"Oh. Nothing wrong with a bit of consensual BDSM," I say, lightly, "although I don't think cigarette burns are very good for you. It's not very clean."

"No. It was quite gross, actually."

"Mm."

"Did you . . . choose . . . for those to happen?" he asks.

I wonder what he'd say if I told him that, yes, it was entirely my idea. That would be a lie though.

"Can't say I did."

"Painful."

"Yes, very."

"Did—?"

"Did I want to talk about it? Nope."

"You don't think—"

"No."

"I only—"

"I appreciate your concern," I tell him. "Honestly, I do. But I don't want to talk about it." I clear my throat. "Tell me about your girlfriend, instead."

"Oh, well. She scared me, a bit."

"Did she? Why?"

"I used to wonder if . . . it's a bit confusing, really, all that stuff mixed up together. I'd never really thought about it before I met her. I wondered what had happened, to make her like that. She said nothing had, but I found that . . . I dunno. That was her thing, though, and she was quite into it. They didn't call it that then, though, did they. BDSM."

"No, I don't think so. It was very niche, wasn't it? Bit more mainstream now. Apparently."

"I used to worry it might all get"—he pauses—"out of hand, you know."

It's easy for us to talk about this because now we have our backs to each other, painting adjacent walls.

"What do you mean?"

"I don't know. I thought she might ask me to do something that . . . would end badly." He clears his throat again. "Not that . . . but I was quite young, and it worried me."

This is interesting. "What sort of thing?"

"Well, you know. I mean, none of it was really bad or anything. But it did . . . progress, if that's the right word."

"I suppose it would. You can't leap in at the beginning asking people to nail you to things, or whatever."

"Jesus. Well, she never asked me to *nail* her to anything, thank goodness."

"But you thought she might? Not nailing—that's me being silly. Although people do nail each other to things. But . . ."

"Yes. Or . . . I don't know what I thought exactly. But it made me quite uncomfortable."

"Imagine it made her uncomfortable, too." I laugh to myself.

"Ha ha. You know what I mean though. Do you?"

"Yeah, I guess. Were you together long?"

"Not really? About a year, I suppose. That's not exactly why we split up, but sort of. I think she . . . well, I wasn't into it, particularly, and I think she felt like she could find someone who was. Which is probably true. She wasn't on my course . . . I mean, there weren't any girls on my course really."

He did some kind of computer science degree.

"What was she studying, then?"

"Illustration. She lived with a bunch of Fashion students. God, they were something."

I grin to myself at this. "Were they? What, hot?"

"Not really. They were like . . . you know you get overbred pedigree dogs who are neurotic and exhausting?"

I laugh. "Yes."

"That's what they were like. Made the art students look pretty sensible. Weird really, because . . . I don't know if you'd choose my university if you were serious about studying fashion. I mean, they all go to art college in London, don't they? Saint Martins or whatever. I think they had to compensate. They were very . . . Fashion."

"How did you meet her?"

"Fell over her in the Union."

"Fell over her?"

"Yeah, she was sitting on the floor. I was off my tits, obviously."

"Obviously."

❧ ❦

Later, as we're clearing up, the painting complete, he says, "When was that, then?"

"How do you mean?"

"Your arm."

"Oh God. One in the spring. The others, last year."

"Why didn't you leave after the first time?"

This question makes me angry, although it's not an unreasonable one.

"Why do people stay? I don't know the answer. I was . . . afraid." I rub my arm through my sleeve and look away. "My brain stopped working."

"I'm sorry," he says, "I know it's a stupid question. I didn't exactly mean it how it sounded."

I shrug at him, irritated.

"I'm not . . . I don't mean to pry, or . . ."

I shrug again. We look at each other in silence for an awkwardly long time. Eventually, he shakes his head. "It's weird, isn't it," he says. "They'll be gone eventually. But always reminding you, while they're there."

I clench my jaw. I don't want to talk to him about any of this. It's nothing to do with him, however kind he is. And anyway, if I started talking about it, who knows what would happen.

"Everything's always in your head."

"It isn't, though, is it? You can forget things, all kinds of things. Even terrible things. You can make it fade, I think. If you talk about it?"

"It's none of your business, is it."

He looks at me sadly. "I suppose not," he says. He turns to pick up the paint trays. "Do you think those potatoes'll be ready?"

❧ ❦

Later, after we've eaten our jacket potatoes, he shows me some pictures of Persian rugs. We're going to see some in real life on Monday, when he gets home from work. I'm quite excited about this. Persian rugs have always been a long way out of my price range.

His new job's going well, he says. I think he's very relieved not to be spending the week in Cardiff any longer.

"Do you miss your friends? In Cardiff?" I ask, as we scroll through photographs of antique floor coverings on his iPad.

"Lots of them were Vanessa's friends, so I mostly find myself dropped," he says.

"Oh. That's a bit shit."

"I don't really mind. It's quite . . . cool? To be seeing people here . . . loads of 'em I hadn't seen for years. I don't know why, really. They're mostly a good bunch. But she was keen to leave. She'd already lived away for ten years or something when I met her, and she didn't like to come home."

"Not even at Christmas?"

"We'd usually have everyone to ours. Her folks, my folks, Abby and Si, her brother and sister, everyone's kids."

"Has Abby got kids?" I don't know why this hadn't occurred

to me, but of course it's Gethin and me who are unusual, not having any.

"My nephew. Leon. He's twenty-three. Lives in Manchester."

"What does he do? This is a good one," I add, pointing to a rug. "The colors are lovely."

"Save it to 'favorites' then and we'll have a look at that one. Anyway, graphic design. Works for an agency. Seems to like it."

"And your parents live here?"

"My mum does. Dad died—not last summer, the one before."

"Oh. Sorry about that." I look at him, but he's concentrating on the rugs. My own father's been dead for such a long time I can't quite imagine what it would be like to have just lost him, or indeed to have known him as an adult.

"Yeah. What about your dad? You've never mentioned him," says Gethin.

"No, he's been dead for years; I was still at school."

"Shit, really? That's tough."

"Yeah, my mum didn't deal with it very well. Whatever that means." I think about this. It's hard to look back at that long-ago time with any kind of objectivity. "That's when my brother left home. I've only seen him a couple of times since then."

I don't know where Luke is these days, and I've always kind of felt I shouldn't look for him in case he doesn't want to be found. After all, he could get in touch with me, couldn't he (well, maybe not at the moment; no one can), or with Natalie, if he wanted to. He's the eldest, so I feel it's his responsibility. I wonder what Gethin, without a brother through no fault of his own, will think about this.

"That's a shame."

"It's not like I know him, really. I haven't seen him since I was twenty or something."

He shakes his head. "I'm sorry. That must be hard."

"Yeah, well, can't blame him. He was old enough to go, so he went. We'd have gone too, if we could've. My sister and I."

"Is she older than you? Or younger?"

"Five years younger. She was only ten when Dad died. I think we let her down, Luke and I. I mean, I know we were kids too. Anyway. Natalie's—we get on okay, but I wouldn't say we've ever been close. Five years is quite a big age gap."

He nods.

"She's got two little kids," I add, "the niblings. Sophie's seven and Max is five."

"And you didn't want to go to hers? Instead of coming here, I mean?"

"No room. And plus, she doesn't live that far from where I was living. I wanted to be farther away."

"Is he looking for you?" he asks.

I shrug. "I doubt it. Anyway, he won't find me."

"You're not worried he will?"

"How would he? No one knows where I am. Except you. And you don't know my other name, do you?"

He looks surprised. "I suppose I don't. That's odd, isn't it? I never thought about it."

"I guess I might tell you one day," I say, thoughtful. "If we're going to be sharing a house."

"You don't need to if you'd rather not. I'm not going to make you sign a contract or anything."

"If I pay my rent in cash."

"Oh, yeah. I guess I'd see it, otherwise. Anyway, you'd tell me, if you were worried?"

"About . . . him? I might. But I'm not."

Chapter Seven

I've moved into my bedroom, which has blinds now, and shelves, and a tiny, tiny Formica-topped table under the window, with an old kitchen chair that I've painted orange. The walls are very pale pink, like strawberry ice cream. I have some books from charity shops and jumble sales, and I've put out some bits and pieces, small objects that I brought with me: Bear, of course; a framed photo of Noosha and her kids; one of my family before Dad died, faded and ancient-looking; the Victorian silver hedgehog pincushion that Johnny gave me when we first met.

Gethin's lent me a laptop, which he brought home from work—he said it was "spare." I'm not sure how true this is, but I'm not arguing about it. I'm pleased with how my room looks, cool but cozy. Every single thing I have feels like a miracle.

We've finished decorating upstairs, painting Gethin's bedroom mostly white, with the wall behind the bed a very dark gray. That was my idea. I could tell he wasn't convinced, but once his bed was in there, and the chest of drawers, and we'd put up some pictures, he agreed it looks pretty smart. The front bedroom is two shades of white, the chimney breast papered in a very, very tiny floral pattern, and it has a little armchair, but no bed yet. A man came and replaced the bathroom floor, and the walls, half-tiled with the original shiny rectangular white tiles, are painted a sort of pale sage green above.

I've never had the responsibility of choosing colors for a whole house before, and it's a huge relief that it looks so great. In fact, I can't really believe I did it.

⚒ ⚑

The dining room is decorated, too, and although Gethin hasn't decided what to do about the horrible fireplace, it all looks much nicer now everything's painted, the ugly electric fire removed. He bought a table from the antiques center in Llandeilo—Ercol, very nice, and there's a sideboard, too, vintage teak. The inside of it smells exactly like the one we had at home when I was a kid, with its green-baize-lined cutlery drawer and drop-down cupboard for drinks.

The walls in here are white, except the chimney breast, which is a very good sort of green—like the inside of an avocado. The plan is to buy another, small sofa for in here—dark green, I'm thinking—but even people with loads of money have to pause occasionally, so he's going to wait for a bit to get that. I saw a very smart dark green velvet one on Apartment Therapy, but I don't think velvet is very practical, for furniture.

Yes, I am obsessed with this house. And no, I don't think it will end well.

Chapter Eight

Next week it's Christmas. Work's been busier than ever. I think I might need to get a job where I don't have to stand up all day.

I bought a wreath for the front door from a stall in town. Gethin bought a tiny Christmas tree for the sitting room and ordered a box of miniature glass decorations from the internet.

"Do you like Christmas?" he asks me, stepping back to admire how it looks.

"I like decorations."

"I'm afraid I don't have many. Or any, really." He frowns. "All the stuff we had before was . . . I don't know what happened to it. It was always very matching. And a different color every year, you know."

"Oh, like, themed?"

"I suppose so. A bit dull."

It sounds it. I don't say this. Instead, I say, "I think you should build up, with Xmas decs. Collect them gradually. It seems wrong to buy them in a big lump."

He laughs. "D'you think so?"

"Yes. Anyway, there's not much room on that tree." It's less than three feet tall and stands on the smallest table of the nesting set (1970s Ercol knockoff) he bought at the flea market last week. It's topped with a tiny tinsel star I found in a box of odd-ments in one of the charity shops.

"True. I might get a bigger one next year. Or I suppose that one will grow. Will it?"

"It should do, although it still won't be very big next year."

"Might plant it in the garden."

"You could get a new one every year and plant them out and have a row of them in descending order of height."

"A tiny plantation."

"Just say 'pine forest'; it sounds much more romantic," I suggest.

"Ha."

"I've often thought it would be fun to fill a garden with trees. Or bamboo. We went to a garden in Cornwall, once, with an amazing bamboo grove, all different types, you know, abso-lutely filling the space, rattling in the breeze. It looked brilliant, and I thought how fun it would be, to fill a suburban garden with bamboo."

"That sounds great actually." He pauses, then adds, "I love Cornwall. We used to go every year. Vanessa's got a mate with a house down at Sennen." He frowns, and I assume he's think-ing about how he won't be going there anymore.

≫ ≪

On the Sunday before Christmas we eat chicken casserole for dinner. Gethin says, "So it's Christmas next week."

I nod.

"I'm going to Mum's on the twenty-fourth, probably come home on Boxing Day. Or maybe the twenty-seventh."

I nod again.

"When are you working?"

"We're closed Christmas Day. Open for lunch on Boxing Day."

"Do you want to come to Mum's for the twenty-fifth, then?"

I stare at him, and then take a piece of bread from the basket and dip it into the gravy on my plate.

"That's very kind of you. Your sister doesn't like me, though. Is she going to be there?"

"She probably will be for Christmas Day, yes. I can talk to her, if you want."

I shake my head. "I don't want to spoil her Christmas. I'll be fine by myself."

"Are you sure?"

"I'm quite good on my own," I tell him. "I lived here for a month by myself, don't forget, and at least I can have the heating on."

"Sorry, I don't think I can allow that," he says, in a serious voice.

"Pfft."

"But really, I don't think Abby—"

"It's okay; I don't need her to like me." I smile at him. "I understand why she doesn't. But it would be awkward. And your mum doesn't know me."

"No, but she doesn't like to think of you being on your own. She'd like you to come. I'd like it too."

I feel my face turning pink and shovel food into my mouth to distract myself from my embarrassment.

"We never have turkey," he adds, "if that tempts you."

I laugh. "I've definitely eaten as much turkey as I'll ever want. And all the mince pies I can handle."

"Oh, come on, always room for more mince pies."

❧ ❦

On Christmas morning, I don't wake up until gone nine. I
didn't get in until half one, because there was a need for post-
service drinks and jollity with my colleagues. I'm endlessly impressed with their stamina. Hospitality is hard work. Everyone
on their feet for hours, the heat of the kitchen, the speed at
which everything happens, the having to be pleasant to custom-
ers. It's exhausting, and I don't even do anything difficult. Anyway, it would have been rude to rush off, so I drank two
ridiculous (but delicious) cocktails and gratefully accepted a
festive bottle of wine as a gift from Maura, along with my tips.
I gave everyone cards, and received some back, so I can add
them to Gethin's collection, strung up over the mantelpiece in
the sitting room.

Despite the cries from the waitresses—"Oh no, don't go,
Jess! Have another drink!"—I scuttled off into the early hours
of Christmas morning. It had been raining all evening, but had
finally stopped, and the wet pavement sparkled under the street-
lights. I went home via the new bit of town, where the chain
stores are, to look at the Christmas lights. I didn't feel particularly festive, but I'm not sure I ever do; you wait ages for Christmas, don't you, and then December rushes past and there you
are and then it's over.

I think about when I was younger, the years after my dad
died, when Christmas was pretty rubbish at home. Mum tried
hard the first year, but after that it all tailed off. This was worse
for Natalie, because she was still a kid. I had friends to go to the
pub with by then and was having what seemed like quite grown-
up Christmases. Lizzie and I got into lots of trouble in those
days, but it was definitely more fun than being at home.

I lie in bed and think about these things. I also think about the last couple of Christmases, which have ranged from average to poor. Spending the day on my own is certainly an improvement on the events of last year, anyway, which involved someone throwing a plate at my head. (It didn't hit me, because he was drunk, but that didn't help.)

Eventually I get up and go downstairs. I think my brain is allergic to the coffee machine for some reason, because I still can't work it, even though I've been shown how to do it three times. I'm embarrassed to ask again, so I pretend I prefer to use the French press. That still seems quite glamorous to me anyway, even though I've been using one for decades. I take my pleasures where I can.

When I was a kid, when Dad was still alive, Mum used to cook a ham for breakfast on Christmas Day, filling the house with savory smells as it bubbled away in the biggest pan. It seems odd, now—I can't remember the last time I ate boiled ham. It's a fossilized memory, so incredibly specific I'd probably pass out if I tasted it again. Anyway, I don't have a ham, but I do have bacon. I never have a cooked breakfast, so it's quite a treat. I brought home a whole loaf of the sourdough from the restaurant, too, because it makes the best toast. I'm happy, making my breakfast. I ask Alexa to play Christmas music, and dance about to "Jingle Bell Rock." I like Christmas music from the 1950s, weird pictures of Hollywood snow scenes and Cold War comfort filling my brain, Jane Russell or someone dressed in a sparkly red dress with white fur trimmings, you know the sort of thing: an image outdated before I was even born, and one that was never even vaguely reminiscent of a British Christmas.

I carry my plate and mug into the dining room and stare at

the table, which is set for one, with scarlet runner and potted poinsettia. There are two rectangular presents wrapped in plain white paper with crimson ribbons, and hanging from the wall by the ugly fireplace, there's a small red felt stocking with my name on it.

"Oh my God." I put my plate and mug down and am almost amused to see that my hands are shaking. None of this was here last night when I got in; he must have come round this morning to do it. I can't believe I didn't hear him.

I pull out the chair and sit down. Okay, breakfast first; them's the rules. I take an arty photo of my breakfast with the presents and plant in the background, fetchingly out of focus, and then another, reversed, where it's the bacon and eggs that are blurry. I've got a new Instagram; basically, all my followers are from the restaurant. I upload the pictures and watch as the likes ping up from people scrolling their phones before they get up for family Christmas.

Then I eat my food, trying not to keep looking at the presents.

For three days, earlier in the week, there was a box in the hall with Gethin's gifts for his family in it. We didn't discuss presents for each other; I bought him a bottle of whisky, which was expensive, but I know it's a good one because I asked Maura for advice. He doesn't drink a lot, but occasionally he likes a malt. We talked about this, at some point, so I know it won't be a waste of money. I also made him a gift—because I didn't really know what to get, and obviously I can't spend much. I wanted to get something more personal, though, because booze is an easy, generic gift, and I wanted to . . . I don't know, demonstrate my gratitude, I suppose.

I bought some supplies from the art shop on Victoria

Street—art stuff is an investment, isn't it, so reasonably justifiable—pencils, a box of acrylics, and some paper and brushes. I haven't done any drawing for ages, and I had to have about five goes before I managed something I was reasonably happy with. I bought a secondhand frame, which was filthy, and consequently cheap. It cleaned up okay though, when I took it apart. Anyway, it's not a brilliant example of the "house portrait," but I thought it was recognizably Sunnyside. I painted the front door the exact shade of cornflower blue that we've chosen but not yet applied, so in some ways, it's a picture of the future. I wrapped it up and put it, and the whisky, in the gift box, hoping he wouldn't notice them until he was unpacking it at his mum's, which would be too late, I thought, for him to get me anything in return. I definitely don't need presents, when he's already given me somewhere to live.

I look again at the stocking. I haven't had a stocking for more than thirty years, and I'm stupidly excited to see what's in it.

My phone buzzes. A message from Gethin.

OH MY GOD DID YOU DRAW THIS??

And then another:

Merry Christmas btw

I did, yes. Merry Christmas.

Thank you so much. It's brilliant. And thanks for the whisky, that's very kind of you.

You're welcome. And thank you for mine, I haven't opened them yet, did you sneak in this morning?

I think FATHER CHRISTMAS will have brought anything you might have found this morning.

>   *Oh yeah, of course. Well, if you see him, thank*
>   *him for me.*

If you haven't opened them, you should keep
your thanks, what if you don't like them?

>   *I'm much too polite to say so.*

Ha ha! Happy Christmas, anyway. x

I open the first parcel, which is a box of nine vintage Christmas tree decorations, delicate glass baubles, three round and six drop shapes. The box is the original, with the price written on it in old money. They're beautiful, in scarlet and blue and gold and green. Perfect. Then there's a small box of very fancy chocolates. The gift tag says *Sorry this is a bit dull*, but they look amazing, so I'm pretty sure they won't be. I turn the baubles in their box. What a lovely, thoughtful gift. My eyes are misty. I'll hang these on our miniature tree in a moment and keep the box for them to live in for the eleven months of the year that it's not Christmas.

I get up to fetch my stocking. I close my eyes and remove things from it one at a time.

A packet of gel pens in sparkly purple.

A very old wooden matchbox that, when I open it, I find contains an amazingly iridescent beetle, nestled on cotton wool.

A Sherbet Fountain.

A glossy navy-blue mug with my initial in gold.

Some tiny LED fairy lights on copper wire.

One of those wooden toys where you press the button underneath and the cow (in this case) collapses as the strings that hold it upright are released.

A key ring with a red and silver tassel.

A bottle of bubble-blowing liquid.

A Fortune Teller Miracle Fish, the packaging surely identical to the ones of my youth.

An orange (traditional).

I look at my gifts, spread out on the table. I think this might be the nicest thing anyone's ever done for me. I don't know what to do with myself. I take a picture of everything and send it to Gethin with a message.

THANK YOU SO MUCH THIS IS AMAZING. x

You're totally welcome.

THANK YOU. (I'll stop shouting now.)
Seriously though this is the best Christmas.
I might be crying.

Oh God, I didn't mean to make you cry, he says.

It's okay. Tears of joy. (I add a blush-cheeked emoji to make this less . . . intense.)

❧ ❧

I have two other presents, too—although they're Amazon vouchers from Lizzie and Noosha, so not something I have to unwrap. Natalie says she'll send something when I give her my address—which is fair—and I rarely get anything from Mum unless I go to hers. I spoke to her last week, anyway, and she seems fine about not seeing me. I'll call her later. I sent her some clothes, as she's terrible at buying anything and will wear stuff until it's in literal rags.

❧ ❧

I have a very enjoyable Christmas Day by myself. There's fancy nut loaf for lunch—yes, I'm so tired of turkey I don't even want any meat—with roast potatoes and tiny baby sprouts and spinach with garlic. I make enough veg that I can have bubble and squeak for my supper tomorrow. This forward planning makes me feel smug and comfortable. I watch *Mary Poppins*, and have an afternoon nap, and in the evening I have a bath with bubbles and a glass of wine. It all feels very luxurious.

Noosha phones, although not for long, as her Christmases are complicated and full of people. It's good to speak to her, though. I don't tell her about Gethin's gifts, although I couldn't exactly tell you why. Maybe if we'd had a longer conversation, I would have got round to it. Lizzie and Marcus are away, in a tiny cottage somewhere with no Wi-Fi, so I send her a message she won't receive. I get a video message from my niece and nephew, to whom I sent toys and chocolate. They sing me a song, which is cute, and Natalie (she also got chocolates) appears at the end to thank me. All in all, I feel it's been a very successful day, and I go to bed happily at ten o'clock, where I listen to Simon Slater reading *Wolf Hall* until I fall asleep.

❧ ❦

At work, Boxing Day lunch, everyone seems a little jaded. Now we're ramping up for New Year's, before what they promise me will be a much quieter January as everyone attempts to recover.

When I get home at half past three, the car's back in the drive and Gethin's slumped on the sofa in the front room, flicking idly through the channels.

"You're back early."

"Too many people," he says. "Or . . . not that many, I suppose. But tiring anyway. Didn't sleep that well. I told Mum she needs to buy a new mattress for the spare bed, but I'm pretty sure I've said that before. How was work?"

"Yeah, it was okay. Busy." I smile at him. "Amazed at how many people go out on Boxing Day, to be honest. Thank you again for my presents. I haven't had a stocking since I was a kid."

"It's always good to get a stocking."

I nod enthusiastically. "That beetle's amazing. Where on earth did you get that?"

"At the flea market. Appropriately. I wasn't sure if you'd like it. I stood there for ages dithering."

"Oh no, it's beautiful. Thank you."

"I was thinking about magnolias, sort of. But . . . bit weird to buy someone a dead beetle?"

I laugh. "No. Well, maybe. But I love it. I loved everything."

"Good." He smiles at me. "I like buying presents. I like getting them, too; I'm going to put your picture in my bedroom, is that okay?"

"Sure, if you like."

"It's brilliant. I didn't know you could draw. I mean, why would I? But what a great idea. You could probably sell those."

"Yeah," I say, amused. "Not sure I could. I'm not really very good at drawing. The ones you see on the internet are properly brilliant."

"Well, I love it. Thank you."

We smile at each other, warm with festive cheer.

"I was thinking . . . you know you said you'd like a job where you can sit down?"

"One day, yes. I'm not getting any younger." I pull a face.

"Only I just remembered that when I went out the other

night, I saw Bruce Cadogan—he's a friend of Vanessa's mum's, actually. Anyway, he said he was looking for someone to do his admin. I wasn't really paying any attention, but . . . d'you think you'd like to do something like that?"

I sit down in the armchair. "What does he do, then?"

"He's got a building supplies firm. Got an office in town, and another one at the yard. Employs quite a few people, I think. Does okay, anyway—or appears to; he drives a very nice vintage Jag. Want me to give him a ring?"

"Probably not on Boxing Day," I object.

"Oh, I shouldn't think he'd mind. I can message him if you like."

"Is it full-time?"

"Can't remember. I'll message him. What else do you need to know?" he asks, getting his phone out.

"Um. Hours. Pay. Er, paid holidays, I suppose. And the scope of the role, if that very HR phrase is appropriate."

"I imagine it's a bit of everything. I think there's an office manager though, so you wouldn't be in charge, I'm afraid."

"Yeah, I don't care about that."

He texts rapidly. "There. Sent."

"Thanks. Soon you'll have solved all my problems," I joke, "and then what will I do?"

"Well, I'd love to be able to do that, but I suspect it might be a bit beyond me."

"What are you saying?" I ask, mock outraged.

"Just that . . . nothing . . . I'm not saying anything—"

I laugh at his expression of horror.

Chapter Nine

The new sofa arrives at the beginning of January. Two men come and fit the folding doors in the dining room—very quick and efficient, which is good, because it's cold. Gethin wants to have his mum round to see the house, and we've discussed what this might involve, but the kitchen is coming on Monday, which means by the end of January everything will be done, so we may as well wait, right? I have no particular opinion about this. He wants me to meet her, which is disconcerting. Although I suppose I don't really have any choice. I think they're quite close, so she's bound to come here, isn't she? I find myself hoping the kitchen will take ages, even though, logically, that would be a pain in the arse. Anyway, it doesn't take ages; it's not quite three weeks before it's done. It looks fantastic.

There's no putting it off any longer: Everything's finished. She's coming on Friday evening. We plan the menu together, although he's determined to do most of the work himself. Which I support. She's not my mum, after all.

Something impressive but not too difficult, was my suggestion. "Soup?"

"I've never made soup."

"What, never?"

"Well, heated it up from a tin—obviously I've done that."

"Soup is very easy to make. If you did French onion soup, that looks impressive. Is your mum funny about food?" She's nearly eighty; it seems sensible to check.

"Not really. I mean, she's been abroad," he says, "and her teeth are okay. If that's what you're asking."

"Ha. Well, French onion soup, and some kind of fruit pie or crumble for dessert."

"Oh, crumble, yes! I love crumble."

"Wrong time of year for rhubarb, but we could have apple. Do you want to go mad and make custard from scratch?"

He stares at me. "With powder?"

"No, you heathen. With eggs and cream."

"Oh. Is that how you make custard? I've never thought about it. Is that why it's yellow, because of the eggs?"

I nod. "But not if you make it with custard powder. Mr. Bird—the man who invented custard powder—his wife was allergic to eggs. That's why he invented it. So no eggs in custard powder."

Sometimes I almost hate myself for knowing so much useless information. I'm not sure why though, because mostly the people I've known have quite liked this about me. It's only Mitch who thought it was pointless, and that I was an idiot for caring about stuff like this. I don't think Gethin thinks it's pointless though; he's willing to engage in discussions about basically anything. He smiles at me.

"Ah. That's lovely. That he invented it for his wife."

"It is, isn't it?" I agree.

"I like the fancy stuff in a tub."

"That's definitely easier than making it; it can be a bit unpredictable. Crumble, on the other hand, is very easy."

❧ ❦

When I get in from work on Friday—the first week of my new job, working for Bruce, complete—I go upstairs immediately to get changed. I still don't have many clothes, and most of what I do have leans heavily toward "practical," so I don't have many options when it comes to choosing something to make Gethin's mum think I'm a nice person. Black skinny jeans and a black long-sleeved top with a ballet neck. I have a cardigan in a very dark red with a waterfall front—it's a bit big but it was only a fiver from the Heart Foundation shop. I don't like to spend more than five pounds on clothes at the moment. I dress quickly and comb my hair. It's good to have found a hairdresser—well, a barber. I have it cut very short, usually, but before Christmas it was getting quite out of hand. It grows quickly, but I didn't know where to go, or even whether I should maybe change the style. I did think about shaving it all off—Gethin has some clippers—but I worried I might look like I'd escaped from a secure unit somewhere. Anyway, Maura recommended me a barber when I said I didn't like salons, so I look like myself again. I even think, sometimes, that I feel like myself.

Downstairs it smells deliciously of onion soup. I stand for a moment in the hallway, listening to the voices from the sitting room. It's silly to be nervous about meeting an old lady who has nothing to do with me. I take a deep breath and push open the door.

"Ah, here she is," says Gethin, as they both get up. "Mum, this is Jess; Jess, this is Marian."

"How lovely to meet you at last," she says, coming toward me and offering both hands. She's perhaps half a head shorter than I am, with curly gray hair and very twinkly eyes, dressed in a long dark skirt and a cream silk shirt under a navy cardigan that looks like cashmere to me. Like her son, she has good skin, and could easily pass for seventy.

"Everything's looking so wonderful," she goes on, as we all sit down. "I've been telling Gethin how impressed I am at how much you've managed to do, between you."

"We've had plenty of help." I smile at her. "We didn't really do it all ourselves."

"Oh, but I know you did lots of it! Even stripping wallpaper is such a big job."

"It's not difficult, though—just time-consuming. And I don't mind," I say. "I quite like decorating. I couldn't manage all the landing though."

"Oh, the stairwell drop!" she says. "The most terrifying part of any house, isn't it? I hear you had Richard Vaughan's boy do that," she adds. "How was he?"

"Yeah, he was good. Very quiet. I think he was embarrassed that I wanted to talk to him."

"He's always been very shy," she says. "I wasn't sure he'd be able to cope with meeting people all the time. You have to be quite chatty, don't you, in that sort of work?"

"I don't see it matters," says Gethin. "No one's employing a painter and decorator for his banter."

This makes me laugh. "No, but it's easier for him if he doesn't find the whole thing utterly excruciating."

"He did a good job, anyway," says Gethin, "very neat. How was work, Jess?"

"Oh, it was fine. Getting my head round it all. It's nice to sit down. I miss everyone though, from the restaurant."

"Ah, yes," says Marian, "you were working at Cenhinen Bedr before, Gethin said."

"Mum's always in there, aren't you?"

She nods. "I often go for lunch with my friend Joyce."

Gethin has told me about Joyce. She lives opposite his mum, and since Marian was widowed, they spend a lot of time together. She's extremely dull, according to him, but I say that's not really his problem.

"Yes, it certainly seems to be very popular," I agree. "Always very busy."

"But now you work for Bruce? That seems like a better use of your talents."

Unconvinced, I say, "I don't know that I have any talents."

"Oh now, I'm sure that's nonsense."

"You could project-manage people's houses," says Gethin, which makes me laugh.

"I doubt I have the vision for that. Anyway, they'd all come out like this," I say, looking round, "because I can only pick things I like."

"What did you do before?"

"Jess used to do antiques fairs," says Gethin. "Didn't you?"

"Really? Selling things? I've always thought that must be fun. But isn't it cold?"

This makes me laugh, too. "Yeah, it mostly is. Unless it's boiling hot, or raining so hard no one comes."

"Do you think you might do that again? I suppose you need money to buy things to sell."

"And you need a van, and contacts. I was just the assistant, really. It was my boyfriend at the time who was the dealer. After that I worked in a library."

"We have a library!"

"Yes, a good one, too. They'll be trying to avoid taking anyone on, though, I expect, because of the cuts. Anyway, I didn't really mind dishwashing, although split shifts are awkward. The hours are better at Bruce's."

"Restaurant hours are terrible," says Gethin, "really. She didn't get home until midnight, or later, quite often. Walking by herself in the dark."

Marian frowns at this, concerned. "By yourself?"

"Yes. It's pretty quiet here, so it didn't bother me." I shrug. It's true; I've never really been scared of walking alone in the dark. I walk fast, and I'm quite sturdy. And I've been lucky, I suppose.

"I'm glad you don't have to do that anymore," she says. "It's not safe."

There's a pause while we all consider this, and then Gethin says, "Right, I should go and do this bread thing."

"Do you need a hand?"

"No, it's all under control," he says, getting up, "at least, I think so. Famous last words, et cetera."

"Should we go into the dining room?"

"Oh, yeah. Light the candles, would you?"

"Yes, chef."

In the dining room, the table looks elegant, I think, with a green cloth and a round brass tray with the candles on it, entwined with ivy from the garden. This was my attempt at seasonal styling, and it could be worse. I indicate that Marian should sit wherever she likes, and I light the candles. In addition, there's a standard lamp in the corner, and a very pleasing West German ceramic lamp on the sideboard, so we can have the overhead light off. Knowing how much fuss my own mother makes about eating by lamplight, however, I check that this is acceptable.

"Oh, of course. No, I can see well enough not to eat a placemat by mistake," Marian assures me. She looks about. "Those doors look wonderful. They'll be lovely in the summer, won't they, when you can open them right up."

"I hope so," I agree. "They certainly look a lot better than what was there before."

"He's full of ideas," she continues, approvingly. "I'm sure he never paid any attention at the other place."

"I suppose he didn't really have to? It all seems a bit different when you live somewhere . . . bigger."

"Vanessa has very definite notions," she says. "I expect he just agreed with her."

I can't tell—even remotely—what Marian's opinion of this, or indeed of Vanessa generally, might be, and I'm not sure how to respond. "He did say it wasn't completely to his taste," I say, cautiously.

"No, it was very . . . well, I always thought it was quite boring," she says. "You know, in an expensive way. Like a hotel or something."

"That does seem a waste," I agree.

"I can't believe he's cooking," she says. "Although I suppose he doesn't have much choice these days. It wouldn't be your job to cook for me, would it." She smiles at me. "I thought he'd just buy something, though. I can't imagine him chopping up a pound of onions. He says he's bought lots of cookery books on your recommendation."

"Well, he said he wanted to learn, so, yes."

"Vanessa never really had time for that sort of thing."

"No, I'm not surprised. You don't always feel like it when you work full-time. And she must be very busy."

Gethin comes in with a steaming bowl in each hand, swathed in tea towels. He puts one in front of each of us. "Don't touch 'em," he says. "They're really hot." He retreats to fetch his own and soon we're all cautiously eating.

"Bloody hell," he says, and laughs. "This is actually good."

"It's very good," says Marian. "I'm proud of you."

He laughs again. "Ha. I should open a restaurant. This is amazing. A soup restaurant."

"You see. Next time you can make custard," I tell him.

"Yeah, well, I wouldn't want to overreach myself. Maybe build up to custard."

❧ ❦

We eat our dinner, talking about Gethin's nephew's new girl-friend, whom no one has met yet, and Marian and Joyce's recent weekend in Bristol, which was wet. I thought perhaps she'd ask me awkward questions, but either Gethin has briefed her very effectively, or else she's not that sort of person. We talk about books we've all read, which is more than you might expect, although none of us has read any of last year's Booker nominees, or the winner, for that matter, which is what started the conversation.

Gethin makes coffee, and I take the dishes out to the kitchen. I admit it's great to have a dishwasher. I'd got a bit bored of washing up. They both come out and stand about while I begin to stack it with the dirty bowls and dishes.

"You really don't need to stand out here, Marian," I say, "honestly. This will take me two minutes. Go and sit down."

They disappear off to the front room while I finish fiddling about in the kitchen. It all seems to have gone well, and it seems odd, now, to think about how nervous I was. It must be nice to have such a **str**aightforward parent. I always look at other people's families with real curiosity, because although most are just as dysfunctional as mine, the way that manifests is often very different.

I go into the dining room to blow out the candles, stack the placemats, and remove the tablecloth. Should I go back into the sitting room with them, or take myself off upstairs? I suppose that would be rude. I turn out the lamps and follow them into the sitting room.

"Who've you seen, then?" she's asking him as I enter. "Have you had anyone else to dinner, or round for drinks?"

He stretches his legs out in front of him, sitting in the armchair. "Not yet. Been waiting for everything to be finished. I went out with Sam Williams and his wife last week; that was cool. I'd never met her before."

It's interesting how many of Gethin's old friends—some of whom he hasn't seen for nearly twenty years—are keen to reacquaint themselves with him. I don't know if this is nosiness—after all, he's bound to have good stories, isn't he?—or whether they're genuinely pleased by his return. He thinks it's because they're all sick of the people they see all the time and are keen to welcome new blood that's not completely unknown. I suppose it might be that. Apparently there are various recently divorced women he knew in his teens who've reappeared seemingly from nowhere, which is entertaining. I can't say I blame them, either. He's so nice. And really very attractive. I imagine they'll be queuing up.

"Sam Williams! That's a name I haven't heard in a while," says Marian. "Do you remember that car he had when you were at college?" She laughs. "I don't know how many times your dad had to come out and rescue you when that old heap broke down." She laughs again.

"Yeah, because Sam's dad refused to help," says Gethin. "Bastard. Thank God for Dad. It seemed like it was always raining, and dark, when it broke down. I suppose you don't remember the times when it was a sunny afternoon."

"I remember he drove all the way to Cardiff once."

"Yeah, we went to a gig, didn't we. Was that when we went to see the Sugarcubes? Might have been. On the way back, luckily," he adds.

"Nothing more annoying than breaking down on the way to a gig," I agree. "We broke down once when we were going up to London to see New Order. The tickets were really expensive, as well. Or they seemed like it, at the time."

"Was that when you were living in Brighton?"

"Yeah. That van . . . we had several, but that one was awful."

"Gethin's father and I went to Brighton once, before the children were born. We went on the train; it took forever."

"I should think it would have done, if you went from here. Good grief."

"Yes, hours and hours. I remember we stayed in a guesthouse that said it had 'sea views,' but you could only see the sea from one of the landing windows." She laughs.

"Ah, classic guesthouse-owner behavior. You could see the sea from three of the bedrooms in the house I lived in. But you had to stand quite close to the windows." I think of the glass in those windows vibrating under the force of winter gales, every one stuffed with wads of newspaper to stop them rattling, the drafts howling through the high-ceilinged ruinous rooms, chunks of decorative molding thumping onto the floorboards.

"That house sounds great," Gethin says, "even if it was in a bit of a state."

"Ha, yeah, well. I'll look the street up," I say, "and show you.

All very nice, extremely faded grandeur. You know how every-thing looked before it got gentrified in the nineties."

"Aberystwyth is still a bit like that. Some fabulous houses there. Worth a visit," he adds, "when the weather improves."

"It's a beautiful town," says Marian. "A nice drive up the coast, as well. Do you know Wales at all, Jess?"

"Not really. I mean, no. I've been to Tenby, but I was tiny; I can't say I remember anything about it."

"Ah now. Tenby is lovely. You should go there first. Even in the winter it's lovely."

"I can't really go anywhere at the moment; I don't have a car. Or any money, for that matter."

"Gethin would take you, wouldn't you?"

"Sure," he says. "We should go."

"Oh, well. I don't suppose you much want to drive me about the place; there's no need. Thanks." I look across at him. He grins at me, shaking his head.

"No, it's good to go exploring. Even I haven't been to Tenby for ages. Mum's right, it's lovely. We should definitely go. Hey—we could go to loads of places. Saint Davids. Cardigan. Aber-aeron. All the castles in the valley."

He sounds quite excited at the prospect. It would be cool to visit places, I expect—I really can't see why he'd want to take me, though; he must have better things to do. I change the sub-ject, and we talk about the garden.

❧ ❧

When Gethin returns from dropping Marian home, he comes into the sitting room, where I'm idly watching a BBC Four doc-umentary about ABBA.

"That went okay," he says, "d'you think? Thanks for your help."

"Very successful. The soup was excellent. And you're welcome. Your mum's nice. Aren't you lucky?"

"I suppose I am," he says. "She's certainly no trouble. I haven't thought about it for ages, but I do remember being grateful when I was younger. That my parents were . . . well, like she said, that Dad would come and rescue me if I needed it. I hardly ever fought with them. I suppose that's because of Evan."

"Did they fight with him?"

"I dunno. There was . . . stuff." He looks awkward. "I don't think . . . he did used to row with Dad, when he was at school, I guess. He got grounded, a couple of times. Once him and a mate broke into the school and smashed up the trophy cabinet. I think that was supposed to be . . . subversive? And he got arrested once, for drunk and disorderly, when I was about . . . thirteen? Mostly, though, they were really worried about him. Mum used to cry. It was . . . awful."

I nod. "Yes."

He sighs. "It's funny, isn't it? It's only when you're older that you think about your parents' lives with them as the, like, main part. For ages you're the main part and everyone else is just a supporting role."

"I'm not sure I've ever seen myself as the main character," I say, doubtful.

"You know what I mean, though. Thinking about your parents as people takes a leap of imagination."

"I suppose that's true. When you look at pictures of them before you were born, it's freaky, isn't it? A whole existence before you began."

Chapter Ten

So now it's February. Sometimes when I think about my life in October and how it contrasts with my life now, I can't believe it. In fact, it seems as though my old life happened to someone else. Past Jess is almost a mystery compared to present Jess, who owns a bicycle and works for Bruce at his building supplies firm. I input orders into a very basic database, file things, and answer the phone, and am definitely enjoying having a job where I'm not on my feet all day, even if there's less gossip. The woman who had the job before me was bewilderingly inefficient, which has the advantage of making me look like an administrative superstar. Bruce is entertaining and avuncular, and the (mostly) men who work for him are also quite entertaining, with their safety boots and hard hats. I'm learning all kinds of thrilling stuff about aggregate and insulation and dampproofing. Dawn, the office manager, is friendly, and all in all, it's good.

I could run the place myself with my eyes shut, if I'm honest. I feel the slightest stirrings of . . . I wouldn't call it *ambition,* precisely, but something.

I have lunch at the restaurant once a week so I can see my hospitality pals. And I've been to Maura's house for dinner twice, introduced to her other friends, who look at me with curiosity but are welcoming and funny. We go out in the evening, too, sometimes—on her nights off, when she likes to check out the other restaurants in town before going on somewhere for cocktails.

The front-of-house team from the restaurant continue to suggest I might like to go clubbing with them; I assume this is a joke. Sometimes they mention elderly (to them—my age, obviously) relations they think I might want to go on a date with. ("My Uncle Mal's just got divorced; what about him? He's all right.") As yet I have resisted.

My wardrobe now quarter-fills the cupboard in the box room, with its smell of new particle board on the inside and fresh paint on the outside. I even have some clothes (although not many) that aren't from charity shops. We've applied the cornflower-blue paint to the front door—it's perfect—and, the dumpster removed, re-turfed the front lawn. The new windows are in, too, and I'm still excited every time I go into the kitchen, admiring everything about it, from the glossy cupboards to the handmade wooden worktops.

The Persian rug in the front sitting room, though, is old—a hundred years, maybe—and cost more than I've ever, personally, spent on a car. It's astonishingly beautiful. Living here really does mean I'm being spoiled, getting used to having nice things. I lived somewhere really nice once before, and it didn't make it easier when that ended—I was doubly bereft. But that's a while ago now, and, like a lot of my past—almost all of it, in fact—I try not to think about it.

❧ ❧

Sometimes Gethin has people round, for drinks, or to eat. He likes to introduce me to people, offering me a selection of potential new pals. I tease him about this, suggesting he work out a rating system so I know which ones I should concentrate on. He says he doesn't know them well enough himself, yet, to be able to do this.

When he has dinner parties (they're not really dinner parties; or, not exactly—I call them that because it makes him laugh), I help him with the food but don't join in. He says this is "pointless" and we almost had an argument about the last one. When I said, "Who invites their lodger to dinner parties?" he said, "Is that all you are? A lodger?"

"Yes," is what I say in reply, and he says, "Fine," in a way that makes it fairly clear it isn't fine at all. I don't really know what to do with this; I'm finding our relationship increasingly difficult to quantify. We're friends, I think, but I'm more grateful to him than one usually is to one's friends. I'm not sure it's very equal, no matter how often he claims that the work I've done in the house, as well as the cups of tea I make, the cooking lessons, my willingness to go on small adventures to castles (the valley really is full of them) or B&Q, and my eagerness to discuss color schemes and choose furniture, means I've paid him back for his kindness. I pay market rent, although he didn't want me to. He offered again to put me on his car insurance, and sometimes we have lunch out, but never dinner, although he did ask me once.

"Dinner is for dates," I said.

"Is it, though?"

"Isn't it?"

Then we glared at each other for a minute or two before he shrugged and said, "Okay, no dinner."

❧ ❦

Gradually the weather improves. It's exciting to watch spring arrive in a new place, to see what all these sleeping plants are, in the gardens along the street as well as at Sunnyside. The garden is full of the thrusting green spikes of snowdrops and daffodils, forsythia blaring over the fence from next door. Out the front there are crocuses in the new lawn, survivors from the old lawn, and rosebushes that I've pruned harder than they've had to cope with in years.

March turns to April. It's my birthday soon. I've written it on the calendar in the kitchen. I bought the calendar cheap, in January, and we both solemnly write things on it as though we're a family—dental appointments, annual leave, other people's birthdays.

I'm not sure what to do about mine. I'm ambivalent about birthdays at the best of times.

One evening while we're making dinner he says, "So it's your birthday next week."

"It is, yes."

"What are you going to do?"

"I'm not sure." I open the dishwasher and begin to fill it with knives and chopping boards.

"Would you like to go out for lunch or something? Or have people round?"

"I don't know. I thought about tea, or sort of tea—everyone eating scones standing up. But then I'm not sure I can face that."

"You definitely shouldn't do anything you can't face. That would be a mistake."

He takes glasses from the cupboard, and an open bottle of Sancerre from the fridge. "You could go out in the evening," he says. "Drinks with the girls? By which I mean Maura, I suppose?"

"Yes, I don't know, I'm not . . . I think birthday celebrations with Maura tend to get out of hand. Or out of hand by my definition anyway. I'm not as much fun as Maura and her mates."

He laughs. "I don't think that's true," he says, handing me my glass. We go through to sit in the front room.

"You know what I mean, though. She likes loud places and buzz and that's why she runs a restaurant."

"True."

"Whereas I like . . ."

"Yes, what do you like?"

"I don't know really." I lift my eyes to his face. "I think I've sort of forgotten. Although some of it's coming back to me."

"That's good. No rush. We could go out for the day? I mean—sorry—I've invited myself." He frowns at me. "Now I'm embarrassed," he says.

"Ha, don't be. Look, I'll invite you. Please come to my birthday something."

"Thanks. I will. What would you like to do? Day trip to Swansea? Or Tenby? It always rains when I go to Tenby but it's still good. Cardigan? That's farther but it's very pretty. I suppose it might be too early in the season though. Abergavenny? There are good restaurants in Abergavenny."

"Are there?"

"Well, just outside. The Hardwick. And the Walnut Tree. Both quite famous."

"Have you been?" I look at him, interested. We both like to eat, which is why we go out for lunch quite often. Now I'm earning a bit more money I like to do this, although part of me feels like I should be stricter about saving.

"Vanessa loved the Hardwick. So yes, I've been there a lot."

That sort of puts me off, but I don't say so. I just look inquiring.

"Couple of times to the Walnut Tree. That's Shaun Hill. He used to have a restaurant in Ludlow."

"Oh. I think I've heard of him?"

"Yes, Michelin stars. Or one, anyway. We could go there. Would you like to?"

"Is it very expensive?"

He shrugs.

"Is that a yes?"

He shrugs again, smiling. "Cheaper at lunchtime. And obviously we wouldn't go for dinner, because dinner is for dates."

"Yes. Well—"

"Anyway, it's your birthday, so you wouldn't be paying, would you?"

"I don't know if—"

"Abergavenny is pretty, some nice shops, galleries, there's a castle, of course . . ."

"Of course," I agree, solemnly.

"So if you wanted to go, I could see if we could get a table?"

"All right. But you must let me take you out for your birthday."

"It's a deal," he says, getting his phone out. "I'll call them now."

❧ ❦

My birthday's on a Saturday this year, the best of all possible results, especially now that I work office hours. Last night Gethin asked if I wanted him to bring my presents up to my room with a cup of tea in the morning. I'm massively tempted by this, actually, but I also feel it's . . . overly indulgent? Somehow inappropriate? So I get up at half eight and go downstairs in my pajamas.

I'd . . . not forgotten, but put to one side, the memory of what he did at Christmas, so when I go into the kitchen, and he shoos me away into the dining room, telling me he's making my breakfast, I'm not thinking about the arrangements he made in December. As soon as I enter the room, though, I remember, because he's done the same again. A helium balloon, in shiny green Mylar with my name on it, is tied to the back of the chair, and the table is laid for two, with a runner I've never seen before, green and gold sari fabric. There are candles, and an enormous spherical vase of scarlet tulips. A pile of cards sits by my plate, and parcels, some in their outdoor wrapping, so they've arrived through the post, and one in shiny green paper with gold ribbons.

I refuse to cry, although it wouldn't take much to push me over the edge. I go back to stand in the kitchen doorway. "I've never had a balloon before," I tell him, "or not one like that. Thank you."

"Go and sit down, for God's sake."

I obediently return to the dining room and sit down. He follows me in with breakfast.

"Smoked salmon," he says, "hollandaise, spinach, muffin. Happy birthday."

"Oh, perfect. Thank you so much."

He retreats to the kitchen to fetch the coffee.

"This is so lovely. Thank you. This is my favorite breakfast."

"I know." He smiles at me. "You said."

"Did I? When was that?"

He shrugs. "I don't know, can't remember. It's a good choice though. I thought perhaps eggs Benedict, but this is better, isn't it."

I nod enthusiastically, stuffing food into my mouth. "A balloon," I say, indistinctly, "with my name on it!"

"Yeah, to be honest, I don't really approve of balloons, but I decided you probably wouldn't let go of it outside to get tangled in a tree or strangle an owl or anything."

I shake my head vigorously. "I definitely won't. I shall save it, anyway, when it's deflated."

He grins. "Hoarder. I thought you might."

"Archive; not hoard. Anyway, how can you say that? I barely own anything at all."

"Ha. Archive," he says. "Ha."

"I only keep important things." I feel my face burn. "I mean, you know, stuff that—reminds me of something nice."

He puts down his cutlery and picks up his mug. "Mm-hm," he says, noncommittal.

I finish my breakfast, mopping up hollandaise with the final piece of muffin. "That was completely lush," I say. "Thanks."

I turn my attention to the parcels. I open the Amazon ones first: books from Lizzie and Noosha, fancy bath stuff from Natalie and the kids. Then the green and gold parcel, carefully peeling back the tape, hopeful I might be able to salvage and reuse the wrapping.

I gasp, and then I really am crying. It's a copy of *I Capture the Castle,* to replace the one I had to leave at Mitch's. I told Gethin about this, months ago, when we were putting his books away on the newly painted bookshelves. I had a lovely Folio Society edition, replacement for the battered secondhand paperback I'd had since I was a teenager.

This one's much older, an actual first edition. I can't believe it.

I turn the pages cautiously. It smells deliciously of old book. It has its original dust jacket, a bucolic rural scene with the castle(s) in the background and a figure in a red dress—Cassandra, presumably—in the foreground. On the flyleaf, the original inscription—*To dearest Peggy, Christmas 1949, love from Uncle Richard and Auntie Dot*—is followed by a newer one: *To Jess, with love from Gethin,* and the date. I close the book and clasp it, sentimentally, to my bosom, weeping foolishly.

"Jess," he says. "Please don't cry."

I shake my head but can't speak. I put the book on the table and cover my face with my hands.

"Hey," he says. "Lucky I didn't save it for you to open at lunchtime. Everyone would think I'd done something awful." He puts his hand very lightly on my shoulder. It's probably the longest physical contact I've had for six months. He squeezes gently, then pats me softly and takes his hand away.

After a while, I stop crying, wiping my eyes on my sleeve and sniffing elegantly.

"All right?" he asks. He passes me the box of tissues from the sideboard.

I nod, still unable to speak, and mop at my face. I blow my nose.

"I really didn't mean to make you cry."

"I know." I smile damply at him. "It's okay. I'm not sad. Thank you so much. You're very good at gifts."

"Oh, I don't know about that. You know. I just pay attention."

"That in itself," I say, "is a . . . it's a skill."

"It's not hard. I don't know why people pretend it is. I see the crap people buy each other and wonder what they're thinking."

"Most people don't pay attention."

"Yeah, I dunno why. It isn't hard to listen to people when they talk about the stuff they like."

"You remembered this from January." I really can't believe it.

"Well, yeah, I made a mental note. I mean, I didn't know when your birthday was, then, but I thought I might . . . that I might get you a present." He shrugs. "I didn't think about getting a first edition, though; I planned on getting a new copy. But then there were loads of different ones and I thought—aha!"

"And it's amazing, and perfect. Now you've set the bar pretty high, haven't you. I'd better start thinking about what to get you."

"Seriously, don't worry about that. I don't need anything."

Chapter Eleven

It's Saturday, a week after my birthday, and I've spent the morning in the garden. We replaced the broken glass in the greenhouse, and oiled the door, which was stuck, and Gethin drove me to the garden center and told me to buy whatever I wanted. I justified this by telling myself it's his greenhouse, and therefore the stuff wasn't actually for me. We bought some staging, which is what those slatted benches are called, and seed trays and pots and a watering can, plus a sieve for the compost from the wooden compost bins at the bottom of the garden. A wheelbarrow, and some tools. And some seeds—nasturtiums, cosmos, and poppies. Some plants, too—tomatoes, to live in the greenhouse, and foxgloves and cowslips to plant. He spent nearly three hundred pounds and laughed when I asked if he was sure it was okay. Imagine not worrying about money. Well, I can't, not really. Anyway, I've planted loads of seeds and had a lovely time. The sun's shining, and although it's not exactly warm, there's a hint of summer in the air.

I hear Gethin calling me. He went to town earlier, to buy cheese from the cheese stall in the indoor market.

"Jess? Jess, where are you?"

I walk up the garden, shading my eyes. "I'm here, what is it?"

He's standing in the kitchen doorway, gesturing to me. "Come in," he says, "there's someone I want you to meet. Oh— are you busy?"

"No, just finished."

"Planting things?"

"Yep."

I scrub my hands at the sink before following him into the front room.

Standing by the fireplace, looking at the bookshelves, is a tall, slender woman with white hair piled on top of her head in a deceptively effortless twist. I think it's natural, although when she turns round, I'm not completely sure, because she looks very young to be completely white. Unless she has that thing, though, that deficiency. She's wearing a beautiful slate-gray linen pinafore dress (Toast? Might be—they have a discount shop in Llandeilo) and a striped T-shirt, and a pale pink vintage suede jacket with big, covered buttons. I've rarely seen anyone so stylish. She also has a stick, a walking stick, covered in red and white painted flowers.

"This is Kate," says Gethin. "Kate, this is Jess."

"Hello," I say, looking curiously from one of them to the other.

"Gethin's been telling me about you," she says with a smile. "Isn't that the worst thing to say to someone?"

I laugh. "It might be."

"I bumped into her in town," he says. He sounds delighted. "I haven't seen her for, I don't know, twenty years?"

"More like twenty-five," she says.

She shifts her weight, and I say, "Oh, sit down, won't you? Can I take your coat? Shall I make some coffee?"

"I'll make it," says Gethin. "What would you like, Kate? Are you still a tea drinker? There's Earl Grey?"

"That would be lovely, thank you," she says, draping her jacket over the arm of the chair before sitting down. "That's an excellent sofa," she adds, looking at me. "This is a *very* nice room." The emphasis convinces me she isn't just being polite.

"It is, isn't it?"

"Geth said you chose everything."

It's funny how everyone always says this. It's funny that this is what he tells them. Is he trying to deny responsibility? "Oh— not exactly. He chose the sofa, really—I just helped with the color."

"It's a great color."

"Isn't it? It works really well in here." I look round, too, admiring the room as I do every day. "So—are you another of Gethin's school friends?" I don't think she is; she doesn't have a Welsh accent. She sounds more like me.

She shakes her head, smiling. "No, I'm from Surrey. I moved here after college; that's when we met. It was very unexpected to run into him. I don't think we have any mutual friends, these days, so I had no idea he was back. He said he's been meeting up with all sorts of people from his past."

"Yes, there are loads of them still here—people he went to school with, and sixth form. Which is nice, I think. Although it's always odd, isn't it, to have missed pretty much all the big things in people's lives, all the weddings and babies."

"I suppose it is," she says. "Back in time for the illness and divorce?"

We grin at each other. "Exactly."

Gethin comes in with a tray of mugs. He sits down on the other angle of the sofa and beams at both of us.

"I'm so pleased," he says, "I can't tell you."

Kate laughs. "Which is always good to hear."

"So what do you do?" I ask her. "Do you work in town?"

"I do. I work at the gallery on Priory Street," she says. "And I run art sessions, too, some for schools, and some during the holidays."

"Oh, how lovely." I'm surprised I've never seen her in there, but I guess she doesn't mean "in the gallery shop." "The gallery is great. You're very lucky here, with the other galleries, too, and all the shops with art in them. In . . . where I come from, there isn't a gallery. Even though the town is bigger. But I buy all my birthday cards in your shop."

She laughs. "It's good for cards, and presents, too. Yes, it's a good place to work."

"I'll get those pictures," says Gethin suddenly, jumping up.

"Oh Lord," she says. She leans back, laughing harder. "He says he's got photographs of my youth. *Our* youth, I should say."

"Always fun to see photos you haven't seen before. Or haven't seen for ages."

"I suppose I must have copies of some of them, but I dread to think."

He's thumping back down the stairs with a fat green photo album.

"Come and sit over here," he says, "so you can see."

She pushes herself up from the chair, slightly awkward. I wonder what's wrong; is she injured, or is it something permanent—arthritis, perhaps? She doesn't use her stick though, as she walks cautiously across the room.

He pats the sofa on both sides of him. "Come and look," he says to me. "If you want to see how handsome I was in my twenties." We all laugh, although I can't see why he wouldn't have been.

He opens the album and flicks through the early pages. "Oh look," he says. "Here's Julia; remember I told you about her?"

I lean to look at the photos, careful not to touch him.

Julia is a dark-haired girl with heavy bangs, a shift dress in dark purple, fishnets. She cups the elbow of one arm with the hand of the other, a cigarette held in her free hand, smoke coiling upward.

"The art student?"

"That's her."

"Oh yes. I can see exactly the sort of trouble she might have been."

He laughs. "Right?"

"Is that you?" I point at the photo next to Julia.

"Yeah, I know," he says, laughing again. "Before I got contacts."

He has little round glasses and wears a white shirt and the waistcoat from a dark suit, his hair pushed behind his ears.

"You look so *young*," says Kate. "How are we ever old enough to go away to university? My eldest does her A-Levels this year," she adds, "and she already looks older than you do in that picture."

"Ha." He flips the pages. "These are Julia's flatmates, look."

"Oh, the Fashion people. Gosh, look at them." The women are wearing those chunky-heeled shoes that were so fashionable back then, and a selection of self-consciously avant-garde outfits. They're angular, with sharp, asymmetric haircuts. There's one boy, in a hat.

"I lived with some Fashion students in my final year," says Kate. "They didn't look much like that, though. They were all really obsessed with tailoring. Alexander McQueen was doing his MA while we were undergraduates."

I know about Alexander McQueen; Noosha and I went to the exhibition at the V&A the other year.

"You went to Saint Martins?"

She nods. "I did indeed."

Gethin flips more pages. There he is sitting on the roof of a Land Rover in a field of rapeseed; squinting into the sun on a beach somewhere; laughing in a crowd of people in the rain, at a festival, I suspect; smoking in a variety of ugly student rooms; in his robes for graduation. I'm trying to work out what I'd have thought if I'd met him then. A bit straight, perhaps. It's hard to say. He wasn't bad-looking, even with terrible early nineties hair and, in some of the photos, a little goatee beard. Although he's better-looking now—an annoying habit of men, to get more handsome.

"Here we go," he says.

"Oh my," says Kate, looking at a picture of herself in one of those floaty seventies Indian cotton dresses with bell sleeves, the exact color of her eyes—dark cobalt blue like a willow pattern plate—her hair a mass of scarlet ringlets. She's utterly stunning.

"Oh," I say. "How beautiful! Directions. Pillarbox Red? Or Flame?"

She laughs. "Flame. I thought Pillarbox Red was too harsh."

"Looks great."

"Yeah, it was easy for me, no need to bleach it. My hair's always been like this"—she puts a hand to her head—"or since I was sixteen, anyway."

"I remember you telling me your hair was white," says Gethin. "I don't think I could really imagine it." He turns the page again, and there they are together, arms round each other, her head on his shoulder. Another where they're in a pub, talking to different people but holding hands. In a third, they're kissing. Kate tuts.

"You used to go out?" I ask. I don't know why this surprises me; of course they did.

"Yeah. Nearly two years, wasn't it?" she says, and he nods.

At some kind of event, here, she's dressed in something more conventional, hair up.

"My brother's wedding," she says, and there they are together, Gethin in a suit that doesn't fit him as well as the ones I've seen him wear later, in the press photos. There are more: Kate on a beach in a bathing costume; drinking a glass of wine in the sun; clambering on rocks.

"Saundersfoot," she says. "Remember how hard it rained?"

"Warm though," he says. "That was a good day."

"It was a good summer," says Kate.

Here they are outside a tent with some other people in festival clothes and dirty feet.

"Megadog," says Kate. "Oh my God, so messy."

"You don't look like a Megadog person, Gethin," I tease. "What year is that? I might have been there too."

"Kate's influence," he says. "I don't remember much about it, if I'm honest. That would be '96, I think."

"I used to go every year," says Kate. "We used to go to Club Dog, when I was in London."

"I was in Brighton then," I say. "We went to loads of festivals. My boyfriend knew lots of festival people. We had a van." I peer at the photographs in case, freakily, our van might be visible in the distance. "I mean, it wasn't meant for festivals; we did house clearances mostly. It was for moving furniture. But we slept in it quite a lot."

"I wish I'd had a van to sleep in," says Kate. "That would have seemed quite luxurious, compared to my shitty tent."

"Kate widened my horizons," says Gethin.

"Oh, come on, I don't think that's true, is it," she says with a laugh. "They already seemed fairly wide when we met."

I suddenly feel very awkward. They're flirting, and I feel like they might find it easier if I wasn't here. I sit back and finish my tea, wondering how I might escape from the room.

They laugh at some more photos, and then Gethin says, "And that's it, I guess—these are after we split up."

"Ah, well, it was lovely to see them," she says. "I have some of you, somewhere. I'll dig them out. I'm sorry, Jess, it's always a bit tiresome to have to listen to people reminiscing."

"Oh, no, it's interesting to hear about people's youth. Especially when you didn't know them at the time."

"I suppose he probably seems quite sensible," she says, "if you haven't known him long." She twinkles at both of us. She really is extremely attractive.

"I don't know about that. I've heard a number of stories about hallucinogen-related shenanigans," I tell her.

"Oh Lord. That reminds me of . . . well," she says, "all a long time ago." We're silent, for a moment, considering the truth of this statement. She changes the subject. "So, Gethin was saying you're taking on the garden here?"

"Oh . . . just—I thought I'd plant some stuff, you know. Tidy things up a bit."

"It's not that I'm not interested," says Gethin, "but I wouldn't know where to start. Jess has Plans."

"I don't know about Plans," I object. "I mean—"

"Did you garden before?" asks Kate.

"Not recently. And not much, but—"

"She used to video *Gardeners' World* when she was at college. Who does that?" He's laughing at me, but I don't mind.

"You sound like my partner. Sam used to spend all his pocket money on plants."

"I can't say I went that far." I smile at her.

"She knows the Latin names for things!"

"*Some* things. I just"—I look at Kate—"pick things up, when I'm paying attention."

"He says you mentioned you might like to do some kind of course?"

I flush, uncomfortable at the thought that they were talking about me. And how long were they together already, in town, if they got this far? I'd mentioned it only in passing, a vague idea about doing something more creative. Gethin and I were talking about "the future," and he encouraged me to think about what my life might be like if I could do anything I wanted. It wasn't exactly a serious conversation, or hadn't felt like one. It seems weird he'd tell someone else what I said.

"We did talk about it, a bit. But I can't afford to go back to college."

"They do apprenticeships at the Botanic Gardens. My partner works there; I could introduce you—then you'd have someone to ask, if you have any questions. They pay you while you do it, which might help?"

"That's . . . thanks, but I really don't know if—"

"Well, think about it; it's a lovely place to work," she says. "Anyway, I should probably make a move. I didn't mean to be out for so long; they'll be wondering where I am."

"I'll give you a lift," says Gethin, and they both get up.

"Do you live in town?" I ask her.

"Yes, down by the river. You'll have to come and visit," she says, putting on her jacket and collecting her stick and her handbag. "Sam was talking about barbecues in the summer. Really good to meet you." She looks at me as she says it, quite intently, I think to show she means it.

"You too," I say, and off they go.

I look at the album on the coffee table and am tempted to look through it. I wonder if it goes as far as Vanessa's arrival on the scene. Probably not, if Gethin and Kate didn't go out for very long. If she's married—although she didn't say "husband"—then maybe she wasn't flirting with Gethin. Sometimes you do flirt, anyway, with people you used to flirt with. Anyway, it's not any of my business if she was. He was properly delighted to see her, though.

❧ ❧

Twenty minutes later, he's back.

"Hey," he says. "What's for tea?"

"Salad, I thought. What cheese did you get?"

"Hafod. And Caws Cerwyn."

"Oh nice, that's my favorite."

"I know. Hey, so . . ." He leans against the worktop to talk to me while I begin to assemble salad. "Ah, wait—can I do anything?"

I always make him help, because I'm not his housekeeper, or his girlfriend. "Croutons," I say, "you could make croutons."

"I dunno if I could. How . . . are they bread?"

I explain the complexities of croutons as I chop cucumber.

"Yeah, so, wow," he says, digging a baking tray out of the cupboard. "Amazing, huh? I'm so glad I bumped into Kate. It's made my day."

"I see that."

"Yeah, and as soon as we were talking, I was like, Jess would like Kate! I should introduce them. I thought maybe she wouldn't come with me. I mean, I guess it is a bit odd." He laughs. "Hi, look, it's your ex-boyfriend from when you were twenty-four! You haven't seen him for decades! Why not come to his house to meet his housemate."

"You managed to persuade her, though."

"Yeah, well . . . d'you know, it's mad, isn't it, because we were only together for eighteen months or something, and obviously it didn't work out, but that was probably the best relationship I've ever had. Does that sound weird? I mean, it does, doesn't it. I don't think we ever had an argument, though."

I pause to look at him. Interesting. "Really? Why did you split up?"

"Oh." He frowns. "Very stupidly, I slept with someone else."

"Oh my God! I'm shocked."

"I know. What a tit."

"I'm really surprised. Although I don't know why; men are idiots."

"I know. It's the only time I've ever done anything like that. So stupid."

"How did she find out? Did you tell her?"

"Not straightaway. But I felt so rotten about it. So, after about a week, I had to tell her. And she was like, yeah, no, that's that, mate. Couldn't blame her really. It was—I think we were both upset, but she was more disappointed than angry, like. I remember her saying that 'she'd had such high hopes' for us, and you know, I had too."

"That's sad."

"Yeah."

"Who did you sleep with?"

"God, I don't know—well, I think her name was Becky? It was at a stag party." He shakes his head.

"Oh Lordy. Gethin, really."

"Yeah, I know."

"That's . . . rubbish."

"It's really rubbish. Yeah. I think maybe it was the stupidest thing I've ever done." He looks genuinely quite sad at this. I shake my head.

"Yeah, it sounds stupid."

"What's the stupidest thing *you've* ever done?"

"What, apart from staying somewhere I should have left a lot sooner?"

"Oh yeah. Shit, sorry."

"No, it's fine. If you mean in a"—I pause—"less dramatic fashion? Are you asking if I ever cheated on someone and re-gretted it?"

"I suppose I am, really. Or finished with someone when maybe you shouldn't have, or messed up through—"

"Idiocy?"

He grins. "Yeah, all right."

I think about it. "I've never cheated on anyone. There are some people I wish I hadn't slept with."

"Hm. Really?"

"Yeah, not for . . . but because sometimes it's like a waste of energy, isn't it. Psychic energy, I mean." I laugh. "Sorry, that's a bit . . . but you know what I mean. Do you? When you spend ages thinking about someone and then—if you get to know them better, it's disappointing. All the time you've spent talking to your friends about them and wondering what they're like and talking to them awkwardly in pubs and then—"

"And then it's not worth it?"

"Exactly."

Chapter Twelve

I'm lying on the sofa reading my book. Sometimes we both lie on the sofa reading and it's the nicest thing. Anyway, this afternoon I'm by myself, because Gethin's gone to his mum's. He asked if I wanted to go, but—although he always asks me—I don't like to. I mean, I do go sometimes, and it's very pleasant, because Marian's lovely, and she's always really nice to me without ever saying anything awkward or nosy. She's definitely one of those very friendly, relaxing sort of people, the sort who's interested in you but not in an intrusive way. She's never once made me feel like I shouldn't be living here, like I've somehow inveigled my way into Gethin's life. You could say, "Why would she?," but it's not as simple as that. And it's one of the reasons I don't always go, because she really has nothing to do with me, and if I go a lot, she might start thinking . . . well. People don't take their lodgers round to their mum's house, do they.

Plus—and this is feeble—I'm always slightly concerned that Abby might be there, and there's only so many times you can cautiously say "Will it just be us?" before it looks a bit pointed.

I hear the front door open and look at the clock. He usually stays for tea, when he goes to his mum's, so he's home unex-

pectedly early. There's a certain amount of banging and shuf-
fling.

"Are you okay?" I call. "Need a hand?"

"No, don't worry," he shouts back. Then the door opens
and he's in the room. He's carrying a huge cardboard box and
grins at me over the top of it.

"Hello. What have you got there?"

He puts the box down on the floor and kicks it gently. It
rattles.

"Guess," he invites.

I look at him. "From the noise, I'd have to say . . . Legos?"

"Ha, yes. I thought she'd got rid of it," he says, "but it's been
in the garage."

He shrugs his jacket off and drops it on the arm of the sofa,
and then sinks to his knees and peels a strip of parcel tape from
the top of the box.

"Mostly Space Legos," he says. "Ooh, look. Instructions."

"Oh wow, you kept the instructions?"

"How else would you be able to put it back together after
you made a massive space station out of all the bits?"

"Fair enough." I get up and move across to the other end of
the sofa, perching where I can see into the box. "Wow, there's
loads."

"Yeah, I think I had all of it. Up to a certain point, like."

"Oh yeah, until you discovered girls?"

"Music, certainly. Ah." He stirs the pieces with his finger. "I
might put some together, is that mad?"

"Oh my God. No, it's not mad. Can I do some?"

He grins at me. "'Course you can. Here." He passes me a
pile of dog-eared, much-folded sheets of paper, printed with

the beautiful exploded diagrams that are part of what makes Legos so pleasing.

"Excellent. Should we tip it all out and sort it?"

"Bloody hell, what kind of monster are you?" He pulls a horrified face.

I laugh helplessly at this. "No, I'm just . . . don't you think that would be sensible?"

"The tipping it out seems a good idea." He suits the action to the words and sends the pieces rippling and crashing onto the rug. We look at each other.

"That's done it," I say.

"Best thing about being a grown-up, isn't it? Doing whatever you want."

I sit on the floor and begin to pick through the pieces. "Did you ever think about being a grown-up? When you were a kid?"

"Not really. I mean, it's all"—he pauses—"you don't really know what it means, do you. Having a job and a wife and a car—but at least two of those things sound rubbish when you're nine."

I laugh. "Yeah, it seems completely unfathomable that you'll ever be an adult, doesn't it? And I suppose you don't—well, what I mean is, we didn't have many blueprints for that stuff, did we. For how you might imagine a relationship? Only your parents, who are old, so they don't count; and what's on TV. Where loads of stuff you watch is sitcoms, so the relationships are skewed to be funny. Everything was very basic. Young people these days are lucky in some ways. They all know there's more than one way to be—romantic, or whatever. Noosha's younger daughter's had girlfriends and boyfriends at school and as far as I can tell no one even cares; it's brilliant. She's never had to worry that a lad with highlights and a terrible mustache will give her a padded Valentine's card. Or worry that he won't."

He's laughing now. "Oh my God. Did you have a boyfriend with highlights?"

I grin at him. "No, by the time I was old enough everything was different. And I never managed to be fashionable. Or at least, not high street. So that sort of boy wasn't interested."

"What sort of boy was, then?"

"Oh, you know. Curtains, Stone Roses T-shirt. And then a bit later dreadlocks and a Spiral Tribe T-shirt."

"Oh yeah," he says, "when you were a traveler."

"I really wasn't. Well, none of us were; no one ever went anywhere, or at least, not in their trailer, or no farther than a different bit of vacant land. I was astounded," I add, "when I went to university and met a whole bunch of crusty types who ran sound systems and went hunt sabbing and on demos; it was amazing. Activists! They were organized! The people I lived with were very much not organized or active. Or cool."

"Not even a little bit? They must have been. Why else would you have moved there?"

"I moved in with someone, didn't I. I did it for love, or thought I did." I glance across at him. We've stopped making Legos to talk, kneeling opposite each other on the rug. "I thought it would be, you know, freeing, but actually it was a bunch of non-rule rules and misogynist bollocks. I assumed everyone would be extremely right-on. Vegetarian anarchist feminist collective. My arse."

He grins at me. "Disappointing. How long did you live there?"

"I dunno, a year? Most of my A-Levels."

"I can't believe you lived on site and still passed your exams. Impressive."

"I used to be quite driven, if you can believe it. That's one of the reasons I gave that up, as you might imagine. My life there. When he said we should have a baby." I look at him, interested to see his reaction.

"Shit. How old were you then? Eighteen?"

"Yeah, just about."

He shakes his head. "So what did you do? Move home?"

"Yeah, luckily I never actually fell out with my mum—she wasn't really concentrating, to be honest; I don't know if she even noticed I'd gone to begin with. Anyway, yeah, I thought, *Oh, hang on, why am I even doing this?* So I just moved home again. It was strange. I'd been . . . I won't say I was unhappy; I wasn't really, although I was often cold, and sometimes hungry, and I thought a lot of the people I lived with were—I don't know, I tried really hard not to think they were wankers, but quite a lot of them were."

"Ha ha."

"I suppose I'd fallen out of love with Fitz and not even noticed."

"Yeah, that's a strange feeling, isn't it."

"Better than messing things up, though." I grin at him. "Like people do sometimes. By sleeping with bridesmaids."

"Oh God, don't. Not that she was a bridesmaid. But like I said"—he looks wistful—"I really feel like I messed that up badly, me and Kate. It's a shame. I think . . . but maybe it's a weird thing to think I'm bad at relationships when I just came out of fifteen years with the same person."

"Um. I think perhaps you're a bit hard on yourself, yes."

"I don't know." He begins to stir through the Lego pieces again. "I think—perhaps—I just can't really imagine . . . meeting someone else. I suppose it will probably take ages. If it ever happens at all."

I'm not sure what to say about this. He wants to be reassured, but I don't know if I'm the right person to do it.

"It depends what you want, doesn't it? If you want to meet someone like Kate, who's arty and used to do the sort of things you did, that would take longer, I s'pose, than trying to meet—I mean, I know Vanessa's famous, so it's not like I'm suggesting you'd easily get another TV girlfriend. But a straight sort of person—someone who likes *Mamma Mia!* and cocktails and has a couple of kids? Maura has friends like that. They're nice, some of them. You know, quite fun." I sort bricks into piles, separating them by color.

"And there's nothing wrong with that. But maybe I'd like to meet someone who used to dye her hair pink and wore Doc Martens, you know, and likes the same sort of music as I do."

"If I was looking for a girlfriend, those are certainly the sort of criteria I'd be using."

"Ha, yeah, well. How do you even find out? There might only be one in West Wales; I'll fight you for her."

I laugh. "You'd win. You're much nicer than I am."

"God, am I?" He looks startled.

"Of course you are."

We look at each other, slightly pained. I'm not going to pretend, though, that I don't think he's pretty great. He is, and he'll make someone a brilliant boyfriend.

"Yeah, well, I'm not sure it helps," he says. "Being nice." He pushes some flat gray pieces toward the heap I've already made and then begins to pick transparent bricks out of the pile.

"I've had both kinds of boyfriend and I can tell you for nothing the nice ones are loads better."

He laughs unwillingly. "I guess."

"Anyway, you're being cynical." I lean across the pile of Legos to reach some white cylindrical pieces. "I assume you were being nice when you got all the girlfriends you've ever had. And they were all okay, weren't they? It doesn't matter whether things worked out or not; it's not like any of those relationships would have been more successful if you'd been a shit."

"I s'pose not. Did you ever have pink hair?"

I look at him. "Hm. Maybe."

"Are there pictures?"

"I suppose there are. I'll dig them out. There are some on Facebook."

"I'd like to see what you looked like when you were young," he says. "I can't really imagine you in combat boots and suchlike. Is that what you looked like?"

"Piercings, loads of layers, stripy knitwear, my clothes had holes in them—yes, you know the kind of thing."

We both reach for the same set of tiny wheels and our fingers touch. An electrical fizz shoots up my arm. It's embarrassing.

"Sorry," says Gethin. I try to ignore the tingle and rub my arm. Gooseflesh. Ridiculous. A moment later, it happens again. This time he doesn't say anything, and we both concentrate on our sorting.

"Ow," he says, about ten minutes later. "D'you know what, I'm massively uncomfortable." He shifts, stretching his legs out in front of him. "What time is it, anyway?"

"I don't know. Half four?" I reach for my phone. "Yeah, nearly five. What shall we have for tea? I thought you'd be out."

"I needed to come home and play with my toys." We smile at each other.

"I thought I might have a cheese toastie. You fancy that?"

"That sounds perfect."

"Cup of tea?"

"You always know what to say."

"Ha, yeah. Don't I." I get up, stretching. "To be honest I haven't been that comfortable myself for the last fifteen minutes."

I go out to the kitchen and wrestle the Breville out of the cupboard. I plug it in and open the freezer for four pieces of bread. I slice up some cheese and go back to ask if he wants tomato.

"Oh, yes. I love a lavalike bit of tomato. Can I do anything?"

"No, it's fine."

I slice a tomato, put the kettle on. I feel a bit . . . I don't know. I make the toasties and then lean on the worktop. I wrap my arms round my head. Everything's stirred up, which is my own fault. It's not that I mind talking about this stuff—actually, I like it, I think. I like talking to Gethin. That's the actual problem. The more I talk to him, the better we know each other, the worse it all gets. I'm such an idiot. All this "Oh yes, why don't you get a girlfriend like this?" and then his fingers brush mine and I'm all over the place. Sexual tension, I suppose. It's not helpful, whatever it is.

Because of the noise of the kettle, and because my arms are wrapped round my head, I don't hear him come into the kitchen, and when he says, "Jess, are you okay?," I jump wildly. He puts out his hand, touching my arm. I jerk away, backing into the counter on the opposite side of the room.

"Shit," he says, "sorry, I didn't mean to—"

"You startled me," I say. We stare at each other.

"I'm sorry. You don't need to flinch, though, I'm not going to—"

"I know, sorry."

Here we stand, apologizing to each other about . . . what, exactly, I'm not even sure. Sometimes I feel very naked and exposed when we're together. Even though we're alone together all the time. My heart's thumping as though I'm afraid, but it's not that.

The kettle clicks off.

"Tea," I say, and take two mugs from the cupboard.

Chapter Thirteen

Gethin's birthday is twenty-eight days after mine, so it's also on a Saturday. We congratulate ourselves on this double good fortune.

I bought a sewing machine for forty quid from a woman on Facebook, much to his amusement ("You're so crafty, Jess! What next, a spinning wheel?"), and made some birthday bunting, which is twee, but I was extremely pleased with how it came out. For breakfast I make boiled eggs and soldiers, and he opens a pile of gifts from his family and some of his mates—including a rather unexpected bottle of champagne from Vanessa.

"Bloody hell. I thought I might get a card. I wonder if Rachel arranged it."

"Who's Rachel?"

"PA."

"Blimey." I stab my spoon through the bottom of my eggshell to prevent witches from going to sea in it, and regard him with some curiosity. "I suppose she would have a PA."

"Yeah, she's not full-time, or she didn't used to be. But she organizes stuff—you know, books hair appointments and liaises with people."

"Lawks."

He laughs. "Your exclamations are hilarious," he says.

"Crikey O'Reilly," I respond. "Fuck off."

He laughs harder. "You can't say that on my birthday; it's just rude."

I'm immediately contrite. "Oh God. I'm sorry."

"Idiot, I don't care. Anyway, it's a bit odd to think Vanessa thought enough about my birthday to send me anything."

"You were together for a long time," I point out. "It's not like she'd forget."

"I suppose," he says, doubtfully. "She didn't send anything last year, not even a card." He opens another one. "Oh, and this is from her folks—look." He fans out five tenners for me to see.

"Wow, fifty quid? For their daughter's ex? They must have really liked you."

"Yeah, I think so. I got fifty quid last year as well. I must absolutely not fail their birthdays," he adds, "or I'll look like a right thoughtless shit."

I nod in agreement. "Are they on the calendar?"

"Yep."

"Good. Anyway," I say, "look at you with nearly twenty cards. Popular."

"Ha ha, right?"

I spent ages (and I mean it; literally hours and hours) looking for something to buy him. I wanted it to be a proper gift, something personal. I looked at loads of vintage china, and boxes, and Welsh cawl spoons, which people collect, and which are supposed to live in these special things like auricula theaters, tiered boxes with holes in them, spoon racks. Those are most definitely at the fancier, more antique end of kitchenalia. A good spoon rack is really expensive: two hundred quid or even more. In the end, after much agonizing, I abandoned the idea of getting something old, and instead bought a Lego X-Wing Fighter. Which was also not very cheap, but it does look amazing. I'm excited to see his reaction.

⅋⅋

We drive to Tenby for lunch. Maura recommended the restaurant, and as per her advice, we have two starters each instead of a main course. I pay for this, like I said I would. It's nothing like as expensive as my birthday lunch at the Walnut Tree, but I suppose that's not the point. It's satisfying to pay for it, though, to treat him. I enjoy the feeling.

It's raining when we get there, but the sun comes out in the afternoon and we go down to the beach to walk off our food. Tenby is as pretty as everyone told me, and it's one of those places with amazing light, like St. Ives—even in the rain, the sea is an astonishing color. There are lots of pastel-painted houses, and rocks, and it's much more seaside-y than the beaches nearer home. There's a huge expanse of flat empty shore, and I find a bit of driftwood and use it to write HAPPY BIRTHDAY GETHIN in huge letters in the sand. Then we climb the steps back up to the esplanade and take photos of my transient graffiti.

We lean on the railing to look down at the beach.

"Biggest birthday greeting I've ever had," he says.

"Yeah, well, there's not usually space to write things with letters, like, five feet tall."

"True. I can't help feeling robbed that no one's ever tried before, though. I mean, who even are these so-called friends and family who've never made the effort?"

I laugh. "Yeah, God, you're treated like total shit, aren't you? I mean, that massive pile of gifts and all those cards . . ."

"Right? It's appalling. I shall complain," he says, "to my ombudsman."

"Ombudsman" is one of those words that makes me laugh every time, and I grip the railing, approaching hysteria. I know that's why he said it, and this . . . what even is that? This tiny gift of laughter seems to me to somehow encapsulate the whole thing, the way we are together, the basis of all of it. Or if not the basis—that's me not having to sleep in a tent, isn't it—then the thing we've built over that basis. I'm not sure if I'm explaining this very well even to myself.

❧ ❦

We go home, and if we both have a sea-air-induced nap on the sofa, that's fine, isn't it? And at least it means we're reasonably alert later, and able to eat cake (brownies, with forty-eight candles, which makes him laugh, as they bristle intently at us).

I have a plan for the evening, but I need to check again.

"And you don't want to go out?"

"God no, I've been out already." He shakes his head at me.

"I thought you might want to go to the pub with your mates?" I watch him carefully, trying to read his expression.

"Pfft, no. Why, anyway?"

"I thought of something."

"Something to do this evening? We could make the X-Wing."

"We could," I agree.

"Or?"

"I thought maybe you'd like to go to an indie disco. Or an alternative disco, anyway."

"Ha, I would quite like to do that, but God knows where the

nearest one would be. Wouldn't we have to go to Liverpool or Brighton or something?"

"Not if you didn't mind there only being two people there. Because I bought this—look." I open the cupboard by the window, removing a cheap disco ball lamp I got from the market. He laughs.

"I did a playlist," I say. "And I bought two cans of Carling."

"Carling? Jeez."

"I couldn't exactly remember what they used to sell for a pound a pint, but it was probably Carling. But I definitely won't be able to drink more than . . . actually probably two mouthfuls. So obviously you can drink what you want. Although champagne would seem . . . inappropriate."

"A bit," he agrees. He laughs again. "I've certainly never drunk champagne even at a fancy nightclub."

"No? I assumed you and Vanessa would be"—I search my brain for details culled from reading scraps of tabloid newspapers at the nursing home where I worked before I ran away— "er, necking Cristal at Chinawhite?"

"Oh yeah, with Prince Harry? No, weirdly." He grins at me. "Luckily Van had already had her nightclub phase when we met."

"In the nineties?"

"In the nineties."

"I can't really imagine what your life was like."

"It was . . . I don't know, it was pretty fun at first. I've said before, haven't I, there are loads of people I've met and places I've been that would never have happened if I'd been seeing someone else. But it's hard work, you know. She works so hard. She's one of those people who never really relaxes; I think she's forgotten how. And it takes a lot of upkeep."

"What, having nice hair and stuff? Has she got nice hair?" I've never told him I looked her up, and it's true I still haven't seen her on the telly.

"Oh, yeah. It's long, you know, dark, and—"

"Glossy?"

"That makes her sound like a horse," he objects.

"Ha. Sorry. Is she very pretty? I suppose she must be?" I'm interested to know what he thinks about this. Presumably he does think so—I mean, she's objectively attractive. Actually I don't know why I asked, and now I'm quite embarrassed. He doesn't notice though, because he's thinking.

"Yes," he says, "or maybe pretty's not the right word? Attractive, though. She's very attractive—beautiful, even. Much better-looking than I am," he adds.

I raise my eyebrows. "Is she? You're quite good-looking."

He laughs. "Yeah, no. She's proper telly attractive, you know. But it does take a lot of work. She goes to the hairdresser's once a fortnight or something. And then there's massages and manicures and getting her eyebrows done and everything."

"It must be weird to have to look at yourself all the time."

"I'm not sure it's very good for you. I sometimes worried—it gets in your head a bit, all that stuff. Not healthy."

I feel unexpectedly sorry for Vanessa. I wonder if she misses him.

"Anyway," he says, "we seem to have got a long way from the point, which was you asking me if I wanted to go dancing."

"Oh yeah. And do you?"

"I do like dancing," he says, "and I can't remember the last time I danced to stuff I really liked. I mean, you dance at weddings, don't you, but you don't have much control over the playlist."

"Depends on the people getting married, doesn't it. When Natalie got married there was lots of Take That and suchlike. Steps and S Club and stuff. Because she's younger than me and more . . . normal. There was a tiny bit for the weirdos. 'Should I Stay or Should I Go' and 'This Charming Man' and that annoying ska medley that you only hear at weddings when it would be better to have the whole song."

"Oh yeah, a bit of 'One Step Beyond,' a bit of 'Ghost Town.' "

"Yeah, and 'Too Much Too Young.' "

"I love 'Too Much Too Young.' And 'Mirror in the Bathroom.' I know they're by two different bands," he adds, "before you point that out."

"I put that on the playlist, 'Mirror in the Bathroom,' " I say, pleased with myself. "So—would you like me to put the music on? Or is it odd, to dance in your front room?" I'm a bit worried now that it might be. But that's because the light's on. I turn off the big light and perch in the armchair to lean over and click on the disco ball lamp. Immediately there's more atmosphere. If we have a drink, and I start the music—

"Alexa, play Gethin's Birthday Playlist from Spotify, please."

The shouty brass intro to "Reward" by The Teardrop Explodes begins.

"Oh, okay," says Gethin, "well done." He gets up and pulls me to my feet. "Yes, I always like to dance to this."

Eight tracks later, I make the international sign for "Want a drink?" and shout, "I'm going to the bar. Do you want anything?"

"Wouldn't say no to that beer."

I dance out into the kitchen and open the fridge. I'm delighted with how well this is going. I love dancing. I'd forgotten.

And how could I have forgotten? Really, it makes me cross, I reflect, as I slam the ice-cube tray onto the worktop and pick up ice for my pint of water, that Mitch made everything in my life shut down so easily. I thought I was better than that, and it infuriates me that I wasn't.

❧ ❧

We dance for nearly three hours. I wasn't sure how much music to put on the playlist. If it was a real nightclub in the 1990s, of course, we'd be there until two, or three. I usually stayed until the end, when I used to go to indie discos. Because I really like dancing, and you might miss the best tunes. But five hours is quite a long time to dance in your house. And I'd assumed I'd probably want to be in bed before midnight.

I'd spent hours trying to remember what various club nights played as their "last song" to tell you it was time to bugger off home. "New York, New York," at one in my hometown. "Summer Wine" by Nancy and Lee, somewhere farther north. In the end, though, I chose "Say Hello, Wave Goodbye," and we belt it out at each other in a heartfelt way before "ad libbing to fade," as it used to say in the lyrics printed in *Smash Hits*. As the song finishes, I turn the big light back on for that realistic end-of-the-night feeling. It's suddenly quiet and I can hear the slight grinding noise as the disco ball revolves. We blink at each other, sweaty and exhausted.

"Happy birthday," I say, "I hope you've had a good one."

"Ah, it's been brilliant, thank you so much." He looks at me for a moment and then steps forward, wrapping his arms round me. We hug, squeezing tightly. "I'm a bit warm," he mutters into my hair, "apologies for that."

I laugh. "No warmer than me, don't worry."

It's nice to hug people; I'd forgotten.

He squeezes me again and then lets go. "Honestly, got to be one of the best birthdays ever. I've had such a great day."

I'm delighted to hear this, of course. I believe him, too. We smile happily at each other.

"Let's do it again," he says.

"Next year?"

I wonder if I'll be here, this time next year. If not here, where?

"Oh, before that, surely? I'll do the playlist. Not that yours wasn't great," he adds hurriedly. "It was pretty much perfect. But doing a playlist is fun. I always loved making compilation tapes."

"Yeah, me too. Even though it's showing off, isn't it, really."

He laughs. "Trying to impress people?"

"Don't you think?"

"You always impress me with your music choices."

"Ha, that's easy enough, isn't it, when you like loads of the same things."

"Oh yeah." He grins at me. "I suppose so."

Chapter Fourteen

May turns to June. Now it's often not raining at all, and sometimes the sun shines for several hours. Most weekends, Gethin and I drive about so he can show me the countryside, the places he went to as a kid, the local area. We go on small adventures, climbing the hill to Paxton's Tower, gazing out at the valley, spotting other places we've been to or might go in the future. We go to the beach at Llansteffan and splash about in the sea before eating quite a breezy impromptu picnic and then climbing the hill to the castle.

I read out the words and place names on the road signs and he laughs at my pronunciation. I think I'm improving. I've even learned what some of them mean.

Last weekend we went to the antiques center at Llandeilo, and he bought a vintage picnic set—tartan flasks, floral china—in a pale blue suitcase. Wildly overpriced, in my opinion, but it was essentially brand-new, with its original tags and keys and the corrugated cardboard between the plates and saucers. A wedding present, probably, given and received in 1965, maybe, and never used. Kept for a special occasion, a special occasion that never happened. It makes me kind of sad, but Gethin says it's been waiting for this opportunity to live a wild and adventurous life with us. Or him, anyway.

He's surprisingly . . . what? I don't know, poetic? sometimes. Maybe that's the wrong word. Fanciful? Romantic? That's not right, either. He has a nice turn of phrase, I think, for someone who works in IT—not that I'm suggesting this is unusual. I don't know anyone else who works in IT. And he's got a slight twist of silliness—fun, even—that I find very appealing. We often make each other laugh, sometimes quite uncontrollably. It's . . . nice. I feel like the last eight months have been a huge exhalation of breath, as I gradually relax into my new life.

Sometimes I wonder what things would be like if he'd bought a different house and I'd never met him. Although logically I know that I'd have been fine—eventually—it's frightening to imagine a different kind of new life, where I exist in a room somewhere rather less pleasant, and where I've had to try a lot harder to make new friends. I admit he makes me lazy. I don't need to make too much effort, because he's there most of the time, always happy to talk, and to introduce me to people. That's a lot easier than making friends by yourself. And because he hasn't seen lots of these people for ages, it's not like it would be if he'd been here for the last fifteen years; he's reaffirming friendships, too, and meeting new people himself, so I don't feel as if I'm totally dependent on a whole scene that he already had.

Plus none of these people knew Vanessa, or barely, even though they all know *of* her. I should think it would be quite hard to be the new partner of someone whose ex was well known.

Although that's not relevant, of course.

❧ ❧

Today we're going to have a picnic at Dryslwyn Castle. Gethin's never been there as an adult, and couldn't remember much about it. There are castles everywhere, round here—nearly every hill is topped by a ruin.

While I make sandwiches, he's looking up the weather forecast.

"Says it might rain," he says.

I peer out of the kitchen window. "No, really? It doesn't look like it."

"Ten percent chance of a thunderstorm."

"That's not too bad."

"No. Says it's going to be hot, anyway."

It's already quite hot. I had to water the garden, earlier, soaking the Acers in their pots.

We load up the car with blankets and cushions and the picnic set, plus a basket with additional food.

"Sometimes I wish I still had a convertible," he says, as we drive along the country roads of late spring.

"I've never been in a convertible," I confess.

"What, never?"

I laugh. "Is that so bizarre? I don't know anyone who's got one. I'm not sure it's practical in Britain."

"Admittedly, there were years when we only took the top down twice, like. It's nice though, in the summer."

"What kind of car was it?"

"Oh, it was a Boxster. A Porsche."

"Oh. Blimey." I always . . . not exactly *forget* that he's wealthy, or reasonably so, or that he used to live a quite different sort of life, but whenever something happens to remind me, it's kind of odd.

"Vanessa's car," he adds.

"Oh." I know you don't have to be rich to own a Porsche—the guy who lived in the flat above us had one—but I'm confident Vanessa's Boxster wasn't fifteen years old, or secondhand.

"Yeah, she likes a little sports car. What sort of car did you used to drive?"

"A really ancient Polo. And before that, an equally ancient Astra. I've never had a brand-new car."

"Cars are just for getting you where you're going, aren't they. I mean, I'm not that interested."

"Just rich." I laugh, although I know it annoys him, to be accused of this. I suppose because Vanessa earned more money, he feels like he isn't. (He is, though.)

"I'm not rich."

"Yeah, okay, well-off then."

❧ ❧

The castle is quite ruined. Heaps of rubble and broken walls like teeth are mostly unrecognizable as rooms or anything. There are earthworks—a protective ditch, grassy and scattered with pale mauve scabious and yellow hawkbits. It's very hot, and we struggle up the steep hill to look around, blanket and baskets and picnic set abandoned at the bottom, jumbled in a heap on a grassy sward.

It's a Welsh castle, built defensively by the Welsh, unlike all the ones aggressively built by the English. There was a siege here in 1287, an almost unimaginably long time ago. I try to visualize trebuchets ranged around it, but it's difficult. It's been ruined since the fifteenth century, and it's very hard to picture it full of soldiers and shouting and injury and death. I read an interpretation board that shows a reconstructed image of the building in its heyday and am startled for the fiftieth time by the fact that castles used to be rendered, or limewashed, white, not gray, against the hillside or the horizon. Rooks—or crows, I'm not sure—fly over us, black punctuation against the blue sky. The setting is great, on a high protuberance above the lazy loops of the river, fabulous views of farmland in every direction.

"This is good," I say, "I like it. Even if it is stupidly hot." I can feel the sweat trickling down my back, my dress sticking to me. I wish I had a hat, or a parasol. "Shame there's no shade."

"Hm," he says, looking across the valley. "Hopefully we'll have finished before that lot gets here." He gestures toward the black clouds glowering to the south.

"It does look quite . . . threatening."

"Come and have some lemonade, then," he says, and we hurtle unsteadily down the stony track to where we've left our stuff. We spread out the picnic blanket and collapse, sweating. Here, lower down, it's even hotter, no hint of a breeze. Gethin unpacks the cooler, handing me a plastic cup of cloudy lemonade and a Scotch egg.

"Sandwich?" he offers.

"Oh, yes please." I take two cherry tomatoes from a Tupperware container. The sky shimmers above us.

Gethin regards his Scotch egg. "Have you ever made one of these? How do they work?"

"You sort of mash the sausage meat round the egg. Made some at school. They're not difficult, but they're messy. Want to try? We used to make veggie ones when I was at college, when you couldn't buy such a thing."

"Veggie sausage meat? How does that work?"

"Sosmix. It comes dry in a packet and you mix it with water. If they still make it."

He looks faintly disgusted. "Sounds grim."

I laugh. "No, it's fine. Anyway, you squish it round your hard-boiled egg, and then you dip it in beaten egg and roll it in breadcrumbs, and then either you deep-fry them or you can do it in the oven. We could make some if you want to."

"What about pork pies?" he says, rummaging in the basket.

"What about them? Hot-crust pastry. I've never made a pork pie, but I've made hot-crust pastry."

"Why's it called that? Isn't all pastry . . . hot? I mean—"

"You make it with hot water. And lard. That's what makes pork pie pastry so short and crisp."

"It's the best pastry. Do you want some of this one?" He's cutting a pie in half.

"Go on, then, I'll just have a quarter."

"One of the most satisfying feelings in the world, cutting a pork pie, isn't it."

I smile at him. "It is."

"Sometimes Mum put a pork pie in my lunch box. It was always a surprise and a proper treat."

"Nice."

"God, I'm boring," he says. "Sorry."

"Oh no. No, you're really not. This is the sort of thing I like to talk about. Perhaps I'm boring too. But I don't care if I am, really. I never *get* bored and that's the important thing."

He laughs. "Don't you?"

"No, hardly ever. There's always stuff to look at, isn't there, and think about." I nibble the crust of my pie.

"Like pork pies."

"Well, but, yes? I mean, look at the pork pie. Someone invented that. Someone invented hot-crust pastry. Think of the regional differences. Think of that weird aberration, the gala pie, with the eggs in it."

"Oh yeah, I'd forgotten those. The eggs were always gray. In the ones I've eaten, anyway. I used to pick the egg out."

"I wonder if we could make one of those and have it not be gray," I muse. "I suppose the egg gets overcooked because they go in hard-boiled. I'll have to look that up."

He grins at me. "Pie planning?"

"You see, I'm much duller than you are."

"You're absolutely not," he says. "You're easily one of the most interesting people I've ever met."

There's a pause here, and I feel a warmth in my face that's not due to the blazing sun. Luckily, a distraction occurs in the form of a low, distant rumble.

"Oh, hey, did you hear that?" he asks.

"I thought I did. Thunder? Or maybe it was a plane?"

We both sit up straighter, straining our ears. Now that we're down here there's no view of the valley, so we can't see if the sky is darker.

"Maybe."

I open a tub and spoon pasta salad onto my plate. "Do you want some of this?"

He holds his plate out.

"A woman I used to work with gave me the recipe," I tell him. "We'd sometimes have picnics when I worked at the library."

"You must miss everyone."

"Oh, well. Yes, sort of." I look across at him. "I haven't

worked with her for years, but I know what you mean. My friends. Yes."

"It must have been—"

"You did the same thing though, didn't you, really. I mean, I know you have friends here but you"—I wave my fork—"unrooted yourself from your life."

He screws up his face. "It's not really the same. I could easily have stayed if I'd wanted. I didn't have to get away."

I shrug, concentrating on my food.

"Do you think you'll ever go back?" he asks.

"Not to live, I shouldn't think. Might visit eventually, I suppose. But not for a while."

"Do . . . is . . . do you think," he says, awkwardly, "would you be . . . are you afraid?"

"To go back? I would be, yes." I know he's really curious, about all this, my life, and I don't blame him for that. I would be, too. This doesn't mean I want to talk about any of it, though.

"That's . . . bad. I know that's a meaningless understatement."

I shrug again. "It's okay. I appreciate the sentiment."

"I just can't—this will sound stupid, but . . . I don't know. It's so hard to understand why people hurt each other. I mean emotionally, as well as . . ."

"Usually I don't think people exactly *mean* to. I don't even think he . . . I think if you asked him, he'd say it was my fault, of course. But when we first met, even though he'd done it before, I don't think he . . ." I pause, looking for the right words. "I don't think he anticipated it would all go to shit in quite the same way."

His face very serious, he says, "I'm sorry bad things happened to you."

"Thanks." I smile at him cautiously. "Good things happen too. I'll be fine. I'm already much better."

"You look loads better than when we met." Again, he looks awkward. "Not that I'm saying . . . what I'm saying is, you don't look so anxious. Or so thin. Not that there's anything wrong with being thin. I don't mean to make personal comments," he adds. "I'm not . . . I wouldn't have said anything, if you . . . but you look . . ."

"Healthier? Yeah. I don't mind, you're all right. No, I'm quite pleased not to be so . . ." I press my fingers to my collarbone. "I'm not a naturally skinny person. And I'm definitely not so anxious. I'm hoping to improve further."

"Have you ever thought . . ." he begins, but then there's a much louder rumble, unmistakably thunderous, from much closer.

"Ooh." I look up. Still blue sky above us. "Will it rain, d'you reckon?"

"Pretty sure it will, yeah."

"We should get ready to run, then." I stuff the last bit of my chicken sandwich into my mouth and begin to fasten tubs and wipe plates with a bit of paper towel.

"I don't know about running," he says, but then there's an oddly unnatural flicker of light that suggests somewhere not far away there's lightning. Thunder crashes even closer, and the sky is suddenly black and threatening.

I drain my cup and cram the crockery back into the picnic set. An enormous raindrop, surely the size of a pigeon's egg, splats onto the lid, followed by another that lands on my shoulder. I gasp in surprise and then laugh. I love storms, and I like summer rainstorms especially, if it rains in a hysterically over-the-top fashion.

"Right," he says, "come on, then." We stand up, and he grabs the rug, shaking it to dislodge crumbs and grass, and picks up the basket. "Are you okay with that?"

"Of course." I grasp the handle of the picnic set and we hurry down the narrow, uneven path toward the gate. The rain begins in earnest, the smell of petrichor filling the air. It's not cold, really—it's just that the afternoon was so hot. A cool blast of wind follows us down the path and across the road to the parking lot, lashing at the trees. There are several other groups of people jamming their belongings into the trunks of their cars and heading away, tires swooshing through the water already collecting on the road.

I sling the picnic set into the car and Gethin slams the trunk shut. There's another curiously yellow flash from the lightning, the light an odd sickly color, and the thunder crashes again.

"I'm going to look at the river," I tell him, and hurry off between the trees.

"In the rain?" I hear him call after me, and then suddenly it's pouring, like someone's turned on a tap. I laugh, exhilarated. The river, so calm and flat when we crossed the bridge earlier, is a dancing mass of agitated water. If the world was a different sort of place, I'd be out of my clothes and in there, although I admit I'm not sure whether that would be a risky thing to do with all this electricity in the air. I'm pretty much drenched, anyway, without needing to actually get in the river. I turn my face to the sky.

"You're going to get very wet," says Gethin, appearing beside me.

"I don't care," I shout, over the sound of the rain hammering into the river and the wind rushing through the trees. I fling out my arms expansively, laughing at his expression.

Another jagged flash of lightning rips across the sky above the castle.

"Wow, look at that. Amazing." Thunder cracks again, booming along the valley, and there's another flash, lighting up the gray ruins. It looks spectacular, the sky livid as a bruise.

"Right overhead now," he says. "Aren't you cold?"

"You can go back to the car if you like." I grin at him and run back across the grass to the entrance of the car park, crossing the road and pelting along the pavement to the bridge. Everything looks completely brilliant from here; there's an excellent view of the castle looming above the floodplain, the rushing black clouds, the inky water of the river jumping beneath the raindrops. I lean back on the railing and turn my face upward once more. The rain runs down my already wet cheeks like enormous tears, and I feel an immense sense of excitement and joy.

"Wait up," says Gethin, splashing through the puddles. "You're always running away from me," he complains when he catches up, leaning on the rail beside me, looking into the water.

"Pfft, no I'm not."

"You ran away the first time I saw you."

We look at each other for a moment longer than is quite comfortable. The rain runs down his face, and I can feel it doing the same on my own. I lick water from my lips, and am very determined to not, in any way, imagine doing the same to him.

"Didn't you?"

"Oh, that." I flap my hand, dismissive. "You're soaked," I add, changing the subject. He ruffles his hair with his hands and droplets of water spray out between us.

"Pretty much. So are you."

My dress sticks to my legs much more conclusively than it stuck to my back earlier, running with water. I pull it away from my body and attempt to wring out the front. It makes no difference, as it's still raining heavily.

He pulls out his phone. "Drenched," he says. He takes a photo, and another.

I stick out my tongue. "Oh, seriously, I must look a right state." I drag a hand through my hair.

"No, you look . . ."

"Show me."

"My phone's not really waterproof." He pushes it back into his pocket.

Thunder rumbles again, quieter this time.

"Oh, boo, it's nearly over," I say, and almost immediately the rain eases. I click my fingers. "Show me the pictures."

He sighs. "So demanding."

"Right?"

He pulls his phone back out, thumbs it open, and steps closer. I wipe my face and flap my hands, raindrops spinning away.

"There. See."

"Good background."

"Foreground's not bad, either."

I look at him. He's looking at the picture, where I stand sodden and grinning, the castle behind me. It's an okay photo.

"Want me to delete it?" he asks.

"No. You can send it to me."

"All right."

He thumbs the phone to show me the next one.

"Huh," he says. I've got my eyes closed and look kind of . . . ecstatic, like a mad saint.

"You might need to delete that one," I tell him. It's not that it's a bad picture—it just feels a bit . . . personal.

"I dunno, it's kind of . . . I like it," he says. He looks at me. "D'you hate it? I'll get rid of it if you do?"

I shrug. It seems an overreaction to demand that he delete it. "Take one of both of us. You're easily as wet as I am."

"Okay. Castle in the background?"

We lean against the railing and he puts his arm round me. We push our cold, damp faces together, and he takes a picture, then another. My skin prickles at the proximity; I feel the heat rising in my chest. I ignore all this, and we dip our heads together over the phone to consider the images.

"Ha, we look ridiculous." I laugh.

"This one's good."

"Now the sun's out? Yeah."

"You look like you're having a great time."

"Well. I am."

"Good," he says, serious. Again we're caught in a moment of . . . something, before I move away and turn to look back at the castle. Within five minutes there's a rainbow behind us and the black clouds have lifted, rolling away to the west. The road steams.

Gethin shakes himself like a dog. "I think there's a towel in the car," he says. "Come on."

I patter along the road behind him, energized. I've been grinning so hugely that my face hurts.

"That was brilliant."

"You're not normal," he says, and I laugh.

"You could've sat in the car. No one made you stay out."

"I know. I'm not complaining really." He opens the trunk. "I'm sure there's—yeah, here." He hands me a towel.

"Is it clean?"

"Of course."

"Huh. Efficient." I rub briefly at my hair. Being short, it doesn't need much to stop dripping.

※ ※

Back home, I have a shower and get dressed while he changes into dry things. It's rained here, too—there are huge puddles everywhere and the garden sparkles. It's warm again, although the air feels fresher.

"Even though it's like twenty-eight degrees," he says, "I feel I might need something cozy. D'you want some hot chocolate?"

"Ha. It's more like ice cream weather."

"Could have hot chocolate and a cold drink? There's lemonade left from the picnic."

"Oh." I think about this. "That is quite tempting. Okay."

"Yeah? Is it dry enough to sit in the garden?"

"I think so."

"I'll bring it out, then. And we can finish the picnic food."

"Good idea." I take the remains of the picnic out to the table on the patio and unpack what's left. The cat from next door, a handsome gray creature, watches with interest from the roof of the coal shed.

Gethin comes out with the hot chocolate and sits down beside me.

"I was just thinking about how we used to have hot chocolate on Thursdays when I was young," he says. "We'd have a bath and come downstairs to watch *Top of the Pops* and *Tomorrow's World* and have hot chocolate. Probably only had that in the winter, I suppose, but it seems like it was every week."

"We had baths on Thursdays, too," I say, rather entranced by this coincidence. "Thursdays and Sundays."

"You know, sometimes I think about my childhood," he says, "and it seems like it's impossible it can be forty years ago."

"I know."

"And some of the memories seem . . . nearer . . . than more recent things? Some of the time I spent with Vanessa seems longer ago. Some of that seems like a hundred years ago. Everything's so different."

I eat my sandwich, watching him. He stares down the garden. I can't tell whether he thinks this is a good thing or a bad thing and I'm not really comfortable about asking.

"This time last year I could never have even begun to imagine the way everything is now," he says.

"No."

He turns to look at me. "I know that's true for you as well; I'm not trying to hog the whole 'wow, isn't life weird' thing."

"Ha, no, I know. You're just as entitled to reflect on the changes in your life," I say pompously. "It's probably weirder for you, isn't it, because of . . . how did you feel, this time last year?"

"I was pretty miserable. Living in Abby's spare room at the weekend, staying with my friend Justin during the week—it wasn't great. I suppose maybe I'd been to see the house for the first time? It felt like it took ages though, finding somewhere. And six months before that—everything was even more different, and worse. Couldn't quite quantify it, though. I kept telling myself it was weird to be so . . . unengaged in everything. You know, 'your life is good and you're lucky' and all that made it worse, because I didn't feel that way. I knew there had to be more, or something else, or . . . you know. I was worried that was it, though."

"Mm."

"Which is a horrible feeling. Sometimes I remember that, you know, there might only be another twenty years. Or less. And then . . . well, it's terrifying, isn't it, to think you might be miserable for loads of it. When did you decide you were leaving? Was that . . . I know you bought your tent and everything. Were you planning it for a long time?"

I consider whether I want to talk about this. I take a fork and stab at pasta twists.

"I wasn't sure what to do. For ages . . . it's not that I thought it was my fault, or not exactly. I'm not an idiot; I knew what he was doing. I was scared though."

"I really hate to think of you being frightened."

I raise my eyes to his face. I believe him; he looks . . . what— pained? I shrug. "It's okay. I'm not frightened now. Or hardly ever."

He frowns at me. "When are you frightened?"

I consider. "I have nightmares, sometimes. So I wake up frightened, you know. I'm not scared when I'm awake."

"Okay. Good. You needn't . . . you know I . . . if there's anything you're frightened of—would you tell me?"

"I shouldn't think so."

"Why not?"

"Not your business, is it?"

We look at each other for a moment. I feel I may have sounded a bit harsh or dismissive. "But truly, I'm not afraid. There's nothing to be scared of."

"Good. Well. I'd like to make it clear you could talk to me about it if you wanted. I realize you don't want to. But if you did."

I duck my head in acknowledgment. "Thank you."

He sighs. "Was he nice to start with? I suppose he must have been."

I wrinkle my nose. "Yeah. Not for very long, maybe. Long enough. I was always hopeful—stupidly—that, you know, he'd . . . that it would all be okay. Anyway," I continue, "I'd rather not think about that."

"No, okay." He thinks for a bit. "You know you can invite them to visit, if you want to? Your family. Or your friends."

"I was going to ask, actually, if you could recommend anywhere for people to stay. Noosha wants to visit."

He looks at me. "She can stay here, can't she? This is your home, Jess. Your friends can stay here if you want them to."

"Oh." I'm embarrassed. "You don't want my friends here, though, do you?"

"Why the hell not?"

"Because, um . . . actually I can't think of a reason. It just never occurred to me."

"It's not like there's anyone in the front bedroom. Wasted space. You wouldn't rather be in there? You could swap if you wanted."

"Oh, no. No, that would . . . no. I like the box room." I can't really explain the sense of cozy security I get from my little bedroom. I fear it might sound rather pathetic.

"Okay. But you can certainly have your friends to stay."

"Thanks."

He shakes his head. "You don't need to thank me."

"Yeah, I do, though."

"You pay to live here. You have rights."

"Oh, well." I'm embarrassed. "Okay."

Chapter Fifteen

Gethin orders a print of the photo of us standing together on the bridge. He finds a frame for it and stands it on the mantelpiece in the dining room. I come home from work one day and there it is, among the other things: the carved wooden elephant he bought in Thailand, the fallow deer antler we found on a walk, the George VI coronation mug I bought for fifty pence from a charity shop.

I look at the photo for ages, the pair of us grinning at the camera, hair and faces wet with rain. It's a good picture, a nice moment to have captured, and unexpected to see, because nowadays no one buys prints. I look at it and remember how I felt, our faces pressed together, his arm around me. I purse my lips at the Jess in the photograph. She doesn't look like an idiot, but I know better.

"You got a copy of that photo," I say later as we eat our dinner.

"Yeah, I thought it was a good one," he says. "You don't mind, do you?"

"No, of course not."

"I remembered in one of the shared houses I lived in we had a whole wall of pictures of us—the housemates, I mean."

"A whole wall might be a bit much," I suggest.

He laughs. "What about if we had one blown up, you know, poster size."

"I really don't think I need to see a poster-sized photo of myself," I say, slightly horrified.

"Ha. With faces bigger than our actual faces?"

"Let's not do that."

"No, you're right, I don't think I need to see my crow's-feet at one and a half times real size."

"Pah, you barely have any wrinkles, do you. And if you did, that would just be craggy."

"I know craggy's kind of a compliment," he says, "but I don't think I'd care to be described like that."

"I don't think you have that sort of face." I look at him, considering. "Or not yet, anyway."

"Happy to put it off, to be honest."

"At least no one minds when men look older. I mean, I expect Vanessa has to look younger than her colleagues."

"Yeah, she's got a whole plan," he says, reaching for another potato. "You know, a tuck here and a tweak there. Eyelids, chin."

"What a ridiculous world."

"I know. I don't really think . . . well, it's a personal thing of course, and there's all sorts of pressure, isn't there, with expectations and notions of beauty and everything. But getting yourself jabbed with poisons or sliced up for nonmedical reasons. I don't like it. We had a big row about Botox once."

"Really?" I don't know why I'm so fascinated by insights into Gethin and Vanessa's life together.

"Yeah. It was awkward. I mean, she was right that it was none of my business. But I didn't like the idea, and it took me a while to get used to how she looked afterward."

"Was it very noticeable?"

"No, I don't think so, not really—not to anyone else. She did look . . . younger, I suppose. Smoother. I don't know. The lines on your face are . . . I don't know. It's evidence of your life, isn't it, laughing and frowning, good things and bad things."

I nod. "When I was crying a lot my eyes used to swell up," I tell him, "which never happened when I was younger. I used to wonder if you'd be able to see it on my face, how unhappy I was. It's got to be aging, hasn't it, being miserable." I eat my last piece of tuna and mop up tomato salsa with my last potato. We had a debate about whether roast potatoes were a suitable accompaniment for this meal but luckily both agreed that roast potatoes go with more or less anything.

"You cried so much your eyes swelled up? Christ," he says, visibly appalled.

"Yeah, but . . . I mean, I did cry a lot, but I think it was worse because I'm old. I've probably cried as much at other times. I cried quite a lot when my dad died."

"Shit, of course. I'm sorry," he says, "I feel like . . ."

"What?"

"I don't think I can ever say the right thing."

"God, I hope it's not me making you feel like that. I wasn't trying to do an 'Oh, my *dad* died when I was a *kid*, Gethin, you heartless monster.'" I pull a face at him and he laughs.

"No, I didn't . . . I wasn't saying you were. I don't know. What I mean is, I realize your dad dying was a terrible thing to happen, and I acknowledge that other bad stuff has happened too, like it does to everyone, but really what I always want to say is, that bastard, how dare he."

"Now you're calling my dad a bastard?" I laugh at him. "I know you're not, I'm sorry. Mitch. Yes, he was a bastard, you're right."

"Mitch. You've never told me his name before."

I sigh. "No, well. There we are. Mitchell . . ." I hesitate, suddenly worried, again, about giving the whole game away, although really, what would it matter if Gethin knew both Mitch's names? He's not going to find him and tell him where I am, is he? Of course not. "Mitchell Brooks," I say. "It sounds like an estate agent's or something, doesn't it."

He laughs. "It does. Or a trucking company."

"Mitchell Brooks Logistics."

"Yeah."

"He wasn't a trucking company though, sadly. He was, as you say, a bastard."

❧ ❦

Gethin's throwing a party. A housewarming. It seems a bit late—he's been here eight months, after all—but he was waiting for all the work to be done, and for the weather to improve. Now it's really summer, he says we should entertain.

He mowed the lawn and I researched and then bought solar-powered garden lights. We put them up yesterday, and they look so lovely, I felt quite emotional. He asked me if I was okay and I said, "It's so pretty," and was horribly embarrassed to hear the wobble in my voice. Since it was dark, though, he couldn't see that I was nearly crying. I worry sometimes about being overwhelmed by emotion. Several times he's said or done something that's made me have to bite my tongue or pinch myself. I don't think he's noticed, though. And the things are never anything spectacular—him getting me a better job didn't make me cry. But my birthday; and when he bought me two big bars of Dairy

Milk because I was having really terrible cramps. I suppose that was hormonal.

It's the way he pays attention, I think, that makes me like this. I'd forgotten what it was like, when someone pays attention to what you say, learns things about you, and doesn't use those things against you but instead uses them to make your life . . . more pleasant. He buys things I like if he goes shopping, remembers which brand of toothpaste I prefer, that sort of thing. None of it's . . . it's not like you could misinterpret any of it, think it had large or significant MEANING—it's just kindness. I've spent a lot of time with hardly any kindness, and so the people who have been kind to me—Johnny, at least some of the time, and Gethin himself—that makes them stand out, doesn't it.

I realize I shouldn't list him with Johnny; he fits better with Lizzie and Noosh. Due to us being friends. I should be more careful about that sort of thing.

⁂

We've spent the day making party food and arranging everything to look nice. One of Gethin's friends has made him a firepit, a sort of large rusty dish—looks quite cool—and he's bought and borrowed extra garden chairs. I think it might be a bit cold to sit outside, but I expect they're all hardier than me—after all, if they're not, they'd never go outside at all.

On the invitations he said people should dress up in their best clothes, so I bought a dress from eBay to wear. When I put it on, though, I'm not really sure. I had my hair cut very short, yesterday after work—it's so nice to be back in a position where

I can run a crop effectively. I bought a bright scarlet lipstick, too. I can't remember the last time I wore makeup, and my face, with its slash of red and extra-extendable mascara (fifteen pounds! I actually laughed in Boots at the thought of it—and that's nothing like the most you can spend on mascara in Boots, either), looks rather odd to me. My skin isn't as good as Gethin's, but it's not too bad—although I have to say that if you are an irregular wearer of makeup, one of the most disturbing things about aging is a sudden close-up view of what's happened to your eyelids and jawline. Anyway, no one's going to be looking at me, are they. The dress is black velvet, knee length, and just off the shoulder with a swoop of fabric across the bust that looked, in the not-very-good photographs, as though it might be flattering.

It's "vintage" (oh really—like me), from the late eighties or early nineties, the kind of thing my friends are wearing in photographs of eighteenth and twenty-first birthday parties, or the sort of university balls I very much didn't go to. I worry it might be too dressy, in fact, and spend a long time in my bedroom wondering whether I should take it off and wear skinny jeans and a T-shirt. I do have a black T-shirt with sequins on it . . . that might count as dressy enough?

The conversation I had with Gethin about the scars on my arm, back in December, makes me self-conscious about that, as well. I don't bother to hide them from him—and I don't suppose anyone will comment tonight, because there's a space between meeting people and knowing them when they're not meant to make personal comments. It doesn't always stop someone, but at least you know they're being rude, and you can be rude back. I suppose a pair of elbow-length gloves would solve that (and in a nicely late-eighties way, too), but I didn't think of it in time. I've painted my toenails and fingernails in a sunny, happy orange. It clashes with my lipstick in a way I find extremely pleasing. For someone who rarely looks very femme, I'm quite done up. The late afternoon sun streams through my bedroom window and shines on the dusty mirror that leans against the wall. I suppose I look okay. When you dress up it ought to be for yourself, and as I don't really know anyone here, and am firmly in my fifth decade, it's not as though I've done it for anyone else.

Outside, I hear cars arriving and the slamming of doors. I look cautiously out of the window and see the first guests, two couples in fancy shirts and bright wedding-reception dresses. I'm glad people have paid attention to Gethin's request—at least I won't look completely out of place. The front door opens, and the hallway is transformed into a complex mass of greetings. I should go downstairs.

The doorbell rings again. More greetings, louder, and footsteps, and now there must be enough people down there, surely, that I can slip into the dining room and no one will particularly notice me. I take a last look at myself in the mirror. I was what's best described as scrawny for some time, but I've put some weight on and I think I look better. Although this frock would probably suit Lizzie, who's very curvy, better than me. However, Lizzie's not here, and even if she was, I'm not sure it would fit her. I don't know why I'm even thinking any of this.

I go downstairs. Gethin's in the hall, calling to someone in the kitchen to help themselves to booze. He's wearing a beautifully patterned shirt: tiny flowers, like a Liberty print. It might even *be* a Liberty print; it's not like he can't afford expensive shirts.

He looks up at me and says, "Oh my God, Jess! You look great!"

I'm embarrassed, naturally. "Is it okay? I'm worried it's too . . ."

He holds out his hand, and I take it, although I'm not sure why; I don't need help down the last two stairs.

"It's great. Wow. I mean," he says, "you always look nice."

"Ha ha."

"No, you do. But I've never seen you dressed up."

"I know. I'm not a natural dresser-upper."

"I wouldn't say that," he says, and unexpectedly raises my hand to his lips. He holds my gaze as he kisses my hand, and I have to say it's the most intensely erotic thing that's happened to me in years. This is awkward. I'm flustered; I can feel my ears burning.

"Oh now," I say, "you charmer." I pull my hand away and clear my throat. "How many people are here?"

"Davey and Nic, Rick and Lisa, Julie, Angela and Angela's brother, whose name"—he lowers his voice—"I've forgotten already."

"Oh, Davey? Davey the electrician? I'll know one person then. That's good."

"There will be lots of people you've met," he reminds me, "even if you don't feel like you 'know' them."

The doorbell rings again.

"You'd better get that," I say. "I'll just make sure everyone's okay."

I sidle into the dining room. The table is spread with a huge snow-white cloth that I had found very difficult to iron, and piled with a variety of party food.

"Ah," says Davey, spotting me. He introduces me to his wife, a narrow woman with exuberant ginger curls, wearing a green silk shift dress that makes her freckles look incredible. Totally nothing like I'd imagined her.

"Hello, Jess," she says, "good to meet you. And wow, doesn't the house look great? Davey was telling me how different it was last time he was here! The kitchen's amazing!"

"It's good, isn't it? Hello. Yes," I say, "I think . . . Gethin's done a good job."

"I heard it was you that did all the work," says a tall blond-haired woman who's shoveling potato salad onto a plate. "I'm Angela, by the way."

"Hello. I wouldn't say that. I just gave him my opinion; he pretty much knew what he wanted." I smile at her. "I'm afraid I still don't know many people. How do you know Gethin?"

"Ah, now, we're a friendly bunch," she says, "you'll be fine. I know him from school, and my ex-husband used to work with him, about a hundred years ago. Don't look for him though," she adds, "I was promised he won't be here." This makes me laugh. She grins at me and goes on: "The floor in here is great, isn't it?"

"Yes, I love parquet; it's come up really well." I've definitely told more people how much I like parquet than I ever would have thought possible before I moved here.

"This is Lisa," she adds. "Lisa, turn round. This is Jess."

"Oh yes, hello." A shorter woman in a brilliantly fuchsia jacket smiles at me. "Gethin's new girlfriend."

"Oh no," I say, panicked, "no, no—I just live here. He's my landlord."

"Oh, shame. Be good for him to go out with someone nice for a change."

"Lisa," says Angela. She pulls a face at me. "Vanessa divided opinion."

Another gaggle of people arrive, and the air is full of the sound of greetings once again.

Much as I'd *love* to hear exactly what all Gethin's old mates thought about the dreaded Winslade, I can't think that showing too much interest is sensible. Or polite. I make sure the new arrivals know where the plates and glasses are, tell people they're welcome to go outside, and generally behave like a gracious hostess, or, failing that, a restaurant manager. Within half an hour, the house is full of people. There are lots of crisply ironed short-sleeved shirts, bright frocks, strappy, sparkly tops, middle-aged bosoms, and tattoos. It's very loud. Gethin's turned the music up. We made a playlist yesterday, rather more mainstream than the one I did for his birthday, long enough to last until half one tomorrow morning, so no one would have to think about it, or holler at Alexa midway through, and carefully calibrated to peak around nine in case anyone wants to dance.

"Do you think anyone will?" I asked him when it was finished.

"Have you ever met a Welsh woman in her forties?" he said, very serious.

This made me laugh. "A couple. It's true Maura and her mates were dancing when I went to hers last weekend."

"There you are, then."

※ ※

Everyone's very friendly, but as the evening progresses I'm beginning to find it tiring. It would be tiring even if I knew all these people. I try to remember the last time I gave a party, with people I know. Not for years. Mitch didn't really do socializing, or at least, not anything more complex than watching international soccer with his mates. If you can count that as socializing. I'd get horribly anxious, because you certainly can't rely on England to win things, and it didn't help his temper if they lost. I shiver.

Who on earth kisses someone's hand? I can't stop thinking about it. It wasn't the kiss, even; it was the way he looked at me. This is . . . well, it's confusing, isn't it. Although a voice in my head tells me cynically it's hardly confusing. It would be naive to claim there's no tension between us, no attraction. I know there is, but I think it's better to ignore it. I don't think it would be helpful to indulge it. Because what would be the point? I don't want to jeopardize my comfortable place here in this nice house. And nothing ruins things quicker than sleeping with someone. I mean, if you can't—or won't—get involved or attached. I really don't want to get attached, do I. It's one thing to fancy someone—there's nothing wrong with that, it's fine—just don't do anything about it. Don't give anyone any power over you. It's true he already has some, because I live here. But I can always move out. I'd rather that was my choice, though, rather than something he makes me do, or that I feel obliged to do—anyway. It makes me feel odd because of all these people looking at me and wondering.

I've more or less managed to avoid Abby. I did say hello to her, as it would have been rude not to. And she did tell me—quite convincingly—that she thought the sausage rolls were excellent. Si said, "All the food's bloody amazing, like. You should cater my birthday, shouldn't she, Abbs?" and she laughed. I think it was a joke; I hope they don't ask me (us?) to do any such thing.

Now I'm talking to Marian. We've discussed the garden for a bit, standing on the terrace, and now we're back indoors, perching on chairs in the dining room, talking about curtains and the plans for replacing the fireplace. Gethin decided we should get a wood-burning stove of some kind, but we're doing endless research into what's the most eco-friendly option.

"He's so lucky to have you. You know I was worried about him, when he first bought the house."

"I'm pretty sure he can look after himself!" I reply brightly. I would say he doesn't "have me," but that feels like a weird thing to say to someone's mum, however innocently she might mean it.

"Yes, but there's getting by, isn't there, and enjoying your-self. I didn't think he'd enjoy sorting the house out; he's never had to do anything like this before."

"It's not that hard if you can afford to buy what you want, is it. It isn't as though he had to save up and then buy the least expensive kitchen."

"Oh, I know he's very fortunate. He could have paid some-one to sort all of this out for him, but I'm sure it's better for him to be distracted. He seems very happy."

"Was he unhappy before?" I know he was, but I'm interested to know how much of that was apparent to his mother.

"I think it's been hard for him, yes. It's sad, isn't it, when people break up, and they'd been together for a long time. But I don't think he'd been very happy for a good while." She laughs. "Not that he ever talked to me about it. It was quite a shock, when he told me they'd split up."

"You weren't expecting it, then?"

"No, they always seemed . . . I won't say they were one of those couples who were always together, or, you know, pawing

at each other. She's always been very busy. And last Christmas—
not this one just gone, the one before—they did have quite a
row, while we were there. That was a strange year though, because it wasn't long since Alun died, and her mother had been
ill, and I put it all down to that, to the stress, see. I suppose
there was more to it though. Is that why you moved here?" she
goes on, a question I can't quite follow the sense of.

"Sorry?"

"I mean, you had a husband, or a boyfriend, or something,
didn't you? He says you split up with someone. Is that why you
came here?" She pauses for a moment. "I know I'm not supposed to ask you."

"Er, that's . . . I don't mind, since it's you." I smile at her.
"But yes, I suppose I did. Yes." I wonder, again, exactly what
he's said to her about that. About me.

She looks at me seriously for a long moment. "I'm glad you
chose to come here. You've made a good team, haven't you,
with the work on the house."

"I suppose so, yes. I've been very lucky, to meet him, and to
be able to live somewhere so . . . nice." These are things that I
always say, and they're true, always, but I'm beginning to think
they might not sound it. The trouble is, when you believe something wholeheartedly and sincerely, you can sound both insin-
cere and like a bit of a prick when you say it. I don't think this
is exactly the moment—and probably not the person—to attempt to fully engage with my often-overwhelming gratitude.
Even thinking this makes my eyes fill with tears. *For God's sake,
Jessica. Get a grip.* I smile at her, slightly wobbly.

"Now, where is he?" she says, looking round. "I should think
about making a move."

"Oh no, really? It's still early."

She laughs. "For you young people, perhaps. I like to be sitting down in my own front room by nine o'clock." She glances round the room again, and leans to pat my arm. "Anyway, I'll say goodbye," she says, and moves away through the crowds of people.

I'm quite warm now, and rather jealous of the idea of anyone being by themselves in their own front room. That's not going to happen here for a bit. I fetch replacement food from the kitchen and top up the plates and dishes on the table, pour myself another glass of wine, and, after hesitating for a moment, step back out onto the terrace. There are quite a lot of people out here, sitting round the firepit, or standing smoking on the patio. There's a bit of a breeze, too, enough to make me wish I'd brought a wrap or something. Not that I really own anything suitable. I used to have a beautiful crimson pashmina that would have gone perfectly with this outfit, but, like a number of nice but unimportant things, I left it behind.

I remember there are extra, less aesthetically pleasing outdoor chairs stacked in the garage, so I slide the door open, just enough to slip inside, and stand for a moment in the semidarkness. It's relaxing to be hidden. No one's going to come in here and talk to me. The chairs glow faintly, white plastic in the gloom. It's warmer in here, too, and there's a faint smell of oil, the ghosts of old tools. Gethin doesn't keep tools out here; they're all in a toolbox in the cupboard under the stairs. I suppose you'd keep things out here if you did stuff to your car, but he doesn't.

The smell reminds me of my dad, a man who did do things to his cars. I've been thinking about Dad a lot recently. Wondering how different things might have been if he hadn't died. Sometimes I think my life would be unimaginably different. If

Mum hadn't started drinking, and Luke hadn't left home so early—all kinds of things would be different. I might still be here, though, because I didn't end up with Mitch because my dad died. Or I don't think I did; it's hard to say. You could say that everything that's happened since I was fifteen, all the choices I've made, have been because of his death. He wouldn't be very impressed though. "You make your own luck" was one of his often-repeated beliefs. I do sort of agree.

I take a chair from the top of the stack and put it down on the cracked and pitted concrete floor. I could just sit down for a moment.

I can hear a dozen conversations interlacing outside, loud laughter, long-term private jokes that make no sense to me. There's a man with a very loud voice telling an apparently hilarious story about a trailer full of sheep, egged on by people who've clearly heard it many times before. Everyone's even more Welsh than they were at the beginning of the evening. I hope Gethin's pleased with how it's going. It was a risk to come back here and hope he'd be able to pick up the threads of his long-ago, less glamorous life. If he ever actually planned to do that, which I'm not sure he did.

They've been nice to me, too, full of compliments about the house, and again, I guess I don't blame them for wondering whether we're together. I'd wonder the same. Or would I? If I knew someone whose previous girlfriend was rich and beautiful, I don't think I'd expect him to have settled for someone like me. You kind of assume people are sleeping together, though, don't you, if they share a house like we do. I rub my arms. It's really quite chilly. I'm about to stand up and take my chair out to the patio when I hear a voice I recognize, out on the driveway.

"Yeah, so I'm quite happy with it. There's another year to go on the lease; I suppose I'll get the new model when that runs out."

Gethin, talking to someone about his car. That can't have been his idea; he really doesn't care about cars.

"I always think they're a bit boring, like," says someone else, a man.

"I don't care. I'm not that interested in cars." Ha, there you go: confirmation.

"You could afford something a lot more fun. You could get a Mazda. Or an Audi TT."

"Yeah, I had one of those," he says. "There's no room in the back though, or hardly."

"No one to put in the back," says the other person.

"No, well, true enough. Anyway. This is fine."

There's a pause. I imagine they're drinking.

"So this woman," says the other person.

"What woman?"

"The one in the dress."

"There are lots of women in dresses here this evening, Mike. It's kind of a theme."

"There are; that little black number's a bit special though, isn't it. Your housemate."

There's a pause. I wonder what he's thinking and hope he doesn't say anything awful. I don't know what I'd do, if he did. A surprisingly large black hole opens up at the front of my head and I have to fight quite hard to close it again.

"Jess. What about her?"

"Yeah, Jess. What's the story there, then?"

"There's no story," says Gethin. I think of earlier, his lips on my hand. Not *completely* no story, I think to myself.

"Isn't there? She's single, is she?"

"I guess . . . yes."

"And you two aren't . . ."

"No. I don't know why everyone's so obsessed with this," Gethin complains. "You'd think in the twenty-first century you could rent your spare room to a woman without everyone thinking you're sleeping together."

"No chance. Anyway, so that means you wouldn't object."

"Object? To what?"

"If I . . . put the moves on her, you know."

In the darkness of the garage, I'm shocked. Really. Do men ever stop being like this?

It seems Gethin thinks something similar, as he says, "Honestly, Michael, can you not go to a party without trying to get laid?"

"Hang on, let me think about it . . . no. And why should I, anyway?"

"There are other single women here."

"Teresa Hughes. Slept with her in the nineties, not keen to do it again. Angela Whatsit—she's never liked me. Carol Morgan. Slept with her as well. And Donna Taylor."

"Bloody hell," says Gethin, and who can blame him. "Should think you'd do better in town."

"Probably I would. But I'm not in town, am I, see? Nothing to stop me trying, though?"

"She's never said anything to me that would suggest she'd be up for a one-night stand with a dick," says Gethin, which makes me laugh to myself.

"You might think I'm a dick," says Mike, clearly unoffended, "but I'm surprisingly successful with women."

"I had heard that, yeah. But anyway. If she tells you she's not interested, please just . . . leave her alone."

"All right. Where is she, anyway?"

"I don't know. She was talking to my mum last I saw."

"I'll go and look for her."

"You do that, then." There's a pause, presumably while Mike leaves. "Dick," says Gethin again, to himself.

I wait for a minute or two before cautiously peering round the garage door. They've gone, anyway, and no one's looking in my direction. I'll go back into the house and find somewhere to sit. Then I'll see if this bloke comes to find me. He doesn't sound like the sort of person I'd like to have sex with, but this morning I'd have said no one did. Probably.

Maybe the best way to deal with being attracted to my landlord is to have marginally regrettable sex with someone I've never met before. That would make this like a proper party, the sort I went to in my late teens and early twenties. Mostly anticipation and disappointment, of course. And that's not even the ones where I managed to find someone to have sex with. Ha ha.

Back in the house, things are feeling a bit looser. There are people in groups who've moved furniture around so they can sit together, and in the front room there are, indeed, a couple of women dancing enthusiastically to Beyoncé. I like to see people dancing, even when they're not great at it. In fact, I think I like that best.

I stand by the table and eat the last of the cucumber crudités, and then I sit in the corner of the old sofa (which was in the garage for a while but has been reinstated for the party). I tuck my skirt neatly round my legs and hitch them up beside me. It's quite dark in this corner, and there's hardly any food left now, so the room is empty, everyone either outside or in the front room with the music. There's an occasional waft of the thick green stink of weed from the garden, and I wonder which of these very normal people is the smoker. Maybe most of them are, though; it's not like people my age have never taken drugs.

A man comes in from the garden and looks round the room.

"Hey," he says, "all right." He waggles a bottle of Budweiser at me. "I'm getting a beer; can I get you anything from the kitchen?"

I consider him for a moment. A big man, with close-cropped hair and a wide, friendly face. I think this is him, Mike, the man who would like to have sex this evening, and for whom it seems I'm pretty much the only option.

"I did have a glass, but I've put it somewhere."

"Reckon I can find a glass," he says, "even wash one up if I have to."

"If there's any white wine left in the fridge. Otherwise a glass of water. Thanks."

"Can't drink water at a party," he says.

I blink at him. "I can do whatever I like."

He grins at this. "I'm sure you can. Glass of white wine, then, if there is some," he says, and disappears through the door.

I scratch idly at my scars and wait for him to return. When he comes back, he presents my glass of wine with a mock bow. I take it from him.

"Thanks."

"You're welcome. Mind if I sit down?"

"Help yourself."

He sits beside me and raises his fresh bottle of beer to me. I move my glass toward him and we clink, solemnly.

"Cheers."

"Cheers."

"So you're Jess," he says.

"That's right."

"I'm Mike."

"Yes," I agree. "Hello. How do you know Gethin? Did you go to school together too?"

"No," he says, "but my brother was at university with him. I went to the other school."

"I suppose all his telly mates are too fancy for West Wales," I muse.

"They probably think they are, yeah. You met any of that lot, then?"

I shake my head.

"No, me either. Never even met Vanessa. I was surprised he came back, like."

"Starting over," I say. This gives me a yawning glimpse of melancholy for some reason. I ignore it.

"I suppose so. Well, telly people aren't better, but you'd think they might be more fun."

"These people not fun enough for you?" I grin at him.

He laughs. "Ah, they're all right. I've known 'em a long time. You get used to people, don't you?"

"You do. They're all new to me, though."

"You not got any friends here?"

"Mostly they work in a restaurant," I tell him, "so they can't come to parties on a Saturday."

"Oh yeah, which restaurant? Locally?"

I tell him the name of the restaurant, and he says, "Oh yes, Maura's restaurant."

"Everyone knows everyone else here, don't they?"

"She had a party, didn't she, couple of weeks ago. I was supposed to go to that, but it was my niece's little girl's christening."

I grin at him. "Great-uncle Mike?"

"Yes. God." He laughs. "She's not even that young; it's scary. My great-uncles were ancient."

"Were they really, though? I bet they weren't."

"I don't know; they seemed it. Older than my grandparents, anyway." He frowns at his beer bottle. "So," he says, "what brings you to Wales?"

"Oh, you know, looking for adventure."

"Really?"

I laugh. "No, not really. Not at all, in fact. The opposite. Just thought it sounded okay. And so I came to see, and it looked all right, and here I am."

"What do you do, then? Do you work at Cenhinen Bedr?"

"I did for a bit. Now I work in the office at a building supply. What about you?"

"Oh yeah. You work for Bruce, I remember." He nods. "Got a little plumbing business. Do high-end bathrooms and stuff." He grins at me. "Geth says you told him he didn't need a new bathroom."

"Yeah, sorry, cost you a sale, did it? I think he's going to get a new loo for outside."

"Yeah, that's not really worth my while, to be honest."

"S'pose not. But the bathroom here's great—period, I reckon—could do with a better shower, but I guess that's not worth your while either."

"Not really, no. I can give him the name of someone who could probably help him, though."

I shrug. "It's not up to me, is it."

"I heard you pretty much project-managed all this." He gestures with the bottle.

"Not really. Just gave my opinion when he asked."

"Looks good, though."

I nod. "It does. It's a nice house," I say, for the fiftieth time.

"So you going to live here permanently, then?"

I shrug again. "Who knows. Permanently is hard to quantify, isn't it. It's a good place to live and handy for where I work, so we'll see how it goes."

❧ ❦

Now Mike's showing me photos on his phone. He went to Crete on holiday last year, and rather surprisingly—although maybe that's me being a snob—did all the stuff at Knossos. I've never been but I'd love to, so from being slightly cynical about our conversation I've transformed into someone who really wants to know, and we're sitting closer together while I scroll through the pictures, and he tries—quite well, I think—to remember what everything is.

"Oh, there you are," says Gethin, and I look up.

"Hello. Mike's showing me his holiday snaps. Did you want me?"

He looks annoyed, but luckily, because of the overheard conversation earlier, I don't think he's annoyed with me. I smile at him.

"Just wondering if there was any more Coke anywhere," he says, although I don't exactly believe him.

"There should be a box under the stairs. D'you want me to look?"

"Oh, no, I could look. It's fine. Don't let me disturb you."

Again, I know why he's said this, so I don't have to worry that I might have annoyed him in some way. I used to spend a lot of time wondering what I'd done wrong; it's very tiring. He disappears off to look in the cupboard under the stairs, or not.

"So how does this all work?" says Mike.

"All what?"

"You and Geth."

"Well, I live here in exchange for rental payments."

"Right."

"It's not very complicated."

He nods. "Do you go shopping together? Like, to Tesco?"

"Sometimes. Mostly he goes."

"Do you eat together?"

I nod. "Now that I work normal hours, yes."

"Breakfast too?"

I laugh. "Yes, even breakfast."

"But you're not . . ."

"Not what?"

"You know."

I shake my head. "No, what do you mean?"

"You don't . . . share a bedroom."

I laugh again. "No. I've seen pictures of Vanessa. I should think he could do better, don't you reckon?"

He rubs a hand over the top of his head. "I dunno about that."

"Are you flirting with me?" I ask him.

"Jesus, yes, of course I am."

This makes me laugh a lot. "Oh, okay. I can't always tell. That's kind of you."

"It's not kindness," he says, and I think he'd kiss me now, if I indicated any interest. I can't quite do it though. He's a bit too beery, too . . . blokey.

"Well, I'm flattered," I tell him, although this is not entirely true. I suppose it's not entirely untrue either. I never think of myself as the sort of person anyone might flirt with, although I do recognize his options are limited.

He laughs. "Not interested?"

"I don't think . . . my life's a bit complicated, Mike, or it has been. I'd rather not do anything . . ." I hesitate, trying to think of the right words.

"You might regret?" He laughs again. "No one ever regrets me, honest."

At least he's good-natured about it all. I'm not worried he'll get arsey, like some people do if you reject them.

"Anyway," I say, "I haven't finished looking at your photos." He thumbs his phone back on and I take it from him. He puts his arm round my waist, stroking the fabric of my dress. I'm not really getting anything from this, though, and I ignore it. When all the pictures have been looked at, I say, "I might get another drink. What time is it?"

He opens his phone again. "Nearly eleven."

"Is it really? Bloody hell." I yawn, suddenly overcome with tiredness. I stand up, and he follows me into the kitchen. I get a glass of water.

"I might go to bed, actually."

"Yeah? Want some company?"

I smile at him. "You're a tryer, aren't you? Nice of you to offer. But I don't think so."

"Oh, go on. It'll be fun, I promise."

This makes me chuckle. "Yeah, I think I might be a bit too old to pick people up at parties."

"Bollocks," he says. "Why would you be? Anyway, that's like saying I'm too old to get picked up."

I laugh again as I head out to the hallway. "Thanks for asking, anyhow, but I'd rather not."

"Jess—"

"What?"

"Go on," he says, "let me. I'm good."

"Ha, I'm sure you're brilliant," I say, although this isn't strictly true. "But if I'm honest, I'm not really in the right place to be having sex with people. I mean mentally and emotionally and all that." He pulls a sad face, which makes me laugh. "So anyway. I'll say good night. Thank you for showing me your pictures."

"Kiss me," he says, "before you go?"

"I'm not sure that's sensible."

"I'm not really bothered about sensible."

I find this quite easy to believe.

"Go on," he continues, "take me to bed." He leans toward me, and I put my hand on his chest.

"Thank you, but no. Good night."

I turn and begin to climb the stairs. I glance across the hallway and see Gethin, standing in the sitting room doorway, his face carefully blank. I raise a hand in acknowledgment and proceed up to my bedroom.

❧ ❦

There's a short queue for the bathroom, so I go and get undressed and put my pajamas on before coming out again and lining up to wait to clean my teeth. It's funny to queue for the bathroom in your own house.

Soon I'm back in my room. I don't go to bed though. I've been writing some notes, about my life. Sort of a diary of daily events since I started living here officially, plus notes about other things as I think of them. Not exactly a memoir—that sounds a bit pretentious. And as if my memories might have value, which they mostly don't.

I bought some cheap hardback notebooks from a stall at the indoor market, and nearly every night, I write about my day. Not that it's terribly important or fascinating, or it wouldn't be to anyone else. I feel the need to trap it though, to pin it down, the way things are. It's interesting to write about past events, too, although I always find that as you write it you change it, and it's hard to be precise about how you felt. Anyway, writing about things years later can't show how you felt at the time, usually—only how you remember feeling, which can be very inaccurate.

Tonight I write about the party, and also about a number of other house parties, long-ago teenage parties held in the homes of holidaying parents, parties that make you realize that having a big detached house in a village just makes people careless about your possessions.

I try to remember how various events made me feel. Excitement, disappointment, nausea. I went to a sixteenth birthday party at a church hall once and Frances got off with the boy I'd fancied for ages. She fancied him too—and I was self-aware enough to know that what seemed like betrayal was in fact nothing to do with me. I remember the feeling of desolation though, sitting on a swing in the dark, wondering if anyone would ever want to kiss me. If I could send a message through time to my past self, what would I say? "Of course they will, but watch out"?

I'm distracted from my memories by the sound of the front door shutting. I listen. There are taxis outside, people laughing and saying goodbye to one another. Is that the last of the guests? What time is it, anyway? I look over at the clock, stretching. Ten past one. I can still hear music from downstairs, but even as I think this, someone turns it down, or off. The house breathes out.

I might go down and start sorting things out. Post-party mornings are grim, even without the overflowing ashtrays of the past. I stick my head out of my bedroom door and listen. Nothing. Gethin's down there, though—or at least, I haven't heard him come to bed. I put my slippers on—I anticipate that the floors will be dirty—and drift slowly downstairs. He's not in the front room, but the lamps are still lit. I begin to collect glasses. We borrowed thirty extra from the restaurant, and although I know they'll go through the dishwasher again when they get home, I still feel the need to wash them up before I pack them away. I find a stray cardigan behind the sofa, and a string of beads against the baseboard, which must have been dislodged by dancing. There are paper plates everywhere. I take an unsteady stack of glasses to the kitchen, which looks like a bomb's hit it, if bombs were made of cardboard and beer bottle lids and crisps. I pile the glasses onto the worktop and go back for more.

"Oh, hey. I thought you'd gone to bed," says Gethin, emerging from the dining room with a rattling armful of beer bottles.

"No, I was reading," I say, which is easier than saying "writing," because if you say you're writing, people ask you about it. "Thought I'd come down and get ahead of all this."

"Yeah, look at it all, the monsters," he says. "There are literally a million empty bottles."

"You know that's not what 'literally' means, right?"

He laughs at this. "A hundred. At least."

"Someone's left their cardi," I tell him.

"Yeah, I found a phone, and a pair of shoes in the garden. People are shit at looking after their stuff."

"A pair of shoes?"

"Yeah, I put them by the folding doors. No idea who they belong to. A woman, of some kind."

This makes me laugh. " 'Of some kind'?"

"I can't tell much from the shoes." He grins at me. I collect the remaining glasses from the front room, take them to the kitchen, and return with a trash bag for the paper plates. They're going in the compost, but I need something to collect them in.

"I'm glad we took the rug up," he says, looking at the scatter of bottle tops and food.

"I know, right? I won't hoover until tomorrow; I expect next door hate us enough already." I plump the cushions on the sofa and rescue a half-full can of Coke from behind the telly. "Is there any food left?"

"Not really."

I follow him out to the dining room and regard the table, covered in empty plates and dishes.

"That all went okay, then."

"Bloody gannets. I didn't get to eat hardly any of the stuff we made," he complains. "I didn't have a single sausage roll, or any of those salmon things."

"No, neither did I. Still, good that it all got eaten." I swipe my finger round the edge of a bowl that once had dip in it. "This is good, the bean dip." I lick my finger. "I might make that again so we can eat it."

"Danny Jenkins said the guacamole was the best he's ever

had. And he's been to Mexico," says Gethin, and we laugh, rather hysterically, at each other.

Two more trips to the kitchen with bowls and dishes, and then he folds the tablecloth up before shaking it out of the back door. Everything looks better now that we've more or less sorted it. I retreat to the kitchen and begin to stack the dishwasher.

"Three loads easy, I reckon," I say, "but at least we don't have to do it by hand. I think I might have reached my limit with dishwashing."

"Mm." He stands in the doorway, watching me. He's got a pint glass of water, and he drinks most of it as we stand there.

"You don't have to stay up," I say. "I'll just finish this; the rest can wait."

"Yeah. Thanks. Oh, er . . . so . . ."

I look over my shoulder at him.

"Yes?"

"So, Mike . . ."

"Oh yeah. I heard you talking to him. You're probably right about the dick thing."

"Oh God." He laughs. "Where were you?"

"In the garage, getting a chair."

"I hope we didn't say anything embarrassing. Did we? Shit."

"I gathered what his plan was."

"Yeah, he . . . I know it's totally up to you, whether you . . . you know, what you do, and who you do it with, like," he says, "but I'm not sure I'd recommend Mike as a . . ."

"No? He says he's really good in bed." I wash my hands vigorously to remove the smell of beer.

"Yeah, well, he might be," says Gethin doubtfully. "I mean, I think he's had loads of practice. But what I'm trying to say is . . ."

"Yes, it's okay, you don't need to say it. I don't always make terrible choices. He was a potentially terrible choice that I managed to avoid making. Go me."

There's a pause before he says, "You were kissing him, though. Weren't you? In the hall?"

"No, I wasn't. Although I did think about it. Kissing's quite nice, isn't it. Haven't kissed anyone for ages. But then it seemed . . . anyway, so I didn't." I look round the kitchen as I dry my hands. "I think that's everything for now." I flick the lights out and head for the hallway.

"I didn't realize you might be thinking about kissing people," he says as I pass him.

"I didn't either. It was a bit of a surprise, to be honest."

"If I'd realized . . ." he says, and stops.

"Yes?"

It's very quiet. The hallway is lit only by the light from the landing, and we stand in the fuzzy dusk.

"I might have wondered if it would be a good idea to kiss you myself."

I close my eyes, briefly, feel my heart thumping. "Might you?" I'm amused by this hedging. "And what might you have decided?" I fold my arms and lean against the wall.

"I'd probably have asked, anyway."

"Are you going to ask?"

"Jess . . ."

"What?"

"Is that . . . something you might be interested in?"

I laugh. "Sweep me off my feet, why don't you."

"It's a long time since I did anything like this."

"Yes, me too." I step toward him and reach up, my fingers on the back of his neck, pulling his face to mine.

It's funny how completely different the idea of kissing Gethin is to the idea of kissing Mike. I suppose that's what happens when you really like someone. My knees are literally weak, and I mean this in the true definition of the word. He holds my face, his hands cupping my jaw. His tongue is cool from the water he was drinking in the kitchen. We kiss for what seems like forever, an endless perfect moment. I slide my hand under his shirt, skin on skin.

I'd do it here, now, against the wall, if he wanted to. I'm surprised at myself, sort of. If you'd asked me—even five minutes ago, when I was pretty sure we'd be kissing—I'd have said I didn't want to have sex, not with him, not with anyone, not ever. I'm not sure who I thought I was fooling. I begin, awkwardly one-handed, to unfasten his belt.

"Jesus, Jess," he says, pulling away. We blink at each other in the half-light.

"Ah," I say. "Sorry. Is that not . . ."

"We could go upstairs," he says. "If you . . ."

"Okay. Yes."

"You . . . ah."

With that we're kissing again. Upstairs seems a long way away. He kisses my face, my eyelids, my throat. There's a strange noise and I think I'm making it.

"Wow," he says, after a bit. "Are you okay?"

"Yes."

"So . . . I've got to say . . . your hair really looks amazing, and this evening you were . . . you looked absolutely stunning. I mean . . . uh . . ."

"No," I say, "go on."

"I think . . . did you want to go upstairs?"

"Yes."

Chapter Sixteen

In his bedroom, I kick off my slippers, and he pushes me backward, tripping me, cautiously, so I fall onto the bed.

"Jess, look . . ."

"I might not be able to," I say.

"You . . ."

"I don't know if . . . so, the last time I had sex," I tell him, "it was . . . not very nice?"

I look up at the expression of concern on his face.

"Right. Shit," he says, "I'm sorry . . ."

I shake my head. "And I don't know if . . ."

"Okay. Well . . . just tell me, if you want me to stop, or do anything differently, or . . ."

I'm worried, now, that I've moved past the moment. Maybe we should have done it down there, against the wall. It would probably be over, now, and . . . but that makes it sound like I want it to be over. Which I don't. We stare at each other. It's funny to look up at someone. He looks worried. That'll be my fault.

"Is this . . ."

"You could kiss me again," I suggest, so he does. After a while, it seems like it might be a good idea to actually get into bed, so, after he wrestles his shirt over his head and extricates himself from his trousers, we do. The curtains are open, and a flat slab of moonlight falls across the end of the bed.

He strokes my face, my shoulders, unbuttons the top button of my pajamas.

"Is this okay?"

I nod.

"You'll tell me, if . . ."

I nod again.

"The thing is," he says, "I really like you."

"Yes."

"I didn't want you to think I was taking advantage or . . ."

I shake my head this time. My hand rests against his chest. I am astonished to touch him, to be here, in his bed.

"And I know we haven't talked loads about why you . . . left, but I'm not a complete idiot . . ."

I shake my head again.

"And I know . . . bad things . . . have happened to you."

"Yes."

"I don't want to be a bad thing. I really don't . . ."

I close my eyes. "I think you might be a good thing."

He dips his face to mine and we kiss, slow, deep kisses.

"I'd like to be," he says, after a while. He leans to rummage in the drawer of his bedside table and produces a condom, which seems unexpectedly well prepared, although I'm happy to see it, of course.

It's warm in his room. We kick the duvet off as we move together, all unexplored yet familiar places. Things are slow, and then faster, almost silent, mouths and fingers. The demons I worried about do not appear. The two of us are alone and, in my head at least, unaccompanied by any complications. I am grateful for this, as the sweat cools on my chest, as I lick salt from my upper lip.

"All right?" he says.

"Thank you."

"You needn't thank me," he says. "You're always thanking me."

"I'm . . . always grateful." I smile, but I fear it may be tremulous. I feel oddly delicate, elevated. I am so thankful for this, for everything. I touch my finger to his cheek, and he turns his head to kiss my palm. I close my eyes.

"Ah, Jess, I . . ."

I feel his breath on my shoulder. Then I sleep.

❧ ❦

When I wake, drawn from sleep by my bladder, I sit up cautiously and look at his face, closed in slumber, distant despite his physical proximity. Would other people's dreams be at all comprehensible if one could see them? I swing my legs over the side of the bed and pad quietly to the bathroom.

I wonder about what I've done and whether it was a sensible thing to do, or merely a pleasurable one. I look at myself in the bathroom mirror, in the gray light of four-thirty. I've always thought how strange it is that nothing you do is visible on your face. I remember going into school the day after I had sex for the first time, absolutely astonished by the fact that no one could tell.

It's the same with rooms—the bedroom looks exactly the same as it did last week. The walls have no memory of love or pain. Perhaps Mrs. Evans—Bronwyn—died in there? Who knows? Not me. I let the tap run for a moment and drink thirsty gulps of cold water.

I return to Gethin's room. Since we've been sharing the house I don't think I've ever been naked on the landing, always very cautious not to be caught even in a towel, and to be naked in the doorway of his bedroom seems oddly transgressive. I hesitate on the threshold. Perhaps I should spend the few hours left of the night in my own bed. I think . . . I think I've allowed myself to be carried away by events.

He stirs, raises his head. "Jess?"

"Hey." It occurs to me as we look at each other that perhaps he's forgotten what happened earlier—maybe he was a lot drunker than he seemed?—and now he's wondering what the hell's going on, and why I'm in his room, naked.

"Where are you going?"

"I'm not going anywhere," I say. "I've been to the bathroom."

"Come back to bed," he says, sweeping his arm across the sheet.

❧ ❦

We do it again. Quicker, dirtier, more—desperate? We gasp and mutter. It's daylight, more or less, early sunshine.

"Wow," he says afterward. "It's a long time since . . ."

"Mm?"

"Well, you know."

"Not bad for an old fella."

"Yeah, thanks."

We smile at each other, drowsy. More kisses. I'm glad to overwrite less . . . pleasant . . . experiences with this. Now I needn't think about before; now I remember how it feels to do this stuff with someone I like. His hands on me, his lips, the taste of him.

❧ ❦

When I wake again, it's six o'clock. This time, I think, I need to get up, go to my own bed. I don't think this is . . . if I fall asleep again, and we wake up, and it's, like, nine or something, then what will happen? There'll be a whole awkward coffee/break-fast thing, and it will be . . . I'm not sure how that will work, so it seems best to go. I gather my pajamas and slippers and head to my own room. My sheets are cool; my bed feels very small compared to the expanse of Gethin's king-size. I lie on my back and look up at the ceiling, so white and clean and freshly painted.

I close my eyes. The muscles on the insides of my thighs ache, just a little, from my unexpected exercise. I'm not sure what we're going to do about this thing we've done.

❧ ❦

When I wake up for a third time, it's because Gethin has put his head round my door and called my name. I blink at him.

"I brought you a cup of tea," he says. "Can I come in?"

"Oh . . . yeah." I push myself up on my elbows, making sure the duvet covers my chest, conscious that I'm still naked, which, considering that three hours ago we both were, and very close together, might seem odd. "Thanks, you didn't need to . . ."

"I wondered where you were."

"Yeah, I thought I should . . ."

He puts a mug of tea on the bedside table and pulls the chair from the desk over toward the bed. He has a cup, too, and he sits down.

"So, look . . ."

"I thought I might have a hangover," he says, "but I guess I sweated it out."

I laugh. Although I didn't exactly mean to. "Were you . . . very drunk? You didn't seem it."

"No, not really. It's physically impossible to get drunk at your own party, have you ever noticed that?"

"Actually I have, yes."

"Yeah, weird, isn't it. Responsibility, I guess."

"I guess so."

"Anyway," he says, "I was thinking we should go out for breakfast. Or brunch, or whatever. We could go out for a drive, maybe. Looks like it's going to be a gorgeous day."

My stomach swoops with . . . something. Anxiety, I suppose.

"I don't think . . . look, the thing is, Gethin, I think maybe . . ."

"What?"

"I think . . . I don't want you to think I didn't enjoy myself. I really did."

There's a long pause. I try not to look at him.

"But?"

"But maybe it would be better if we . . . pretended it happened, like, five years ago, and that's fine, and we're not pretending it didn't happen, just that it was . . . in the past?"

"Oh."

"Is that . . . would that be a problem?"

He looks at me for a long moment. His eyelids flutter, and he looks away. I see the muscles in his jaw tighten for a second.

"Not a problem, no. A shame, maybe," he says. "Anyway. I'll

leave you to it, then." He gets up and returns the chair to its place by the desk, picks up his cup, and leaves the room.

I slide back beneath my duvet, head and all. I know this is the most sensible course of action. I don't want to be involved. I don't think Gethin is a dick, obviously, so I'm sure he can cope with this. I don't expect him to take it badly; in fact, if he thinks about it, he'll be relieved. Yes.

※ ※

Not long afterward, I hear the front door bang, and then the sound of the car. He's gone out, then, and that's probably a good thing. I stare at the ceiling for a bit, telling myself that I feel fine—better than fine, actually, because whatever else happened, I had sex, and not only was it extremely enjoyable, but it didn't freak me out or make me uncomfortable or fill my head with unpleasant images or anything. This is a definite win, because of what happened last time, which wasn't much fun at all.

After a while, I get up, shower. It would be a good idea to get a better shower; maybe we should ask Mike for the number of this other bloke . . .

I go downstairs and wrestle the hoover out of the cupboard under the stairs. I vacuum carefully, then heave the rug out from behind the sofa in the front room and re-lay it. This is hard work; it's heavy.

I open the folding doors and sweatily, awkwardly fight with the old sofa, dragging it onto the patio and back into the garage. That was much easier with two people, but I want it to be done. I empty and restack the dishwasher, box up the borrowed wineglasses, mop spills off the kitchen floor. I wonder if Gethin will come home for lunch but think, on the whole, that he won't. I make myself some toast and another cup of tea and sit in the sunny garden for a bit. Then I do some washing. The house is back to normal, more or less, although it still smells slightly odd, of other people's perfume, overlaid with cleaning products.

In the afternoon I go for a walk, as the weather's so nice. I'm still exploring; I like to walk round the streets, learning everyone's cladding and garden ornaments, looking out for interesting stuff. There are some good houses round here, as well as lots of quite ordinary ones. There are several streets of what I assume is ex–council housing: plain, efficient, probably 1950s. The way people personalize these very standard spaces is always interesting. I take pictures of good plants, and make notes, so that one day, if I'm feeling brave, I might come back and ask for a cutting, or some seeds.

If you walk for about fifteen minutes, you pass the old workhouse, which is a fine building, although dilapidated, abandoned. There's been a fire at some point, and I expect eventually it will be demolished, although this seems a shame. On the other hand, I don't know if I'd personally want a flat built into something so drenched in misery. I suppose it was better to be in there than outside, dying of hunger. At home, they converted some of the buildings from the old asylum into flats, and they look really great: fine redbrick mid-Victorian things with high ceilings and big windows, representative of a particular kind of municipality. But surely the walls weep with sadness? Perhaps I'm oversensitive.

᪥ ᪥

Back home, and no sign of Gethin. I wonder if he'll be back for dinner? I fetch my washing in from the line—is there anything better than line-dried bedding? I really don't know how I lived somewhere for three years with no outdoor space. (I admit that wasn't the worst thing about my time there, but you know.) If I'm cooking only for me, I'll just have pasta.

We've mostly cooked together for the last six months, because I've been teaching him how to do stuff. I wonder if this might have been a mistake. I think I've miscalculated the closeness of our relationship. I've allowed myself to be seduced by companionship. Being . . . friends . . . has been extremely pleasant and relaxing. Ignoring the attraction between us has somehow made what happened last night seem infinitely more significant.

I think of him muttering "I really like you" into my ear. I really like him, too. Rather too much, if I'm honest. I wonder what would have happened if I'd said yes to brunch. Is there a world where we'd be talking about whether we might be together? I stand in the kitchen for a long time, blankly staring at the contents of the open food cupboard.

If Mitch hadn't been like he is . . . but that's no help. If Mitch was nicer, or I'd never met him, I wouldn't be here, would I. So if I'm broken (which I am), it's not like there's any magical thinking that will change how things are.

I've been very attracted to Gethin since . . . probably since we met, if I'm trying to be honest. I guess this was mutual. We both pretended there was nothing going on there, and we've probably swerved a number of situations that could have found us in bed together much earlier. I think of my birthday, and his, dancing in the front room . . . or just a month ago, when we went to Dryslwyn and got soaked in the rain. That was kind of . . . I wonder if he was thinking of it then, wondering if he should kiss me. I was certainly wondering if I should kiss him.

It's a good job I didn't though. I'd have been even more confused and conflicted if this had happened even a few weeks earlier.

※ ※

At eight-thirty, I hear the car pull into the drive. It's nearly ten minutes, though, before the back door opens. Was he sitting out there trying to decide whether to come in? I hope not. What I really want is for everything to be how it was yesterday, before all this happened. Even though I can't say I wish it hadn't. If I could go back, and not do it? Yeah, I'm not sorry we did. I wouldn't change it. It's a strange mixture of feelings. It's been difficult to put it out of my mind, despite all the practice I've had with not thinking about important things.

I hear him in the kitchen, filling the kettle. Then he's looking round the sitting room door.

"Making some tea," he says. "D'you want one?"

"Oh, thank you. Yes, that would be great. There are cookies," I add.

"What kind?"

"Those chocolate ones you like? Granny Boyd's."

"Oho, homemade?"

"Yeah, they're in that box by the toaster." Why did I make cookies? It's like an apology, and I'm not completely comfortable with that. I had all the ingredients out before I'd really thought about it.

"Cool," he says, and vanishes again.

Okay. So maybe it will be fine. *Please let it be fine.*

Even though I'm anxious, it's interesting not to be afraid. I'm never afraid he'll be angry with me. It's one of the best things about him.

Chapter Seventeen

I'm meeting Kate in town, after work. We're going to walk to her house, and Gethin's going to meet us there, and she's going to feed us and introduce us to her partner and any of her children who might be about, as well as some other friends. She didn't come to Gethin's party because they were away, and it's a while since I've seen her.

I'm dead nervous. Not sure why exactly, apart from the fact that she's very cool, and I want her to like me, I suppose. I like Maura and the restaurant girls, but their idea of socializing is very different from mine. I can't handle too many nights in too-loud pubs that mostly sell cocktails, or indeed that end up in a provincial nightclub.

I walk slowly up Victoria Street, enjoying the sunshine. Kate's waiting outside the gallery, leaning against the wall. She waves, and I hurry over to her.

"Hello," she says, "how are you? Good day?"

"Oh, well. Yes, it was fine. My job's not very exciting. Although I do quite like it. How was yours?"

"Yes, a good day today. And such lovely weather. I admit I was worried."

"Worried?"

"Usually if you mention any sort of outdoor event it guarantees rain."

"Oh yes," I say with a laugh, "I've already been to two indoor barbecues this summer."

We cross the road.

"I'm lucky to live so close to work," she says. "It only takes me ten minutes, and if I could walk properly it would probably only be five."

I'm not sure whether to ask about her leg, so I don't.

"Being able to walk to work is a great thing," I agree. "I've never fancied commuting, although I did have a job I needed to get the bus to for a while."

"What did you do before you came here? Oh, you did the antiques thing, didn't you? That must have been fun. You must have seen loads of cool stuff."

"Yes. And some fab buildings, when we did clearances. Johnny knew all sorts of people. Useful connections."

"Why did you break up?"

"With Johnny? Oh . . . he started sleeping with someone else. Imagine."

"Were you together for a long time?"

I wrinkle my nose. "Yes, but it was a long time ago. It annoys me that it was the longest I've ever been with someone. He was . . . well, we did have a lot of fun. I wish we could have lived somewhere warmer though. Our house was a bit . . . broken."

She laughs. "Was it? How?"

I explain the house to her, finishing with ". . . and it was freezing cold nine months of the year. No heating, huge windows, howling drafts."

"Being cold sucks," she says. "I couldn't live somewhere without heating."

"I've done it more often than I'd choose. It doesn't get any better."

❧ ❧

Kate's house is lovely. It's Victorian, elegant, with blindingly bright white render, like a house at the seaside, or an old-fashioned wedding cake. There are huge bay windows and intricate railings. Inside, as anticipated, everything's very, very stylish. It's painted in shades of white, and there are beautiful original tiles on the floor of the hall. A hugely imposing mahogany banister curls up the stairs. As we walk along the passage, I catch glimpses of the sitting room and the dining room, both equally pale, with big abstract paintings in blues and grays. I wonder if they're Kate's own work. The back has been extended to cover that side return thing you get on Victorian houses, so there's a huge kitchen diner with a vast skylight and exposed brick and yards of worktop. Plants everywhere, a big pine table. Through the open glass doors, a hint of barbecue smoke. You can tell she's got a great eye; everything is so beautiful. You could slap the whole place on an interiors website without even tidying up.

"Now," she says, laying her bag on the table, "I'll get you a drink, and introduce you to people. What would you like? We have most things." She opens the fridge. "Gin? Homemade lemonade? Or there's wine, or Coke, or fizzy water, or . . ."

"Lemonade's fine, thank you," I say, looking round rather enviously. Why on earth didn't Gethin buy something like this? Then I feel a bit disloyal to Sunnyside. And if he had bought something else, we'd never have met. That's a strange thought. I feel suddenly dizzy. I can't think there's anyone else in the world who would have reacted to my presence the way he did. Someone else would have called the police, perhaps, and thrown my belongings away. I close my eyes and breathe deeply to calm myself. That didn't happen. I don't need to worry about things that didn't happen.

Since the party things have been . . . not as awkward as I feared. Although for a while I retreated to my room, it didn't last long, because he'd come upstairs and knock on my door to say, "Fancy watching *Bill and Ted*?" Or, "If you had to choose a Muppet film, which would you choose?" Or, "Hey, *Jurassic Park*'s on. Do you know how to make popcorn?" I'm grateful to the films of my youth for enabling us to reframe things, or construct a new version of the way we are together, or something, and everything seems to be fine, which is a relief.

Kate leads the way out to the garden, which is partially paved, with a square of grass and some topiary, a garage at the back covered in Virginia creeper. There's a big, fancy barbecue, a smaller, less fancy one—for vegetarian barbecue, I guess— a variety of tasteful garden furniture, and a number of people. A tall man in jeans and an ancient band T-shirt stands at the barbecue, talking to another, shorter man with a glass of wine and a linen shirt–cargo shorts combo, which leads me to anticipate, accurately, boat shoes. The bigger man is Sam, presumably. Sitting at a circular stone table are two women, one with short orange hair (satsuma-colored, I mean, not ginger) and one with expensively ashy blond tresses in an artfully messy bun. On a sun lounger farther away on the grass, a teenage girl in sunglasses is looking at her phone.

"Sam," says Kate, "this is Jess."

He looks round from his conversation and grins at me. He's very attractive, with good hair, longish, graying, and a big smile. He hooks the giant pair of tongs he'd been using on the barbecue and wipes his hands on a tea towel before striding toward us, hand held out for me to shake.

They introduce me to everyone else. The man is Steve; he's married to the blonde, who has one of those posh nicknames that I don't quite catch. Plum? Pom? The woman with orange hair is Tanya. The teenager is the younger of Sam and Kate's daughters, Lamorna. She doesn't look up, but who can blame her; she's here for the food and maybe a sly glass of wine, not to chat with her parents' mates.

"So you're a plant person," Sam says, smiling at me. "Always good to meet a fellow gardener."

"Oh, well . . . that's a . . . I suppose I am a bit? I do like plants. And . . . stuff." It's almost embarrassing to say this to someone who gardens professionally.

"You're doing your garden, though?"

"Yes, kind of." I consider this statement. *Come on, Jess, be more assertive.* "No, I am . . . or fiddling with what's there already. It's a good size; there are some nice trees . . . it's been fun to think about what might suit it. I've never had the opportunity before, really."

"Kate said you'd been thinking about maybe coming to do our apprenticeship?"

"I don't know. I'd just been thinking about doing something new. But I might be a bit old to start again."

"Never too old," he says, laughing. They make a horribly attractive couple. He's definitely the best-looking bloke I've seen since I moved here, almost movie-star handsome.

"I don't know. It's quite physical, isn't it?"

"You can soon move on to telling people what to do," he says. We smile at each other.

"I ought to look into it," I say. "I think I need to do something more . . . something I can be more engaged with . . . than office admin. I've always loved gardening, and gardens . . . I don't know."

"Well, if you want to come up for a look round, let me know."

⊰⊱

I talk to Sam and Kate and the others. More people arrive—a gay couple who are both called Robin, which seems confusing, or maybe not. They live in Llanelli and own a beauty salon. One of them works there, but the other one—who has amazing tattoos of birds (birds of paradise, I think—or maybe they're invented?) on both forearms—does book illustration. He sees me looking at his tats—they really are stunning—and winks at me. He's known Sam since school. As well as the Robins, I'm introduced to a very pregnant woman in a hijab, Parandis, who works with Kate at the gallery, and her husband, Hasan, who's a junior doctor and works at the hospital.

I watch Sam begin to cook things, and help Kate bring bowls of salad, plates of bread, and trays of dips and sauces out to the garden. I feel . . . I don't know. I wonder if I'll ever be fully relaxed and comfortable ever again. Eventually, perhaps. I don't know how long you have to know people before you can be completely yourself in their company. I'm still cautious, worried about making people like me, even though that's not actually a thing. People like you or they don't.

I think I imagined that leaving home would be like when I

went to university, when you're thrown into a mass of other people your age who don't know anyone, all on an equal footing. Instead, of course, I'm an interloper, an extra. Then again, I wonder if it actually never occurred to me to think about this side of it at all. Did I imagine I'd be making new friends? Not really. I just wanted to be somewhere else; I'm not sure it ever crossed my mind that I'd need to build a social life. I don't remember this being a problem when I moved to Brighton, but again, it's much easier when you're young, and everyone else is young, and anyway, Brighton's always full of other people who've just moved there.

I'm waiting for Gethin to arrive and worrying about this. Even if he's the person I know best, I should try not to be so . . . needy. When I hear his voice, I sit up and look round, like a dog. I can practically feel my tail wagging.

It's because he's the only person I really know, I tell myself, but I know it's not just that. He's talking to a second long-legged and beautiful teenager, who must be Kate and Sam's eldest, Zennor. She's laughing at whatever he's saying. I watch as he looks round the garden, taking everything in, until he sees me and smiles a wide smile of relief.

"Oh, you're here! I tried to ring you," he says, coming over. "Is your phone off?"

"It might be. Hello. How was work?"

"Oh, you know, same old same old," he says. "Is there room for me?"

I'm sitting on a wicker sofa beside a man called Matt, who works with Sam. We've been talking about gardens, unsurprisingly. I shift up slightly, and Gethin squeezes in beside me. There isn't really room for three people, or at least, for three people who don't want to touch one another. Especially when two of them are men, who are no good at sitting neatly. Gethin and I are pressed together, hip to knee. I try to ignore it but it's tricky. And what do we do with our arms?

"Sorry," he says, "I thought there was more room than this. It's a bit cozy, isn't it. Are you okay?"

I know he's asking because of what happened. It's not like he can say "Do you mind if I touch you?" while Matt's here. And what would I say? It isn't that I *mind*, after all.

"I can move, if you want?"

"God, no. No, it's fine." I elbow him gently in the ribs. "I mean, it *is* a bit snug. Lucky you're not one of those beefy rugby types."

"Pfft."

❧ ❦

"Do you want me to phone a cab?" he says. "Or shall we walk? It's a fair way."

"Oh, we can walk, can't we? It's not cold, and it's easier to walk home when you've had a drink, isn't it, because you don't notice so much."

"This is true."

We say goodbye to our hosts, and Kate says, "We really should have lunch, Jess. I'll message you."

"All right," I say, "I'd love to. Thank you." I try to imagine myself as Kate's friend, her actual friend, not just a peculiar add-on. I almost can. We might go to exhibitions, perhaps, and shopping. She could advise me about elegant linen-based outfits and we could discuss documentaries we've watched, and the latest novels.

She probably has all the friends she needs, though.

Things are loud and confusing for a moment, too many people in the hallway, others leaving too. Then we're outside in the cool darkness.

"There," says Gethin. "Okay? Did you enjoy yourself? Sam's nice, isn't he?"

"He is. Very handsome."

"Did you think so?"

"Yes. No wonder their kids are so beautiful; they're both extremely hot."

He laughs at this. "Do you think Kate's hot?"

"Yes, definitely. You punch above your weight."

This makes him laugh even more. "I've got good taste and a persuasive manner," he says. There's a pause that's almost—but not quite—awkward, before he goes on, "But everyone seemed okay, didn't they? I thought maybe that Matt guy was a bit of a dick but actually . . ."

"Yeah, he just looked like one."

He laughs again. "I thought you'd like them. The other lot—from school and that—I like them, but they're . . ." He pauses as we cross the road. "If I said they're not as interesting, would that sound bad?"

"Maybe. I know what you mean, though. It's okay to like people for different reasons. It doesn't make any of them less . . . worthy."

"Yeah, I guess so. Is it about moving away? I always think . . . well, there's nothing wrong with always living in the same place. But it's good for you to spend some time away, I think. If you can. Makes you appreciate home more, as well."

"It *is* good for you to see somewhere else. Especially if you're southern," I add. "It's good to live in the north for a bit if you get the chance. And it was so different for me to live in a city, I couldn't believe it. The depth of people, the endless streets."

"Yeah, I definitely felt like that about Birmingham," he says. "It seemed huge compared to here. Even compared to Cardiff. Well, it is, I guess."

"I'd never really seen a shuttered shop before I moved up north. Like, shuttered at night? They don't do that at home. Or not where I lived, anyway."

"Ah, the leafy quiet of the Home Counties."

"Piss off," I say, laughing, and push him. We tussle in a childish fashion, risking turned ankles as we fool about up and down the curb. It's very silly. We're through town now, and beginning to climb the hill. It's colder, and I shiver, glad I brought my jacket.

"Clear skies."

"Yeah, it's good, isn't it," he says, pausing to look upward. "Or it would be if there was no light pollution. We should go out somewhere and look at the stars."

"Not tonight, though," I say, amused.

"No. But we could go camping. Couldn't we?"

I laugh at this idea. "Really?"

"You've got a tent. There's a Dark Sky thing in the Brecon Beacons National Park. We could go there."

"My tent's tiny," I object. I can't imagine what it would be like, sharing a tent with Gethin. Or maybe I can—and I suspect it would lead to trouble.

"Is it not a two-person? I could buy a bigger one. Or another small one. I expect you'd rather not share."

I think about this for a while, as we reach Sunnyside and

turn into the drive. "I don't mind if there's enough room, but two-person tents are quite tight for two people."

"A three-person tent then," he says. "Or one of those big ones with a window and separate bedroom." He laughs at the idea of this. "Do you actually like camping?"

We're inside now; the house is surprisingly warm.

"I haven't been camping for years. Proper camping, I mean—holiday camping, festival camping. It's . . . I wouldn't necessarily choose to do it; it's not that comfortable. I'd rather have a bed. But if you want to look at the stars"—I take off my jacket and go into the kitchen for a glass of water—"it's probably better to camp. More immediate. If you stay in a house you have to get up and go outside, don't you? Whereas you can just put your head out the door of the tent."

"That's true."

"One of the things I liked best when I lived on site," I say, "was looking at the stars. It wasn't the proper countryside, but it was quite dark. Everyone thought I was mad." I sigh. "That's one of the things that made me realize I didn't fit in there, either."

Chapter Eighteen

"Oh, hey," says Gethin. "You know we talked about camping?"

"Yes?"

"What about not-camping?"

"Er, in what sense?"

He laughs. "We could go away not-camping?"

"Go away?"

"Short break. Weekend away. Or long weekend."

"Oh, well . . ."

"Because Abby's husband—"

"Si," I say, because I do know who he's talking about, after all.

"Yes, him—so, his grandparents used to live in Laugharne. They're dead now, but him and his siblings share their house. Like a holiday home, you know. It's good. We used to go sometimes, with them. They're going down next weekend and he asked if I wanted to go. It's only like half an hour away."

I look at him carefully. "Abby would be there?"

"Yeah."

"She doesn't like me, Gethin."

"I think . . . I know she was a bit off to begin with, but—"

"I'm pretty sure she still doesn't." Not that I've seen her, or not since the party. If you asked if I avoid situations where she might be, the answer is yes. They've been here to dinner, twice, and both times I've gone out, to prevent any sort of issue.

"I'm pretty sure whatever she was worried about categorically hasn't happened, has it, so she needs to get over that. Anyway, Si said I could bring someone."

"I don't suppose they'd expect that to be me, though." And who could blame them?

He shrugs. "We don't have to spend any time with them. Do our own thing. It's right by the beach, and there are two sitting rooms. And a garden. I mean, it's up to you."

"Will you go anyway?"

"I don't know; I've never been on my own. I know I wouldn't be on my own. You know what I mean."

"You could take Mike or someone."

"Well, I could, I suppose. Probably not Mike, though." He laughs. "He's entertaining but we're not . . . I wouldn't choose him for my best mate or anything, like. I wouldn't want to spend the weekend with him. Christ knows what kind of shenanigans he'd want to get up to. I dunno, most people are couples, aren't they."

"I suppose they are."

"Do you want me to ask Abby if she'd mind if you came?"

"What would she say, though? Would she say if she did?"

He shrugs. "I've never known her to be tactful."

"Ha ha, right, no, I have heard that." I grin at him.

"So?"

"I don't know. Why do you want me to come with you?"

"I thought it might be nice." He shrugs again. "You know. Or not." We frown at each other. I feel like I'm cautiously testing my way as I answer.

"I think . . . I think she definitely wouldn't want me there.

And I'd feel uncomfortable. So thank you for asking me, but . . ."

"Okay, well. Okay," he says. I think he's annoyed. He shakes his head. "Okay. You'd better invite your friend down, then. Noosha. You said you were going to invite her—have you?"

"Not yet, I . . ."

"Message her now," he says, "don't put it off."

I look at him and he grins. "Sorry, that sounded . . . I mean, only if you want to, obviously."

"I would like to see her. And she wants to see the house," I add, "and to meet you."

He laughs. "Does she? I hope she copes well with disappointment."

❧ ❦

Lizzie's my oldest friend, from home; we've been friends since junior school. I haven't known Noosha as long, but we're closer. I met her when I moved back home after university, when she was pregnant with her eldest. Her baby's father was best mates with the guy I was seeing very briefly that summer. Both those men are long gone, but Noosha and I have been friends ever since. The last nine months is by far the longest we've been apart since we met, and I'm excited to see her.

The station in Caerwyddon is inconveniently situated (in my opinion), being on the opposite side of the river from the town itself. Gethin kindly gives me a lift down there, and we sit in the car park, waiting. I keep checking my phone to see if the train's arrived, even though, as he points out, I will actually see it when it gets here.

"It's cute how excited you are," he tells me.

"Pretty sure nothing I ever do is cute," I object. He doesn't respond to this, probably wisely.

Finally, the train is here. I spring out of the car as passengers begin to appear in the car park, scanning the faces. If I ever have to meet someone I worry, foolishly, that I somehow won't recognize them, and I have to look carefully at everyone, even the people who are quite clearly not Noosha. But there she is, unmistakable in a leopard-print mac, dragging a violently pink wheeled suitcase. Nearly six feet tall, with peroxide-blond hair in a Tippi Hedren updo, Noosha is never understated. She spots me and abandons the suitcase, rushing toward me for a hug. I wrap my arms round her and find, to my embarrassment, that I'm weeping.

"Hello, gorgeous," she says. "You look great!" She holds me at arm's length so she can see me better, before hugging me again. "I've missed you, darling. Hey, no need to cry; Noosha's here now."

"Oh God, I've missed you too. Thanks for coming."

"Yeah, it's quite the adventure, isn't it," she says, retrieving her case. "Oops, we're in the way," she adds, as a car tries to pass us. "All right, mate, calm down!" She smiles brilliantly at an aggrieved driver. "I couldn't believe how much farther it was from Cardiff to Swansea. And then even farther. Are we getting a cab," she asks, "or the bus?"

"Oh, no, Gethin's here. Come on."

He's out of the car, leaning against the trunk, which he opens as we approach. I introduce them.

"Charmed, I'm sure," she says, putting her hand out for him to shake.

"Welcome to Wales," he says. "Good to meet you. Let me take your case." He swings it up into the car.

"Thank you very much. Now we need to go somewhere with flowers, so I can buy some for you both. I did see some at Cardiff, but I already had too much to carry."

I laugh. "We don't need flowers; it's okay."

"A guest without flowers, though. Is that even a guest?"

"Of course it is. Do you want to sit in the front?"

"Oh no, darling, I'll be fine in the back." She opens the door. "Is it far?"

"Noosh gets carsick," I explain to Gethin.

"About five minutes. Shout if you feel rough," he says, "and I'll stop."

"Oh, we should be okay if it's only five minutes. I can sometimes manage ten, or even fifteen," says Noosha, as she folds herself into the back of the car. "I haven't actually been sick in a car since . . . last week. Ha ha, don't worry," she adds, poking him in the shoulder. "I merely josh."

He looks across at me. "She's the funny one, is she?"

We both laugh. I'm so pleased to see her, I can't even explain it, and I crane round in my seat so I can look at her.

"Was it awful, on the train?"

"Oh, no, not really. It was too hot from Reading to Bristol, something wrong with the air con. But the other two trains were fine. It's a pain in the arse, though, changing three times."

"You don't drive?" asks Gethin.

"I'm one of those idiots who's scared of the motorway," Noosha tells him. "Or at least, I am if I'm by myself. Tits offered to come with me, but I didn't think you'd want a teenager in your house."

"Tits?"

"My youngest."

"Tatiana," I explain.

"Does she mind being called Tits?" Gethin's laughing.

"Oh, I wouldn't do it to her face; she'd kill me."

"She doesn't like 'Tatty' either," I say. "No idea why."

"How many children do you have?"

"Three," says Noosha. "Madagascar—that's not her real name, don't worry—Madeline, she's the eldest; she's twenty-three. Ed, he's nineteen, and Tits is seventeen."

"Are you old enough to have a twenty-three-year-old daughter?"

"Ooh, he's good, isn't he? I already approve of you," she tells him. "Carry on. Of course, I was a child bride."

"Hardly a child," I say with a snort. "You were twenty."

"Hardly a bride, either, darling."

"Do they all live at home?"

"Ed's at university. Mads lives with her boyfriend. So it's mostly me and Tits these days."

"And Nathan," I add.

She cackles from the backseat. "Oh yeah, I forgot about him. He's my fella," she explains. "Not responsible for any of the offspring, bless him."

"They don't all have different dads," I say, "but—"

"But they may as well have," she finishes for me. Gethin laughs.

"It's basically an accident that Eddie and Tits have the same father."

"I won't ask what kind of accident," says Gethin, trying to concentrate on the road.

"It was very much a sexual sort of thing," says Noosha.

Gethin is approaching hysteria.

"I'm afraid this is what she's like," I say, grinning at him.

"Are you dreading the weekend?" asks Noosha. "I can tone it down."

"Not on my account," says Gethin, "please."

"There's the park," I say as we drive past it. "There's a Gorsedd. Do you know what that is?" I ask her.

"No idea."

"It's a stone circle for druids. For the eisteddfod."

"Haven't you gone native. What's that?"

"They do poetry and stuff."

"In Welsh."

"Yeah."

"Does everyone speak Welsh? Do you?" she asks Gethin.

"*Dipyn bach*. A little bit."

"More than a little bit," I say. "He can do it properly if he wants. And all the young people do," I tell her. "Pretty much everyone at the restaurant did. They do it at school. One of the secondary schools is all Welsh."

"Really?"

"Yeah, so you could learn French in Welsh, and I know that's not weird, but it seems weird."

"Did you learn it at school, then?" she asks Gethin.

"Yes. It's mandatory at primary school. And then you choose. I did it at secondary too, but I've forgotten loads."

We turn up Henllys Street. "Nearly there," I tell her. "It's just at the top of the hill."

"You can walk to town, then."

"Yes. And I did, every day when I first got here. Here we are," I say, as Gethin turns into the drive. "Sunnyside!"

"I love a house with a name," says Noosha. "Ah, I can't believe I'm here!"

We get out of the car, and Gethin fetches the suitcase.

"We usually go in the back," I say, "but since it's your first visit . . ." I lead her back up the drive to the front door.

"Oh, the VIP treatment, is it. I like the stained glass," she says, "and the tiles."

"I'll take this up for you," says Gethin, adjusting the handle of the pink case and heading up the stairs.

"Oh, thank you. He's very well trained, isn't he?"

"He's a nice man," I say solemnly.

"Nicer than any landlord I've ever had, certainly." She takes off her mac and I hang it up for her.

"I'll give you the tour, if you like?"

"Oh yes, please. Shall I take my shoes off?"

"Up to you," I say, regarding her scarlet suede wedge sandals with a certain degree of envy. I could never wear any of the things Noosha wears; I simply don't have the brio.

"I will, then—my feet are fecking killing me."

"You should wear comfortable shoes for a journey, Noosh," I say, leading her into the sitting room.

"Ha, I'll be dead before I do anything sensible, as you well know. Oh my God, that sofa! What an amazing color. Oh, Jess, this room is so you! Did you choose all this stuff?"

"Well, some of it." I'm embarrassed.

"Nice art."

"The paintings are Gethin's."

"I like this one," she says, peering at the one over the fireplace. "Ha, now I'm too close." She steps back. It's a kind of stormy seascape, almost abstract. We put it in here because there's a strip of tumultuous wave that's almost exactly the same color as the sofa. "Very good. Do you sit in here, then?"

"Yeah, mostly."

She drops her handbag on the armchair. "Those curtains are good. Are these your books? Or are they all at Mitchell's still?"

"Oh. Yeah." I rub my arm. "Had to leave most of them."

"That's a bugger."

"Yeah. Well." I shrug. "I know they're just . . . things."

"Want me to go round there?"

I laugh. "No. Really, they're only books. I expect he's thrown them away. And some of them are still at Nat's. Plus I've bought loads more since I've been here. There are some good charity shops."

"What did you bring? Hardly anything, I suppose."

"Not much. Some clothes. Photos. I took some stuff to Lizzie's—letters and that sort of thing." Anything I could get out of the flat without him noticing. I probably could have moved more, to be honest, but I was a bit paranoid toward the end.

"I saw Lizzie," she says. "Did I say?"

Lizzie and Noosha don't really get on; they're kind of opposites. Lizzie thinks Noosha is loud, which she is, and Noosha, I'm sure—although she's never actually said this—thinks Lizzie is boring. "Did you? When was that?"

She looks round the room again. "I dunno, April? Saw her at Redwoods. Had a chat about you."

"Oh no. Did you."

"Obviously. Anyway, yeah, it was mostly going '*Thank God she's out of that!*' I like the carpet," she adds.

"It cost nine grand. Can you imagine."

"*Nine grand?*" She stares at me.

"Yeah. It's antique. Hundred and thirty years old or something."

"Thank God I took my shoes off. Are you sure it's okay to stand on it?"

"Ha ha, yes."

"Nine grand, though?"

I nod.

"Wow."

"Come and see the rest," I say, and take her back into the hall.

❧ ❦

When she's dutifully admired the kitchen ("Great cupboards. Ooh, I love a wooden worktop. What's this? Coffee machine? Can you work it? Ha ha!") and the dining room ("Ooh, is that Ercol? I love those chairs. Did he put those doors in? I like the floor.") and we've stood on the patio to look at the garden ("It's bigger than I expected, as the actress said to the bishop. I like this tree. What's in that shed? Outside lav? Nice."), we go back in and upstairs to see the bedrooms.

"Ah, cute," she says about the box room. "How come you don't have the big bedroom?"

"I like the small room. The front bedroom's for guests. You're the first one," I tell her.

"Really?"

"Mm. Anyway, I think you should have everything you might need. There are hangers in the wardrobe. Everything in the bathroom is straightforward; the shower's not brilliant but it's okay."

She stands, hands on hips, and looks round the room. "This is a lovely room," she says. "The house is so nice. I can't believe you broke in." She shakes her head, pretending to be shocked.

"Yeah."

"And I really can't believe he let you stay."

"I know." I look away, tears pricking.

"I mean, you might've been anyone," she says, opening her suitcase and beginning to unpack her things.

"I know."

"He's lucky, though, I bet it would look shit if he lived here by himself."

I laugh at this. "I don't suppose it would. He'd probably have paid someone to sort it out for him."

"Is he rich? Nine grand for a rug! He must be."

"He sold a much bigger house. I'll show you a picture," I say, and get my phone out, looking for the article about the house he shared with Vanessa.

Noosha empties her case and shoves things into the chest of drawers, then slides the case behind the stumpy pink armchair we—Gethin—bought from the antiques center. We sit together on the bed while I scroll through articles. There's one here about the breakup and Winslade's new fella—I haven't seen that before. I'll have to remember to look at it later.

"Here you go." I pass her the phone. "That's his ex."

"Whoa. Do I recognize her? She looks really familiar . . . what's her name?"

I tell her, and explain about Vanessa's career.

"Yeah, maybe I saw her on *The One Show*. And this is where they lived? Bloody hell."

"Right?"

"Flip. I guess nine grand for a rug is par for the course."

"I dunno about that, but he can definitely afford it."

"Bloody hell, look at that kitchen."

"Yeah. He says it was shit, though."

"It doesn't look shit. I mean"—she widens her eyes at me—"not to my taste, darling, but even so."

"It's all a bit bland, isn't it."

"At least it's not *vulgar*."

"Ha. No, that's fair. Just a bit"—I shrug—"generic."

"Wow, though. You've fallen on your feet."

I don't know what to say to this, and anyway, we're interrupted by Gethin, who knocks on the open door and puts his head round. I imagine we're the picture of guilt, as Noosha presses my phone to her bosom so he can't see we've been prying into his life.

"Shall I put the kettle on, then? Or would you like a coffee?"

"Ooh, from the machine? I *would*," she says, "yes please."

"Are you coming down?"

"Yes, of course," I say, springing to my feet.

❧ ❦

Later, we eat a snacky sort of meal—cheese and salami, figs in prosciutto, good bread—sitting outside, as it's actually quite warm. Noosha asks Gethin a million questions about his job and his life generally, which he answers good-naturedly.

"You'll have to excuse me," she says, "I'm insatiably curious." She leans her elbows on the table and props her chin on her hands, batting her eyelashes at him.

He laughs. "I don't mind. As long as you answer my questions too."

"Ask away, darling. I'm an open book, unlike Secret Squirrel over there."

They both look at me, grinning.

"I'm not secretive," I complain. "I'm . . . discreet."

"I don't suppose you know anything about her at all," she says to him.

"She didn't tell me her surname for about six weeks," he confirms.

"Jessica! Really?"

I shake my head. Noosha laughs. "Oh my God. And you still let her live here?"

"I thought it didn't really matter what her name was." He smiles across at me.

"What did you do when you changed your mind, then? Fling into the front room and announce, 'It's Cavendish'? Drumroll playing on your phone?"

I laugh. "No, I felt like . . . well, when he said he thought he could get me a job, I had to tell him, really, so he could introduce me to Bruce. You can't really say 'Give my lodger a job—by the way, I don't know her surname.'"

"I would've given it a go," says Gethin, "but he'd have needed to know so he could pay you."

I nod. "I felt a bit guilty. But I was very . . . cautious . . . to begin with."

"She was," he agrees. "Every time I asked her anything, I could see her working out whether it was safe to answer. Mind you, can't blame her for that."

"No," says Noosha, and we all sit quietly for a moment. I know what they're thinking about and I'd rather they weren't. I need to distract them.

"I thought we might get the bus out to the Botanic Gardens tomorrow. The weather's supposed to be good. Or Aberglasney, maybe."

"The bus? God, how long does that take?" says Gethin.

"I don't know—forty-five minutes? I don't think it's too bad. Farther to Aberglasney, obviously. At least there *is* a bus."

"I can take you, if you like. I mean, if you don't object to my company. Or if you do, I could pick you up when you're done."

"Oh, but . . . that would be better. I mean, it would be easier, and it would be nice if you wanted to come too? But you really don't need to. Do you want to? Object to your company, seriously." I roll my eyes.

"I just want you to beg me to join you," he says, straight-faced.

"Ha ha. Seeing as how you'd be doing me another massive favor . . ."

"Hardly massive. Anyway, that's agreed, then."

"Have you got any other shoes?" I ask Noosha. "You might not want to wear those red ones to a garden."

"I've got some sparkly flip-flops."

"Of course you have. But yes, that would be better. Cool."

Gethin cuts a piece of very soft brie and balances it on a slice of sourdough. "What are you two doing this evening, then? Going out on the town?"

"Oh gosh, you don't want to go out, do you, Noosh? There's wine and cake and stuff here."

"I'm happy to do whatever you like. Is Caerwyddon a throbbing center of nightlife?"

"I think it's okay if you're young. There are loads of pubs. The girls at the restaurant always seem to enjoy themselves, or not enjoy themselves in a dramatic way that makes a good story."

"Ha. Do you go out at all?" Noosha looks from one of us to the other.

Gethin looks over at me. "We've been to the pub a few times, haven't we? I'm not that fussed really, but sometimes people have birthdays and stuff. I'm trying to reintegrate myself into what passes for society."

"Gethin's got loads of old school friends; they're always inviting him to things. And me too, sometimes. And I go out with Maura. You know, she was my boss at the restaurant. She's fun—you'd like her."

"Oh yes. That's nice, then. Making new friends? I know you love that," says Noosha.

"Yeah, I hadn't really thought about how I'd have to make an effort and everything. It's been, um, well . . . it could have been worse. Everyone's very kind."

"Yeah, they're all right," he says, "most of 'em. Anyway"— he looks at his phone to see what the time is—"I'd better get off. Told Abby I'd be there for six and it's five past already."

"Oh no, will you be in trouble?" I grin at him. "You can blame me."

"I reckon I can handle it without resorting to that. Have a good evening. I'll see you later."

Noosha waits until he's reversing the car out of the drive before she says, "And who's Abby?"

"His sister."

"Ah. Thought it might be his girlfriend."

"He hasn't got a girlfriend. I did tell you this."

"Yeah, but that was months ago—and why hasn't he got a girlfriend? Seriously, he's lovely."

I shrug, deliberately avoiding her eye. "It's not that long since he broke up with Vanessa."

"Oh, come on, when was it? Last year? Ages." She stabs at an olive. "So are you two banging or what?"

"Noosha—"

"Yeah, look, I'm good at subtext and undercurrents," she says. "He watches you the whole time. He made you blush twice."

"No, he didn't, what the hell—"

"Yes, he did. He's clearly not just your landlord."

"He's been very kind," I begin.

"Oh kind, schmind. And?"

"And nothing." I glare at her. "Don't make me wish you hadn't come."

"Oh, as if you ever would. I've improved your weekend, haven't I? Unless you two usually spend it in bed, in which case . . ."

"Look, can we . . . not . . . do this?"

"Why not? Tell Auntie Noosh all about it. What's the story, what's going on—the truth now."

"There's nothing to tell."

"Right. But you have slept with him?"

"I . . . no, it—"

"You're a terrible liar, always have been." She pops another olive into her mouth. "You may as well just tell me all about it. What have you got to lose?"

"I don't like telling people things."

"And that's worked well for you in the past, hasn't it?"

"This is hardly the same as—"

"Right, so you admit there's something to tell?"

I sigh irritably. "Okay, yes. But it was . . . not a mistake, but I decided that . . . it would be better if we behaved as though it happened ages ago. Like, years."

"And when did it happen?"

I explain about the party.

"Were you drunk?"

"No."

"Was he?"

"I . . . I don't think so. He said he wasn't."

"And how did he react when you said you should pretend it happened years ago?"

I shrug. "He was okay about it."

"What does that mean?"

"He agreed. I don't know. He's been fine with me, since, I mean. It hasn't made any difference. I don't think."

We sit in silence while Noosha thinks about this. I feel itchy and awkward. I meant not to tell her, which was naive. She always finds out about stuff. I don't really want her watching him for his reactions to anything, though; I don't want to feel self-conscious.

"He seems very nice," she says eventually. "I was worried, you know. When you first met him and everything."

"I know."

"But he seems genuinely . . . genuine."

"Yeah, he is. Yes."

"And it was . . . how was it? The sex?"

I shrug again, grumpily.

"Jess."

"Yes, okay, look, I was . . . worried I might not . . . ." I screw up my face, unwilling to cry, and blink at the sky until I can speak. "I thought there might be a problem. But there wasn't. It was . . . well. I enjoyed myself."

"So, that's good?"

"Yes. Yes, it was good, great, whatever."

"And . . ."

"And I was relieved, you know, that it was okay, because . . . but it was fine, completely fine."

"Well, that's good, isn't it?"

I nod.

"And . . ."

"The thing is," I say, rapidly, "the thing is, it's not fair, is it, on him, I mean. I'm not a normal person, I can't do normal things, I'm a bit broken, I'm scared, I can't be . . . even if he was interested in . . . anything, I'm not . . . there's no point to me."

"No point to you? Sweetie, whatever do you mean?"

"I wouldn't be able to . . . it's too risky. He's been very kind to me; I don't want to . . ."

"He seems to really like you."

"I think he does like me, yes, but that doesn't mean it would be okay for me to . . . try to be . . . I can't be anyone's girl-friend, Noosh, I can't. And it wouldn't . . . it's not fair to faff about, is it. It's better to go, look, thanks, that was nice, maybe not sensible, but pretending it was longer ago means it's safer, like we've got past it, and . . ."

"Yes, but . . ." She frowns. "I do get what you're saying, but . . . the thing is, it's not true, is it? It didn't really happen five years ago, so the idea of that . . . like, you're saying, if it was in the past, all the"—she waves a hand—"feelings . . . would have dissipated. Is that the right word?"

I nod, miserable.

"Yes, but they haven't, have they? Because it's not five years ago; it's, like, what? Five weeks?"

I nod again.

"So instead you're both pretending not to have feelings about it?"

I shrug again. "He might not be pretending."

"Oh my God."

"Well, it's true."

"Right," she says. "I'll monitor the situation and let you know the results before I leave."

"Please don't say anything to him."

She shakes her head. "What do you think I am? I won't say anything. Unless he brings it up." She grins at me, but I can't grin back; it makes me anxious. After a moment I guess she realizes this and leans to stroke my arm. "Don't worry, darling, I'm not going to screw this up for you."

"No, I—"

"And don't worry that you'll screw it up. I don't think you will."

I shake my head. "There's nothing to screw up."

❧ ❦

Now I'm nervous about leaving them together. It's certainly not beyond Noosha to sit Gethin down and interrogate him about all sorts of things. I really don't want that. The idea of them even vaguely talking about me gives me an anxious clenching in my belly. I lie awake worrying about it. Ironically, this means I wake later than usual, and when I get up, Noosha, resplendent in a very Doris Day–style yellow gingham housecoat, her hair tied up in a matching yellow scarf, is drinking coffee in the garden with Gethin, who is rather more soberly dressed.

It's another beautiful day, still fresh, the dew still on the grass. I stand awkwardly in the doorway.

"Hey," I say, "morning."

"Hello, sleepyhead," says Noosha. "I looked in at you but you had the duvet over your head so I didn't wake you."

"The duvet over your head? It was roasting last night. What are you even doing with a duvet? I had the fan on all night."

"She always sleeps like that." I watch her look sideways at him, judging his reaction.

"Not always," I object. "Were you too warm, Noosh? There's a fan in the cupboard in your room."

"I know, I found it," she says. "It was okay with the window open, anyway."

"Have you had breakfast?"

"No, just coffee. Gethin showed me how to work the machine and I grasped it instantly, so I guess that proves I'm better than you." She smirks at me.

"You *think* you've learned how to do it. But if you try in a couple of hours, you'll have forgotten. Guaranteed."

"Want me to make you one?" he asks.

"Oh, please, that would be lovely." I sit down and look at Noosha. "Been up long, then?"

"Half an hour or so. Don't panic," she adds, grinning. "We barely talked about you at all."

"Ugh."

Chapter Nineteen

It's Saturday. I ate my solitary lunch (Gethin's gone to his mum's) and then sat at the table, looking out at the rainy garden. It's windy, too, and the trees thrash. It's been raining all week, and in a fortnight it will be a year since I arrived here, a year since I got off the train and looked about and tried not to be terrified, and walked up through the town, where everything was strange and new, before setting off to find the cemetery.

∂ℓ ℓ∂

I suppose I might have dozed; I didn't hear Gethin come in, anyway, and when he says, "Jess, are you okay?," it makes me jump wildly.

"Oh, hey. Did you have a nice lunch? How's Marian?"

"Yeah, she's good, thanks. Are you okay? Did I wake you? Sitting in the dark." He comes over and sits beside me, the legs of his chair dragging across the parquet.

"It's not nearly dark yet," I object. "I was looking at the rain."

"Cheery."

"Yeah, well, I like rain," I tell him.

"Lucky. You'd be sick of it by now if you didn't. Seriously, though, what are you doing?"

I shrug and smile weakly at him. We sit in silence for a while. He clears his throat. "Are you okay?"

"I was feeling a bit . . . melancholy, you know."

"It's a melancholy kind of day," he says, looking past me to the window. He puts his hand on mine, very briefly. "I won't say don't be sad, because I'm not sure that's a helpful thing to say. But try not to be too sad. Is there anything I can do to cheer you up?"

"No, I don't think so. Thanks. I was just . . . I've made so many mistakes; I think I've wasted my life. And I tried so hard not to."

"Oh, but . . . you haven't, though."

I shrug.

"No, look . . . okay, so this is selfish, but you've made such a difference to me, to my life, that I can't accept that it's been anything like a waste, in any sense."

"Oh, come on. What bollocks."

This makes him laugh, but he's serious again immediately. "No. I'm being totally genuine. Honestly. You've made a huge difference. When we met, I was . . . I don't think I realized how lonely I was. I know I wasn't *alone,* but it's not the same thing, is it. It was such a long time since I'd had anyone to share things with. Or who'd usually understand what I was talking about. I've always felt like I don't have to explain myself to you, though. You know Vanessa didn't . . . I'm not saying, 'Oh, she didn't understand me,' like some kind of arse. She often did. But not about everything."

I don't say anything.

"And I'm not saying I couldn't have done any of this"—he gestures at the room—"without you; I know I could. But I wouldn't have enjoyed it."

"You might have done."

He shakes his head. "And maybe by now I'd be doing okay, but having your friendship made the first months I was here a positive experience, instead of a negative one, or even a neutral one."

"That's a nice thing to say." I smile at him. "But I don't really—"

"I mean, to be totally fair, I do find your inability to take a compliment extremely boring," he says. "Especially when I'm trying to tell you big serious truths."

"Hate big serious truths."

"Jess."

"Also I'm quite annoying?" We look at each other. "Were you lonely? Really?"

He nods. "I wouldn't have said so if you'd asked me though. Like I say, I didn't realize. To be honest, I haven't had much idea how I felt for about the last . . . five years?"

"Haven't you? Why not?"

"I'm a middle-aged man and I work with computers." He pulls a face. "No one would expect me to, would they? But since I moved here, I've . . . hopefully I'm improving myself. I know there are things I need to work on. I think I could have worked harder at my relationship. Which isn't to say I wish I had," he adds. "I think it was the right thing for both of us, that it ended. Perhaps if I'd paid more attention, we'd have split up earlier. That would have been just as good a result as if we'd been able to fix things."

I tilt my head, thinking. "It's good that you don't blame her or yourself anymore. I think you were doing both when I met you."

"You're probably right. I was a bit resentful. Although I'm not sure why."

"You said you were relieved, that it was over."

"I definitely was."

"I felt like we had that in common." I laugh. "Even if I was a bit sarcastic about it."

"Yeah, well, like I said, I know my relationship was very different from yours."

"It was good to be reminded that normal people can be unhappy too."

He grins at this. "Nice to know you think of me as a normal person."

"Ha ha."

"Anyway," he says, "I'm just reminding you that your existence is not pointless."

I sigh. I'm not convinced.

"Kate messaged," he says, changing the subject. "She thinks we'll like the new exhibition. Do you want to go to the private view?"

"I've never been to a private view," I say, briefly distracted.

"Well, it's just wine and standing about really, but I said we might."

"Did she invite us both?"

He looks at me, puzzled. "Yeah?"

"I mean, you're sure she didn't just invite you and you're assuming . . ."

He takes his phone from his pocket and reads from the screen: "'. . . and the PV's on Wednesday if you'd both like to come'—seems fairly clear to me."

I admit this and agree that I might like to go.

I've wondered, a couple of times, whether maybe Gethin has . . . unfinished feelings about Kate. Stirred up by meeting her again. She really is great—funny and clever and interesting, plus so attractive, and everything about her just a quarter turn off. I wouldn't ever use the word "quirky" in cold blood, but she is, a bit. Maybe I should ask him. I hesitate.

"Are you . . . in love with Kate?"

"What? God," he says, "no. No. Why would you ask that?"

"I just wondered. Not suggesting you'd do anything about it, if you were, or . . ."

"All that's a long time ago, those feelings. I mean, I'm really glad to have her as a friend, but . . . that's all."

"It's probably easier not to be," I agree. "It would be tedious to be unrequited about someone you used to go out with."

"It massively would. It's bad enough anyway."

"What is?"

"Being unrequited." He stares out at the rainy afternoon. "It basically sucks, doesn't it."

"Yeah, it always seems—it's annoying, isn't it? Although I don't know—some of the people I've felt unrequited about might have been crushes. I'm not sure that's the same thing."

"No," he says. "I don't think it is."

"I suppose sometimes you don't know people well enough for it to be more than a crush. Like, if you got to go out with them, you'd go, 'Oh, ha ha, what was I thinking.' There was a man I used to work with, at the library—I had quite a thing about him." I shake my head, amused at this thought. "But I never did anything about it."

"Do you regret that?"

"Only when I'm feeling melancholy." I smile at him. "You

know, when you pick through your life for places where you could have made a different choice or decision and things might be . . . better."

"What would you want, then, if things were different?"

I look back out of the window, the branches of the trees buffeted by the wind. "Just to be safe," I say, "just to be safe."

"You're safe now," he says.

I shake my head. "I never will be."

"Jess . . ."

"It's okay, I'm used to it."

Chapter Twenty

Gethin's bought a PlayStation. He plays and I watch, making helpful suggestions. As it's a Saturday, and neither of us is going out, and it's been raining all day, we've mostly eaten popcorn, lying on the sofa, while he improves his archery stats and I say things like "Watch out! On the left!" It reminds me of my twenties, when I lived for a while with a couple of lads who played lots of *Micro Machines* on the Nintendo. I didn't play it myself—there's really no point playing something for the first time with people who've obsessively played it for months—but I didn't mind watching. This is more fun, though, because the games Gethin plays have more narrative and also, have you seen video games recently? They really do look amazing.

We slump on the two angles of the sofa, which keeps us usefully far apart and makes all these comfortable intimacies seem perfectly safe and reasonable. The curtains are drawn, the lamps are lit, and I'm shoveling popcorn into my mouth and squealing every time a dragon attacks. When the doorbell rings, Gethin, busy fighting fireball-flinging mages, says, "Who the hell can that be?," without looking away from the screen. I can't imagine. People don't pop round, really—you generally get a message if anyone's thinking of calling in. I get up, brush crumbs from my jeans, and head out to the hallway.

When I open the door, there's a woman on the path with her back to me. Hearing the door open, she swings round to face me and frowns.

"Oh," she says. "Who are you? Have I got the wrong house?"

I look at her for a moment. I think . . . is it Vanessa? She looks a bit different from the pictures I've seen, but that might be because she's wearing normal clothes and has (presumably) done her own makeup. Behind her, parked on the street, there's a very shiny car, all curvy lines—a sports car of some kind.

"I don't know. Who did you want?"

"I'm looking for Gethin? Gethin Thomas?"

"Oh, right. Yeah, no, this is the right place. Come in?"

She frowns again. "Who are you, then?"

I step backward to make room for her. She smells expensive, a waft of perfume and . . . I don't know, hair product? Her hair is amazing, like an advert.

"I'm Jess," I say. "Who are you?"

"I'm Vanessa, of course."

As I thought. ("Of course"? All right, madam.)

"He's in the sitting room," I say. "First door on the left."

I follow her into the room, in time to see Gethin, still not looking up, say, "Who was it, then?" before he realizes there are two of us and takes his eyes off the screen. I won't say he jumps, exactly, but he does jerk in surprise, dropping the controller.

"Bloody hell," he says. "Hello, Van, what are you doing here?"

I walk past her and stoop to pick up the controller, pausing the game.

"I came to see Mum. Thought I'd pop in, like. How are you?" She's looking round the room, taking in the furnishings, the art, the bookshelves. Then she looks back at me, clearly puzzled.

"Shall I put the kettle on?" I offer.

"Oh, hey, would you mind?" He looks rather shell-shocked.

"What can I get you?" I ask her.

"Oh—coffee'd be great, thanks. Have you got soy milk?"

"I'm afraid we don't, no."

"Oh, well, dairy's fine. No sugar."

I go out to the kitchen and fill the kettle. No chance I'll be able to hear what they're saying, which is a shame. I wonder if I've always been this nosy. I suppose I probably have.

I put two mugs on a tray and make coffee. I guess I should take their drinks through and then retreat, even though I have every right to be in the sitting room and would clearly love to know what they're talking about.

❧ ❦

I carry the tray cautiously into the room, where Gethin and Vanessa are sitting, tensely, with her in the armchair nearest the door. I place the tray on the coffee table, gather up evidence of debauchery—almost empty popcorn bowl, three empty glasses, packet of Tunnock's tea cakes—and whisk back out of the room.

I stand for a while in the kitchen, and then go into the dining room, where I curl up on the new green velvet sofa and scroll through Facebook on my phone. I've started posting again, occasionally, since Noosha was here, interacting with some of my other friends. It's hard to grasp that I've been in Wales for a year.

I've tightened and reduced my virtual social circle, checking everyone's mutuals. I don't blame people if they still want to be friends with Mitch—I know Facebook friend does not equal actual friend. And anyway, if you don't know anything about what happened, why would you care about this? I doubt any of them has ever seen him lose his temper.

Speaking of temper, I'm startled out of my perusal of social media by the slamming of the front door, which echoes through the house in a much louder way than usual. I look up as Gethin appears in the room.

"Jesus Christ," he says.

"Are you okay?" He's pacing, hands pressed to his head. "What did she want?"

"I don't know. Some kind of . . . I don't know."

I wait. He pulls a chair out from the table and sits down heavily. "Flipping heck," he says.

I'm not sure what to say, so I don't say anything.

"God," he says. "I don't even know why this has upset me so much. I don't care, I haven't cared for ages, I'm not . . . it's not like she broke my heart or anything."

"Well . . ."

"She really didn't, though. I don't know why I'm so angry."

"Are you angry?" He doesn't look it. I've never seen him angry.

"I'm furious," he says, and laughs.

"So what did she want?"

"I don't know. To tell me how much better her life is now?"

"Is it?"

"Apparently."

"That's nice, then."

"I mean, it is—I'd rather she was happy, God knows I'm loads happier now, even if . . . but anyway, that's . . ."

"So her boyfriend's left his wife, then? Are they living together?"

"They're getting married."

"Wow, really? Okay." I think about this for a moment. "And . . ."

"I don't care, I'm just . . . I think I'm angry that she thought I would care. Like she was—and she'd definitely deny this—but a whole thing about how it's all going brilliantly?"

I nod.

"And I was like, things are pretty great here actually, Vanessa . . ."

I nod again.

"And she . . . I mean, this is the whole point, isn't it? I didn't want to live in a stupid big house with loads of money and no . . . love. I'd much rather be here."

"In a perfectly reasonable-sized house with extremely adequate levels of money and no love?" I raise my eyebrows.

"Yeah, I know my life isn't difficult. But anyway, it's loads better. I mean, I wish there was some love," he says, "but it's not going to kill me."

"No, and that won't last forever, will it. You'll meet someone, of course you will. If that's a thing you . . ."

"Yeah, anyway. It's not even about that. Why am I so angry?"

I shake my head. "I don't know."

"It's like . . ."

I prop my chin on my hand and watch him wrestle with this, whatever it is.

"It's like she assumes I'm miserable about it? Like, how

could I not be, you know? I've lost everything. Even though I bloody haven't."

I laugh at this. "She probably wanted to reassure herself. Maybe it's not as great as she's pretending."

"Ugh. Maybe. I mean, yes. Perhaps you're right. I don't even know why she thought I'd be interested, and you know, if I *was* brokenhearted, her skipping round here to flash her engagement ring at me wouldn't help, would it? In fact, it's a horrible thing to do."

"Why didn't you get married?" I've wondered this before, because most people do get married, even the ones you don't expect.

"I don't know, really. I'm not that bothered, and I didn't think she was. People usually tell you, don't they? If they want to?"

I shrug.

"You didn't marry that man, did you?"

"Which one?"

"The . . . the last one."

"Ha. No. He was still married to someone else. Luckily." I stretch.

"You wouldn't have married him, though?" He looks faintly worried.

"Probably not? I'd like to think I definitely wouldn't. I've never married anyone else, after all. And Johnny did ask me— more than once, actually."

"Did he?"

I nod. "He was quite romantic, especially if he'd had a good day, or was slightly . . . you know."

"Why didn't you?"

"I think . . . the thing about Johnny is, he's really flaky. Plus,

I told you about where we lived. That would never have improved. I think I always felt he was unreliable, which is a bit unfair now that I look back. He never actually did anything to make me think that. Except not have a proper job and so on." I pull a face. "Which I realize is a strange thing for me, of all people, to say."

"He made you live in a house with no heating."

I shrug again. "I dunno if that counts as 'unreliable.' In the end, though, he did sleep with someone else, so I suppose I was right, really. Although he was a lot more reliable than Mitchell. Mind you, everyone is. Anyway," I say, aware that I've said too much, and pushing everything back behind the locked door in my brain. "So, she's getting married?"

"Yeah. Next summer."

"Is he divorced now, then?"

"I didn't ask."

"Hm." I don't know why, but I'm still dubious about this, which is odd, considering I don't know her, or care, and I don't even know what her boyfriend's name is.

Gethin's phone rings, and he stands up and takes it from his pocket.

"God," he says, "why do people always want to speak to you?" He closes his eyes, breathes deeply, and then answers the call. "All right, Mike, how are you?"

I laugh and head for the front room. He follows me, continuing his conversation.

"I wasn't going to, no. No, playing on the PlayStation. No. Yeah, she . . . no."

I sit down on the sofa and check the time. How can it be nearly half six? I really don't know where the day's gone.

"Yeah, no, to be honest I . . . yeah, Vanessa was just here, it's freaked me right out." He laughs. "Yeah, right? I don't know. Anyway, I . . ."

I lean to pick up the controller and un-pause the game, saving it in case he doesn't want to play anymore.

"Yeah, I doubt that will help. Seriously." He laughs again. "No. Well . . . maybe. Could do, I suppose. Just for a couple, like. Yeah? Okay. Yeah, I'll ask her. All right, then, see you in a bit."

He finishes the call and looks across at me. "Want to go for a drink? I'm going to meet Mike."

"Oh, no," I say, "no, thank you."

I've seen Mike a couple of times since the party—he came round and watched a film once, and another time he and a couple of other people came for drinks. The second time he asked me for my phone number, which I thought must be evidence of some kind of drought in his sex life. I didn't give it to him, anyway.

"Sure?"

I shake my head. "I'd rather stay in. Thank you."

⁂

At half past nine, I go to bed. I'm tired, even though I haven't done anything today. I read my book for a bit, but I feel strangely restless. I think about a conversation Gethin and I had recently, about happiness and contentment, and how it's nice to be happy—properly, noticeably happy—but being content is just as good, or I think it is, anyway.

I know things will change—things always change; there's nothing you can do about that, and you shouldn't want to, not really—so I'm trying hard to enjoy every day, to pay attention. To be grateful, like they say. I am grateful. Actually, in some ways, that might be a problem. As we progress further and further from my old life, I wonder if it's this gratefulness that is preventing something else, something we could be doing.

Although Gethin is very careful never to do or say anything about what happened before, I'm pretty sure he thinks about it. As I do myself. I wonder how things would change if we did it again. If we did, it would be harder to pretend none of this matters. I still think I did the right thing, though—I don't think I'm quite where I'd need to be, to live here and have a convenient and enjoyable . . . whatever it would be. I mean, we are both adults, and we could talk about it, and make agreements, about levels of closeness, about . . . romance. But it would get complicated, wouldn't it.

❧ ❧

I'm awake, suddenly, heart thudding. I'm confused about where I am for a moment, and what time it is—half twelve, apparently—and by what woke me. Then I hear the second door close and realize it must have been the front door. Gethin's back, then—his "couple of drinks" turning, like they do, into several, or even loads.

I relax, and then I hear laughter, and I'm tense again, because that wasn't him laughing. He must have brought someone with him, and it certainly wasn't Mike. That was a woman's laugh. I can hear voices, muffled, more laughter. Who can it be? He's never brought anyone home after the pub, ever.

I listen, hearing footsteps, the tap in the kitchen, voices.

The stairs creak, and someone makes a hushing sound. I lie there, rigid. He's brought someone home and now they're going to bed.

I don't know why it's never occurred to me that this might happen.

Voices on the landing, and then his bedroom door closes. I try very hard not to imagine him and this unknown other person fumbling with each other's clothes. I stare at the ceiling, fists clenched, trying not to listen. Will I hear them? The bed, at least, surely. I think of other times I've had to listen to people having sex. I think of the people next door, when I was first at university (luckily none of my housemates ever got laid), and then my flatmate in third year. I had to play tapes (tapes! Good Lord) quite loudly to drown her out.

A faint rhythmic squeaking penetrates (poor choice of words) my bedroom door.

I can't believe how upset I am. I'm horrified, sick with jealousy, furious with myself. This is entirely self-induced. It's my own fault I never thought of it; it's my own fault I'm so completely stupid.

I can hear her, now. Did I make noises like that? I used to be quite loud, in bed. I can't remember if I was noisy when Gethin and I slept together. Perhaps? I remember him saying things, but I don't think he was loud. I wonder what he's saying to her, now.

What if he likes her, properly likes her, and then she's here all the time? I put my hands over my ears so I can't hear her. What if she's nice? She might be. I don't have any objection to people having sex the night they meet. And it might not be the first time they've met. It might not even be the first time they've had sex. I don't know everything he does, after all.

If he had a girlfriend, could I live here? More important, would he *want* me to? I think the answer to both questions is no, to be honest.

Why has it never occurred to me that this might happen?

In the morning, I wake up feeling rubbish—hungover, almost. That's down to not getting enough sleep, and fretting. It's half eight. I open my bedroom door and listen carefully. I can't hear anything. I go downstairs to make coffee and find the kettle's hot, the back door open. I can smell something sweet, like cotton candy. I peer out cautiously and see her, wearing a shirt of Gethin's (she must be freezing) and no shoes, standing on the edge of the patio, blowing scented smoke upward at the gray sky. She hears me and turns round. I suppose I shouldn't be surprised that she looks a bit like Vanessa, same glossy dark shoulder-length hair and careful eyebrows. She's a lot younger, though. Late twenties? Early thirties? Huh. Her eyeliner must be industrial strength as it's not even vaguely come adrift, although she's taken her eyelashes off—I can see the white line from where they were applied before the eyeliner went on. Glamorous, is how I'd describe her, even when standing in a suburban garden wearing nothing but a shirt.

"Oh, hey," she says, "all right?"

"Uh, yes. Hi." I gesture vaguely. "You've got a coffee, then?"

"Yeah, cheers. He said I could help myself, like. Came down for a smoke."

I nod, helplessly.

"I'm Charlotte," she says. "I'm sorry, he did tell me your name, but I've forgotten."

"Jess," I manage. "I'm Jess."

She rubs her arms. "Chilly out here." I back into the kitchen to make room for her. "Brr," she says, "proper autumn now, isn't it."

"It is." I turn back to the kettle, which has boiled again, and make my own coffee in the smallest French press. "Did you want some toast or anything?" I ask her, although I can't really see that it's my job to get her breakfasted.

"God, no." She pulls a face. "Too early for me." She sips her coffee, watching me. I don't really understand why she's still here and hasn't buggered off back upstairs. I can't think of anything to say to her, and it seems very odd that there's an almost naked woman in my kitchen.

Not that it's my kitchen.

"Right," she says, "I'll make him one, shall I? How does he take it?"

"Milk, no sugar," I tell her, putting the lid on the butter dish and picking up my plate and mug. I'd usually eat my breakfast at the table, or on the sofa, but I think today I'll hide in my room. Unless it looks like they're going to spend the day in bed, in which case I might cycle down to the footbridge and throw myself into the river.

I don't mean that, obviously.

I think I'd better find somewhere else to live.

I turn on the laptop—yeah, I guess I need to buy a laptop; this is going to be expensive, isn't it—and eat toast with one hand while I scroll through SpareRoom and Gumtree with the other. There are lots of big Victorian houses here, with five or six bedrooms, but I'm not sure I can handle that. I'm pretty old to be house-sharing. I'd be better off somewhere smaller, or maybe I can find someone else who needs a lodger. Next time I'll keep to myself. Which will be easier, because I do have some friends now, and won't accidentally find myself hanging out with my landlord. Or stupidly sleeping with them.

I find a couple of places that don't look too awful and send messages. Then I text Maura and ask if she knows of anyone who might want to rent me a room.

Are you okay? What's happened? she texts me back.

> *Oh, nothing, I'm fine. I just think I should think about finding somewhere else.*

I thought you liked living there?

> *I do.*

So?

> *So yeah, but Gethin won't always want me here, and I've been thinking about how I should get ahead of that.*

Have you fallen out?

> *No, of course not.*

Really?

I try to imagine what we might actually fall out about.

> *Really. But if you could ask around?*

Okay, I will. But phone me if you want to, yeah?

> *Okay.*

And we'll have to go out soon.

> *Okay.*

❧ ❧

Later, I call Noosha. I mean to tell her about all this, but instead she has stuff to tell me about her kids and her dad, who's not well, and what's going on with her new bathroom, which Nathan's brother is putting in with a certain lack of efficiency.

Then it's time for lunch and she's off to eat roast potatoes. I hang up and wonder if I should call Lizzie. Then I wonder what I should have for my own lunch. Gethin went out about an hour ago, giving Charlotte a lift home, I suppose. I'm not sure what to do with myself at all, and then I remember that there's a bag of daffodil bulbs in the garage, along with some alliums. They need to be planted, even if I won't get to see them come up.

Shit.

It doesn't matter, though. It's like when I stripped the wallpaper even though I wasn't sure I was going to stay. It's a task that needs doing, so I'll do it.

It's not so cold now, although it's still pretty gray. I arrange my bulbs and then dig holes for them. I feel better. I hack holes in the lawn around the fruit trees, then peel back some turf at the end of the garden and scatter the exposed earth with snowdrop bulbs. I climb back up the steps and arrange a wide swathe of fritillaries, and then cut spaces for them in the grass. It's quite tiring, and the trowel gives me a blister on my palm. It's satisfying, though, and I think it will look wonderful. I wonder if I'll be able to come and look at it, in the spring. I sit back on my haunches and stare up at the sky.

❧ ❧

It's half past one. Gethin's not home, and I wonder if he's at Charlotte's house, and what they're doing if he is. I scrub my hands clean and then go and change my muddy leggings. I get a message from him.

Hey. I'm in town. Do you want to come and have lunch? I thought we could go to Cenhinen Bedr.

I regard this for some time. Does "we" mean him and me, or what?

Who's "we"?

Us. You and me.

This is something I'm supposed to be avoiding, now, isn't it? I can't though.

Okay. What time?

Well, if you leave now—twenty minutes? Or are you busy?

Ha. No. All right. See you in twenty minutes.

I comb my hair and put on some mascara, frowning at myself in the bathroom mirror. I get changed again, this time into a long skirt and a linen shirt. It's still just about sandal weather—or possibly it isn't, but I like to hang on as long as possible—but it's really not very warm, so I find a jacket, and then pick up my bag and leave the house to hurry down the hill and into town.

Maura's working, and I wish I'd thought to tell her not to mention to Gethin that I'm looking for somewhere else to live. She probably wouldn't have though, would she? She hugs me hello and points over to the corner, where he's reading the paper. He looks up as I walk over, and, as always, his smile of recognition warms me.

"Hello," he says, as I pull out my chair and sit down. "I thought I'd left it too late to cook or anything. You hadn't eaten?"

I shake my head and look at the menu. Alys comes over to take my drink order, and we have a chat about how she is and how the kitten—a recent arrival with its own social media presence—is doing. I wonder if I should mention Charlotte, and what I should say. But really, there's no reason to be shy about it.

"Where've you been, then?" I ask. "Did you take that girl home? Woman, rather?"

"Yeah, I gave her a lift," he says, eyes on his menu. "Then I went to see my mum."

"Oh, right. She okay?"

"Yeah, she's good, says hello."

I try to decide whether I should have hummus or avocado.

"Are you going to see her again?"

His eyes flick up from the menu for a moment. "What, my mum? Should think so, yeah."

"Ha ha. You're funny."

His mouth twitches. "Ah, d'you think? Nice of you to say so."

"And?"

"And?"

Alys brings my lemonade and asks if we're ready to order. I ask for the flatbread and hummus with pomegranate, and he orders a Reuben sandwich.

"Gethin."

"What?"

"Charlotte. Are you going to see her again?"

"I should think that's very unlikely." He pours water into his glass. "Why?"

"I just wondered."

"Yeah, it's not really my style, picking people up."

"That doesn't mean you can't see someone again."

"I don't think we had much in common, to be honest."

"And again . . ."

"Someone put Nirvana on the jukebox," he says. "I told her my Kurt Cobain story. She said, 'Oh yeah, my dad loves Nirvana!'"

"Pfft. He probably does." I grin at him.

"Yeah, I'm sure he does, but it made me feel pretty old."

"It's not you being old, is it. It's her being young," I say, amused.

"Yes. So, that's not better. She's like fifteen years younger than me."

"Congratulations."

He looks at me. "It's not . . . yeah, okay, so . . . I'm not sure what was in it for her, but she was definitely up for it."

"I'm not suggesting she wasn't."

"I mean, it is weird, isn't it."

I shrug.

"I'm not really . . ."

"I'm not trying to make you feel bad," I say, although that is slightly mendacious.

"Hm."

Our food arrives, and for a while we're busy eating.

Something else occurs to me. "Did Mike pull as well, then?"

"Oh, yeah. It's kind of his thing, isn't it. In fact, I'm pretty sure if I'd gone out with anyone else it wouldn't have happened. He got talking to her mate."

"Ah, right."

"It was probably some awful joke for them."

"What, like, 'I bet we could shag those old guys'?" I try to keep a straight face.

He nods, chewing.

"Well," I say, tired of the subject, "she seemed perfectly nice."

"Oh, I'm sure she is. Just . . . you know. I don't . . ." He frowns at me. "I don't usually . . . one-night stands are not my thing." He sighs. "Although clearly that's what I get, at the moment."

Chapter Twenty-one

After work on Monday, I go to look at the rooms. The first one is much smaller than it looked on the website, and the kitchen is . . . grotty. The second one is in a house where all the other inhabitants are men in their twenties, and—although they seem nice enough, or reasonably okay, anyway, the two I met—I can see they no more want to live with a forty-six-year-old woman than she wants to live with them. I walk home and look at the websites again. I can't see anything that looks any better, and I try not to worry. There isn't actually any rush, after all. And if there is, it's only that, having decided, I know I should go as soon as I can, before I sink back into the easy comfort of my life here.

On Tuesday evening I get a message from Maura.

Friend of my aunt's is looking for a lodger. She lives in one of those big houses up Springwell Road.

Really?

Yeah, do you want her number?

Yes please.

She texts the number, and her aunt's friend's name, Bea, and I ring immediately.

The woman who answers the phone sounds efficient and friendly, and I arrange to go round at once. Gethin's not home yet, so I don't have to tell him where I'm going. Not that I have to tell him anyway. I get my bike out of the garage and cycle off through a thin drizzle. Springwell Road starts in town, but it soon gives way to almost country, with fields on one side of the road and some large double-fronted Victorian houses on the other, hiding behind discreet hedges, some of them with their backs turned to the road, looking out over the town. The one I'm looking for is called Pen y Bryn, and I peer at gateposts as I cycle up the hill. After a bit it's too steep for me, and I have to get off and push my bike. And here we are: a big oak tree, a sweep of drive, beautiful borders, even now, at the end of the season, and a large—very large—double-fronted detached house with a central porch ornamented with pierced wood and a pointy finial. The name of the house adorns the glass above the front door in curly gold writing. The house is not as well presented as the garden—as I lean my bike against the wall behind the bins, I see peeling paint and a broken downspout.

The doorbell is a ceramic button that says PRESS, so I press it. I wonder if it works. It's a big house; I wonder how long it would take to get to the front door if you were upstairs, at the back. Or even in the kitchen. Built for a doctor, perhaps, or some other moderately important Victorian, big enough for a servant or two as well as a large family.

Eventually the door is opened by a small, round woman of maybe seventy. She has short gray hair, very blue eyes, and is wearing jeans and a bright red shirt.

"Hi, I'm Jess. We spoke on the phone just now."

"Hello, Jess! Come in, come in."

I follow her down the hallway, which, like Kate's house, has lovely original encaustic tiles on the floor. That's about the only resemblance, however; whereas Kate's house is all soothing shades of white, Pen y Bryn is busier, with bright green anaglypta beneath the dado, and broad stripes of blue and white painted on the wall above the rail, where it's visible between the many, many paintings. The kitchen is equally bright, with red and white gingham curtains, bright yellow cupboards, and a huge mural—expressionist blossoms—on one wall.

She offers me a cup of tea, and we sit at a very battered pine table to drink it.

"You're a friend of Maura's, then," she says. She smiles at me. "I've known Maura since she was a little girl."

"Yes, I used to work for her, at the restaurant," I explain, "when I first moved here."

"And where do you live at the moment?"

I tell her about Sunnyside.

"Oh yes, I know those houses. So why do you want to leave? It sounds lovely."

For a moment I'm tempted to just say it. *I think I'm in love with my landlord and I know he likes me too but for some reason I can't fix this in my head and . . .*

"I think the guy I live with—my landlord—well, I don't want to live there when he meets someone. I mean, that probably sounds weird. Um. The thing is, once he gets a new girlfriend, it will be awkward, and I'd rather get ahead of that."

She looks at me.

"And . . . he's been really kind and helpful, but I'd like to move ahead on my own."

That sounds better, I think.

She drains her mug and stands up, saying, "Come and see the room. It has its own entrance, so we'll go outside and I'll take you round."

I finish my own tea and follow her back down the corridor and out of the front door. She turns left and walks to a tall wrought iron gate in a beech hedge. She pushes it open with a squeal of complaining hinges.

"There," she says. "I keep meaning to bring the WD-40 but I never remember."

We walk down the side of the house. There's a one-story, flat-roofed extension in front of us, with a shiny red front door, which she opens.

"This was my husband's studio," she says, "hence the sky-light."

It's a large, bright, rectangular room, with paint-spattered quarry tiles on the floor and a huge, floor-to-ceiling window taking up the whole wall at the far end, looking out onto the back garden. Thick, heavy curtains swirl at each side of the window; there's a squat wood-burning stove with a shiny steel chimney, a double bed against one wall, a large chest of draw-ers, an elderly armchair, a Formica-topped drop leaf table, a pair of kitchen chairs and two kitchen units with a sink, a shelf above, and a tabletop oven with a two-ring hotplate. There's a smaller, rectangular window in that wall, too high to see out of. A door leads into a tiny bathroom with a shower.

"This door"—she moves a curtain by the bed—"goes through to the house. It's locked; there are bolts on this side. I'll give you the key though, and you can come through to the house if you want. There's no fridge out here, but you can use mine. And you're welcome to use the kitchen whenever you like."

"I didn't realize it was an annex." I look round curiously, trying to imagine myself living here.

"Yes. And I won't say it's cozy exactly—but it's not too bad with the burner going."

"Your husband was an artist?"

"Yes, he painted, mostly, did a bit of sculpture. He died nearly ten years ago."

"I'm sorry." I consider the room. It's a lot better than I'd imagined. I can see it might be cold, but it's not winter all year. And the garden!

I head for the window. "How beautiful," I say. There's a wide terrace in York stone, and then a joyful explosion of late autumn color and mature trees.

"That's my passion," says Bea.

"It looks wonderful."

"This opens," she says, sliding open the window and stepping out onto the terrace. "You're welcome to sit in the garden. I mean, when the weather's suitable."

"It all looks great. Yes. I'd like to live here, if you'd like to have me. Are you seeing anyone else?"

She shakes her head. "A girl came up yesterday, but it's too far from where she works. When would you like to move in?"

"As soon as possible. Next weekend?"

"Okay, that's fine."

We discuss details like deposit and rent, and then I cycle home in the dark.

❧ ❧

"Oh, hey," says Gethin, as I open the back door. "Wondered where you were. Is it raining?"

"A bit, yeah."

"Been out on your bike?"

"Yeah. What are you making?"

"I thought risotto. I've prepped everything like on the telly." He shows me a dish of finely chopped onion.

"Nice."

"Do you want some?"

I nod. "Yes, please."

"What have you been up to, then?" he says. I take off my jacket and carry it through to drip in the hallway.

"Tell you later," I say, ignoring the clutching anxiety in my belly. I go into the dining room and set the table. It seems like a meal we should eat at the table. Surely telling him won't be too bad. He doesn't need my rent, after all. The three hundred pounds a month I pay him is money for sweets, essentially.

I go to stand in the doorway of the kitchen, watching him stir the rice. Risotto is one of his favorite things to make. I taught him that. I suppose our relationship's not entirely one-sided.

❧ ☙

"Where'd you go, then?" he asks, as we eat our dinner. "Bit miserable for a bike ride."

"Yeah, it's not great out there," I agree. "I went to look at a room."

"A room? What d'you mean?"

"Um. I've been thinking, and it seems like maybe I should find somewhere else to live."

He stops eating. "What?"

"I'm . . . the thing is," I say, "at some point, you know, you'll meet someone, and then you won't want me here, and I'd rather go now than wait for that to happen, and . . ."

"What the hell are you talking about?"

I blink at him, uneasy. "You know I'm . . . you've been so kind, and helped me so much, and I don't want you ever to wish I wasn't here, so I thought, you know, if I go now, then . . ."

"What's this about? I don't understand."

"You don't need a lodger, do you? I mean, financially. And when you bought this house you thought you'd be living in it by yourself. And I'll never not be incredibly grateful for everything you've ever done for me. I just think . . . it seems like it's time for me to do stuff on my own. For myself."

"That's all bollocks," he says. "I don't want to live on my own. I like living with you."

"Well, yes, but . . ."

"There aren't any buts, Jess."

"I'm in the way of your life."

"No, you're not. Is this about the weekend? About . . ." He waves his spoon. "Is this about Charlotte?"

"No, it's . . ."

"Because you know I didn't expect that to happen, and it won't happen again."

"Yes, but . . . you're perfectly entitled to bring someone home, of course you are. And I am, I suppose, I mean if I wanted to, which I wouldn't, but anyway, the thing is, she might be personally irrelevant, but she's . . . representatively"— I frown; I'm not sure that's a word—"significant."

"What? You're talking nonsense."

"I'm not. I'm just saying, when you get a girlfriend, you won't want a random woman in your box room."

"No, I wouldn't want that," he says, "but you're not a random woman, are you."

"I very much am, though. Anyway, when you said I could stay, and asked me to deal with the woodchip, you weren't expecting me to still be here ten months later, surely."

He frowns. "I didn't expect anything. I didn't know what would happen or how it would be."

"It's been . . . good." I blink hard, determined not to cry. "But it's time for me to go."

"But why? I don't understand. Seriously, Jess . . ."

"You've given me loads of things," I say. "More than I could ever have expected. Time, to sort myself out, and somewhere to stay, and things to do. You've introduced me to your friends, and got me a better job, and taken me about to see the countryside, and let me make plans for your garden, and I could never have imagined any of that. And I don't want to spoil it by staying when I should leave."

There's a long, intense silence.

"Please don't leave," he says.

"Yes, I have to, because I'm . . . I don't want to get too attached, you see, to the house, and everything, because then when you want me to go, it will be much worse. Much worse." I stare at the tablecloth, unable to look at him.

"So you're leaving because you think I'll want you to leave at some hypothetical future point?"

"But you will. Say you meet someone and want her to move in . . ."

"Jess, this person doesn't exist."

"She does. You just haven't met her yet."

"This conversation is ridiculous. I don't know why you think . . . look, I'm sorry I slept with that girl—"

"You don't need to apologize; it's not about that, it's none of my business. I don't . . . care what you do; you can do what you like. And we can still . . . if you want . . . we can have lunch, and . . . you know, visit places, and . . . be friends. If you want? But I have to . . . I can't stay. I feel like a parasite."

"Jesus Christ."

"Well, I do, and I don't like it. I need to be in charge of myself."

"How are you not in charge of yourself now? You pay rent, you do loads of stuff in the house, we . . . uh . . . we have a nice time, don't we? I thought you liked it. I thought you were"—he blinks at me, clenches his jaw—"not unhappy."

"I'm not. I'm just . . . anyway, this is pointless. I've found somewhere to go, and I'm going."

"Great," he says. He stands up. "Great, well, I hope it all works out for you." He picks up his bowl, still half full of risotto, and goes out to the kitchen. I sit and look at my own bowl, from which I've eaten maybe a spoonful. That went a lot worse than I was expecting.

Chapter Twenty-two

I pack my things. I have my rucksack, a big blue IKEA bag, and a large cardboard box. Luckily my sewing machine has a handle, since it doesn't have a case. I own three times as much stuff as I did when I arrived, but it's still not much.

I think Gethin isn't speaking to me, but as I'm avoiding him, I might be wrong. I haven't told him when I'm leaving; it feels strangely melodramatic to go down to the sitting room and announce it. I thought about messaging him, but that felt even stranger. So I've done nothing. On the remaining evenings of the week, I sit in my bedroom or go out, walking endlessly. I buy a memory stick in town and transfer my stuff from the borrowed laptop. I buy myself some towels and bedding from one of the discount shops. I eat toast for my tea before he gets home from work.

I'm quite miserable.

On Saturday morning I get up very early and call a taxi to take my things to Bea's. Then I'll walk back and pick up my bike. I've started to worry that I won't see Gethin at all before I leave, which would be . . . well, it would be rude, if nothing else. I've ordered some flowers—men never get flowers, do they, which seems harsh—so I need to be in for when they're delivered.

When I get back to the house, the car is gone. I wonder where he is. I could text him, but somehow that seems impossible. I check that I've got everything, strip my bed, and then pace, nervously, waiting for the flowers. When they arrive, I arrange them in a jug on the dining room table and sit down to write him a note.

Dear Gethin

It feels like years since I read the note you wrote me back in November, standing in the garden and horribly frightened that I'd lost all my things and would have nowhere to sleep. I was so surprised—and suspicious, I admit—to read what you had to say. I don't think I've ever met anyone else who would offer their home so generously. I'll never be able to explain exactly how grateful I am for that, and for all your kindnesses. I really hope you've never regretted the impulse to help me. I think I've failed to explain why I have to leave, and I'm truly sorry if I've hurt your feelings. I would never want to do that. I'm sorry I can't explain myself properly, or express myself in a satisfactory way. I've loved living here, and so enjoyed the time we've spent together.

I pause here, and think for a long time about what I'm trying to say.

I'd like it if we could be friends, but I completely understand if you don't want that. I wish I could have seen you before I left, but I don't know where you've gone or when you'll be back.

Yours

Jess

A large and unexpected tear drops onto the paper at this point, which is embarrassing and melodramatic. I press my sleeve against it and then fold the paper in half and write his name on it. I prop this against the jug, put the laptop neatly on the sideboard with my keys, and write my new address on a Post-it Note, which I stick to the bulletin board. I look for a long time at the photograph of the pair of us, soaking wet from the storm. Then, after standing for a moment in the sitting room, looking blindly at the things I chose and helped to arrange, I leave the house. The sound of the door closing behind me is rather final. I collect my bike from the garage and cycle toward my new home.

Chapter Twenty-three

It takes me a while to get used to being by myself. Although Bea is friendly, and quite willing to sit and drink tea in the kitchen, I don't really like to impose. So I'm on my own a lot more than I have been for a long time. And although those six weeks when I first arrived were much lonelier in some ways—I remember when the only people I ever spoke to were shop assistants and the people who work in the library—I was also in a dizzying rush of relief. And anyway, I soon had my job at the restaurant, and then I met Gethin. This is different.

I don't think I'd thought about how I might be lonely. I suppose I panicked. I suppose I've run away, again, really, and I think I might have . . . not made a mistake—I'm confident I've done the right thing, however hard it might be—but that I might have rushed into it. Although I can't imagine I could have found a better place to live, since I definitely didn't want to share. It feels like the most independent I've ever been—Bea's not a flatmate, more like a neighbor. This feels important. I have to be able to construct my own life, not just hermit-crab my way into someone else's.

I've been at Pen y Bryn for a few days when I come home to find a padded envelope with my name on it in the porch. The porch door doesn't lock, and so my post (such as it might be) will wait for me there, we agreed, and I'll check and collect it myself, rather than expecting Bea to bring it to me. There's no mail slot, anyway, in my own front door. I carry the envelope back to my room and look at it while I boil the kettle. The address is typed, a printed label. I make my tea and then open the Jiffy bag. Inside there's a bundle of cash, and a note.

> *Jess*
>
> *This is the money you paid me as rent. I don't want it, and I thought you might need it. If you're going to stay in Caerwyddon you'll probably need a car. If you give Steve Jones a call he'll probably have something suitable. Remember to haggle.*
>
> *Best wishes*
> *Gethin*

I look at the money. One hundred and fifty twenty-pound notes. Three thousand pounds. Ten times three hundred. My immediate reaction is to stuff it back in its envelope and cycle to Sunnyside and shove it through the mail slot, but then I think, well, he's right.

I look at the stack of twenties on the table.

I think I'm a pretty terrible person.

I check the time. Will he be home from work? Maybe. I scroll through my phone and find his number.

I drum my fingers on the table as the phone rings.

It cuts to voicemail, so I leave a message.

"Hello. It's me. Look—thank you for the money, I'm not sure I should accept it, though. Maybe you could call me when you have a moment?"

I wait all evening for him to call, but he doesn't. When I wake up in the morning, however, there's a message from him.

No need to thank me. It's your money. I never
meant to keep it. I told you I didn't need it.

I know, but that's not the point. Thank you.

That's it though; he doesn't reply. I look at his message for ages, and scroll back and look at other messages we've exchanged, which are mostly about what we were going to have for dinner, or whether to go out for lunch.

I miss him.

It's been only three days though—of course I do. It will be fine. I've got over more complicated things than this, after all. Or harder things, or . . . but anyway. It will be fine.

❧ ❧

I slowly develop a routine. Bea and I have breakfast together on Saturday mornings, when we talk about gardens, mostly, and planting, and art. During the week, I go to work, continue to have lunch at the restaurant once a week, hearing all the latest gossip, and spend the rest of the time on my own, unless Maura asks me to go out for a drink, which I might do if I'm in the mood. She's curious though, convinced "something" must have caused my sudden exit from Sunnyside. Well, she's not wrong, is she, but I still don't want to talk to her about it, any more than I want to talk to Lizzie ("But I thought you liked it there? Did he try something?") or Noosha ("So come on, something must have happened? What was it?").

It's cold in my room, as Bea warned me. Even with the wood

burner lit, it's never exactly cozy. One corner of the skylight leaks if the wind's in the wrong direction. This probably sounds bleak, but it isn't too bad, really. I bought an electric blanket, and spend a lot of time in bed, because it's warmer. I also bought a secondhand laptop, and I'm working hard on my memoir. I need to think of something else to call it; my brain shies away in embarrassment from calling it that. I think it helps though, to write about my life. There are some things I've never talked to anyone about, and it's . . . cathartic . . . to write them down. I should probably have some therapy, but that's expensive. So I'll do it myself. I try to be honest when I write about my life, and sometimes it's painful. It seems odd to make yourself cry just by writing things down.

૪ૐ ⁊ૐ

There's a big shed at Bea's, round the other side of the house from the studio. It's jammed with all sorts of abandoned treasure. She said I could look through it, and I found an old turntable and speakers and I buy old records from junk shops and charity shops—although most charity shops have stopped selling vinyl, you can still find it sometimes. I play things I've never heard before, things I've only read about, and things I used to own—some things I suppose I still do own. I think there's a box of my records in Natalie's attic. Sometimes I find stuff in charity shops that's good enough to resell on eBay.

I spoke to Steve Jones about cars, and I am now the proud owner of a twelve-year-old Vauxhall Corsa. It cost me fourteen hundred quid, and I was a bit worried I'd have forgotten how to drive, but fortunately not. Now I can visit other places, like Llandeilo or Swansea.

I am reassembling my life again.

I try not to think too much about Gethin, who hasn't messaged me and presumably isn't going to. Sometimes I write him letters, but I never send them.

I really miss him.

I have lunch with Kate, but I feel bad about that, because she's his friend, isn't she, and I don't want to make her feel awkward. Also, when she asks me why I don't want to live there anymore, I can't explain it without telling her things I don't want to tell her.

"You know he really likes you," she says.

"I really like him, too."

"So—this might seem like a stupid question—how come you're not speaking to each other?"

"I think he doesn't want to speak to me."

"He thinks you don't want to speak to him."

I shrug. I've decided it's easier that way. Although I miss him, I don't think seeing him would help the ache in my chest.

"He was terribly upset that you left without saying goodbye."

"I wrote him a letter."

"I know. It's hardly the same, though, is it?"

I think she's . . . what? Slightly disapproving? She thinks I've behaved badly. Maybe I have?

"I thought he'd gone out so he didn't have to see me," I say, although I'm not sure this is true.

"He didn't know you were leaving so soon. You didn't tell him, did you?"

"I might not have done."

"I thought you'd get together. You always seemed so . . . comfortable together."

I shrug again. "I don't think that was ever in the cards."

"Really?" She picks at her salad. "He told me you slept together."

I'm a bit shocked by this. I can't imagine him talking to Kate about that. Although maybe it's easier to talk about that sort of thing with someone else you've slept with.

"Did he? What did he say?"

"He said he was sorry it was only once."

I open my mouth to speak and then close it again.

"He also said he was confused because—excuse me—you seemed quite keen, and that made him very happy, but then afterward it was like you thought it was a mistake."

"I didn't think it was a *mistake*," I say. "I wanted to. I was keen, if you like. Yes. But it wouldn't have worked out, and I didn't want it to spoil everything."

"Can you . . . why would it?"

We look at each other for ages, until I'm embarrassed and have to look away.

"I don't have anything to give."

"Jess, that's ridiculous."

"No, it isn't. Look, Kate, I don't really want to get into loads of . . . you know that . . . so, fourteen, fifteen months ago, I was living a completely different kind of life. And it might look like all that's gone away, but it hasn't. I really like Gethin, and he's been . . . extraordinarily kind to me. But everything about me was smashed to pieces, pulverized, turned to dust. There's nothing left, and what you see . . . is just a really wobbly simulacrum, a faked-up thing, a stitched-together monster."

She regards me silently for a long moment.

"I don't think that's true," she says. "I think you're scared."

There's a tight feeling in my chest as I look at her. "Of course

I'm scared. I'm terrified of absolutely everything. My ex-boyfriend took everything away from me. He made me—" I stop. "He lives in my head."

"Yes, that's awful," she says, "but it's nothing to do with Geth, is it?"

"It would be, if we'd ever tried to . . . anyway," I add, "you know his sister was right, wasn't she, when she told me about Vanessa."

Kate looks puzzled. "What d'you mean?"

"She was basically saying, 'Look at what he's used to.'"

"I don't think—"

"And it's fair enough. Did he tell you about that girl he slept with?"

She doesn't say anything.

"Well, she looked a lot like Vanessa."

"Yes, but—no offense to Vanessa," she says, "but lots of people look like her. Don't they? And hardly anyone looks like you. Or me, for that matter. So what's your point about that? Are you saying he's got a type and it's not you? Because frankly, Jess, that's bollocks."

"I'm not sure I see the point of this conversation."

"I'm just trying to . . ." She closes her eyes. "Okay. I know it's none of my business."

"It's kind of you to try to help. But there's no point."

"All right. I'm sorry. I won't mention it again."

※ ※

One Saturday, I'm shopping in town. It's November already, and I'm looking for presents for my niece and nephew. I said to Natalie, last time I spoke to her, that I'll visit in the New Year.

She was surprised. I think she'd decided they might never see me again. It's not like that's never happened before in our family. After my brother left home and never came back, I suppose it's easy to think this might happen again. I wouldn't do that, though. I don't know the kids very well, but I wouldn't vanish from their lives, especially when they have such an unreliable grandmother, a missing uncle, a dead grandfather. I want their aunt, at least, to be a regular purveyor of stuff. Stuff they might not need, but nonetheless.

I always remember their birthdays: I send them postcards if I go anywhere; I look out for things they might like. I've been in Waterstones and bought some books, and now I'm going to buy some bits and pieces, barrettes for Sophie perhaps, in Claire's, maybe some coloring pencils.

I'm walking up Victoria Street in the rain, huddled into my new coat, which is like a beautiful cozy quilt with a big fake-fur-lined hood. Although I know quite a few people now, I pay no attention to anyone hurrying past me. I never expect to see Gethin, for example, and I never have. I know he still goes to the restaurant, sometimes, because Maura tells me if he's been in. He doesn't go on Tuesdays, which is the day I go. I assume this is deliberate.

"Jess!"

Someone is calling my name. I look round and am rather horrified to see that it's Abby, waving at me from across the road. I pause, and wave back, uncertainly. She darts across the street, narrowly avoiding being run over.

"Jess, hello," she says.

"Uh, hi. How are you?"

"Good thanks, yes. Come and have a coffee," she says, most unexpectedly.

"Oh, well, I don't know if . . ."

"No, come on," she says, "get out of this horrible rain." She hurries me down the alleyway and across the square to the coffee shop on Gwelfor Street. I've never been in—I hardly ever come this way, and always forget it's there.

"Oof," she says, "what an awful day. I hate the winter. What can I get you?"

I'm confused by this friendliness, wary. I ask for an Americano and find a seat while she goes to the counter. I really don't want to have a coffee with Abby, of all people.

She brings the coffee on a tray with two almond croissants.

"I didn't know if you'd want one," she says, "so I chose something I could eat two of."

I nod, as this seems fair.

"Help yourself," she says, cutting one in half. "So how are you?"

"I'm good, thanks," I say cautiously.

"How's your new place?"

"It's okay. A bit cold at the moment. No central heating."

She looks vaguely appalled. "Really?"

"It's an extension," I explain, "not part of the house. But it's fine."

"I was so surprised when Geth said you'd moved out."

I look at my coffee, too hot to drink. I don't know what to say to her. I glance briefly at her face to see if I can tell what her motivation is for this conversation. No clues there.

"I suppose I thought you'd be there forever. After all the work you did on the place."

I clear my throat and lift my shoulders in a half-shrug.

"I think maybe I was a bit . . . I know we didn't really get off to a good start," she says, "when we first met."

I stare at her. Is she going to . . . apologize? Surely not.

"But I'm sure you understand why I was worried about him."

I nod slowly. I do, of course.

"You know, he'd been at ours for a while, and I knew how . . . they'd been together for a long time, and it was . . . I was worried about him being on his own. And we didn't know anything about you."

"Yes, I understand."

"When he said he was helping a homeless woman . . . well, you know what happened. With Evan. Our brother?"

I nod.

"I didn't want him to get involved in anything . . . complicated."

I nod again.

"But I know I was wrong about that. Mum says—and I agree—that you were a . . ." She looks uncomfortable now, awkward. "You know, a breath of fresh air and everything."

"It was very kind of him to let me live there," I say dully.

"I know it helped you," she says, "but it helped him too. It made such a difference to him, I think, to how he felt."

I look miserably out of the window. "Did it? That's good."

"He was much happier, as soon as he moved in. And I don't think that was just because he didn't have to live with us anymore," she says.

I glance back at her. She's frowning at her croissant.

"What I mean is, I think it really cheered him up, having you as a . . . housemate."

"It was nice. I was really lucky to meet him."

"It was good for both of you."

"I suppose so."

"And we wondered," she says, "you know. What happened."

"Who's we?"

"Oh, me and Si. And Mum. She likes you."

"Your mum's lovely," I say, pleased to be able to be honest. She smiles at me. "She is, isn't she?"

"Yeah. You're lucky."

"Is your mum—is she still alive? Gethin said your dad died when you were young."

I nod. "I was still at school. Yeah, Mum's still going. Amazing really." I see her trying hard not to ask nosy questions. "She drank too much for a long time; I don't think any of us expected her to make seventy. Her included."

"Oh," she says. "That must have been difficult. Was that . . . when you were young?"

"She started drinking more after Dad died, so, yes. Anyway," I say, "she's not a straightforward person. Even when she's not drinking."

"Have you seen her? Since you moved here?"

I shake my head. "I call her sometimes."

"I can't imagine not seeing my mum."

"No, well, like I say, you're lucky with Marian. She's a . . . nice lady."

She eats another piece of croissant and takes a sip of coffee. "Yes, so anyway—I expect you think I've done nothing but interfere, and not in a good way, and I know you probably don't want to talk to me about what happened."

"What do you mean?"

"I mean . . . the thing is . . . we don't really understand why you left? Geth's been . . ." She clears her throat, awkward. "I know he liked living with you. He won't talk about it, about why you left. I know it's none of my business. It just seems like . . . I don't know. I wondered if you met someone."

"Met someone?" I laugh. "God, no. No. Anyway, Gethin knows why I left, so if he doesn't want to talk to you about it . . ."

"Does he though? I'm not sure he does. Or if he does, he doesn't understand?"

We look at each other. Abby pushes the plate with the remaining croissant on it toward me and I shake my head.

"I did explain. He might think my reasons are . . . peculiar. Stupid, even. But they're real reasons."

"I don't think *stupid*'s the right word. I wasn't trying to . . ."

"Sometimes things are untidy," I say. "Or awkward, or not what anyone would have . . . wanted, exactly. But you can't force life into a neater shape."

She sighs. "No. No, that's for sure."

Chapter Twenty-four

My friends at the restaurant have finally persuaded me to go on a date. I'm not sure why I said yes, apart from the relentlessness of their insistence. It's the middle of December, and I suppose at the back of my mind is the fact that I'll be on my own for Christmas, not that I really care. I'd rather not sit around thinking about last Christmas, though, and how it seemed like—how it was—the beginning of something quite pleasant.

Anyway, I did think that if this guy—recently divorced mate of Alys's uncle—is all right, we might be able to spend Christmas together, or some of it, even if that doesn't lead to anything else, which it probably won't, because I don't even really want it to. It's six months since I slept with Gethin, though, and I'd be lying if I said I didn't think about this a lot. If I slept with someone else, maybe that would go away. Actually, the idea that Gethin might be replaced as "the last person" makes me unbearably sad, and that in itself is probably a good reason to do it.

So Alys gave my phone number to her uncle, and his mate—Owen—phoned me up, and we had an awkward conversation and we're going out to dinner. Not to the restaurant, though, because, as he said, we don't want to be the entertainment. We're going to the Griffin, which is an upmarket sort of dining

pub. Gethin and I went there for lunch once and had a hilari-
ously bad time, because they didn't have either of the things we
ordered, and then they got our second choices wrong. We had
quite a lot to drink, and he had to leave his car in town.

Anyway.

I'm not sure what to wear. I don't really have any going-out
clothes—when I go to the pub with Maura I usually wear jeans
and a vaguely dressy top. I feel like I should make a bit more
of an effort. I've only got the black dress I wore to Gethin's
party, and I don't want to wear that. I go shopping at lunchtime
the day before and trail miserably round the shops. Why am I
doing this to myself?

The shops are full of Christmas party clothes. I remember
when I thought my life might involve the sort of events that
would require such outfits. I go into Monsoon and find a black
dress with embroidery and net sleeves. I try it on and look at
myself critically in the mirror. It's a good length, although . . .
will I have to buy shoes? The long, flat boots I wear to work,
bought from eBay, won't really cut it. I'd forgotten how this
stuff snowballs out of control if you let it. The dress is pretty
though, so I buy it. Then I buy some strappy sparkly evening
shoes, and a bag. I haven't spent this much on clothes in years,
and it makes me feel a bit anxious.

❧ ❦

Owen's a year younger than I am, and he's been divorced for a
year. He's had a couple of dates with various friends of friends
and one woman he met online. He's very shy—I don't know if
this is always true, or if it's me, or the situation. He also has a
really quiet voice, and I'm worried I won't be able to hear him

once it gets a bit busier. We sit in the bar for one drink before going through to the dining room, and I already feel a bit despondent. I think my dress might be wasted. He's perfectly nice, don't get me wrong, although he has one of those droopy handshakes that I can never understand. It's not hard to shake hands firmly, surely. It's not encouraging when a man doesn't, and I know that's a weird psychological thing, and probably unfair.

We've ordered our food, anyway, and we're making (very) small talk about Christmas and work when he says, "Wow, is that Vanessa Winslade?"

I'm sitting with my back to the room (rookie error) so I can't see, and I don't want to look round in case she sees me.

"If it looks like her," I say, "it probably is. She's got family here." I can see other people have noticed her, too; the people at the next table are craning their necks in a very unsubtle way.

"I know, my cousin was at school with her." (Of course.) "But she hardly ever comes home, see?"

"Who's she with?"

"I dunno. Some guy."

I wonder if it's her fiancé. "Don't you recognize him? Her new fella's meant to be famous."

"No, I don't think so. Who does she go out with?"

"I don't know. I can't remember if Gethin told me what his name is."

"Who's Gethin?"

"Oh," I say, embarrassed. "Her ex. I used to live . . . share a house with him."

"What, here?"

I nod.

"Gethin Thomas?"

I nod again.

"I didn't know he came back," he says. "He was at school with her, wasn't he."

"Kind of. The same school, yes." I want to turn round, but I really can't. I don't know if she'd recognize me. We didn't exactly spend much time talking when she came to Sunnyside, but still.

"Have you met her, then?"

"I did once, yes, for about five minutes."

"Huh," he says. "She's like our pet famous person."

"I know. Okay. I'm going to turn round."

He laughs. "Everyone else is."

"Oh God, poor woman." I look casually over my shoulder. I can just about see Vanessa, in a very tight red dress, but not the person she's with. I'll have to move my chair. I pull a face at Owen and shift a little, and then look again.

They're sitting sideways on to me, so I can see them easily. She's not with her mysterious or otherwise new boyfriend, though—she's with Gethin, looking unnaturally smart and, yes, very handsome, in a white shirt and dark jacket.

I'm shocked, and I gawp at them foolishly, my heart banging absurdly in my chest. Perhaps he hears it, because he looks round, and our eyes meet. He smiles immediately, his face lighting up, and I feel my own face do the same—a huge and delighted grin. He raises his hand in greeting, and then, as though remembering why it's nine weeks since we saw each other, frowns. I've waved back by this point but feel suddenly very awkward, and turn back to my own dining companion.

"That your old housemate, then?" says Owen.

"Oh, er, yes. I wonder where her new fella is," I say, distracted. "He was supposed to be leaving his wife."

My phone vibrates on the table. We both look at it, and I

decide—with some difficulty—that it would be rude to look at the message. Anyway, at this point, our starters arrive, and so we talk about those instead. When we've eaten them, Owen asks, "So he's her old boyfriend?"

"Yes." I try to think of something else to talk about but my mind's completely blank. "I've still never seen her on the telly," I manage. "I always find local news a bit . . . I mean, not as depressing as national or international news, obviously, but . . ."

Owen doesn't have much to contribute to this. Or indeed the conversation as a whole. It's quite hard work, and now we're on to places we've been on holiday, which in my case isn't many. Still, I encourage him to talk about a family holiday to Florida until it makes him think too much about his children. I don't think he'd have left his wife, if she hadn't left him, even though from what he says they weren't very well suited. I feel quite sorry for him but there's definitely no spark between us. When they come to take away our plates, he asks if I mind him going outside for a cigarette. I might do, if I was finding him fascinating, but the truth is, of course, that I don't mind at all.

As soon as he's gone I unlock my phone to see who messaged me, but I haven't even managed to open Messenger before Gethin's beside me.

"Jess," he says, "hello."

I drop my phone and stand up, my chair scraping awkwardly. Once I'm up, though, I don't really know what to do, as I'm not sure if he'd want me to hug him, or if I want to, or exactly what's going on.

I sit down again with a bump, and he looks round for a spare chair, borrowing it from the table behind. Our knees are almost touching.

"Hey," I say. "How lovely to see you. Hello."

"Hey."

"Look, I'm sorry I . . ."

"Who's that you're with? Are you on a date?" he asks.

"Oh, yes . . . well . . ."

"Sorry to interrupt," he says, "I just . . ."

"No, no, it's fine, no. It's not a very good date," I say, leaning toward him, voice lowered. "The girls from the restaurant suggested it."

He doesn't react to this, instead saying, "You look great. That dress is excellent."

A horrible, desperately rushed feeling comes over me. I'm not sure what to say, worried that we have only a moment, and we're filling it up with pointless pleasantries.

"Are *you* on a date?"

"Well," he says, and laughs. "I'd tell you all about it but it's a long story. But . . . so is this the first time you've been out with this guy?"

I'm concerned Owen will be on his way back now.

"Yes. He's Alys's uncle's mate. I mean, he's perfectly nice."

"Oh dear," he says, and grins at me.

"It's not funny."

He laughs, but then he's serious again. "Can I talk to you?"

"Always. But probably not now?"

"No, okay . . . look, so . . . you won't be taking him home?"

I raise my eyebrows. "I think I'm getting a lift, but I'm not going to shag him, if that's what you're asking."

He laughs again, looking over my shoulder. "He's on his way," he says. "Okay, look, could I come to yours? Later?"

"What, tonight?"

He nods.

"I suppose I . . . if you like. Do you know where it is?"

"Yes, I've been there, haven't I. Delivered your money."

"Oh! Of course. Yes. Well, all right. Message me, then, when you get there, because I don't live in the house."

"Okay." He stands up, twirls his chair back under its table. "See you later."

With that, he's gone, Owen returns, and our main courses arrive.

I don't imagine I'm much company for the rest of the meal, full of doubt and confusion. We talk about schools—Owen's kids (they're twins) are about to start secondary school. I don't have many opinions about this, but I have taken in some level of information about the town's secondary schools by osmosis. I try hard to seem interested, because it's rude to go out with someone and then get enormously and fundamentally distracted. I turn down a third glass of wine, and am tempted to forgo dessert altogether.

I think my eagerness to leave is probably quite apparent. He asks me if I'm okay. I apologize, although I'm not exactly sorry. Or maybe I am . . . I shouldn't have let the girls persuade me to come out with him really. But it's not his fault.

In the car, as he drives me home, I try to communicate this.

"Thank you so much for inviting me out."

"Got to keep trying. Hope you enjoyed yourself."

"Thank you, yes," I say, which is fairly noncommittal.

"Let me know if you want to go out again."

"Thank you," I say again. "I'm not sure I was ready, really."

"I had a nice time," he says, although I think he's being polite. We sit for a moment at the end of the drive, and then I thank him again and escape from the car. I watch him drive away and then hurry across the gravel—not ideal, in these shoes—creak through the gate, and let myself into my room.

I'm very nervous. Anxious. Excited? I try to work out what's going on. It was hard to think about while I was having dinner. But Gethin's coming here—so keen to talk to me he couldn't wait until tomorrow, or next week. Despite almost three months of silence, he didn't hesitate to come over to speak to me. I'm very pleased about this. I've been trying to make myself accept that he wasn't going to call or message or drop round, and that this was entirely my fault, and I shouldn't expect him to. I've known, really, that it was down to me to contact him, but I haven't, because why would he want me to? But I've forgotten the most important thing about all of this, which is that he likes me, and I like him. I think again of his face as he realized it was me, earlier. It reminds me of that time at Kate's, when I felt like a dog delighted to see its owner. He looked like I felt, then, unfiltered happiness, a true reaction, no need to apply social neatness or any of that stuff from when you're younger. No need to be cool, or mysterious, or to play complicated games. Just wag your tail when you're happy to see someone.

I flit round the room making sure everything's tidy, kneeling awkwardly in my party frock to light the burner. It's cold; when I first got in, I could see my breath, and my feet, clad in only sheer tights rather than my usual opaque, plus socks, are freezing. I'm not going to put my slippers on, though, or not yet anyway. And what's that about? Vanity.

I fill the kettle and get out two mugs. The lack of fridge isn't a problem at the moment, as it's never warm enough to turn the milk. I flip jerkily through my records, wondering if I should put some music on.

I remember the message I got at the restaurant and open my phone to see what it says. It's from Gethin—which I suppose is not a surprise—and it says:

Can I talk to you?

I think about an evening about twenty-five years ago, waiting for my ex-boyfriend to arrive at my house. It was my third year at university, and we'd been split up for a while. He lived in a different town, and I'd invited him to my birthday party—probably a stupid thing to do. I was very determined in my attitude of "Hey, it's totally grown-up to be friends with your ex. We're not going to do anything—stupid." My flatmate was sarcastic about this. Who can blame her? Anyway, I carried on pretending we weren't going to have sex right up until the point we were in my bedroom taking our clothes off.

Not that I anticipate anything like that happening tonight, obviously. Nothing's changed, has it, to make any of this less . . . complicated. I waver between denial and finally, fully acknowledging something I've been avoiding for months.

I hear a car crunching on the gravel, listen as the engine is switched off, and hear the sound of the expensively firm slam of the driver's door, and I go outside to stand shivering by the gate.

Chapter Twenty-five

"Over here," I call, diverting him from his walk to the front door.

"Oh, hey," he says. "What are you doing?"

I creak the gate open.

"I don't live in the house; I told you."

"Where do you live, then?"

"Through here. Behold, my humble abode. It's a studio," I add as I usher him in, "or it used to be."

"Oh, okay." He looks round. "You've got your own kitchen."

"Sort of. Did you want a cup of tea or anything? There's red wine, but it's very cold."

He wanders about, looking at things. "Tea's good, cheers."

"I'm afraid the chair's not very comfortable. It needs to be re-sprung or something. You can sit on the bed, if you'd like."

"Thanks. Oh, hey, record player. Is that new?"

"I found it in the shed." I explain Bea's shed to him, and then show him some of my other treasures—the 1960s drinking glasses in their wire rack; a chunky glass vase, knockoff White-friars, that's almost but not quite the same as one I had to leave behind in my old life.

He picks this up, weighing it in his hand. "Have you been to collect your things from your sister's house?"

"I'm going to see her in the spring, so I suppose I should. Now I've got a car it'll be easier." I still can't quite imagine going home.

"You bought a car, then? The one out front?" Gethin tries out the armchair and pulls a face. "I see what you mean about this. They had a couple of good armchairs at the flea market last month. I took the guy's card; I'll find it for you."

"Yeah, I've looked at a couple, but armchairs are either broken or really expensive." I give him his tea, and then pull a kitchen chair over toward the bed. "It would be useful to be able to reupholster things. Maybe I should do a course."

We look at each other for a bit, and then I clear my throat. "So hey," I say, "it's good to see you. I'm sorry I didn't say goodbye properly. I know I messed up."

"I didn't realize you'd be gone so soon," he says. He frowns at his tea. "I wish you'd said."

"Yeah, I was . . . I should've done. I just . . . you know, I was worried you were angry with me, and—"

"I wasn't angry, Jess, I was . . . upset."

"Yes. I'm sorry."

"I've really missed you."

It's hard for me to respond to this. There's a lump in my throat, which is something people say but I'm not sure I've ever really experienced before.

"I've missed you, too. I know that probably sounds stupid, when it was my decision. I didn't know whether to contact you or not."

"I assumed you didn't want to have anything to do with me."

"I did say I wanted to be friends," I object.

"Yeah well, I wasn't convinced you meant it. I've never . . .

I've never been sure how you wanted to . . . Look," he says, "I came here to say some stuff and I think I should say it."

"Oh, okay, yes." I feel a bit sick at this, like when your boss says, "Can I have a word?" Although really, what can he say, now, that would make things worse than they've been?

He sighs, leaning to put his mug on the floor. The bed's a bit low for him; he doesn't look that comfortable. Mind you, that might not be furniture-related.

"I know when we met, you found it bizarre that I wanted to help you."

I nod.

"And I understand that. I suppose it was, a bit. Or, not that I wanted to help, but that I'd do it in such a direct and personal way."

I nod again.

"But as soon as I'd spoken to you I felt like . . . I know you say it's impossible to know anything about someone when you meet them . . ."

I'm still nodding.

"But that's down to experience, isn't it. It's because you met someone who hurt you and you didn't know that was going to happen and you feel . . ."

"Stupid," I provide.

He shakes his head. "Cautious, is what I was going to say. But I've been lucky, in my life. I've never met anyone like that. I knew as soon as we were sitting outside the house, drinking coffee—before that, maybe, when I saw your library books, and your bear . . ." he turns, slightly, to look at Bear, who's perched jauntily on the shelf above the bed, ". . . and how clean the bathroom was—I felt like I could trust you. And I was right, wasn't I?"

"Only by accident. I mean, you didn't know any of that, and I still think it was foolish of you, and a terrible risk."

"Maybe, but a risk that worked out."

"Well."

"Don't you think?"

I nod reluctantly.

"At first I thought maybe it would be odd to share a house with someone I didn't know, but I've done that before—most people have, at least once."

"I suppose so," I admit, unwillingly. I drum my heels on the floor. My feet are cold.

"And it wasn't odd, or awkward, or weird. It was fun. It was brilliant to have someone to help me with the house. If I'd had to buy carpet by myself—that would have been rubbish."

"I'm sure you'd have managed." I smile at him.

"Yes, but it was fun, because you were there." He pauses, picks up his mug, and drinks some tea. I watch his hands on the mug, the contrast between the dark collar of his jacket and the white of his shirt. His hair, neat in the restaurant, is more tousled now; he looks more like himself.

He sighs and begins again. "Okay. This bit is harder. At first I was like, this is cool, isn't it great to have made a new friend? I mean, there are loads of people I know here, who I hadn't seen for ages, and it was good to get back into knowing them, but I really enjoyed having a properly new friend. Someone who didn't know anything about me, or anything about Vanessa, who didn't have any opinions about any of it. Someone whose life was completely different. Someone I could . . . help, maybe. Or maybe that's arrogant. I don't know."

He looks at me, questioning. I shake my head.

"I wanted to ask you, about your life, but whenever I tried, you were very definite about not wanting to talk to me about it. So I was like, okay, that's fine, if she wants to, she will. I knew I needed to give you loads of time, and space, and that was . . . that was good. I was confident we might get to a point where maybe you'd be happy to talk to me about it. Every small thing you did say, I was grateful that you felt like you could tell me."

He closes his eyes for a moment, and then continues, "I wanted you to be somewhere calm, and safe, where you could . . . get yourself back. I could see how you were . . . relaxing, if that's the right word, and I thought, you know, eventually perhaps you'd feel like you did before you ever met him. Not with those experiences gone—we talked about that, didn't we, about time not being wasted—but so it wasn't pressing on you."

I open my mouth to speak—not that I know what to say— but he carries on.

"And then I was like, oh shit. I really like her. And she's not . . . she won't be . . . that's not going to be a thing. I have to . . . work round that and not make her feel . . . I didn't want you to feel uncomfortable. I was like, okay, I can do that, I can carry on like this, and if we ever get to a point where it seems . . . we can talk about it then. It's fine. I mean," he says, "it wasn't easy, but I'm not a teenager, or an idiot. And sometimes I thought . . . that perhaps you liked me, too. That there was a bit of a connection, something between us."

I swallow, nervous.

"When I thought you were kissing Mike, at the party—that was a bad moment. I was . . . it upset me. But I knew it was none of my business," he says, looking at me, and then back down at his mug, "what you did, or who you did it with. I was . . . that was hard. So I was delighted when you said you hadn't. And when you kissed me. You know, obviously I've . . . there have been people I've really liked before, and I've even slept with some of them. But it felt . . . special, and I was devastated that you . . . about what happened afterward. But again, I was determined not to be an arse about it. Not to add to your . . . worries. I wanted things to be okay between us."

A tear slides down my cheek, followed by several more. I wipe my face with the back of my hand and blink hard. I can't quite stop though. He looks up at me and notices this.

"Shit, I'm sorry. I should probably shut up. But I . . . now we don't live together it doesn't matter, does it? I need to tell you this stuff, and I'm sorry if it's selfish. I've got to say it though. I've been a lot more unhappy since you left than I ever was about Vanessa. I know that probably sounds stupid."

I wipe my face with my palms and shrug. I've been quite unhappy, too. I sniff. I need to stop crying; it's not . . . helpful. We look at each other.

"Didn't mean to upset you."

I shake my head. "It doesn't matter."

He takes a deep breath. "Anyway," he says, "so yeah. It was difficult to pretend it was . . . what did you say? Five years since we slept together? That was hard, but it did sort of make sense. I could see how it might work to . . ."

"Make things easier," I offer. I reach for my handbag and find a tissue, blow my nose.

"Yeah, I guess. Anyway, I thought it would be awkward but it wasn't, really, because—and I may have mentioned this already—I really liked living with you. I liked those Saturdays playing on the PlayStation, and I liked you teaching me how to cook—which, you know, that was kind of . . . I might have been a bit better at that than I pretended." He tilts his head, a half-smile lurking.

"What?"

"Yeah. I wanted to spend time with you, and it seemed like a good way of . . . anyway, you definitely helped me improve."

"You made it up? Bloody cheek. I spent ages thinking about useful recipes and handy things to teach you. And I was impressed with how quickly you picked it up."

"I know." He grins at me. "I wanted to impress you."

I shake my head. I can't believe anyone would ever want to impress me. It's like a doorway to another world, a different kind of existence.

"Yeah. But anyway, what I'm trying to say, what all this is for . . . is that I wanted to tell you something."

"Okay, go on then."

He closes his eyes for a moment and takes a deep breath. "I'm not expecting any kind of response to this," he tells me. "I just need to say it."

I wait, puzzled.

"Yeah, all right, so I just . . . I love you, Jess. I'm in love with you. I think you're . . . everything about you is . . . well. You're exactly what I . . . I mean, I didn't know that was what I wanted, what I was looking for, but it was. You are. You're . . . you've been very important to me. And maybe I should have mentioned it before. Or maybe I should never have mentioned it." He stands up. "Anyway, it's late. I should probably get going."

"What?"

"I should probably . . ."

"No, what did you say before that?"

"Oh, come on," he says. "You know this. Don't you. I'm pretty sure you do."

I'm astonished. Is this what Abby was talking about? Or trying to talk about? Am I very stupid? (Yes?)

"Why the hell would you think that?"

"Because I followed you about like a dog for six months?"

"No . . . what . . . no, you didn't. What are you talking about?"

He comes two steps closer.

"Okay, so it's a horrible surprise. Whatever. Anyway, so now . . ."

"I wouldn't say it's a *horrible* surprise." No.

"Yeah, well, that's great. Anyway. It's late," he says, "and you're cold . . ."

It's true—I'm shivering now.

"So I should leave." He ducks his head in a weird kind of nod, and heads for the door.

"No, wait. Wait."

He pauses, one hand on the latch.

"No," I say again. "I don't . . ."

"You know where I am, if you want to talk to me." He opens the door and is gone, out into the darkness. He closes it behind him and I stand there, foolishly, once again alone in my room. I chew my lip and press my nails into my palms. I don't know what to do. Should I go after him? It feels like . . . are we grown-ups? Is that what grown-ups do? It feels a bit . . . but then again, like I said before, what's the point of trying to be cool? I'm not cool; I'm desperately confused and uncool. I wrench the door open and run awkwardly down the path.

"Wait!" I shout. I drag the gate open and hear the *thunk* of the car door. He switches on the headlights and I shade my eyes. Shit.

"Wait! Gethin!"

He's started the engine and is reversing to turn the car round. I can't chase a car, for goodness' sake. He's seen me, though. He stops and opens the door, half getting out.

"Wait," I say again, flapping my hands at him.

"You'll freeze to death," he says. "What are you doing?"

"I need you to not go away," I say elegantly.

"I've said everything I want to say."

"Yes, but I haven't said anything."

His face is in shadow, so I have no clues about what he's thinking.

"Couldn't you . . . couldn't we . . . look, I need to say things too," I tell him. I'm shaking uncontrollably now, teeth chattering.

"Do you, though? You've never wanted to say anything. I never have any idea what you're thinking."

I wrap my arms round myself. "It's usually not very interesting."

He shakes his head. "Well, so, go on."

"Won't you come back inside?"

"It's late. I don't know if . . ."

"I don't care how late it is," I snap, as quietly as possible. I've suddenly remembered that Bea's bedroom's right above us and she can probably hear every word.

He sighs, and bends to turn off the ignition. "Go on, then," he says, and follows me back into the studio. Luckily, the door hasn't slammed shut. That would have improved the evening to no end.

"Look," I say.

He folds his arms and leans against the wall by the coat pegs. He looks . . . I don't know. I can't tell what he's thinking.

"Do you want to know about it? Do you want me to tell you?"

"About what?"

I gesture angrily. "About me, about my life before I came here? To Wales, I mean?"

"Not if you don't want to tell me."

"I don't want to. I don't want to tell anyone about it, or think about it. I want it not to have happened. I want it to go away. It won't ever, though. It makes me wrong inside. That's why I can't . . . why I couldn't . . ."

"Couldn't what?"

"Couldn't tell you how I felt."

"About what?"

"About any of it." I glare at him.

"And?"

"Well, bloody hell. You know I . . ."

"No. I told you; I don't know. I've no idea how you felt about any of it, except that after we went to bed you wanted to pretend it happened years ago, and when I slept with someone else you felt you had to leave."

"Some people," I say sarcastically, "might think either of those things was a clue."

He purses his lips, shaking his head.

"Anyway," I add, "I've said about fifty times, I don't care about whatsherface. It would be pretty outrageous if I did." Even as I say this, I wonder why I can't just be honest. I stamp my foot, childishly, and then say, "Shit, I need to take these shoes off. My feet are killing me."

He looks down at them. "Never seen you in heels," he says. "I wondered why you were so tall."

I stamp over to the bed and sit down. "They're okay if all you're doing is walking from the car to your table and back." I stoop to unbuckle them.

"You seem to have gone to a lot of effort for this date of yours."

"There's not a lot of point going on a date if you don't make some effort. I was trying to ramp up my enthusiasm." I unbuckle the second shoe and press my feet to the floor. There's a rug here, by the bed. I stretch my legs and wriggle my toes, and then look up at him. "Oh yeah, which reminds me—how come you were having dinner with Vanessa? You look like you've made an effort, as well." I nod at his jacket.

"It's her birthday," he says. He pushes himself away from the wall with his shoulders and comes toward me, sitting on the chair where I sat earlier.

"Oh, is it? That's nice. Where's her boyfriend, then?"

"Where do you think?"

"With his wife?"

He nods.

"Oh. That's . . . unfortunate."

"Yeah."

"So, what . . ."

"She rang me up. She was in a bit of a state. They were meant to be going away. Three days in Paris or something."

"Huh."

"Yeah." He runs a hand through his hair. "We went to Paris, for her fortieth."

"Very nice."

"Well, it was okay." A hint of a smile there, for a moment.

I gather up the quilt and wrap myself in it. I think the burner must be out, but I can't be bothered to turn round and look.

"Dinner at the Griffin's not quite so glam, is it. Being gawped at by the plebs."

This makes him laugh. "I'd forgotten how much people stare," he says.

"I suppose they're a bit more sophisticated in Cardiff."

"Not so's you'd notice."

"Pfft."

We look at each other.

"Anyway?"

"Anyway what?"

"Bloody hell. So you took your ex out for her birthday 'cos her boyfriend's a prick. How was that?"

"Oh, yeah. I guess she wanted someone to be nice to her."

"I'm sure. How nice? Would she have come back to yours if you'd asked her?"

"I think she might've, yeah." A gleam of amusement.

"Well."

"Yeah, it was a bit odd. Another thing I'd forgotten is what she's like when she's being nice to you."

"Oh yeah."

"Overpowering, if I'm honest. Especially when compared to the sort of woman I'm interested in these days," he adds, "who is pretty much the opposite of overpowering."

"Yeah, so I get why I might . . . have a thing about you. Because you're probably the . . . nicest . . . person I've ever met. But I don't get why you'd have a thing about me."

"*Have* you got a thing about me?"

"If anyone's been following someone about like a dog . . ."

We sit and look at each other. A very intense silence stretches out between us.

He sighs. "It's nearly midnight. Are you going to talk to me or keep deflecting forever?"

"Keep deflecting." I nod.

"I may as well go, then. I mean, not that I don't like"—he gestures—"talking shit, with you—I do really like that. But it doesn't get us anywhere, does it?"

There's a long, painful pause.

"Please don't go." I grip the quilt.

"Talk to me, then."

"What do you want me to talk about?"

"I'd like you to explain how you see all this. What you think about it. How you . . ." He hesitates. "How you feel."

I wrap the quilt round me more tightly. "So about four years ago," I begin, "my car broke down. The AA took it to a garage for me, and they fixed it. And when I went to pick it up, the guy who worked on it came out to tell me about the work he'd done." I clear my throat, thinking. "He was kind of funny. A bit younger than me. Not bad-looking, bit of banter, you know what the sort of bloke who works with other blokes is like."

He nods.

"I'd been on my own for a while. He asked me if I wanted to go for a drink, so I said okay. We went out that evening. It was . . . it seemed to go quite well. I'd been . . . I was worried, you know, that I'd had all my chances. I was forty-two, nearly, I was single again, I was living in a . . . well, it wasn't a shitty flat, but it wasn't great. I mean, I was lucky to have it, I see that now." I sigh. "So it was nice, to flirt with someone, to feel like, you know, like I was . . . worth flirting with. Anyway. We went out again, the week after. He came back to mine and it seemed to . . . go quite well, you know."

Gethin nods.

"So for a month we . . . I was pretty into it. It reminded me of the beginning of other things. I wanted . . . I just really wanted that feeling, you know, when it's all potential."

He nods again.

"Anyway, so I suppose I was . . . vulnerable. Not that I would've recognized that. I guess everyone's always vulnerable. We started seeing each other. It was quite intense. He said I should move in with him and . . . it seemed like a good idea. So I did. We'd known each other like three weeks, or a month. My friends were all 'Are you sure this is a good idea?' But none of them knew him, and I hadn't met any of his mates, yet. It wasn't the first time; I've often moved in with people really quickly, when I hardly know them." I smile a rather wobbly and unconvincing smile. "As you know. And it's always worked out okay. I suppose there has to be an exception." I take a deep breath. "To begin with, it was fine. I mean, not as much . . . fun . . . as before we lived together, but it was okay. We did some of the things normal people do—we went out, we watched films, we went away for the weekend. It was six months or something before I pissed him off enough that he really lost his temper."

He watches me carefully, his hands clenched.

"He didn't hit me or anything, he just really, really lost it. Screaming and shouting. I was shocked. No one had ever spoken to me like that before; I didn't really know what to do with it. I was upset, but I shouted back, told him he couldn't talk to me like that. It seemed to work; he flipped right back"—I snap my fingers—"apologizing. Says he's stressed, says his ex—so now I know he's got an ex-wife, not that she's actually an ex; they weren't divorced yet—anyway, he blames her, somehow, for whatever it was that triggered him. I was like, okay. Cautious, though. Wary? Yes, you could say I was wary. But again, everything's fine, we went on holiday, it was good, maybe the nicest time we ever spent together? I thought, all right, that was bad, but now it's fixed. Then I came home from work late, once—I'd been out for going-away drinks with someone and forgotten to say I was going. When I got home, that's when he did this"—I gesture at my arm, the cigarette burns hidden by the sleeve of my dress—"the first time. I didn't really react though. I mean, it hurt, obviously. Well, you know what it feels like."

He nods.

"After that I was . . . well, I didn't want him to do it again."

We look at each other. I sigh.

"So one minute, things are fine, and then there was all this . . . stuff . . . and I was somehow living with someone who really didn't seem to like me at all. But he didn't want me to go. I still don't understand that. And even though I'd read about this, you know, I still couldn't stop any of it happening. I tried not to annoy him, so he wouldn't lose his temper, but the whole thing was irrational. So it was impossible to do the right thing. But he was always nice to me if anyone else was there, you know, to the extent that some people were like, 'Oh, you're so lucky!' Ha ha." I shake my head. "It's all quite embarrassing really."

"Embarrassing? Jesus, Jess, I don't think . . ."

"Yeah, it is, though." I pull the quilt tighter round myself. "Anyway, then I caught him on his phone, talking to . . . someone. It was obvious they were sleeping together. But I wasn't . . . I wasn't devastated, you know, or even upset—I was just, 'Oh, okay, are you leaving, then,' and he . . . I thought he would. Although it would have been me that had to leave, because it was his flat we lived in. But no. He said he was sorry. Didn't seem very likely, but whatever. I felt like maybe it would balance things out a bit. I mean, it's obviously bad behavior, isn't it; you can't pretend it isn't. So we carried on. Then I got a letter, pushed under the door, saying he'd been sleeping with a woman at work, the receptionist. I asked him if it was true. That time he lost his temper. I was . . . I said, you know, there's no need for any of this, we could split up. So he said he loved me, yadda yadda. He said he'd kill himself if I left. So, on we go."

He shakes his head. I can tell he doesn't know what to say.

"I wasn't sure what to do, for ages. I wanted to leave, but I couldn't quite. For some reason. And in the end, I caught him in bed with someone else. Maybe it's not that surprising. He'd slept with lots of other people while we were together, three at least. Anyway, I came home unexpectedly and there they were. He was absolutely furious with me for catching him. But he must have wanted me to, don't you think?"

Gethin shakes his head again, clearly unable to think of a response.

"I felt a bit sorry for the other woman; I guess she'd never seen him lose his temper. She left pretty quickly. We had a massive row—even though, you know, I didn't care. I was pleased. Because I thought, now I can go, and he won't look for me. I said I was leaving, and he was like, 'You'd better fucking not.' I thought that was quite funny. I was lucky, I suppose. That's when people get killed, isn't it. He didn't kill me, though."

"So then you left?"

"I'd been sort of planning it for a while, but I could never quite . . . I don't know why I couldn't make the decision. I'd bought my tent, though. Hid that in the shed with the garbage cans. He never took out the trash, obviously." I smile at this, although it's not a pleasant memory, thinking of dragging the trash bags downstairs in the dark and across the car park in the rain, just one more utterly grim and tiresome thing, back when my whole life was utterly grim and tiresome.

"But did you leave then? Like, immediately?"

"I should have done. But no. Next day when he was at work. But that's why I said about . . . when we went to bed. Because that last night was . . . it wasn't great."

"Did he hurt you?" He looks so appalled; it's very touching.

I smile reassuringly. "Well, yeah. A bit. But . . . it could have been worse. A lot worse. I was mostly worried that it would hurt my brain, you know. So I wouldn't be able to do anything like that afterward. But as it turned out, it was okay. Because it was you, and you're . . ." I pause. "Because I really liked you, and you're so kind."

"Jess, I—"

"People think that's not important, but it is. It really is." I sigh. "I suppose it was difficult to make the decision because I knew I'd have to leave everything. And although it's not like it would have been twenty years ago—I mean, I am still in touch with my friends—I did have to give up everything: my job, my stuff, my . . . place in the world."

"It's . . . it's a brave thing to do."

I shrug. "I don't know if it is. I think running away is . . . not terribly brave. Anyway, I should have left before. But you know, even though it was awful, it could have been a lot worse." I pause for a moment, my face turned away from him. "He pushed his wife down the stairs. Broke her arm."

"Fuck."

"Yeah. I didn't find that out for a long time. Eighteen months, I think it was, before anyone told me. Bastards. But that's why I was frightened, you know. I thought—" I pause, considering.

"I'm still not sure if it's true, if I really thought this—but I was . . . I did worry that he might try to kill me. You know, and it would seem like an accident? Maybe it would *be* an accident? And I'd be one of those women on the news, and everyone would say how nice he was, and the defense would argue that I'd . . . pissed him off? I'd be very annoyed," I say, trying to be funny, "to be a statistic."

"I'm sorry," says Gethin. "I'm sorry I've made you talk about this. I'm so sorry."

"It's okay. It's probably a good thing. I've been trying not to think about it, but it's always there, of course."

"And then . . . but . . ."

"Yeah, so that was it. I don't think he thought I'd go. Or maybe he did—I don't know, I have no idea, maybe he wanted me to. He was sleeping with someone else, after all. But anyway. I sent him a text telling him I was gone, and blocked his number on my phone, and, you know, twelve hours later I was lying in my tent in the cemetery. And six weeks after that"— I hear my voice crack—"you bought me a bed to sleep in."

"Ah, Christ," he says, and he's on his knees at my feet, grasping for my hands. "Jess."

"Sorry. But there you are: that's my story. And look, it's not that . . . it's not that I didn't want to tell you about it, specifically. I didn't want to tell anyone." I pull a hand away so I can touch his face, my thumb on his cheekbone. "Anyway," I add, "so I'll always be grateful, won't I?"

"I don't want you to be grateful. I'm not interested in gratitude. Is this the problem? Have I . . . sabotaged myself by helping you? Would it be better if we'd met some other way?"

I consider this. "I don't think so."

"So it's just that . . . you don't want me?"

"Oh shit," I say, and laugh. "Have I totally failed to communicate exactly how much I want you?"

"Er, yes? Well, unless it's hardly at all, which is how I've interpreted this whole thing."

"Not really, though?"

"I don't know . . . how am I supposed to know?" He shifts, grimacing. "This floor's not comfortable. And I'm not as young as I was."

"Come here, then."

He gets up, awkward, and stretches. "It's late."

"I know. And cold as well. You should probably take off your clothes and get into bed."

He laughs. "Should I, though?"

"If you'd like. I'm going to."

"Yeah, I don't know if . . ."

"What is it?" I unwrap the quilt and stand up too.

"If . . . look, I think probably I won't stay, if there's . . . if you might decide tomorrow that you wish I hadn't."

"Yeah, I can see why you'd say that. But, um . . . I don't anticipate that will happen."

"You don't?"

I shake my head. We frown at each other.

"Can you help me out here?" he says.

I take a deep breath. I have to get this right. It's important.

"Please come to bed, Gethin. I'd like to spend the night with you and possibly—okay, probably, definitely—other nights in the future."

"Really?"

I hold out my hands. "Really."

He hesitates and then steps toward me. He takes my hands, and we look at each other for a moment, before I step closer again and he puts his arms round me. I lay my cheek against his shirt and close my eyes. I feel his heart beating, the firmness of his flesh beneath the crisp white cotton. It's funny how you live in your own body but nothing feels like someone else's. He smells lovely: fabric softener and expensive soap. He tightens his grip, squeezing, and when I look up, he kisses me.

"I love you," he says.

"Yes. I love you, too." My God, it's a relief to say it.

"You do?"

"I have done for ages. I'm sorry about everything. I'm not much of a catch."

"Oh, seriously. Shut up."

Chapter Twenty-six

"I was freezing," says Gethin. "I'm a bit warmer now, though."

We face each other, just far enough apart that we can focus, the duvet pulled up to our noses.

"Mm."

"I think you're very beautiful," he says.

"Oh, come on," I say, amused. "You mean you think I was, like, thirty years ago, when I had pink hair."

He laughs. "Yeah, but also, no. Now."

"I'm all old and baggy, though."

He laughs some more. "Baggy? You're not baggy."

"I am a bit. I don't mind. Old is better than dead."

"Yeah. But listen, I'm trying to tell you. I really fancy you."

"Ha. Yes. Likewise."

"Funny, and clever . . ."

"Clever? Hardly. And extremely ordinary."

"Not remotely ordinary. Brilliant, amazing. I love you. What's that line? 'You must allow me to tell you how ardently I admire and love you.'"

I laugh. "You're delightful, aren't you? Quoting *Pride and Prej*? When did you memorize that? Thought it might come in useful?"

"Ha. Yeah, I watched it with Mum about a month ago. I didn't think I'd get to use it."

"It's a good line."

"It didn't work for him though, did it."

"Eventually."

"Eventually. Yeah, well that's appropriate, right?" He leans to kiss me.

I close my eyes, still astonished by everything. "I love you. You're the kindest person I've ever met. I know you don't want me to thank you again . . ."

"I really don't . . ."

"But I'm so grateful. For everything, all your kindness." I'm looking at him again now, intent on learning every line and crease and freckle.

"You deserve it, don't you."

"Probably not?"

"Ah, you do, though."

We rest our foreheads together. I'm so happy, I can't begin to describe it. Perhaps I should try.

"I'm very happy." Ah, not an impressive attempt, admittedly.

"Yes, me too. Never been happier."

I laugh. "No, come on."

"Seriously, Jess."

"I feel like . . . I can't remember the last time I felt like this. Please let it be okay."

"It will be."

"You don't know that."

"Yes, I do," he says, and sounds so confident I laugh.

"I hope so."

"When can you move back? Do you have to give notice? I mean . . . do you want to come home?"

"Home. Yes." My eyes fill with tears.

"Hey. It's okay." He leans to touch his nose to mine.

"Can I . . . will I have my bedroom back?"

"If you want? I was kind of hoping you might sleep in my room, with me, like."

"Oh, yes." I laugh. "Yes." I try to imagine this, but I can't really.

"Yeah? I mean, if you want your own room . . ."

"I don't know. I might. Even if I never sleep in there."

"Well, that's fine. If you want. But when will you come home? Tomorrow? You'll be home for Christmas? I've been dreading Christmas."

"Bea's going away," I tell him. "I thought I'd be on my own."

"On your own? Bloody hell, has no one invited you?"

"I haven't told anyone, so, no. Anyway," I add, "she said I could sleep in the guest room. It's got a really amazing bed, and there's heating, so I was going to do that."

"Heating, eh? That does sound better than in here."

"I quite like it here, though. But you're right, it's very cold. I had to buy an electric blanket."

"Shit, do they still make those? Wow." He pauses for a moment. "But when will you come home?"

"I don't know. Perhaps I should stay here for a bit, and we should, you know, go out? Because what if it's awful? Or . . . I don't mean that. I mean, what if it doesn't work out? I'll be homeless again."

"We know we can live together, though."

"Yes."

"But you must do whatever you're comfortable with. I don't

want to put any pressure on you." He kisses me. "Just know that you're very, very welcome to come home whenever you like."

"Ah. Yes."

We lie in silence for a while, smiling at each other. Actually, if you could see us, it would turn your stomach.

❧ ❦

When I wake in the morning I'm briefly confused. It's light, with a bright stream of sunshine pouring through the skylight, so it must be quite late. And there's something—no, someone—in the bed with me and oh my God now I remember. I turn round quickly and there he is, head pillowed on his arm, eyes closed, breathing deeply. My heart contracts. I gaze at him, disbelieving. Is this us, now? I stroke his arm very lightly, put my finger to the tip of his nose, and then to the curl of his ear. He twitches slightly, frowns, and opens his eyes. I see him realize where he is, and then we're grinning at each other.

"Hey, you," he says.

"Hey."

He blinks. "Shit, it doesn't get warmer, does it?" He puts his hand over his face. "My nose is cold."

"Ah, you poor wee thing. I'll light the burner."

I feel under the pillow for my pajamas.

"Oh, don't get up," he says.

"I'll be back, but you can't be naked in this room," I explain, dragging the top over my head. I stand up, step into the bottoms, and push my feet into my slippers. I pull a large, shapeless jumper from under the bed and put that on as well. My breath condenses in the cold air.

"Shit," he says, "this is ridiculous. I can see your breath. It's probably warmer outside."

I laugh. "Yeah, it's chilly all right. Brr." I hurry across the room to hook open the burner. I feed it with wood, light it, clang shut the door. "D'you want a cup of tea?"

"Go on, then, since you're up." He pummels his pillows and props himself up.

"I'm afraid I don't have anything that would fit you, like a jumper or anything."

"That's okay, I'll stoically put up with it."

I put the kettle on and rinse the mugs from last night, make a pot of tea. It's very slightly warmer now that the burner's going. I give Gethin his mug and kick off my slippers before climbing into bed beside him. I lean against his shoulder and drink my tea.

❦

"You should take some of these clothes off," he says, tugging at my jumper.

"Should I?"

"It's warmer now. You must be too hot."

"I wouldn't say I was, actually," I say, but I take it off obediently.

"I love your pajamas," he says.

I look down at myself. "Really?"

"You always look . . . cozy."

"Ha, yeah, that's me. Cozy, not sexy."

"Yeah well, you might think that," he says. "But you'd be wrong. I mean, obviously I tried not to think about them, or . . ."

"I see. That could have been very awkward. I was worried it would be, after the party. But then"—I press my lips to his throat—"then I remembered you're not a dick."

He laughs. "I don't know about that. But I was determined." He sighs again. "When I said I didn't want to be a bad thing, and you said you thought I was a good thing? That was . . . it was a significant moment in my life. Although it did mean I allowed myself to hope."

"I think my body knew better than my brain," I tell him. "That's not always the case. But . . . I had some stuff to do, before I was ready."

"I know. I do understand. Even though it was confusing, and difficult, and even though I've been . . . I've been miserable. I missed you so much."

"I missed you too. But I suppose that helped, really. I kept thinking, of course I miss him, we've been living together for months—and I've been quite alone here, you know." I shake my head. "I knew it was more than that, but . . . I had a lot going on, in my head. I did think it might be better for me to . . . just be me, by myself. For a long time. Because . . . even when I've been very sad, you know, after a breakup, I've never felt like it was too risky to try again. But last time . . . it made everything seem very risky. Frightening. And then there you were, almost immediately. It was confusing for such a long time."

We kiss for a while and then he says, "I feel like this is something we've earned, though. Is that silly?"

I shake my head. "Not silly. And you've been very patient, haven't you? I'll never forget that."

"I wish I hadn't slept with that girl."

"Oh, don't—it doesn't matter. I think I needed to spend some time living somewhere else. I think that . . . I mean, that's why I left, because I suddenly saw how you could meet some-one. But it's this space between us—even if it was horrible, and I'm sorry you were miserable—it's this that's made it okay. I had to be by myself and prove that I could do it. And then—now—I'm still grateful—shut up—but not in the same way. I don't know what would have happened otherwise. If we were still living together—there'd be no catalyst, would there. Per-haps we'd have slept together again, and it would have been difficult, and awkward, and I would have been confused and annoyed with myself, and unsure, and . . ."

"You don't feel annoyed and confused now?"

"No."

"You're sure?"

I look at Gethin, this kind and wonderful person. I smile at him, and he smiles back. "I'm sure."

Chapter Twenty-seven

It's May. May! How can it be May? The last five months have gone in a flash. It's disturbing. But here I am, more than eighteen months into my new life. Everything's . . . well. It's as annoying to hear people banging on about how happy they are as it is to hear them complaining about being miserable, but I'm pretty happy. I got to see the bulbs flower at Sunnyside. My home, where I live. Where we do all the things we did before, except now when we watch films we sit much closer together, and at night we sleep in Gethin's bedroom. We went away to Shrewsbury for Valentine's Day and stayed in a tiny house full of beams. It was cold, and wet, and lots of things were closed, but we still had a lovely time. For my birthday we went out for dinner—not that this was the first time, obviously; we go out to dinner now, because that's an okay thing to do. Because we're allowed to go on dates. It's pretty much a requirement.

Today we're going for a picnic. As we pack the car with food and drink, Gethin says, "We should go to Dryslwyn. It's a year since the last time." He slams the trunk and we get into the car.

"Is it really? I suppose it is."

"Yeah, I thought we should take a picture. To match the other one."

"Ah! What a lovely idea. Yes. Let's do that."

It's not as hot as it was last year, but equally, I don't think we're expecting a storm. Everything's bright and cheerful, the leaves on the trees with that late spring sparkle. I like all seasons pretty much equally, enjoying whatever is actually happening, but there are certain things I love, like the moment the beech trees come into leaf, and then when all the trees are out but everything's fresh. High summer is good, but late spring might be better. We eat our picnic in more or less the same spot as last time, but this year we don't need to rush away as the rain starts. There is no rain, and we lie in the sun for an hour or more, talking about all kinds of things. I'm still surprised, sometimes, by how easy everything is. I wondered if we might have arguments, or bicker, at least, because although he's right, and we already knew how living together might be, things are different once you're seeing each other, and there are things you might get annoyed about that are none of your business when you just share a house. But I needn't have worried. We've never had an argument.

We pack up the stuff and put it back in the car.

"To the bridge?"

"Yes, to the bridge!"

❧ ❦

"Come on, then, photo time. Here." He puts his arm round me and we shuffle to get the castle in the shot behind us. We press our cheeks together, just like we did a year ago, and he takes some photos.

"That was the second time I ever really touched you," I say. "After you hugged me at the disco."

"I know. And you were soaking wet and you looked amazing."

I laugh.

"No, I'm serious, bloody hell. I looked at those pictures a *lot*."

"Did you?" I love hearing things like this. I'm always delighted to know he was—is—attracted to me. I suppose that's slightly pathetic. But what can you do.

"I thought it was so nice that you got a print of that one of us together. No one prints stuff out, do they? It was lovely to see it on the mantelpiece. And that it was still there, when I moved back."

"I didn't want to take it down, even though it made me sad to look at it."

We turn back and look again at the view. "I'm glad we live on a hill. I expect it floods, down here." I sigh contentedly. Saying "we" still gives me a thrill; I can't explain it, really. I don't think I've ever felt quite like this before.

He laughs. "Yeah, I dunno what kind of horrendous weather you'd need for Sunnyside to flood. Anyway, Jess, look, I have some stuff to say to you."

"Shit, do you? Is it bad?"

"No, it's not bad, you idiot, why would it be bad?" He puts his arm round me and squeezes. "No. Okay. So—first of all, if this is . . . if you don't want to, that's fine."

"Don't want to what?"

"Um." He rubs a hand across his face. "Ha. I thought this would be easy."

"What is it?" I know he said it wasn't bad, but I'm anxious now.

"I didn't think you'd want a big fancy speech, or for me to go down on one knee or anything . . ."

I goggle at him.

"But I wondered if . . . would you like to get married?"

"Married?"

"Yeah, look, like I said, if you don't want to, that's . . . I know it's not really . . . I would have said it wasn't mine either, but . . ."

"Are you asking me to marry you?"

"Shit, yeah, sorry, did I . . . is that something you might be interested in?"

I laugh, unexpectedly, at this phrase. "You've said that before," I tell him.

"What?"

"'Is that something you might be interested in.' You said that before I kissed you, after the party."

"Oh. Is that . . . is that bad? Look, what I mean is"—he takes my hand—"will you marry me?"

I stare now. He looks very serious.

"Only the thing is, see . . . I don't think I've ever loved anyone the way I love you. And you know what you said once, about being safe? I know I can't . . . I know there's still climate change, and fascism, and the asteroid, and also I know that people's feelings change—but if we got married, you'd always have somewhere to live. Even if we got divorced, later. But it's not . . . that's kind of an extra. I'm not asking you so you'll have, like, assets. I'm asking you because I'd like us to get married."

"The asteroid?"

He laughs. "Yeah, you know. Like the one the dinosaurs got, only it's for us. I can't do anything about that."

"Okay."

"I'm sorry," he says, "I think I've done this all wrong. Maybe I shouldn't have done it at all." He frowns at me.

"No, I . . . no, I'm just surprised."

"Good surprised or bad surprised?"

"I . . . good surprised? Of course? It's . . . unexpected but . . ."

"You don't want to," he says. "That's okay. I just thought—"

"No, it's not—"

"Or you do want to? I'm sorry . . . you absolutely don't need to decide now. I know it's a bit of a shock." He puts his hand in his pocket. "I brought a ring, in case. D'you want to see it?"

"You bought a ring?" I'm astonished.

"I didn't buy it." He pulls a little red ring box out of his pocket. "It was my grandmother's. Dad's mum." He opens the box. "I looked up when it was made," he says, "from the assay mark? Same year the house was built: 1932. Coincidence, huh?"

"Oh, really? Wow." I look at the ring, which has three small square-cut diamonds and quite a fancy setting, and immediately burst into tears.

"Shit," he says, "look . . . I thought—"

"Would you really give this to me?"

He shakes his head. "Of course I would. If you liked it. Or we could get something else . . . I wasn't sure . . . you don't really wear any jewelry. But I know you like things with significance."

"I do, yes. Yes, that's exactly what I like." I wipe my face, sniffing.

"So anyway," he says, "if you want to think about it—"

"Gethin."

"What?"

"Seriously, you'd like us to be married?"

"Well, yeah. Yeah? I think it'd be pretty cool. But, you know—"

"I've never wanted to be married to anyone."

"I know. I know . . ."

"No, I mean—I've never wanted to be married to anyone *before*."

"Oh. Oh?"

We smile rather shyly at each other.

"Would we have to have a . . . wedding?"

"Um . . . technically, to some degree, but you know, if you want to get some strangers off the street to be witnesses," he says, "that would be fine. We don't even need to tell anyone, if you don't want to."

I look at the ring in the box.

"Or if you wanted to have a massive wedding with loads of guests and a huge frock . . ."

I look at him.

". . . that would be okay too. Whatever you want. If you want."

"Well, I . . ."

"But no need to decide now. Unless you want to."

"Um."

"I mean . . ."

"Gethin."

"Yes?"

"You can stop talking." I put my arms round his neck, stand on tiptoe, and press my face to his. We kiss in the sunshine.

"I think I'd like to be married to you," I say. "I think I've never liked anyone better, or loved anyone more."

"Really?"

"Really." I kiss him again. "Although, I don't know if I'd want to be Mrs. Thomas?"

"Jeez, you absolutely don't have to be. Your name's good."

"You could be Mr. Cavendish." I don't mean it, really, but he says:

"If you wanted me to take your name, I totally would."

"Would you?"

"I feel like a bit of a dick saying this, but the thing is, Jess, I'd do anything you wanted."

I grin at him. "Anything?"

"Pretty much." He takes my hand and kisses it. "I just . . . I really love you."

"Yes." We smile at each other. "Are we engaged?" I ask. "I've never imagined myself as a person who might be engaged."

"Well, yeah. If you want."

"Okay."

"Okay?"

I nod. "Let's get married. Don't worry, I don't want a big party and a frock or anything."

"Give me the ring, then," he says, and I hand back the box.

"Don't drop it," I say, suddenly terrified.

"Ha, in the river? I'll try not to." He takes the ring from the box and puts the box back in his pocket.

I hold out my hand.

"It might not fit," he says, "but we can get it adjusted." He slides it onto my finger. "There. How's that?"

"Yes, look. I think it does fit."

"Not too loose?"

I shake my hand, cautiously. "No. Perfect." I hold up my hand so I can admire the stones, sparkling in the sunshine. It's lovely. I can't believe it.

I look at my hand again. "Never had a fiancé," I say. I look at him, shaking my head. "When I think of all the things that had to happen, for us to meet . . ."

"I know. What if you'd broken into someone else's empty house?"

"I'd be engaged to them?" I laugh. "I don't think." I look at him. "When can we do it, then? Get married, I mean. Could we do it next week? How long does it take to sort out?"

"Ah, well, I did look into it. You have to give notice and wait twenty-eight days."

"Oh." Considering that ten minutes ago I'd never thought about getting married, I'm weirdly disappointed by this.

"Yeah, so not next week. But we could give notice tomorrow. If you wanted. There's a fee, but if you don't want anything too fancy we can probably do the whole thing for five hundred quid. I mean," he adds, "we can spend as much money as you like; I don't have a budget in mind."

I laugh. "We probably don't need to spend loads of money. It's not really about that, is it?"

"Not really. But you might want to invite people? Or not. We could just send an email out to say what we've done and run away somewhere for a honeymoon."

"Ooh. I like the sound of that."

"I know you like running away." He grins at me.

"I don't *like* running away," I say, mock outraged. "How rude."

"Two weeks in France, or Italy? Or Scotland?"

"Ah," I say happily. I kiss him again. "I don't care where we go, as long as we're together."

Author's Note

My mum said I should write this "because people might be interested."

Caerwyddon is almost-but-not-quite Carmarthen, as anyone who knows West Wales will probably have guessed. It shares lots of attributes with its real-life equivalent, but I wanted to be able to make some stuff up. The places Jess and Gethin visit on their small adventures are real though, and the Towy Valley is certainly full of castles. It's also very beautiful, so you should visit if you get the chance.

The people Jess lived with when she was with Fitz would have been described as New Age travelers by the media. In the 1980s and 1990s if you parked up your trailer or caravan (or converted van or bus or ambulance) on an empty piece of ground, you could avoid interference on some level and live in the margins, resisting social rules, or appearing to. Travelers moved around the country attending protests, free festivals, and raves, before the Criminal Justice Bill made this sort of existence much harder.

Acknowledgments

Last time I did this Ollie complained about being last on the list, so I guess I'd better bump him up to the top. All my love and thanks for driving me about and bringing me treats. I like to think we have a nice time, even if I'm mostly typing. Here's to many more years of looking at rocks in fields.

Thanks once again to my parents, Pam and Vic, for being the best, and Stewart and Tess, for also being the best. Uncle David for buying the first book even if he didn't read it. My in-laws, the Frasers, and also the Mansons (Mark, Susan, and Tilly) who live very close to the cemetery that inspired the one where Jess pitched her tent.

I wrote most of *The Beginning of Everything* during the various lockdowns of 2020, when I didn't really see anyone. And unlike other things I've written, I didn't share it with anyone, maybe because everything was so strange. Nonetheless I'd still like to thank Women's Fiction Critique Group stalwarts Ann Warner and Gail Cleare, as well as Margaret Johnson.

I've seen much less of the gang over the last couple of years than when things were "normal," but I still love Sarah Albiston and Mat Winser and am always grateful for their ability to make me laugh until my face hurts. I called Gethin's mum Marian in memory of Marian Warren, always a kind and welcoming presence in my life and one of Sarah's Additional Mums.

Is it too much to dedicate a book to someone and put them in the Acknowledgments as well? Who cares? Anyway, thanks to Katie Ashcroft, who lived in a trailer on various bits of vacant land while we were doing our A-Levels. Inspirational always. Love you!

Penny Austin's brother didn't smash up the trophy cabinet but he did burn the registers. I'm not thanking him, but I will thank Bobbin, whose return to our lives has been a delight.

Many thanks to Gwen Guthrie-Jones, dear small adventure pal, with whom I sometimes discuss plots and titles while looking at churches and chalk streams. We also drink coffee, some of which is of reasonable quality.

Thanks to Iestyn Hughes for his help with naming Caerwyddon and his willingness to answer my annoying questions about Welsh things, and Sara Huws for similar Welsh assistance. Also Donna Wood and Clare Ashton for their continued support.

I'd also like to thank everyone who bought or borrowed a copy of my first novel, *The Bookshop of Second Chances*. I'm grateful to every single one of you, whether you're someone I've known since school, or someone I worked with in the 1990s, someone I know from Twitter, or you used to live next door when I was tiny, or you're my mum's hairdresser or cousin (maybe my mum missed her calling, she's been amazing at marketing!), or you're the friend or cousin or hairdresser of one of my friends, or someone who found the book in a bookshop or online. It's been amazing to think of my words being in other people's brains, and I've been really touched by the number of people I know who've read it, even if it might not have been quite their "thing." Equally touched, of course by the thousands of people I *don't* know who have read it. You're all great!

Many thanks to everyone at Simon & Schuster UK, especially my editor, Louise Davies, and Sara-Jade Virtue, force of nature and publishing powerhouse.

And last but certainly not least, many thanks to the editorial team at Random House: Shauna Summers, Mae Martinez, Ada Yonenaka, and Laura Dragonette for a fabulous and enjoyable copy edit.

The Beginning
of
Everything

A Novel

JACKIE FRASER

Random
House
Book Club

Because
Stories Are
Better Shared ™

A READER'S GUIDE

Questions and Topics for Discussion

1. Despite difficult circumstances, Jess perseveres and manages to stay positive. Do you remember a time when you had to endure a tough situation? How did you get through it?

2. Jess is adamant about not accepting or asking for help from others. Why do you think that is? Can you relate to Jess? Why or why not? When does this get in Jess's way and prevent her from moving forward?

3. Were you shocked by Gethin's offer to allow Jess to stay in his home for free? Have you ever showed a similar act of kindness to a stranger? If so, what compelled you in that moment?

4. Early in the novel, Jess and Gethin have a heart-to-heart about how the fear of wasting time can stop you from making positive changes in your life. Does this resonate with you in any way? Looking back on your life, do you have any regrets?

5. Gethin trusts Jess from the beginning, despite his sister's skepticism and Jess's own hesitations. Why do you think

this behavior seems odd? What events have made you less trustworthy of strangers? Do you find hope in Gethin and Jess's relationship?

6. Jess often takes a moment to be grateful for what she has. She feels that every single thing she has is a miracle. Do you feel this way? Take a moment to reflect on what you're grateful for and what possessions you have that feel like little miracles.

7. Gethin is arguably the best gift giver, mainly because he listens and intentionally remembers what people share with him. Have you ever been given a memorable gift? If so, what's the story behind it? Have you ever given a meaningful gift or gesture?

8. It's pretty clear near the end of the novel that Jess and Gethin have feelings for each other. What's holding them back from taking the next step? Were you surprised by any of their decisions?

9. Why do you think Abby has a change of heart and reaches out to Jess at the end of the novel? In what ways have you changed opinions about people in your life?

10. If you were to cast the film adaptation of *The Beginning of Everything*, who would you cast as Jess and as Gethin?

ABOUT THE AUTHOR

Jackie Fraser is a freelance editor and writer. She's worked for AA Publishing, Watkins, *The Good Food Guide,* and with various self-published writers of fiction, travel and food guides, recipe books, and self-help books since 2012. Prior to that, she worked as an editor of food and accommodation guides for the AA, including the *B&B Guide, Restaurant Guide,* and *Pub Guide,* for nearly twenty years, eventually running the Lifestyle Guides department. She's interested in all kinds of things, particularly history (and prehistory), art, food, popular culture, and music. She reads a lot (no, really) in multiple genres, and is fascinated by the Bronze Age. She likes vintage clothes, antiques fairs, photography, and cats.